The President

The President

Michael J. Walsh

O'Malley & Finnegan
Washington D.C.

ISBN-13: 9780692971109
ISBN-10: 0692971106
Library of Congress Control Number: 2017919146
O'Malley & Finnegan, Washington, DC

To the family

Prologue

FOR AS LONG as he could remember Michael Sullivan wanted to be a trial lawyer. Inspired by biographies of William J. Fallon of New York, the great criminal lawyer, Clarence Darrow, Lloyd Paul Striker, Edward Bennett Williams and other giants of the law he attended Georgetown University Law School in Washington D.C., graduating in 1982. Returning home to the state of his birth he joined a small firm which by 1996 had grown to a dozen lawyers with he and another as senior partners. With each passing year his reputation grew as one of the top trial lawyers in the state and he became what he aspired to be. After 15 years a dispute arose between the partners resulting in Michael withdrawing and forming a new firm with, good friend and fellow trial lawyer, Paul Connolly. By 2002 Sullivan & Connolly had become one of the largest firms in the state with a 100 lawyers. He was at the height of success, worth millions of dollars, thriving in the law with a national reputation as one of country's top trial lawyers.

Early in his career he gained, as a client, John Kennedy a very successful businessman, who at 50, had already made a fortune estimated at five hundred million. Kennedy saw in Michael Sullivan, not only a brilliant lawyer, but someone who was a natural born leader. When a seat in the U.S. Congress became vacant in 2003, he persuaded Michael to run arguing he was already worth millions and had a duty to serve the country at a higher level. While the law remained his love, he ran and won a special election and a few months later the general election of 2004.

With his wife of 23 years, Mary, and four children, Jack, Sharon, Peter and Kathryn, he moved to Spring Valley in Washington D.C. and began serving the first of two terms in the House of Representatives returning week-ends to campaign in his district. While he missed the law, he discovered rather than working for a few clients at a time, he could work for thousands.

In 2008 he challenged his state's incumbent Senator and won. At the Republican convention in 2012 the Presidential nominee, John Madden, opened the floor allowing the delegates to pick the Vice Presidential running mate. At the last minute Michael decided to vie for the nomination and after leading on the first ballot lost narrowly on the second. It was a hard loss. After that experience Sullivan and his team decided to seek the presidency in 2016. In 2014 he was handily re-elected to the Senate by a wide margin.

"The President" is the story of the 2016 campaign for President of the United States and the aftermath. Three previous volumes: *"The Firm," "The Congressman,"* and *"The Senator"* trace his ascent from the court room to candidate for the highest office in the land.

CHAPTER 1

THE RAIN CAME down in waves, as it so often does in the nation's capital, pelting the windows of Senator Michael Sullivan's home in northwest Washington D.C. It was nearing five o'clock in the afternoon January 16, 2015 and huddled with the Senator in the library with a blazing fire to keep them warm were the men who had been instrumental in convincing Michael Sullivan to run for the presidency in 2016. Four of those closest to him were: John Kennedy a self-made billionaire, Tom Galvin, head of a large Wall Street investment firm, Paul Connolly, co-founder of the firm of Sullivan & Connolly and presently the head of Connolly, Wilson and Riley the successor firm and Jack "Jocko" O'Brian, political strategist and campaign manager of Michael's election to the Senate in 2008 and re-election in 2014. Five other men, all senators and close colleagues during his first six years as a United States Senator joined the four. They were Bailey Long, the new Majority Leader from Wyoming, Travis Johnson of Wisconsin, Peter Halvorson, Minnesota, William Martinelli, New Mexico and Benjamin Wisnuskie, Pennsylvania. As far back as 2003 Galvin, Kennedy and Connolly had seen the potential in Michael to eventually become President.

As the presidency of Barack Obama, the first African American to become President, unfolded with disastrous results these men realized it would take a strong man, a man of unquestioned integrity, and leadership qualities to undue the harm inflicted on the Republic in his six years in office.

They believed Michael Sullivan had all these qualities and could bring the country back to what it had been when Obama came to the office in 2009.

During the early part of the day Kennedy and O'Brian had led the discussion using charts and graphs to illustrate how the campaign would proceed. In their outline Michael would cover the country in the first part of 2015 speaking in approximately twenty states with multiple appearances in Iowa, New Hampshire and South Carolina, the first primary states. The pace would be doubled in the second half of the year as Florida, Ohio and Wisconsin were added to the list. Jocko explained, that to win, the Republican would have to carry Florida, Ohio, recapture Virginia and win Wisconsin.

For the Democrats the path was easier picking up several Midwestern states and both coasts for a total of 273 Electoral votes to the Republicans 265; thus Michael would have to win Wisconsin, Ohio and New Hampshire to reach a minimum of 272 votes on Election Day. It was Kennedy who stressed only George Bush and Ronald Raegan had made it a 12 year stretch for one party over the Democrats and no matter who they put up would have a difficult time duplicating that feat. Besides whoever the candidate was he or she would carry the baggage of the Obama years with them.

The discussion turned to who the Democrats might pick as their nominee. The name of Hanna Hamilton, Obama's Secretary of State during his first term, immediately became the center of the conversation. During the latter half of 2013 Hamilton had been making speeches around the country leaving pundits to speculate she intended to become the first woman president of the United States. With Obama essentially a lame duck for the last two years of his presidency and no strong Democrat on the horizon to run in 2016 she could throw her hat in the ring fearing no heavy competition from the Vice President, considered by most to be incompetent and an Obama sycophant. Several other small state governors had already declared their intention to run although given no chance in the eyes of the media. Jocko O'Brian was of the opinion if she declared in early 2015 she could preempt the field. He already had compiled a great deal of research on her and was prepared to fill them in.

"Born in New York, a graduate of the University of Colorado and Columbia University Law School class of '73. No particular distinctions. Joined a New York law firm in 1979 and stayed six years without making partner; joined a smaller firm and ran for the legislature serving six years before running for Congress representing Manhattan's Upper East Side. In 1994 she ran for a vacant seat in the U.S. Senate won and was re-elected in 2000. She won a third term in 2006 and left in 2009 to become Secretary of State, appointed by Obama. As Secretary most of her time was spent travelling the world accomplishing very little while promoting herself with photo opportunities with world leaders at every stop not bothering to hide the fact she might be a candidate for the presidency in 2016. She made a huge mistake in the Benghazi, Libya affair when she became part of a cover up orchestrated by the White House trying to pass it off as a spontaneous uprising rather than a terrorist attack that killed four Americans who might have been saved. Her real blunder, among many, was discovered after she left office and it turned out she had set up a personal e-mail account and a special server at her home in New York unbeknownst to the State Department.

Three congressional committees are investigating what she did with the e-mails and she is stonewalling all three, refusing to cooperate. Finally she's 67 and will 69 in January of 2017 if she wins the presidency and begins her first term.

She's tough as nails and a stranger to the truth. She's all the Democrats have to send into battle and she will be no pushover."

Long before he met Michael Sullivan, Jocko O'Brian had been a force in Massachusetts politics having been responsible for electing 3 congressman, a senator and governor. Brought to Michael's attention by John Kennedy in 2007 he was hired to run Michael's bid for the Senate and had been with him with ever since, devoting almost all his expertise to the Senator's future believing him to be a candidate for the presidency at some future time. That time had now come and he was looking forward to it with great anticipation; he felt no matter who ran he had the best horse in the race. Paul Connolly, 62, had formed a law firm with Michael in 1995 when there was just the two of them and a couple of secretaries. By the time Michael ran for an open seat in congress in 2003 they had built the firm into a powerhouse with over 100 lawyers, Michael being the top trial lawyer in the state and Paul not far behind. Paul remained a close advisor and confidant of Michael and eventually the same to John Kennedy. Kennedy became an early client of the firm and as his business interests mushroomed so did his association with Michael and the firm.

It was he who urged the young lawyer to run for a seat in congress when the sitting representative died in office and a special election was called to fill the seat. Michael was reluctant to give up the law for politics, but Kennedy, recognizing leadership when he saw it, told him he must do it arguing he was tops in his field, had made all the money he would ever need, and had duty to put his talents to work serving the public. Moreover, he said if he didn't like it he could always return to the law. Although Kennedy was a business man and not a lawyer, the argument sounded persuasive to Michael.

As Michael advanced in his political career, Kennedy was becoming a tycoon in his field and as they gathered in the Senator's home Kennedy's wealth was known to be in the billions. With talented managers in all his enterprises he was ready to devote the next two years of his life to seeing Michael Sullivan president of the United States.

The fourth member of the quartet, Tom Galvin, met Michael and his wife Mary when he and his wife were vacationing on Lido Isle across from Venice, Italy. There had been instant rapport between the two men and their wives. Like Kennedy, as Michael's fortunes rose so did Tom's so that at the time of their January 16th meeting he headed one of the largest investment banking firms on Wall Street and along with Kennedy had become a top fund raiser for the Senator. Tom Galvin was trustee of a blind trust Michael set up when he was elected to the House; a trust that started with twenty million dollars and now exceeded sixty million through his shrewd management. He too intended to spend a majority of his time on the campaign for the next two years. Each of these men, at the top of their professions, expected nothing from their service if Michael succeeded in winning the presidency. Their raison d'etre was the same as his---public service.

As for the man they were backing, newspaper and magazine articles described him as 59, six foot one, slender, with a full head of brown hair, a slightly crooked nose from a boyhood accident and penetrating green eyes. Many articles spoke of him as a family man with four grown children, married for 34 years with one grandchild and another on the way. The women's magazines discussing his wife, Mary, labeled her as very attractive in a classic way and a pillar of strength to her family. With no known infidelity in their background many pundits thought of the couple as semi-dull and not great copy. Political pros knew better. They had seen Michael on the stump with Mary demonstrating real charisma with his ability to turn crowds on by virtue of his sincerity and her charm and warmth. His record in the Senate was one of leadership and he, early on, saw the danger in the President now coming to a head after the 2014 off year elections.

In 2010 the Democrats took what the President described as a "shellacking" with the House of Representatives turning Republican by a margin of 33 seats, after picking up 63 seats. When the smoke cleared from the 2014 election Republicans controlled the Senate 54-44 and the House 246-188 plus 31 Governorships and state legislatures 23-7 with another 20 divided between the parties. Instead of acknowledging the crushing defeat at the polls, the President decided, by executive order, to give amnesty to over five million illegal aliens stirring public calls for impeachment. In the view of all the men in the room the President had no regard for the welfare of the Republic and in their unanimous view was bent on bringing it to its knees. Michael had seen this fatal flaw in the President and had taken to the floor constantly to attack his initiatives. Doing so earned him no credit with the media, who for the previous six years had done everything in their power to shield their idol from criticism. As 2014 turned into 2015 some of the older, wiser heads in the media began to see that by shielding him they were tarnishing their own credibility. What they failed to grasp is once you forfeit credibility you can't get it back. They would understand more clearly as the country prepared to undergo two more years of a destructive presidency and would blame him for their loss of face.

The men continued their discussions of Hanna Hamilton and what kind of a candidate she would be against their man. Kennedy went to the bar and took drink orders from around the room while Michael announced he was retiring to a covered patio in the back of the house to start broiling the steaks. Bailey Long, the Senate Majority Leader, shouted loud enough for everyone to hear: "you cook the steaks Michael while we decide the next two years of your life." Good natured laughter followed this remark and others chimed in with similar statements causing more laughter at Michael's expense.

"It better be good gentlemen, because I'm cooking and I don't want to ruin any steaks because of overheard plans to kill me with campaigning the next two years."

Several shouted, getting into the spirit: "don't you worry about us Michael, you just make sure those steaks are done to perfection and we'll take care of the rest."

He wasn't the greatest cook in the world but he prided himself on barbecuing and cooking breakfasts for the family on big holidays. Looking at the flames licking upward on the steaks he thought about the men out in the front room having drinks and talking in loud voices, obviously pleased with a hard day's work. They were taking time out from their busy lives to embark on what would be a great adventure---electing a president of the United States. He was not awed by the thought. He had gone over it enough the last year, especially after having lost the Vice Presidential nomination of his party when John Madden opened up the nominating process for Vice President at the Republican convention in 2012. The team in the front room had almost pulled it off, but it was not to be. And as it turned out, probably for the best, John Madden failed by a good margin to defeat the President in his re-election bid for a second term. Michael gained national attention and in campaigning doggedly for Madden won the respect of the party. He knew in the primaries he would be a dark horse, nevertheless, he felt confident with the team in the living room and himself at the helm they would make it. At just the right time he pulled the steaks off the grill and marched into the dining room shouting for the company to join him. Steaks, potatoes, salad and corn on the cob. They all said afterward what a swell party it was, especially the steaks.

• • •

As they had on six prior occasions, the five Senators who met with Michael in Spring Valley now met again the morning after the President's State of the Union speech, in the office of the newly elected Majority Leader, Bailey Long. "Welcome Gentlemen to the new digs. In honor of the occasion I've had the chef prepare a fitting breakfast for you before we deliberate."

"Nice view Bailey," Travis Johnson mused as he looked out the Leader's windows with a view stretching all the way down the mall to the Washington Monument and beyond. The others went to the elaborate table the Leader had prepared and helped themselves to bacon, sausage, scrambled eggs, orange juice, Danish and hot coffee. When they all seemed about through and getting a second cup of coffee Bailey began the meeting.

"Jacks or better to open gentlemen who wants to comment first on what we heard in the house last night?"

"Palaver, pure palaver, Bailey. The guy spent over an hour spinning one cliché after another. He told us the economy is growing. It is not. Employment is higher than before the financial crisis in 2008. It is not. It's worse. Our combat mission in Afghanistan is over. False. We are going to need a troop presence there for years. He said our youth have earned the highest math and reading scores on record. Is that why they have to take remedial reading classes as freshmen in college? Our public schools have profited teachers unions not the students. As for the economy, he lied again to the American people. He said: "We've seen the fastest growing economy in over a decade," instead of telling the people the truth the economy is stagnant. He told us he will be sending a bill to Congress to make community colleges free. That may have been the biggest lie of the night. Everybody in Congress, even the big spenders, know there is no money for that. That was just a shameless reach for Democratic votes from youth hoping to go to college. Shall I go on?"

"I gather you weren't impressed by the speech last night, Travis," Peter Halvorson said with a straight face which generated loud laughter from his listeners.

"You laugh gentlemen but you and I both know this is a tragedy not waiting to happen but happening before our very eyes," the Senator from Minnesota responded.

Michael broke in uncharacteristically saying: "I think the greatest deception of the night was his treatment of what we're doing in Iraq, Syria, and Afghanistan and our effort to defeat Islamic terrorists. And worst of all trying to get an agreement with the biggest enemy we have, Iran. The idea is to prevent Iran from getting an atom bomb. This President is trying to avoid Congress and give our worst enemy a path to nuclear weapons. The only logical conclusion is that he has been and is a clear and present danger to the republic."

The others nodded in agreement. The conversation went on for another hour discussing the dangers that lay ahead dealing with a rogue President with a consensus reached the Senate and Republican House must resist the President with every ploy available to respective legislative bodies.

In late March the *New York Tribune* broke the story Senator Michael Sullivan would be running for President announcing his candidacy in early summer.

"Michael Sullivan, the U.S. the Senator who narrowly missed running as Vice President on the 2012 Republican ticket with John Madden, has decided to try for the first prize in politics---President of the United States. Sullivan, an outspoken critic of President Obama will be a first tier candidate based on his past performances. He has baggage like the charge he is close to the Vatican, which could turn off some evangelicals. On the other hand Catholics will be drawn to him because he is known to be a devout Catholic unlike the first Catholic President, Kennedy. Our reporters followed him on the campaign trail in 2012 when he made close to a hundred speeches on behalf of the Republican ticket.

They reported he has the same kind of charisma Kennedy had. He's a natural campaigner and seems to genuinely enjoy plunging into crowds. He has an attractive family, with his wife Mary rivaling him in pleasing the crowds. His children are all accomplished, the oldest Jack being a successful trial lawyer and a rumored candidate for Congress; Peter, studying for the priesthood at the North American college in Rome, a training ground for future Bishops and even Cardinals, Kathryn a partner In the top financial firm Goldman Sachs and Sharon a breast cancer surgeon at the Lombardi Cancer center in Washington.

He will not go uncontended. Governor Bernard Winslow of North Carolina, who narrowly edged him out of the Vice Presidential nomination in 2012 will certainly challenge him as one of several from the southern states. Inasmuch as the President's term ends in two years as many as fifteen Republicans have been mentioned as candidates. It will be a crowded field but Sullivan will be in the thick of it by March of next year."

Michael read the article in the solitude of his office the next morning. He put the paper down and sipped hot coffee from a steaming mug placed on his desk by Maggie Johnson, his secretary from his days at Sullivan & Connolly. He said: "good morning Maggie" and she responded with a cheerful: "good morning Senator" and with that she retreated silently from his office, sensing he wanted to be alone. From his fourth floor office in the Hart Senate Office Building he could look across the green expanse to the Senate side of the capitol and the dome. The sun held the upper part of the structure in its bright rays. The would be candidate was thinking about what lay ahead. Conventional wisdom suggested you had to have "fire in the belly" if you wanted to be President. You had to really want it they said. He laughed at the thought. He didn't have to have it. He didn't need it. At sixty he had it all. Wealth, a wonderful family, a new grandchild, worldly success as a top trial lawyer and former senior partner of the most successful law firm in his state, a millionaire worth seventy five million and success as a Congressman and Senator. All that was to the good and yet he knew in his heart of hearts he could not walk away from the office he sought. The country was daily losing ground under the sitting President. The morals of the country were being torn to pieces and the base on which the country rested—the family---undermined by those set to kill religion and set up government of men beholden to no one but themselves. Michael Sullivan, confident in his abilities, realized it would take strong determined leadership to turn the ship of state around. Obama would have had eight years to bring America to its knees and it would take at least eight years to bring it back. He knew he was the one who through force of will and the aid of other good men and women could accomplish the task. He would lose everything he had if he won, because the fight would be full time and bitter. Having enjoyed power for 8 years the radicals who occupied the Presidency would do everything in their power to retain it even if they lost in 2016. They would undermine everything a new President proposed and not hesitate to lie, smear, cheat, bribe and subvert every effort to make America great again. Trial lawyers are fighters they don't shirk a fight. He was a trial lawyer. If elected, he looked forward to leading the fight to reduce the grip the left now had on the country. He would lead a government that served the people not a government the people had to serve. It had taken only a few minutes for these thoughts to cross his mind. As he finished his coffee he began working on the documents in front of him. He felt good. He knew where he was going and what had to be done to get there.

CHAPTER 2

In March 2014 Russian President, Vladimir Putin annexed the Republic of Crimea a part of Ukraine but autonomous. By summer of that year the Russian Army moved men and equipment into Ukraine, and in September thousands of troops were massed on the border ready to move into eastern part of the country. Eventually they withdrew after negotiations between The Russian government and the Ukraine president. Michael and several fellow Senators on the Senate Select Intelligence committee became alarmed knowing Putin was willing to move against the interests of Europe and the United States as a result of a weakened foreign policy of President Obama which was leading to chaos all over the world. Sullivan was particularly of the persuasion that Putin wanted Russia to be restored to the stature of the pre-soviet breakup in 1990 when 15 republics broke from the Soviet Union and declared their independence. Knowing Putin would move against the former republics if he could do so without opposition Michael and two other Senators on the committee decided to take a six day trip into eight Eastern European countries to determine if they were aware of the danger they faced if the Russian Bear decided to move west.

Senator Bob Gladstone the senior senator from Vermont and ranking member of the committee had hit it off with Michael Sullivan the first time they had occasion to meet on committee business. A man about Michael's age, he was a partisan but not an ideologue. He felt it necessary to make some independent findings of his own and Michael was delighted to have him as part of the group. The other Senator, Bud Hasson, also a Democrat and a member of the committee was an easy going fellow in Michael's view, and a hard worker. He had been a country lawyer in his native state then served six terms in the House and recently elected to a second term in the Senate. All three men were in their fifties which contributed to their compatibility and they held similar views of where America should be on the world scene and it was not the view the President had foisted on his party and the American public.

Advance people flew to all eight countries to arrange lodging, transportation and routes they would be traveling in each of the eight capitals. Thomas Donovan, a lawyer who joined Michael when they both came to Washington after his election in 2008 and who had been a top associate about to make partner in Sullivan & Connolly, headed the advance team. Their job was to line up appointments with the prime ministers of each country or the deputy, advise the purpose of the visit in general terms specifying the Senators were chiefly concerned about the economic condition in each country. Nothing was said about the underlying motive---to determine their attitude towards the Russians and if they had any concern about President Putin's provocative move into the Crimea and later taking part of Ukraine using the ruse that the Russian speaking people of that country needed Russia's protective mantel. The security side of the trip would be undertaken by the CIA and people Michael had been served by on prior to trips to Columbia, Iraq and Afghanistan. Emory Watson, a short squat man with a deter-mined look was the lead and his second in command, Ken McCloud, were 20 year veterans with the agency and two of their top people. Ken was the taller of the two, level headed and not prone to panic under fire. They had worked for years as a team and knew as much about Michael as he knew about himself. Their loyalty was unquestioned and they were fully aware that they might be protecting the next President of the United States. Without committing their feelings they hoped he would be.

Emory decided four agents would fly with the Senators and four would go ahead to the first capital, Bucharest, Romania and set up shop. Their job was to provide security outside each hotel the Senators would stay in, secure the Falcon 50 aircraft Michael and the other agents would be flying in at the airfield in each country and make sure local police would be used as additional security.

Finally, after a month of planning and coordinating, the Select Committee on Intelligence represented by the three proxy members were set to leave at seven o'clock on a rainy evening in April from Andrews Air Force base just outside Washington D.C. Three aides, one for each Senator, four CIA agents, three Senators and two CIA pilots got comfortably settled and once airborne a CIA steward served meals and drinks. Within a short time all the passengers were fast asleep as the plane headed for Reykjavik, Iceland where it would land for refueling and then 2208 miles to Bucharest, Romania.

They arrived at 10:15 the next morning and were taken directly to the Grand Hotel Continental. The CIA arranged for the three Senators to have separate rooms next to each other with the agent's rooms at either end for security reasons. The same arrangements were made at each of the hotels they would be staying at. Agents would also be in the lobby and outside the hotel. An appointment was scheduled at 2:30 with the Prime Minister and several other government economists and because the time was short before the meetings two of the Senators decided to take naps but Michael decided to do something he did in every place he visited. After unpacking his suit case he took a shower, shaved and proceeded to the street to catch a cab. From past experience he found that cab drivers knew as much about the economy of a city or country as a lot of economists. Emory Watson, when told what Michael had afoot, insisted he go with him. It was luck the two caught up with a cab with a driver who could speak passible English. When the driver asked for directions Michael told him to just drive around the city a bit they wanted to do some sightseeing. A few minutes passed before the driver asked "You from the states?" in a thick accent.

"Yes, I'm just in town for a couple of days. How's business?"

"I tell you the truth, not to good. The Euro is down and city is cheap but not too many come. We need tourist. I make a living but no more."

"How about the general economy?"

"It not too good also. We doing better now but it was bad in 2008, big depression but better since then."

"Were you around when the Russians were here?"

"Those were dark days mister. I tell you now is better and it will get better if the EU can hold together…..but I don't know. If we get some exports out to other countries and you guys maybe we do ok."

As they talked Michael took note of people on the street, how they were dressed, how they looked. He was impressed by the fact there were not a lot of people on the street in what would be a typical work day. The architecture was spectacular and the ride worth it even if he didn't learn too much. It would be interesting to hear what the government officials had to say. He got back to the hotel in time to take a short nap and an hour later the mission was on its way to meet the Prime Minister.

The Prime Minister, Victor Nastase, a man of approximately forty five years, met them as they approached his office with a uniformed escort. He looked older than his years but gave off a sunny disposition and stuck out his hand in greeting. They reciprocated. Once in the office, the three Senators, an interpreter and the Prime Minister sat on ornate chairs in a palatial office that would dwarf any government office in the United States. Without wasting any time the Prime Minister launched into a prepared statement in English pointing out his country had twenty million people and while the country had gone through hard times since World War II, they had survived. A member of the European Union since 2007, the country was prospering and looked forward to continued growth. After an hour of probing the economic health of Romania the conversation turned to politics and foreign affairs and the Prime Minister seemed well versed about happenings in the U.S., Eastern Europe and particularly the Middle East. He pointed to the fact he knew Senator Sullivan might be running for President and without changing expression Michael acknowledged it was a distinct possibility. The Premier, an experienced politician, laughed and said: "I think you will be successful." Senator Gladstone interrupted the talk of Michael's political prospects asking in an offhand manner: "How do feel about Putin's actions in Russia?" For the first time during the two and a half hour conversation, a scowl came over the face of Victor Nastase and his eyes narrowed. For emphasis he was silent for just a moment and then answered: "he is what you Americans call 'a clear and present danger' to us and all of Eastern Europe. He bears watching and if he moves on Ukraine then we are all in for what could become World War III."

Realizing, the moment was at hand to ask the question he was most interested in, Michael softly asked: "what precautions have you taken if what you just described happens?"

"If he took the Ukraine, he would then move quickly into Moldavia and we'd be next." We have a small army, some weapons, mostly modern, but we would be like Poland in 1939 when the Germans invaded. They lasted six weeks we wouldn't last three."

Michael decided to be blunt: "Would missiles stationed on your eastern border make a difference?"

The Prime minister realized instantly two things. First the Senator, in a circuitous way, was asking how he would feel about U.S. missiles being located on his eastern border and second the Senator might be the President in 2016 and could make it happen. He did not hesitate. "We would welcome this deterrent on our eastern border; it might make an invader think twice before trying to dominate us again" and by this he meant Russia without saying it. They said no more about it and moved onto other subjects, but Michael's query was answered in the affirmative. It would be interesting to see what the other leaders in the eastern block bordering Russia would have to say on the subject of deterrent.

• • •

Before leaving Washington each of the Senators was furnished a briefing book containing biographical information on each of the official dignitaries they would be meeting within the eight countries visited; in addition pertinent facts about the political, economic and social conditions of the country were fully detailed. After they returned to the hotel the Senators ate in the hotel restaurant, discussed the day's findings and headed for their respective rooms. Michael, as was his custom, wrote an extensive memorandum on the conversation with the Romanian Prime Minister and what he had observed during travel through the city. When finished he fell into bed exhausted but pleased with the day's events. At 7:30 the next morning after a hurried breakfast of rolls, orange juice and black coffee at the airport, the group boarded the CIA aircraft for the four hundred mile flight to Budapest, Hungry.

They arrived at the Budapest Ferenc Liszt International airport at 9:45 and were driven nine miles into the city to the hotel Le Meridien Budapest. As they entered the lobby they were struck by the old world exterior and the modern interior and were not surprised when they found the rooms to be in the same semi-modern style. On this day they planned to meet with the Hungarian delegation including the Prime Minister, Janos Wekenle who was in the midst of a second term. Before arriving for the appointment Michael had studied the dossier on Wekenle and concluded the Prime Minister had been a professional athlete and after completing his playing career continued in the field as a manager in the sport before engaging in the political arena.

When they met that afternoon the description he had read in the dossier matched the man. Muscular, with a broad face complimented by broad shoulders and a thick chest he was what Michael expected and it turned out he was just as tough as he looked. When he spoke it was in a gentle fashion which contrasted dramatically with his appearance. During the two and a half hour conference he spoke of his country having a difficult time during World War II fighting on the side of the Germans against the Russians losing thousands of men and then being taken over at war's end by the conquering Russian Army. He talked with melancholy about the Communist servitude endured by his people from the end of the war until 1989. With bitterness he recounted the history of the Hungarian uprising in 1956 when Russian tanks came into the city of Budapest and massacred thousands who cried out to the world for help but no nation answered. They listened in sympathy and allowed him to make the case. He noted the country had only 10 million people but they had survived for forty four years under the Soviet yoke and now were on the upswing after a devastating blow to the economy in 2008 when the whole world went into an economic tailspin. A man of optimism he felt his second term would be more successful for himself as well as his nation. Impressed by his firmness Michael asked if he was concerned about Russia's intentions affecting its former captive states in Eastern Europe. Without hesitation he advanced the theory Putin wanted to reassemble the former Soviet Union and become a world power again. It was his opinion Russia was a poor country and only getting worse barely propped up by its ability to sell oil. His caveat: Putin was a former KGB and capable of launching an attack against one or more Eastern states if he thought the Western powers would stand by and let it happen like they did in 1956 in his country. Michael came directly to the point and asked the Prime minister what he thought Putin's response would be if missiles were placed on Hungary's eastern border.

The response was immediate and bellicose. He said he didn't think Putin would risk invading his country or other eastern European countries bordering Russia if he thought devastating retaliation would ensue. He said: "if you are suggesting U.S. missiles, I myself would favor. It is another question whether our Parliament would go along. Of course the subject has not come up before but I'm quite sure it would be given serious consideration." From the tone of his voice and body language Michael took that as an affirmation it could be done and sooner rather than later. Back at the hotel over dinner, discussing the afternoon's conference, they all had the same interpretation of what the Prime Minister said on the subject of the missiles: he would welcome them and would push the plan through his Parliament. Before retiring it was agreed they would make the one hour flight to Bratislava at 7:00 am the next morning for a 10:00 am meeting at the parliament of the Republic of Slovakia one hundred miles north of Budapest. The Republic was part of Czechoslovakia until 1993 when, by agreement, the country was divided into two countries, The Czech Republic and the Slovak Republic. After the split Slovakia joined NATO and the European Union as did the Czech Republic.

At 8:15 the party landed in Bratislava, a city of five hundred thousand people situated on the Danube and the seat of government. The day was resplendent with spring flowers everywhere and a blue sky overhead. Michael and the others were in good spirits as they were ushered into the Premier's office and he apparently felt the same as a gracious smile spread across a broad face highlighted by a large nose, heavy eyebrows and a full head of black hair with tinges of gray streaking on the sides. He introduced some of his deputies who were in the room and Michael reciprocated.

"Ah Senators we are so glad to welcome you not one but three Senators. Is great honor. We are a small country and relatively new, as you know, since the agreement to divide Czechoslovakia in half. We are more rural and not as industrialized but we are better off with our independence. So far my five million people are struggling economically but we at least don't have the Nazis or Communists beating us down."

He went on to discuss what he saw as the threat from the East, Putin. Like his peers in the other capitals he was disturbed by the Russian move in Ukraine. He, like the others, felt if Putin was not stopped he would continue to move west.

"We have always had to look to America for help but it looks to us like your President has withdrawn from world leadership. I mean no disrespect but this is what it seems to us." Michael felt he could not let that go without comment.

"Senator Gladstone and Senator Hanson are of the President's party so they might have something different to say. For my part I have to agree with you; we have reversed our policy of world leader. Even my fellow Senators would acknowledge that."

Bob Gladstone followed up and said: "Michael is right; our foreign policy has changed from proactive to inactive and there are those in my party who feel as I do that this must change. All three of us are of like mind on that point even though he's a Republican and Bud and I are Democrats. The trouble is the policy won't change until an election sixteen months away." Eventually the conversation came around to Russia again and the subject of missiles subtly came to the fore. Bob Gladstone took the initiative to explore the leader's thoughts. It didn't take much probing. He understood as the others did before him. That the Americans were suggesting that the Republic might wish to have missiles on it's boundary as insurance against Russian aggression. Without committing himself he gave them the distinct impression that if missiles were furnished they would be pointed at the Russians. At twelve noon, they turned down an invitation to stay for lunch advising the premier they had a plane to catch.

On schedule they arrived in Prague, and were taken directly to the Hotel King's Court where they had time to shower, change clothes and prepare for their 4 pm meeting at Prague Castle. President Petar Klaus met them in a formal receiving room in the castle. They exchanged pleasantries and heard about the success of the Czech economy anchored by its automobile production. Klaus, a man in his mid fifties with close cropped steel gray hair and built like a fire plug, spoke confidently about the future of his country until the subject of Putin and Russian aggression came up. The Americans had said nothing about Putin or Russia to that point. As he spoke a cloud came over his otherwise ebullient demeanor and he proceeded to enlighten them on the Nazi atrocities and the Russian invasion in 1968 and the occupation that lasted until 1999 when the Soviet Union collapsed. He was bitter and stated that Putin's move into the Crimea and Eastern Ukraine did not bode well for Europe. Missiles? Yes he would welcome missiles that would stop any Russian thrust. The subject went no further because he insisted they stay for dinner including several of his people and Michael's team. The President said the menu would include a favorite Czech dish commonly referred to as *svickova a na smetane* translation: sliced beef sirloin served with a special sauce, cranberries and whipped cream. Waiters in tuxedoes moved among the guests filling their glasses with red *Frankova* wine. To cap it off after several toasts had been exchanged the waiters marched in with plates of apple strudel. Stuffed to the gills they returned to the hotel thinking they had seen true hospitality and Michael made a note to have the American ambassador compliment the President on the fine table he had presented for their pleasure. Michael was so stuffed and worn out from the long day that he skipped his usual recording of the day's events in memo form. He just put on his pajamas, crawled into bed, turned out the light and fell asleep two minutes later.

Of the east European countries, Poland is the largest and most populace counting thirty eight million people within its borders. The country's history is one of sadness and domination by other countries. On three occasions it was divided: 1772, 1792 and 1795. Until 1918, after World War I, there was no Poland. Despite being obliterated as a country for over a hundred years they held together with an indomitable spirit. A good part due to their Catholic religion. Freedom for the Poles lasted until the Nazi invasion in 1939. For almost five years they endured the ruthless German occupation, while their Jewish population was sent to death camps. No sooner had the Germans been chased from their country than Russian hoards stormed in and occupied Poland through puppet communist governments until 1990. All of this history was known to Michael having read several books on Polish history. In his view the Polish people were strong and dedicated to freedom and democratic government. He was anticipating his meeting with the Prime Minster.

Now in its fourth day, the mission showed up promptly at the 2 p.m. meeting with President Eva Pawlak. Like all the heads of State they had met thus far, President Pawlek was gracious and more importantly very interested in the political situation developing in the U.S. presidential election. At home on a subject they too were interested in the three Senators filled her in on the situation explaining the Democrats had one woman candidate, the Secretary of State, who would presumably preempt the field on the Democratic side and ten Republicans who would be reduced to one as the nominee. Senator Hanson intimated his friend, Michael Sullivan, could be the Republican to capture his party's nomination. At this they all looked at Michael for his reaction. Before he could speak the President said with a knowing smile: "So I have heard Senator Sullivan, I wish you great success."

"Does that mean you hope he defeats my party's candidate?" Bud Hanson asked jokingly. This brought laughter and defused any tension caused by the Senator's question. The President quickly moved to a new subject, Poland's economy. "We are the largest economy in Eastern Europe and fortunately we did not feel the effects of the worldwide recession in 2009 as much as other countries. Our workforce is low cost and that is why we enjoy so much outside investment coming into our country. Unemployment is too high at 10% but manageable. Whereas under the Russians every industry was owned by the state, now most is in private hands. We do have one problem we hope to rectify and that is the 'Putin problem.' As you are aware, under your prior administration we and the Czechs were to receive interceptor missiles. That promise was abrogated when your President Obama came to office in 2009." Looking squarely at Michael she asked abruptly: "I hope under the next President the promise might be redeemed."

Michael took the lead in replying since he understood the question was directed at him. "Madame President, I too share your concern and your desire to have the promise made in 2008 made good in 2017. I hope that can be accomplished under a new President and I know my colleagues share in that hope." She looked at the two Senators, knowing they were of the opposite party, for confirmation of what had just been spoken. In tandem, the two nodded their assent. Michael continued: "This is our fifth stop on an eight country mission. The leaders we have talked to in those countries share your concern about the Russians and Putin. He has shown he is willing to risk the world's umbrage by his move into the Ukraine and the Crimea. Russia's goal is not hard to ascertain….Putin wants the former Soviet Republics brought back into the Russian Federation. It is in your interest and ours that he be blocked from reaching that goal. Our policy during World War II until the fall of the Soviet

Empire in 1989 was one of containment. Under the present circumstances we may have to renew that policy in view of Putin's actions."

"Precisely, Senator, you express the sentiments of myself and my countrymen. Let us look to the future with a desire for peace and prosperity with the knowledge that could be shattered by Russian aggression."

They wanted to know what she thought about Pope Paul II's role in the liberation of Poland from the Soviets.

"It could not have come about without his intervention. His appearances here broke the back of the Soviet puppet government. He made the Russians think twice before coming in with their tanks as they did in Hungary in 1956. Because of him Poland was freed and in my opinion the whole eastern block was freed because of Poland's courage and leadership."

As she spoke of the Pope and what he meant to Poland Michael thought back to the trip he and Mary made years ago to Krakow, Warsaw and many other cities in Poland. Their favorite was the little town of Wadowice thirty five miles from Krakow, Home of John Paul II. They visited the church next door to the building where he was born and lived until he was eighteen. The church, Our Lady of Perpetual Help, more like a little cathedral, is an heirloom constructed in the 1790s. After saying a prayer in the church they went next door and up a flight of stairs to the apartment he was born and raised in. There they were greeted by a little nun who let them wander around what is now a three room museum containing pictures of the Bishop of Krakow who later became Pope, the garments he wore in the office, his slippers, his hat and hundreds of other items that were a part of his tenure as Pope. They spent two hours there without another person entering the apartment. Before they left the town they went across the square to a little shop that was just a hole in the wall with just two chairs and were served the town's favorite, Kremowka Papieskia, a cake pudding, that John Paul himself and his classmates sampled many times. The proprietor told them the same shop had been in existence when the future Pope lived there.

The President was speaking when he came back to the present and he heard her say: "It would be wonderful if you could stay a few days in Warsaw. The city was completely destroyed by Nazi Stuka dive bombers. It has been restored to what it was through the work of thousands of Polish workers over five years. In old town the buildings and churches were meticulously built from the ground up just as they appeared in 1939 before the bombing."

"Truly amazing Madame President what you have accomplished here. I have been all over Europe and particular Berlin. They have rebuilt there but it nowhere compares to what you have done here. I congratulate you and your countrymen." Senator Hanson spoke with real admiration when he said this.

When they returned to the Hotel Bristol that night they reminisced about their day over a leisurely dinner in the hotel dining room, the Marconi, with its high ceilings, chandeliers, windows with a view to the park across the street. In this relaxed atmosphere they spoke of Poland and Warsaw and what the Poles had gone through as a nation and non-nation over hundreds of years. They agreed the Poles were a great people and deserved, as a valued ally, all the help America could furnish. When the waiters started turning the lights off and on they knew it was time to retire and get ready for the journey to the Baltic States.

CHAPTER 3

AFTER A 45 minute flight from Warsaw they landed at Vilnius airport, Lithuania, six miles south of the city and as usual a black Mercedes limousine and back up cars were waiting and they were swiftly driven to the Kempinski Hotel on Cathedral Square. Michael had not stayed in the hotel but the other two had on previous congressional junkets and raved about it. After getting his room overlooking the square he told them he had to agree. In the middle of old town a few blocks from the Presidential Palace the town was right out of the middle ages the only difference being cars in the streets instead of horses and carriages. Although exhausted from travel he felt exhilarated at the thought of the two meetings they would have that day; one in Vilnius and a second in the evening in Riga, Latvia. So far he considered the trip a great success from the standpoint of a better understanding of the situation in Eastern Europe both economically and politically with respect to their concern about Russian ambitions. At 10:00 they decided to walk to the Palace since the temperature was in the 70's, the sun was high in the blue sky and the architecture was striking but Emory Watson would have none of it and so the motorcade was brought around to the back of the hotel and they drove the few blocks to their destination. Although they had enjoyed a hearty breakfast of fruit, Danish and hot coffee at 7 a.m. in the hotel coffee shop a midmorning treat awaited them when they arrived at the President's suite. Newly elected President, Greta Kulpa, spared nothing in preparing the table for their arrival.

Presented as a buffet, they helped themselves to a second breakfast.

"It was not necessary to do this for our benefit Madame President but I must say it is one of the tastiest breakfasts I have had in a long time," Michael exclaimed. "My compliments to the chef."

"Oh but it is my pleasure Senator Sullivan. It is right that we treat our distinguished guests with hospitality and be assured the chef will be given due plaudits."

From their briefing book they knew the young woman sitting across from them was a lawyer, former mayor and an outstanding politician although she had only been in office a short time. As a leader, her country was thriving and she was chiefly responsible. The country with a small population of three and a half million people was doing very well for its size. Having obtained their freedom from the Soviet Union in 1991 they were enjoying the first prosperous period since 1944 when the Nazis left and the Russians arrived.

When they had enjoyed their repast the talk turned to world politics. Without betraying confidences of what had been discussed with other leaders, they expressed the thought they had heard at every stop and that was the Russians had learned little from their collapse in 1989 and now were making ominous sounds from their leader, Putin that Russia should again become a world presence. The President voiced the opinion that her country, as well as Latvia and Estonia, would be gobbled up first if the Russians felt the world would stand down should they choose to march into the three Baltic States. The Senators agreed and said her people had suffered so much over a long period of time that it would be cowardly to allow Russia to conquer the Baltic States again. That's when Michael disclosed what they had learned from talking with leaders in Romania, Hungry, Slovakia, Czech Republic and Poland that, a line of defensive missiles facing Russia along its western front would do a great deal to discourage any thoughts of conquest. Behind that line of missiles would be NATO forces. She said, without saying so "count me in." After another hour the conversation came to an end and with thanks for the meal and pledges of friendship they were off for an afternoon rendezvous with leaders in Latvia.

A forty five minute flight landed them in Riga, Latvia, the capital city where they were taken to the Grand Hotel. A meeting with the Prime Minister and President was scheduled for 5:00 p.m. so while the others checked into their rooms for short naps, Michael, with Emory Watson in tow, caught the first cab they hailed in front of the hotel and, as usual told the driver to just drive and they would decide later where they wanted to go.

"You speak English?"

"A little, I learn speaking to tourist."

"You live here long?"

"All my life I live in Riga. You Americans? I got relatives in states. They live San Francisco. You been there?"

"Yes we're Americans and yes both of us have been to San Francisco. I'm sure if you go to visit your relatives there you will love it."

Fifteen minutes into the ride everyone had reached a comfort level where Michael felt he could ask his usual questions without seeming too inquisitive. Fortunately the driver was friendly and wanted to impress his passengers with his knowledge of the city and his English.

"How many people live in Latvia?"

"We not big country, maybe two, three million. A lot of Russians but we the majority. No like Russians. They here when I was young man. They no good for us. Now that guy Putin, he raisin' his Russian head in Ukraine. We next? I don't know."

"How do you like the new Prime Minister?"

"She nice lady, good looks too. She be all right. We had bad times in 09' and next couple year but now we do good. Business is good and people happy. How do you like Riga?"

Michael liked it fine: in fact he thought of it as a little jewel. Never having been in Latvia he was taken with its old world charm. Maybe the way things had been before World War II.

"I think you have a beautiful city; I'd say you're fortunate to live here. We're here for just a few hours and someday I'd like to come back and spend some time with my wife Mary. She would love this place."

"You bring wife back I give you free ride around Riga." When an hour had gone by they directed the driver back to the hotel and Michael over tipped him.

"That was a pretty generous tip Senator did you see the look on his face when he realized it was twice the fare."

"It was worth it Emory. We got to see the town, learned a great deal about the mood of the people, found out the taxi drivers think they have a good looking Prime Minister and to top it off he was a very nice guy."

The three Senators were greeted by the President and the Prime Minister at the appointed time at Riga Palace in an ornate room obviously used on occasions such as the one they were about to engage in. Liam Godanis, the President, was tall, about fifty five or six Michael judged and very distinguished looking in a dark blue suit and gray tie. The Prime Minister, Ruta Balodis, they all agreed after the meeting, was as described by Michael's cab driver—very attractive. Liam began the conversation by giving basic facts about the country which jibed with what Michael had learned on his cab ride. He told of breaking away from Russia in 1991 when the three Baltic States won their independence and the hard road they had endured economically since 2008 when the recession hit his country very hard and unemployment reached 27%. Since then, he said, an amazing recovery had taken place with gross national product reaching almost 3% in 2014. He explained, as the cab driver had explained, that the country had a substantial minority of Russians who felt close to Russia and it was important from a political standpoint to keep them satisfied, coupled with the fact Russia was an important trading partner. At that point the Prime Minister voiced concern over Vladimir Putin's move into eastern Ukraine on the pretext of protecting the rights of Russian speaking people in eastern part of that country. The same could happen to Latvia, she told the Senators, if Russia decided to annex her country as they had in the past. Picking up on her concern Michael told them of what they had learned from other neighbors of Russia.

"I agree you have a difficult situation vis a vis Russia and how important it is to maintain balance. However, I think the time is different than 1941 when the Germans came here in violation of the non-aggression pact they had signed with Stalin. Now you have NATO and the European Union to come to your aid. In talks with your fellow leaders along the Russian border they expressed the same fear you have, Madame Balodis. Each volunteered that having defensive missiles in their individual countries would be a warning to the Russians to confine themselves to their current borders.

"I agree with your premise, Senator Sullivan, but for us with our semi dependence on the Russians for oil, it would be dangerous for us to point missiles at them."

"I understand completely Madame and agree with your thinking. Missiles might make them move against you claiming provocation and a need to protect the Russian minority as they have in the Ukraine."

When the conference came to a close Michael complimented the leaders on the beauty of their city and how he and the other Senators found it to be a special place. He said he would like to come back for a visit with his wife Mary. They beamed at that and said they would welcome such a visit and make it an affair of State but they feared he might not be able to come back if he was elected President of the United States.

"If I'm elected President, I will invite you to visit me in Washington and I will send Mary to visit you here. Is that fair?"

"More than fair Senator, said the President smiling, "we look forward to that meeting in Washington in 2017." They all laughed at the President's quick response to Michael's invitation. The meeting ended shortly thereafter.

Before leaving for the meeting at Riga Palace, Senator Hansson proposed they have a farewell dinner that night at the hotel with their aides and the CIA agents since after the meeting in Estonia they would be leaving for home. All agreed. A separate room was set aside for their pleasure. A round of drinks was ordered by Senator Hansson followed by a few more. They all imbibed except the four CIA agents. Michael and the others made no comment about their abstinence but silently were thankful for these men were, in effect, the designated drivers and more if it came to any harm directed at the Senators. Hansson had arranged for steaks and baked potatoes to be the entre with separate dishes of peas and carrots to satisfy the chef. For dessert, chocolate cake and vanilla ice crème. For thirst he chose

an Italian wine, which he had heard about somewhere---
Chianti Classico Monsanto.

Near the end of the meal when all were in high spirits
Senator Hansson rose and gave a toast to all assembled and
then proceeded to tell them when he went to arrange for the
menu the chef de restaurant, as he referred to him, argued
with him, that the meal was to mundane for such distinguished guests. He wanted to prepare a Latvian specialty.

"I had a hell of a time talking him out of that and I tried
to be as pleasant as I could which you all know can be pretty
unpleasant. I told him that we were simple folk from America
and we had been eating gourmet food for days and we longed
for some home cooking. When I explained to him if he were
in America on a visit he might want some good old Latvian
food. He agreed and that is why you are eating the delicious
food that has been set before you. I'm due the compliments,
not the chef." He sat down to thunderous applause from the
others.

"Here, hear," Sullivan was on his feet raising his glass in
a toast: "to the distinguished Senator for his thoughtfulness.
What a noble fellow he is even though he sits on the other
side of the aisle. He is living proof there is such a thing as a
good Democrat."

"Here here, to a noble fellow," they shouted.

Senator Gladstone rose to his feet in the spirit of the
moment that was gaining speed and bellowed in a voice loud
enough to be heard throughout the entire restaurant packed,
presumably with Latvians, who had to be stone deaf not to
hear him bleat out in a thunderous voice." If my Irish friend,
Sullivan, will yield the floor I speak in defense of my good
friend, colleague and fellow Democrat. Yes, he's a Democrat
and his pappy was before him and his grand pappy before
that. What else would you expect? The gentleman is a proud

Democrat and I'm proud to call him my friend." These last words were slurred a bit as he sat down with a flourish. Michael responded: "Senator Hasson needs no defense based on the explanation by his colleague Senator Gladstone. Loyalty to one's pappy and grand pappy is to be admired and I must confess in the spirit of this colloquy that my pappy was a Republican so it is entirely understandable that we would follow in the learned steps of our grand pappys. Now I would suggest that we adjourn this meeting sine die before the management asks us to leave for disturbing the peace."

All agreed with the Senator's suggestion and they, as quietly as possible, left the room full of food and good cheer. At breakfast the next morning it was decided unanimously that instead of flying home after meeting with the Estonian Prime Minister, Juham Rebane, they would stay that night at the Hotel Lombardy in Tallinn. After a 45 minute plane ride they landed at the Tallinn airport, were met with the usual CIA SUV's and ten minutes later were at their hotel in the center of Old Town. The four story building was imposing and had formerly housed a manufacturing concern until it was completely renovated into a modern hotel. As he had done in other cities on their route, Michael hailed a cab and with Emory Watson close on his heels the two toured Old Town and beyond. Everything he had read in his briefing book matched what the cab driver told them in broken English. For an hour they rode all over the city and saw it was a jewel, situated on the Baltic sea; small in population (the driver estimated about a million and a half) yet bustling and alive. The day was made in heaven, not a cloud to be seen and a blue sky that complimented the profusion of flowers of every color all along their route. Estonia's fate had been the same as their sister republics. They had been oppressed until the end of World War I. After a brief period of freedom they were annexed by the Soviet Union in 1940 and a year later invaded by Nazi Germany whose forces were ousted by the Russians in 1944 who occupied the country until the Soviet collapse in 1990.

At two o'clock that afternoon, they were taken to Stenbock House, the official residence of the government. There they met with Juham Rebane, the newly elected Prime Minister and several of his staff. The Senators were surprised at how young he looked. Only in office a few days he radiated the look of a newly elected politician brimming with confidence. He was fully aware of who they were and their status in the United States Senate and while giving them due deference he held himself out as the head of a sovereign nation. Michael admired the fact he was a young man who obviously new himself and was not intimidated by seniority. It turned out he was a salesman teeming with facts about his country fully knowledgeable of the country's cruel history under German and Russian dominance. He betrayed no bitterness only optimism for the future. Yes, he was well aware of Russia's ambitions under Putin to put back the Soviet empire, and yes, he was concerned about Putin's actions in the Ukraine, and yes, based on past experience he knew if Putin wanted Estonia they could take it easily but he argued this time they might be facing NATO and the European Union both of which his country had joined shortly after being granted their independence. He admitted he had talked with the leaders of the other countries they had visited and they agreed to the presence of missiles. He agreed with the Americans the missiles would serve as a deterrent but too dangerous to be placed in Estonia. It would only serve to affront the Russians and that they could not afford.

"Understandable after your history with Stalin and his successors---a very mean cast of characters. Our interest, as it has been since the end of World War II, is to preserve Europe and that would include the Baltic States. I hope the time never comes when the Russians decide they need to revive their empire in Eastern Europe. I do not think the Russians are in any shape to threaten anyone. If they are stood up to they will back down. I say that knowing our country has a foreign policy of withdrawal which would seem to encourage the Russians and even the Chinese to take advantage of the vacuum left by that withdrawal. I believe that policy will revert to what it was prior to our present administration. That policy has been nothing less than naïve, and worse yet, dangerous. Our elections are eighteen months off. I have faith our foreign policy will change for the better and that my fellow Senators agree with me on that point. They do not however believe my party will win the 2016 elections but we do agree on policy."

Rebane cast a glance at the two Senators and they both affirmed what Michael had said but insisted the Democratic Party would win the election. "I quite understand Senators but I ask you about your presumptive candidate, Hannah Hamilton. She was Secretary of State and it would seem to me she would follow the lead of the President and follow his policies in foreign affairs, am I not right?"

As the senior Democrat, Senator Gladstone felt compelled to answer. "Prime minister I believe, as you have stated, Mrs. Hamilton will be our standard bearer; believe me she is not as reckless as our President. She is more to the center than he is. She is not unaware of the damage he has brought upon the country. And believe me I mean no disrespect to our President and the head of my party but it is no secret in Washington that he has abandoned the party and what the party has stood for. Whether my party wins or loses we in this room agree, as do many of our colleagues back home, that change must come. There is a dangerous vacuum in world leadership, as Michael has pointed out, and the United States must fill it." They turned to discussion of Estonia's economy which the Prime Minister said had been a free market one since gaining independence. Tourism was becoming a huge factor but not the major one which continued to be manufacture of industrial goods. The Prime Minister told them he had inherited a booming economy and it was his hope that with the country's flat tax and balanced budget law foreign investment would come to Estonia. The meeting ended at five o'clock much longer than they had anticipated and they were anxious to get back to the hotel, get some dinner and sleep before their departure for home early the next day.

Although it was only 9:00 o'clock Michael decided to place a quick call to Mary in Washington to update her on their progress and tell her he expected to be home late on the following evening. They had talked about five minutes when he heard what he knew to be an explosion most probably somewhere in the hotel. He told her what he thought had just happened; that he would call her when he knew more and hung up. By the time he put the phone down he heard what was unmistakably machine gun fire and another blast. The phone rang: It was Emory Watson "Senator we're under attack. Lock your door and stay down. It's going to get ugly."

Outside the hotel, Emory Watson had stationed two of his men across from the entrance. Two more were in the lobby. At least 10 of the local police were in strategic positions surrounding the building. At approximately 9:10 the two agents were chatting in an unmarked car across from the hotel entrance. Two SUVs pulled up to the curb in front of the hotel. Men piled out of the cars. They were dressed in black and wore black hoods.

"Jim, we got trouble. Alert our men inside and call Emory and tell him we are under attack by terrorists as many as nine."

Bill Thompson, the speaker, had one Glock fully loaded and a second on the seat beside him. He put two 22 shell magazines in his pockets and headed across the street firing at the SUV's as he neared the entrance. He had just about reached the front when a blast in the lobby blew him back onto the sidewalk. He felt a trickle of blood run down his face. Instinct brought him to his feet and he ran through a hole in the wall that had been the hotel entrance. The first thing he saw were three bodies lying in the lobby with pools of blood oozing from beneath them. A gun battle was raging in the lobby and he saw one of the CIA agents positioned behind a large pillar firing at what appeared to be the reception desk. One of the men in black had his head shot off and it was laying on the desk and the agent counted him as out of the fight. Thompson knelt down behind the stairwell leading to the upper floors and let loose a volley at what he saw moving directly across the room from his position. He got lucky and another terrorist fell out from where he had been firing and slumped on his face dead. All the while the few patrons who were in the lobby when the terrorists burst through the entrance were screaming in fear and several had been wounded. Sirens could be heard wailing in the distance.

After he made calls to the agents in the lobby and to Emory Watson on the fourth floor, the other agent left the car and was immediately pinned down by machine gun fire from one of the two SUVs. He finally dodged the fire and ran for the entrance just as a bullet hit him in the shoulder.

He fell into the Lobby his weapon firing in the same direction as the agent who reached the scene first. Alerted by the explosion the police came running from all directions, but the men in the SUVs pinned them down with continued short bursts of machine gun fire. Before they could get to cover two were shot and bleeding badly on the sidewalk, their fellow officers unable to reach them without being cut down by the terrorists. The battle raged all across the lobby as at least three terrorists remained. After two hundred more rounds were fired silence fell over the area. One CIA man was badly wounded; Bill Thompson had a flesh wound in the shoulder, four terrorists were dead and one lay dying in back of what was once the beautiful lobby. Police reserves arrived five minutes after the initial blast and riddled the two SUVs with at least 500 rounds of fire leaving two junk heaps and their drivers slumped over the wheel.

When the nine men exited the SUVs five entered the lobby firing automatic weapons indiscriminately and killing at least three people with the initial bursts. They were followed by four more men, two made for the stairs and two entered an elevator. After Emory Watson called the Senators and Ken McCloud, he and McCloud left their rooms and took up hidden positions on the floor, one covering the stairs and the other the elevator. From experience they knew this was a terrorist attack and they had a prey in mind. You don't rush a hotel in Estonia trying to intimidate the local citizenry. No their prey was much larger---three United States Senators, one of whom might be the next President. Both knew they would be outnumbered; they also knew they had just one chance, if they didn't kill the terrorists when they reached the fourth floor it would be all over for everyone. When the explosion occurred, senate aides who were on the same floor as the Senators opened their doors to see what was going on. Several were in the hallway when Watson and McCloud took up their positions. When they saw the CIA agents crouching with guns drawn they quickly receded into their rooms. The two who had ascended four flights began firing their automatic weapons at the top of the stairs and headed directly for Michael's room pouring bullets into the door and walls of the room. Ken McCloud and Emory Watson opened fire at the same time catching the two men in a cross fire which threw one up against the wall of Michael's room the other on his stomach at the foot of the door. Within seconds the elevator opened and the other two men came out and seeing their companions slumped on the floor in front of them realized they had walked into a trap. One turned to his right and the other to his left firing their weapons simultaneously. It was too late. They were cut to ribbons as the two CIA agents fired a fuselage of shells cutting them in two in the crossfire.

As he clicked his phone shut Michael knew he and his fellow Senators were the target. All he could do was to follow McCloud's orders. Take cover. If they reached his room they would not bother to knock. Their tactic would be to pour hundreds of rounds into the room hoping the target within would be dead on entry. With that thought in mind he got on the floor at the furthest point from the door, pulled a rosary from the bedside table and started to pray. He could faintly hear the gunfire coming from somewhere below him. Three minutes passed and he hadn't moved. Suddenly gun fire erupted outside his door and then the door was splintered with shells and the glass lamp over his head was shot out. He dug his face into the carpet. More gunfire. Then thirty seconds passed. The door had been shot up so badly he could partially see the elevators across the hall. Suddenly the doors opened and he saw two men in black attire with slits cut for their eyes. He dropped back to the ground feeling he was in God's hands. He heard bursts of fire from automatic weapons. It only lasted ten seconds. Emory Watson quickly moved from his firing position, stepped around the four dead terrorists and motioned Ken McCloud to check on their charges. All business, and totally in charge, he called his agents in the lobby instructing them to bring the cars around to the side of the hotel. A second call went to agents at the airfield alerting them to what had just happened and ordering the plane to be ready to take off in twenty five minutes for the air force base at Wiesbaden, Germany. By the time he reached Michael and the other members of the party they had already changed into street clothes awaiting his orders.

"Gentlemen, we are departing now. The cars will be at the side entrance; leave everything; my men will make sure your things are secure and returned to you. Follow me." No one asked a question or hesitated. They knew only that Watson was in charge and clearly knew what he was doing and they were still to shaken by the gun battle that had just occurred on the fourth floor of the hotel to do anything but follow. They went by way of the stairwell that had been cleared by the police and entered the car. 15 minutes later they were airborne headed for Wiesbaden Air Force Base. For a while silence prevailed, each with their own thoughts about how close they had come to death. Michael had been in the position before in Iraq and Afghanistan but he was no less shaken up by the experience than the others. One hour into the flight they began talking in quiet tones realizing that had it not been for Emory Watson and his fellow CIA agents they would surely be the latest victims of the Islamic terrorist scourge.

She heard the explosion that Michael heard and then he had rung off. She was frantic. He had given her a number to call if she had to get a hold of him in an emergency. She called that number first and it turned out to be a special office at CIA headquarters at Langley, Virginia. They knew who she was and when she related what she just heard the gentlemen on the other end of the line, told her information was just starting to come in and he would call her right back. She hung up and made calls to the children asking them to pray for their father and advising of what she knew. It was 3:10 p.m. in Washington, and like her husband laying on the floor in Tallinn, Estonia saying the rosary, she took out her beads and began to pray. After a half hour, that seemed more like three hours, the phone rang and the deputy head of the CIA related to her what they knew. Her husband and everyone on the mission was safe and in flight to Wiesbaden, Germany. He would make sure the Senator would call her from there. Relieved she finished her prayers and notified the children.

TERRORIST ATTEMPT ASSINNATION
OF SENATORS IN ESTONIA

International Press, Tallinn, Estonia, Two hours ago terrorists rushed the Lombardy Hotel in Tallinn, killing several civilians and Tallinn police officers and wounding a number of security guards who were part of group led by three U.S. Senators, including Michael Sullivan frequently mentioned as a possible candidate for President of the United States. In all, eleven terrorists were killed in gun battles that erupted on the street, in the lobby and on the top floor of the hotel where the American visitors were quartered. An investigation is ongoing. The Senators and their aides safely left the hotel for an undetermined destination. Earlier in the day they had visited with the Prime Minister at Stenbock House.

Hours later the story was picked up by the American Media and by the time they were writing and broadcasting their stories the Islamic terrorist group ISIS had claimed credit for the attack and promised there would be more. The reporters were shocked at such a brazen attempt to kill U.S. Senators. What is going on they asked incredulously? Is no American safe? Even the President commented on how far they would go to intimidate Americans while at the same time he was trying to negotiate with the terrorist regime in Iran over their nuclear program intended to create a nuclear bomb. The Media didn't seem to see the irony in it all. We abhor the terrorist but negotiate with them.

ISIS HITS CLOSE TO HOME

By Milt Smith, Denver Statesman:

"Islamic terrorists tried to assassinate three United States Senators and their aides in Estonia, one of the three Baltic States. This attack was not on their home territory but miles away. An attack that had to be carefully planned and choreographed. They knew months ahead of time where the Senators would be on the day of the attack. What is not known is whether these thugs were home grown or flown in from Iraq, ISIS headquarters. My guess they came directly from Mosul, Iraq; they were that well trained. What this proves beyond a shadow of a doubt is they can strike any-where anytime. All were killed but in their minds they were heroes in the eyes of their fellow terrorists, Our President doesn't seem to understand the danger. He waits. And waits. And waits. For what? ISIS could own Iraq as this lame duck waits out the time to leave the White House playing golf all the while. ...."

Michael was reading accounts of the attack in Tallinn when he received a phone call from John Kennedy.

"Michael, that was too close a call in Estonia. When I heard about it I came to a quick resolution. If you and Mary will go along with it I want to furnish you with protection. I think ISIS has decided you might be the next President and that could result in their sudden demise. You're not a declared candidate so you are not entitled to government protection. What do you think?"

"I don't like the idea John because it looks like I'm already acting like the President. But you're right those fellows were playing for keeps and I was lucky not to have my head blown off. Not my time but there could another. These terrorists don't mind dying for their cause. Do what you think as necessary and I'll tell Mary this is going to be the way it will be for the next year and a half."

As they spoke Ron Fitzgerald burst into Michael's office waving his hands signaling for attention. He placed a copy of the *New York Tribune* in front of him and stepped back awaiting his reaction.

"John hold on a minute, Ron just stuck an early morning edition of the *Tribune* in front of me. They have a story on the front page that may be of interest to you, Jocko and our gang."

"Read it, save me the price."

"The story is written by a number of reporters and it looks like they're going at Hanna Hamilton full bore." He began to read slowly as Buddy Fitzgerald watched his demeanor change from relaxation to one of intense interest as he leaned forward over the newspaper. He read:

"Hanna Hamilton, today announced a second personal e-mail account was used by her during her term as Secretary of State from 2009 to 2013. Contrary to rules of the Department requiring all employees to use government accounts for all State Department business so that at all times e-mails sent or received would be accessible to the government, Ms. Hamilton abused those rules. Ms. Hamilton in fact signed a document with the White House to the effect she would abide by such rules. In using private e-mail accounts and a private server at her home in New York she cheated the government and therefore the people of the right to know what documents she was sending and receiving. She now claims she has turned over 30,000 e-mails to the State Department that she says are government business as determined by her and her attorneys. It is preposterous to think her attorneys would turn over any damaging material that could hurt their client. To make sure nothing will be exposed she said she determined which e-mails were personal and those have been scrubbed from her private server. The Chairman of the House Oversight Committee has subpoenaed the server and all documents handed over to the State Department. However, the chairman has added the caveat that until the server is placed in the hands of the Committee or an impartial third party to see if the contents can be recovered, he will not bring her before the committee to question her about her use of private e-mail accounts and a hidden server. In testimony before Congress, the Under Secretary of State has already testified that it was against Department rules to use private accounts and a private server. These acts on the part of one of the highest officials in government are reprehensible and should not be condoned because this is the way Ms. Hamilton has always operated. This story will not go away and we at the *Tribune* will continue to follow it to wherever it leads." "That's it my friend. Do you have any profound thoughts?"

"I have a couple. The first is it is about time somebody caught up with these two and I include Frank, the husband. That guy has been an unnamed co-conspirator for years. When they shine the light on those two it's not going to be pretty. But don't kid yourself; old Hanna is as tough as they come and she and Frank will just try a stonewall on this obstacle as they have all the others. This time I don't think they'll get away with it"

"That might be true John, the media will do everything they can to obscure the facts and paint it all as a right wing conspiracy while at the same time painting her as a victim."

"We can't do too much about the media propaganda, except to blunt it with the truth, which we will do in every county in this country no matter the cost. Americans are going to find out exactly what they are getting when they vote for Hanna Hamilton. Jocko and his colleagues are already at work on commercials. Hanna can dish it out let's see if she can take it," he said emphatically.

Two days later a more explosive story appeared in the: *San Francisco Bulletin*

"The *Bulletin* has learned that during her tenure as Secretary of State, Hanna Hamilton's Foundation, which she serves as co-trustee with her husband Frank, received hundreds of donations from foreign governments and individuals (all seemingly by coincidence) having business before the government or the State Department. Of interest is that after these governments and individuals received what they were requesting the foundation received large donations, often in the millions of dollars. Simultaneously Frank Hamilton, her husband, a successful trial attorney, would be asked to speak to these entities and be paid as much as half a million dollars as an honorarium. Does anyone see an ethical problem in this if not an outright quid pro quo. The Hamilton forces are all over the networks screaming 'there is no evidence she did anything wrong.' There is such a thing used in a court of law and elsewhere known as circumstantial evidence which is sufficient to convict. We suggest, in this case there, is a great deal of such evidence that would be sufficient to convince a jury that the U.S. State Department was being used. We will continue to investigate what could be just the tip of the iceberg. Other news outlets may try to bury this story; we will not. It is vital that people know about those who seek political office and that is doubly true for one who would seek to lead the country."

Two days after the articles appeared in the *New York Tribune* and the *San Francisco Bulletin* Michael, Paul Connolly, John Kennedy and Tom Galvin each received a packet rapped in brown paper marked: "personal and confidential" and when opened contained a thick note book with a label: "eyes only,"

Michael sat back in his chair and read a summary of the contents. The document was authored by Jocko O'Brian and Associates LLC.

"Knowing that you all have been hearing and reading about the unfortunate situation candidate Hamilton finds herself in I thought it would be instructive to go back and see where all the trouble started. After Frank and Hanna Hamilton graduated from law school, as you already know, she joined a pretty good firm in New York as an associate and started to work toward partnership. Frank, always the individualist, went out on his own as a personal injury lawyer; it wasn't too long before he had a rapidly growing practice. He didn't chase ambulances but he handed out his cards to hundreds of policemen and in return for him helping them on their legal problems at little or no cost they would give out his cards at the scene of an accident and suggest "Frank Hamilton was the man to see." Nine out of ten didn't know an attorney and so would invariably follow the advice of a police officer. After trying perhaps twenty-Five cases, some with major injuries, Frank began getting some pretty big verdicts. Word got around in the casualty insurance business that it was better to settle with Hamilton than go to trial and risk a large verdict. For the next few years while she was still a struggling associate Frank was pulling in thousands of dollars in settlements. Two or three times a year, an insurance company would refuse to settle and Frank would work like a dog in preparation and then convince a jury in his client's favor. A lesson learned, the insurance companies would go back to settling. Meanwhile Hanna was getting bored with the law and realizing she would not be making partner in her firm, left to join a smaller firm specializing in discrimination suits, employment law, and politics. In 1982 she ran as a Democrat for a vacant seat in the New York assembly. It wasn't too long before she understood that a member of the assembly could do quite well by doing favors for lobbyists and getting a little something in return. Before she was re-elected she and her husband set up a charitable foundation that individuals could contribute to and take a tax deduction. People would ask her to push this bill or that bill and while she took nothing for herself those favored made generous contributions to the foundation. Some even hired Frank to conduct seminars in the law or into the intricacies of class action law suits and paid a healthy stipend for his favor. Sometimes as much as $10,000.

After three terms in the legislature Hanna had become a harden politician with an appreciation of how one could prosper as an elected official. She had also become heavily engaged in Democratic politics in New York and with a demonstrated ability to raise funds for the party and herself she began having a say, although minor, on who should be elected and who should not. As the year 1988 rolled around the bosses decided she should challenge a Republican congressman who was barely holding his seat after a 51% - 49% win in 1986.

She won and it was considered an upset by the media. In the nation's capital she found she could do large favors for constituents as well as non- constituents and that larger contributions would come into the Foundation which had been paying out minimum amounts of grants to charity while amassing millions of dollars through investments. The marriage was unsteady when she moved to Washington. Frank stayed in New York coming down once every two months and she going up to New York as frequently. Frank had the reputation of being a man around town and was constantly in the gossip columns being seen with this or that beauty. Hanna didn't mind the whispering for she had found a new love, politics. Frank appreciated the fact she was making a name for herself in Washington and he considered that an asset that could be used to their advantage. Divorce never crossed his mind. Her six years in the house were not wasted; she made all the appropriate contacts in the city and numbered hundreds of lobbyists, politicians, lawyers, and most important national figures in the media who were quite taken with her left leaning positions on most of the issues they favored.

When she was elected to the Senate in 1994 against a Republican tide she became an immediate star to the left wing of the Democratic Party. At that point Frank decided to open a branch of his New York firm in Washington. Instead of coming to the capital every two months he began spending two weeks a month building a practice that would give him some status as "Hanna Hamilton's successful lawyer husband." She was in great demand as a guest on the networks as the new "star" Senator from New York. She was invited to the magnificent homes of the Democrat elite in Georgetown and she relished the attention. Frank, of course, always went along when he was in town, and she made sure he met everyone who even smelled of money. She would move on to the next conquest and it was Frank's job to follow up and cultivate the new acquaintance. This he did with great attention and after four years he had built his Washington office to twenty five lawyers; he found he was getting all kind of out of town clients who seemed to need some favor that his wife, the powerful Senator from New York, might be able to assist on. Frank, of course, would get right on it with a brace of his lawyers and suddenly when a bill was passed it might contain one sentence that might be the difference between his client paying no taxes and ten million in taxes. He was well paid for his services and three or four months later the client would make a hefty donation to the Hamilton Foundation.

At the end of six years they both decided Hanna should run for re-election. She had built a war chest of twelve million dollars in early January 2000 and no Republican of any stature seemed willing to take her on. For the Hamiltons life was good; they were rich with every prospect of getting richer and the Foundation had a client base of five hundred generous donors who knew Washington's power couple could be counted on to get things done. Frank was spending most of his time on the golf course entertaining clients in the afternoon and the two of them would work the Washington circuit at night gaining more and more powerful friends many of whom were foreigners. They were close to two in particular, one a Korean, named Jimmy Chung who raised millions for her senate campaign and later pleaded guilty to a felony and Charles Chan a Chinese who raised another five million for her most of which were illegal contributions. He was the bag man for foreign donors. It was later determined those two gave over a million to the Foundation. Once and a while a question would be raised by some inquisitive reporter about the donations and what they were used for. The Hamiltons always maintained their Foundation had been started years in the past and it gave to good causes. Nobody bothered to go any deeper into the question. A few ethics charges were brought against her for close ties to lobbyists but they were eventually dropped. What is now coming out in the press shows they have given very little to charity and are being investigated by the Charitable Organizations Governing body.

After 14 years in the Senate (she was re-elected to a third term in 2006) the new President, Barak Obama, made her Secretary of State. Now she was in a real seat of power. The pinnacle. And Frank was going right along with her. She was a powerhouse in the party and some even mentioned she could be the first woman President of the United States. It was not a hue and cry but her closest associates were already thinking to the time she might run.

Hanna wasted no time doling out favors. Her trademark through the years has been 'champion of abused women, yet under her countries known for repressing women like Saudi Arabia, Algeria, Oman, UAE and Qatar poured millions into the Foundation to curry favor. Odd as it may seem Frank made speeches in all those countries for the token sum of $250,000 each on such diverse subjects as the U.S. Constitution, The Bill of Rights, American Courts and damages for injuries, his specialty.

The President

When Haiti was devastated by an earthquake in 2010, Frank was first on the ground and a commission was set up with Frank one of four commissioners. Upwards of hundreds of thousands of dollars were channeled to foreign entities for rebuilding much of which was never accomplished. Millions in donations poured into the power couple's Foundation and the Secretary of State and her husband benefited greatly. Even Hanna's brother, Hubert got in on the spoils when he was awarded a permit for mining gold in Haiti, the first one issued in fifty years. The *Tribune* is investigating this story and will be breaking it in a couple of weeks.

Her failures as Secretary of State are legion. In 2009 after the Iranian election, Mahmoud Ahmadinejad, the incumbent, was charged with fraud and voters took to the streets to protest the election results. The State Department and its chief officer said nothing and did nothing to encourage the protesters against our sworn enemy. When the government In Egypt broke down she allowed the Muslim Brotherhood and Mohamed Morsi to take over the government and instill an Islamic State. Fortunately that error has now been reversed. On her watch Libya was allowed to fail when Muammar Gaddafi, the leader was deposed. Her department had no plan to move into the vacuum and save the country which has now succumbed to anarchy. She was in charge when we pulled out of Iraq. She now claims she opposed Obama's decision to cut and run. If she did, it is a well-kept secret. It was her assignment to get a status of forces agreement to allow us to remain in Iraq. She failed. ISIS is now capturing Iraq one city at a time due to her incompetence. Syria was lost on her watch. She and the administration did nothing as ISIS formed in Syria and then moved into Iraq. Worst of all she signed off on an agreement giving the Russian atomic energy agency a controlling interest in uranium mines in the

United States. Investors who were interested in the deal gave heavily to the foundation. Was there a quid pro quo? The press is looking into the story and we'll soon know. In sum the Chinese water treatment has begun with the Hamiltons and it's going to get much worse. Unwittingly the media is helping us expose her for what she is. Available for a price. She will seek to paint Michael Sullivan, as a Catholic, out of step on abortion, same sex marriage, stem cell research. In one of her first appearances she has said religions are going to have to conform to the times. What she implies is that religion stands in the way of the popular will which in her case is the Democrat left wing agenda. War monger, enemy of women, scourge of the middle class and worse will be used against the Senator by her campaign operatives, most as corrupt as she.

What the press has commenced we will continue in spades up to Election Day 2016. Those who shut their eyes and minds to her unscrupulous record are going to know exactly what they're getting when they cast a vote for her."

CHAPTER 4

As MAY TURNED into June the Republican primary lineup contained five announced candidates: George Bruck, a 48 year old Senator from Tennessee. A maverick only two years in the Senate who took controversial stands at odds with the Party. A lawyer by profession, he had been a small town practitioner until he decided, without any prior political experience, to run for the Senate. The man he challenged and beat was 78 year old six term Democrat. He came to town with the label "Giant killer." Two years later he decided to apply his reputation in search of the highest office. Short, pugnacious and a prodigious talker he had a definite following amongst the young.

Bernard Winslow, ex North Carolina Governor, was perhaps the chief threat to Michael having defeated him at the 2012 Republican convention when the two had contested for the Vice President nomination when John Madden opened the convention to allow the delegates to pick his running mate. Still distinguished looking with an erect carriage and young at 64, but older than the other announced candidates, he would have ample financing to go all the way to the convention. The pros figured he would contest the south with the "Giant killer" from Tennessee.

The third candidate to announce, Patricia Swanson, a good looking successful CEO of a Fortune five hundred company left the business world to run for Governor of California in 2012. Although unsuccessful she showed an ability to pull votes from Democrats, Republicans, and Independents. In her early appearances she was turning out large crowds who delighted in her attacks on Hanna Hamilton who she labeled a "title" with nothing to show for it.

Samuel Tortelli, an ex U.S. attorney who managed to upset the Democratic Governor of New Jersey, was riding high in 2014 but started a slow descent just as the campaign for President was getting underway. Too rough around the edges his critics said. He was a big man with a full head of black hair and a commanding presence due to his size. He minced no words when answering reporter's questions and if annoyed would tell them to shut up. His biggest drawback looked to be his state; liberal, Democratic and out of tune with the Republican Party.

The dark horse in the group, Richard Batterman, a young 46 year old, three term Congressman vacated his seat to run for Governor of Wisconsin and won re-election to a second term in 2014. Popular In the state and running well in preliminary polls in Iowa and New Hampshire, his best route to the nomination lay in capturing the mantle of the Midwestern states.

The Sullivan team had decided early on they would not run a primary campaign against the five opponents but a presidential campaign against Hanna Hamilton. This was based on the thinking they would win the nomination and as bad as her reputation was, the Democrats would stand defiantly behind her even if it meant bringing down hundreds of Democrats in the process.

Michael Sullivan sat in church one morning in late May waiting for mass to begin, two body guards sat next to him and one in the pew behind. As often happens with people who are trying to pray his mind wandered to thoughts about his family and the effects his running for the presidency was having on them. They all wanted to help yet he felt it was important they continue to lead their own lives; soon enough they might have real restrictions on their movement should he become President. Jack, a Georgetown lawyer was married to Megan and they had two boys three and four years old and another child on the way. Jack returned to the state after law school and instead of joining his father's old law firm, which he was invited to do, through in his lot with three others and four years later the firm was ten and growing. Like his father he was a trial lawyer and a very good one recognized as such by his peers. Politics was his ultimate goal and a start was made in 2014 by being elected to the state legislature. Unlike some others Jack proved he was his own man not succumbing to the blandishments of the lobbying class. After his first year he was picked as the outstanding freshman and they knew then, he like his father, was meant for bigger things.

His second son, Peter, followed his brother to Georgetown law school and upon graduation obtained a clerkship with a federal district judge in Philadelphia. Where Jack was gregarious and very Irish, Peter was taciturn and a deep thinker but with a wonderful sense of humor like his mother. He was half way through his clerkship when he confided to the family he thought he had a vocation to the priesthood. The subject had never come up before with his parents or in family discussions. When he broke the news Mary and Michael were surprised but whole heartedly supportive and proud that he felt he had a calling. His siblings felt the same way. After a year in the seminary, his bishop discovered the young man had great potential to be of service to the church and decided he should complete his seminary work at the North American College in Rome---West Point for men who would lead the American Catholic Church in the 21st century.

His thoughts focused on Sharon Sullivan a 2006 graduate of Georgetown University like her father and brothers, who, after college decided to stay on at Georgetown and study medicine. Four years later she received her degree, and to her family's delight ranked third in a class of 100. She interned at her alma mater. With a specialty in surgery, she moved on to a three year residency at Sloan Kettering in New York, inspired by her mother's breast cancer. Sharon was a beautiful dark haired Irish girl with flashing blue eyes who attracted many of the single resident Doctors, but little time for dating; her goal being to be the best breast surgeon she could be. And that took most of her time.

The priest came out of the sacristy and onto the altar and the mass began. Michael stood automatically but his thoughts were still on his children. Kathryn was the youngest of the four and the most fearless. She would do anything that promised adventure. She was curious about everything and generous with others almost to a fault. The boys kidded her about being pollyannaish but to every ones delight she always came out on top---the eternal optimist. After college it was a two year stint with the Peace Corps in Cameroon, West Africa. Then onto Wall Street with the firm of Walton & Stafford where they put her to work as a trader. Not too many women are traders but they told Kathryn at the firm: "We want you on the trading floor." Taking everything in stride within six months she was challenging the men. Her first big break came one morning when she spotted a stock on an upward trend selling at $10 per share. She had been watching the stock for a month and felt it had real breakout potential. At 9:30 she bought 2,000,000 shares at the asking price and at 3:50 in the afternoon sold it at $15 per share for a profit of ten million dollars. The partners were ecstatic and by the end of 2013 she was one of the top traders. In

December a trade she made netted forty million. Within two years of joining the firm she was made partner with a growing reputation on the street.

In the years after Michael Sullivan became a Senator the Majority leader, Boyden Johnson, a crusty five foot seven curmudgeon who hated everybody and everything around him, took umbrage at Michael's speeches on the floor against the health care bill the President so desperately wanted and finally got by deception. He saw after a year that this new Senator was going to be a threat to him, his party and the President. He put his men to work linking Michael to the Vatican after he had leaked pictures of his appearances at the Holy See. A spread in *Spy Magazine* appeared the day the Republicans were voting for Vice President in their 2012 convention. Michael lost and John Kennedy became so angry at the low blow the Senate Majority leader had dealt his candidate that he swore, without telling Michael or any of their associates, he would see that Boyden Johnson was removed as Majority leader. In 2014 when Boyden ran for re-election he was defeated by a candidate Kennedy recruited and financed. He brooded a long time after the loss and when he found out Kennedy was behind it he determined to pay Michael Sullivan and John Kennedy back. He found a willing accomplice in the left wing billionaire Mikos Tabor renowned for his financing of the extreme liberal wing of the Democratic Party and contributions to the Hamilton Foundation and its chief beneficiaries, Hanna and Frank Hamilton. It was decided a PAC would be setup to which Tabor would contribute millions to be spent defeating Michael Sullivan in the Republican primary, and if not, in the general election. To give the PAC an aura of respectability small donations would also be made to the Republican Party.

Tabor was a natural for Johnson to approach for his plan to get revenge on the Sullivan group. Back in 1992 he was a well to do Hedge Fund Operator when no one really understood the hedge fund concept. In short it involved making a bet but hedging against losing. In 1992 Mikos, a short fat, balding man with heavy eyebrows and mean black eyes was making money on short sales. In the summer of that year he began buying British pounds after Britain entered the European Exchange Rate that had been put in place by the countries of Europe pegged to its strongest currency, the German Deutsche mark. As a member, Britain agreed to keep its rates within certain parameters of the Deutsch mark. As a world recession reached British shores in 1992, the unemployed rate soared and the economy began to deteriorate. Tabor and his associates saw an opportunity to short the pound betting that it would lose value and they would make a great deal of money. In September of that year Tabor built a position of two billion that the pound would devaluate----It would be only a matter of time. At the same time the British government was guaranteeing the Pound would not fall. In early September the German finance Minister made a speech suggesting the Pound was overvalued and could eventually tumble. Mikos, picked up that speech and decided on September 16, 1992 to borrow enough to up his position to fifteen billion pounds and to sell off this sum in less than twenty four hours. He and his associates believed they were taking little risk if the Bank of England propped up the pound they would lose a minimal amount and if the bank did not or could not they would make a huge profit. Overnight they began selling off and when other traders in New York saw what was happening they too began to sell pounds as fast as they could. When the Bank of England opened on September 17th[h] they knew billions of pounds had been sold. The Chancellor of the Exchequer asked the Prime Minister for permission to raise interest rates which the Prime Minister knew would be political suicide. He refused. The Bank tried to buy pounds to support the sterling but it was useless. Hours later the Prime Minister gave permission to raise interest rates to 12%. The pound continued to drop. Permission was granted to raise the interest rate to 15%. That same evening the British government announced it was abandoning the European Exchange rate and allowing the market to fix the price of its currency. Tabor and his gang in effect "broke the bank at Monte Carlo." Their haul was well over a billion and a half.

Mikos set up an institute in the 90s that began contributing to left wing causes, like redistribution of wealth, the taxpayers, not his own. In the next three decades he became the Godfather of the Democratic Party's extreme left wing. Huge amounts were contributed to defeat President Bush, and his main objective, aside from transfer of wealth, was to make the United States subject to international tribunals. For this reason he became a major backer of President Obama who after six and a half years in office appears to share his views. Mikos was actually glad when Boyden Johnson came to him with a plan to stop Michael Sullivan. The plan was simple; he would do what John Kennedy did to him in 2014, that is, get one of the Republican candidates to turn against Sullivan in the Primary and if that proved unsuccessful, back Hanna Hamilton's campaign to the hilt in the general election. Mikos was no stranger to the ex-Secretary of State having funneled millions into her foundation and received favorable treatment on projects dear to him. He was prepared to do so again.

They picked the most liberal of the Republican candidates to do their bidding. Boyden Johnson knew George

Bruck couldn't get past Iowa without money and was essentially running a bluff with his candidacy and the positions he had taken in the Senate. He had become an abortion advocate, and a friend of Planned Parenthood, responsible for over 300,000 abortions a year. He sought the women's vote. He favored marriage between homosexuals to curry favor with gay voters. Not being a Christian he favored withdrawing tax exempt status for non-profits that hold marriage is between a man and a woman. These were the issues Mikos espoused so it would be a perfect marriage between the candidate and the money backer. Bruck was pliable they saw from combing his record in the Senate. One finger to the wind; he went where it was blowing and would let it fill his sail.

Through emissaries a contact was made and the deal struck. Bruck would act as a counterweight to positions taken by Michael Sullivan. He might not beat him but he would throw enough punches to weaken him in a general election. The money would be funneled in from Mikos though hundreds of donors who would give the money in their own name. None could be traced back to Mikos or the candidate.

As he campaigned thru Iowa, New Hampshire and Iowa Michael kept searching in his mind what should be the central issue of the campaign. He had not yet announced his candidacy although his team thought July 4th would be the perfect day. He agreed. Their idea was to make the announcement with the U.S. Capitol in the background. Hanna Hamilton had opened with 5,000 partisans in lower Manhattan on June 13.th. The media panned her forty five minute speech as leaden and robotic. Michael's announcement before 15,000 would be a great contrast they hoped. Invitations had gone out to 25,000 people in Virginia, Maryland, Pennsylvania,

West Virginia and Delaware. Arrangements were made to bus 5000 in from New York and New Jersey.

As the day approached his thinking led him to conclude the overriding issue must be the state of the nation's morality. Without a change the country would continue to drift down no matter who occupied the oval office. In talking to people on the trail he heard over and over "the country has lost its way, the morality of the people is being undermined. Everything we hold dear, religion, speech, values our very liberty is under attack as being irrelevant; is all we hear is government will decide what's good for us." This theme kept running through his head. He discussed it with Mary and she agreed.

She told him whatever he said about values, religion, morality would be used against him by the media who would accuse him of being a stooge for the Vatican. He reviewed the theme with Jocko, Paul, Tom Galvin and John Kennedy. To a man they agreed with him. Without a change in the country's morality the nation would continue to flounder on the shoals of socialism and nihilism.

"It is a bold move Michael," John Kennedy said, "yet it gives them a reason for making a change from the present occupants of the White House who have encouraged and fostered the denigration of our principles. Once we get the country going the other way everything else will follow. So far nobody has been able to articulate what the voters know in their hearts and mind. That's why every poll you see shows the people feel we are going in the wrong direction. Tell them what you believe and let the chips fall where they may. Let's go over the heads of the media to the man on the street." With Mary and the team behind him he sat down to write the speech that he would use throughout the campaign in an appeal to the goodness and honesty of the American people to throw off the chains of liberalism and return to the values that served the nation so well for over two hundred and thirty years.

When he was finished he read it to Mary. She wept. The speech would only take twenty minutes and would be the most important speech he would make in the campaign. It could rally the people to a new leader or, because the morals had been too far eroded, cast him as another failed candidate trying to appeal to a people who didn't want to hear the message. As July 4th approached he practiced the speech over and over not disclosing the text to any of his advisors. Only Mary. For a trial lawyer, this would be his biggest case. His conviction that the obvious must be stated that the truth must be told and that the people would respond if what he had heard from the voters in his forays around the country was true. Their feelings were pent up; they knew the country was on the wrong track but so far no one had articulated the reason or the solution.

On the appointed day they arrived for the speech. Jocko and his team produced not fewer than 17,000 people on the Mall in front of the west front of the Capitol. Empty busses lined Pennsylvania and Independence Avenues. It was the largest turnout for an announcement of a presidential run anyone could remember and the weather cooperated with temperatures just above seventy degrees with a blue sky blessing the throng below. Jocko and his team had arranged the stage so that just the candidate, his wife, his three children and Megan Sullivan (Peter could not come from Rome) were seated in front of a flag draped background with the dome of the Capitol visible to the assemblage. Large screens were placed on both sides of the stage and all the way down the mall so that people at the far back could see and hear Michael Sullivan. Television Trucks were parked on

Constitution Avenue, representing all the major networks.
Fifty rows back from the stage a huge platform had been
erected to accommodate a hundred or so television and still
photographers. Hundreds of signs dotted the crowd with one
word: "Sullivan." When Michael and his family mounted the
stairs to the stage with Bailey Long, the Majority leader of
the Senate, the crowd let loose with applause and shouting
that could be heard as far as the Washington Monument.
They kept it up for a solid minute. When the applause abated
Bailey Long stepped up to the microphone. In his introduction he explained it would be short because the man he was
about to introduce was the "genuine article." His speech,
as he promised, lasted two minutes and he introduced the
candidate and sat down. Before Michael could speak a roar
went up louder than the first. The placards waved and you
couldn't see the people for the placards. "Sullivan, Sullivan,"
they read. "Sullivan" they shouted. He stood at the rostrum, smiling, his hands resting easily on the sides of the
lectern. He waited patiently for them to settle down. When
they finally did he began speaking without notes or a teleprompter. He didn't need either. He knew what he was going
to say and from the minute he said his first words he had
their attention. After introducing his family he began.

"Today I want to talk about change." I'm not talking
about the environment; that is an issue I will discuss later in
the campaign along with other issues.

No, I'm talking about the most important change that
must take place before we can move forward as a nation from
the morass we find ourselves in. I'm talking about a change
in the mores of the nation. The morality of a nation---the
philosophy by which it is guided in all things.

75% of the people, according to a recent poll, think the
country has declined in its moral principles. Where does that

sentiment come from? It comes from a philosophy that argues there are no truths, no fixed standards, any conduct is acceptable, no principles are absolute, and certainly no self evident truths as stated in our Declaration of Independence. This philosophy is espoused by those elites on the left who believe man is all powerful; there is no higher power. This allows them to decide what individuals can and cannot do without recourse to a higher authority. *They are the "higher authority."*

For them the past is not relevant; the past is what you make it even if in conflict with the facts. The principles and rationale set forth in the Declaration of Independence are outdated and no longer work. For the leftists, the end justifies the means. If you have to lie, cheat, defraud, so be it. Bringing about social change, no matter how much harm it does, is an end in itself. They say government must expand----an end in itself---- no matter the consequences. The leftists want freedom or as they frame it: *"rights."* (without responsibility) Their allies in this endeavor are propagandists in the media, internet, television and the film industry applauding the spread of pornography as free speech, condoning open marriage ; that same sex marriage is good for the welfare of the nation; that speech must be politically correct; that infidelity; adultery and promiscuity are normal; that doctor assisted suicide is de rigueur; that abortion is preferred even though it amounts to a license to kill; that religion stands as a barrier to the new morality and must conform or be destroyed; that past history has no relationship to the present; that America is the new enemy and must be reformed.

These concepts are being taught by these same leftists in our colleges and universities which you support with your taxes. Our graduates matriculate without knowing anything about our history or morals. I remind you nations and empires that have disintegrated from within first saw their morals corrupted. Are we going to allow that to happen here? I say no!"

The crowd shouted back: "we say no. we say no."

"Contrary to what the leftists have told us we are a moral country based on Christian-Judeo beliefs. We are told the way to happiness is to do what makes you feel good. Our reason tells us morality strengthens us for the vicissitudes of life; immorality weakens us and makes us vulnerable to the whims of others and our own destruction. History proves this beyond the shadow of a doubt.

To change what we've allowed to happen we must go back to the beginning, the source. To July 4, 1776 and read what one of the framers of the Declaration of Independence wrote." Here his voice dropped as if he were reading from sacred scripture.

"The unanimous Declaration of the thirteen
United States of America
When in the Course of human events, it becomes necessary for one people.......to assume among the powers of the earth, the separate and equal station to which the Laws of Nature and of Nature's God entitle them..............

We hold these truths to be self-evident, that all men are created equal, that they are endowed by their Creator with certain unalienable Rights, that among these are Life, Liberty and the pursuit of Happiness---That to secure these rights, Governments are instituted among Men, deriving their just powers from the consent of governed......"

Thomas Jefferson
"The premise upon which our country was founded is in the Declaration of Independence. That's why we say in the pledge of Allegiance One nation under God."

Benjamin Franklin, a signer of the Declaration of Independence told us: "A nation of well informed men who have been taught to know and prize the rights which God has given them cannot be enslaved. It is in the region of ignorance that tyranny begins"

Michael spoke these words slowly with great sincerity and clear annunciation. He paused and looked out over the crowd which had grown larger as tourists joined in the back and on the sides of the crowd. For an instant there was no sound no reaction. He knew he had struck a cord. He had reminded them their rights came from a higher authority, not from government. He reminded them of what they knew and believed in their hearts. Now a leader had just told them they had power: government existed to serve them; not for them to serve the government.

Something let loose within them. A roar went up that had not been heard on the mall in long time. They were not clapping, they were yelling, whistling, shouting all it once. Some looked up to where the working press was located and shook their fists. When they finally settled down after a long minute had passed he knew anything he said after that would be anticlimactic but they proved him wrong. He continued:

"The Declaration states in clearest terms that it is based on natural law, the law of the Creator. That all rights come from God. The elitists on the left argue to the contrary that rights come from the government and can be removed. Thus they say social justice requires the redistribution of wealth among the citizens. To this Jefferson says:

"The democracy will cease to exist when you take away from those who are willing to work and give to those who would not."

The same sentiment is found in the words of Patrick Henry, one of the founders:

"The Constitution is not an instrument for the government to restrain the people, it is an instrument for the people to restrain the government----lest it come to dominate our lives and interests"

The crowd roared back approval and he knew they understood. They were hanging on every word knowing he was saying what they felt but didn't have a platform to deliver it.

"Before America begins its climb back the relativism of the left must be overturned and rejected and the principles of the Declaration of Independence be re-asserted. The leftists tell us the past is meaningless and they reject it. I reject their Marxist philosophy and say we must rather re-affirm our principles that have guided us for 225 years. We can do it but it will take the votes of people like you-----people who believe government is not an end in itself but subservient to the will of the people.

John Locke, whose writings were studied by the framers of the Declaration captured the essence of rights and obligations when he said:

'All mankind...being equal and independent, no one ought to harm another in his life, health, liberty or possessions.'

His thoughts and words were incorporated into the Declaration of Independence." Again the crowd responded waving flags, placards and a deep throated roar of approval. Michael continued.

"John Adams, a signer of the Declaration and our second President affirmed the basis on which the nation was formed. He said:

'The general principles on which the fathers achieved our independence were the general principles of Christianity.' (more roars of approval)

"Our third president, Thomas Jefferson said:

"Man has been subjected by his Creator to the moral law, of which, his feelings, or conscience, as it is sometimes called, are the evidence with which his Creator has furnished him….the moral duties which exist between individual and individual in a state of nature, accompanying him into a state of society, the Maker not having released them from those duties on their forming themselves into a nation."

Now a quiet settled over the audience. He told them in a straight forward way he wanted to be their President and asked for their vote and then he concluded:

"We know we have inalienable rights. The fathers who founded the country were wise men. They knew they were not a power unto themselves; that rights they enjoyed came from a higher power and they enshrined that in the Declaration of Independence and the Constitution. We must re-claim our birth right and restore our national values: love, respect for the family, humility, generosity, respect for the belief of others, taking care of the poor, the sick, the suffering, the handicapped, the aging and the dying. Reject those who say government is all knowing. Take back the rights given at the founding; life, liberty and the pursuit of happiness. And let us continue to be a nation of freedom of speech, freedom of worship, freedom from want and freedom from fear. Thank you. And God bless America."

He turned and embraced his family and the audience cavorted with signs and yells of "President Sullivan," "we want Sullivan." In an instant they mobbed the platform as though they were tearing down the goal posts after a dramatic football game. He and Mary plunged into the crowd to the consternation of the forty private security forces staggered though out the crowd. They were finally able to clear a path that the candidate and his wife could walk down shaking hands as they went. All was recorded for posterity and Michael Sullivan was now officially a candidate for President of the United States.

CHAPTER 5

PRESS COVERAGE THE next day was strident amongst the big liberal newspapers. The *New York Tribune* labeled it "an undisguised attack on the media and liberals everywhere. Jeb Berkowitz, writing in the *Washington Star* said: "I was there. He laid down a vision of the past and 15,000 plus people on the mall loved it and rewarded him with thunderous applause and in some cases adulation. The speech was short but it packed a message that the crowd lapped up. His thesis is the country is bereft of morals, with a strong implication that the president, the press and other media are to blame. His target is dissatisfied voters and from the cheers he received there may be a lot of them out there. A gamble has been taken by Senator Sullivan and it will be interesting to see if he's tapped into something that will appeal to the voters or turn them off........."

Thomas Coburn, *Los Angles Chronicle*: "in his announcement that he was running for the republican nomination for president of the United States Senator Michael Sullivan brushed liberals off as the cause of the country's moral condition. He used such vehicles as the declaration of independence as a prop and quotes from some of the founders to ground his argument that the country is going to the dogs, and can only be saved by an all out push for biblical values. He wants the country to move backward into the nineteenth century. He may wind up looking behind him and see no followers." The, *Philadelphia Courier*, *San Francisco Bulletin* and *Seattle Messenger* were of the same tenor. The television political commentators felt he had made a big mistake especially with the younger voters who have been brought up in a climate of morals he obviously doesn't approve of.

The first call he took after the speech was a conference call with John Kennedy, Tom Galvin and Paul Connolly. "A thing of beauty is a joy forever Michael. That speech was a thing of beauty. My congratulations." Paul Connolly chimed in saying: "Michael it had to be said and you said it plainly and clearly. You've put a marker down---they will follow."

"Count me in," Tom said. "Didn't think anyone could do it. You did. You said: 'here's the way follow me.' We will pound that theme home until the Democrats and the media are buried. It's out there Michael, they just had to hear a leader get up and say we need to reform ourselves and our values. People have been intimidated by the liberal press from speaking out and being labeled right wing fanatic. They don't want to hear any criticism of their agenda and now that they have they will attack with a vengeance. I predict it will backfire and the voters will turn on them at the polls. They are blinded by their own elitism."

Not surprisingly, others news outlets were more perceptive and agreed with the Senator's call to arms.

Bert Towers of the *Chicago Times:* "The liberal pundits and smart guys are kidding themselves if they think Senator Michael Sullivan is barking up the wrong tree when he called for a change in the moral compass the country has embarked on. Politically speaking I think he knows exactly the issue that is an elephant in the room no one dares speak about. He has dared. 83% of the people living in this country are Christian and they don't like the way things are going. They hate the propaganda they hear from a nihilistic media every day. His appeal is to that group and they all vote…….."

When all the press outlets were accounted for the dailies seem to grasp the problem Michael highlighted in his announcement and applauded him for the effort saying; "he has singled out the underlying disease and pointed the way to bring back a moral America."

The day after the speech Michael and Mary flew to Iowa to see if it would resonate like it did at the announcement. At the first stop 5,000 were waiting and the response was loud and boisterous. They made two other stops with the same result. That night they flew back to Washington with the knowledge Michael had correctly detected what the people wanted; they were on the right track. Jocko O'Brian called a week after the speech to report his findings from focus groups taken in all parts of the country after the announcement: "I have to tell you Michael I swallowed hard when you said you would open the campaign with a speech on morals. I thought to myself most people don't know what morals are. I guess I'm getting cynical. Been in this business to long. It turns out I don't know too much and you know a lot. The short of it is you've tapped into a vein of discontent. We ran groups of blacks, Hispanics, whites, Republicans, Democrats, Independents and a group made up all three. We found across the board 75% agreed with the speech. Each group viewed the speech in its entirety. Overall we found real discontent with Obama and he's been written off as a failure. There's a vacuum in leadership eighteen months before the election and they are definitely in the mood to change direction. We didn't test on issues Hanna Hamilton stands for but these focus groups tell me they aren't going to buy her view on a variety of issues."

"To be honest Jocko I wasn't that sure myself, your findings make it clear we have to pound the theme home".

Mikos Tabor and Boyden Johnson watched the speech in luxury on the 45th floor of the of the famous Blackwell cooperative in New York smoking *Fuente Don Arturo AnniverXario* cigars. Two minutes into the speech they looked at each other in dismay.

"Is he crazy Boyden? People aren't interested in morals. God is dead. "

Boyden looked at his co-conspirator with a broad grin, drew on his cigar and let the smoke drift into the air. "He's a risk taker Mikos. This time I think he's made a disastrous mistake. The press will murder him and he's given an opening for Hanna to link him to the Vatican as a threat to our sovereignty." They watched in astonishment and delight as Michael, in their judgment, was setting himself up for a fall.

In July the Senator spent most of his days flying back and forth from Washington to campaign stops in Colorado, Missouri, Ohio, Florida Iowa and Wisconsin. The Republican National Committee scheduled nine debates the first of which was to be held in Cleveland, Ohio August 6th He and his advisers began to prepare on August 1st keeping him off the campaign until after the debate. Their thinking, which Michael agreed with, was to win the first debate by out preparing their rivals. In keeping with his training as a trial lawyer he was prepared to spend ten or twelve hours a day studying the issues and practicing delivery. It proved to be grueling work and his advisers felt it would all be worth it if he won. First impressions are lasting ones Jocko predicted. To impersonate the interviewers they corralled three of the toughest radio personalities they could find. They peppered him with every conceivable question and he would respond with the shortest answer in the plainest English and with the fewest gestures. No one could mistake the answer and he was prepared for any follow up by the questioner.

While Michael was preparing in Washington, George Bruck was all over the airways and the national cable stations ridiculing his positions on abortion, same sex marriage, Iraq, Iran...

"Senator Sullivan would take us back to the past" he would answer the interviewer. His views on war and peace and the country's morality stands in stark contrast to the rest of the party."

"His position on abortion and same sex marriage is certainly the same as the Republican Party, you can't deny that can you Senator?"

"I grant you that," he flippantly responded, but in my view our party is out of step with the times and a lot of Republicans agree with me on that point. He's trying to appeal to the white voter, I want to appeal to all voters regardless of their race."

That's pretty sharp charge you've just made Senator about Senator Sullivan wanting to appeal only to whites, can you back that up?"

"Go out to his rallies, is all you see are white faces. That tells me that's who he appeals to. That is not a winning strategy in my opinion."

Ex Governor Bernard Winslow, Patricia Swanson, Governor Samuel Tortelli, and Senator Richard Batterman continued to campaign without attacking each other or Michael Sullivan. With two days to go until debate night they interrupted their campaigning to prepare. Not so George Bruck who looked at it as an opportunity to be on stage by himself while the others, in his opinion, wasted valuable time on debate preparation. On the morning of August 6th Michael had breakfast with Mary, Jocko, Tom Galvin, in from New York, John Kennedy, in from Rome and Paul Connolly who flew from Washington with the Sullivans.

"Are you ready Senator?" Jocko asked with a nod of his head.

"That I am Jocko, and I feel just like I used to feel before a trial. Keyed up, calm and ready to take the case to the opposition." They all knew he wasn't bragging; they'd seen him in action too many times to believe he would ever go into the ring unprepared. They had confidence he would hold his own if not outshine his opponents. As a result of bickering amongst the debaters in the 2012 primaries, the candidates had agreed amongst themselves and their managers they would not attack each other in the debates with ammunition that could be used against the eventual winner by the Democratic nominee in the general election. All except George Bruck who felt he had nothing to lose since summer polls showed him running last in the race,

Time for the debate : 9:00 pm Eastern Standard Time at the Cleveland Convention Hall music center with 3,000 seated ready for the first debate of the 2016 presidential race. Three candidates entered from the left side of the stage and three from the right. The men dressed in dark blue suits, white shirts and various colored ties and Patricia Swanson in a royal blue dress with a necklace of expensive pearls as the only decoration. They took their places behind individual stations and were introduced by the moderator who explained the debate would be two hours in length with an intermission in between. The three reporters picked for the occasion sat facing the candidates with their backs to the audience. George Bruck was the first to be questioned and in answering he got around to attacking Michael's stands on abortion and same sex marriage linking It to his Catholicism. When it came to Michael's first question, the inquisitor, a notorious liberal broadcaster hoping to throw him off stride at the outset asked: "In your announcement of candidacy Senator you said the country had to reform its morals----go back to certain values. What values were you referring to?"

The candidate relaxed, smiled benevolently at his adversary, and said: "I was referring to such values as:

"*Integrity*, sadly lacking in our government and in our Institutions;

Patriotism, honoring our country, and those who have given their lives for it;

Respect for the Elderly, something we see little of in our society;

Truthfulness, something we have not received from our government;

Protection for the family, the strongest unit in our society;

Protection for the unborn; instead of killing 57,000,000 children since 1973;

Respect for Religion, which is now under attack in our secular society;

Protection for the institution of Marriage, which is under attack from those who would seek to destroy the family

Respect for women, rather than allowing the sewage of pornography flooding the country portraying women as sexual objects;

Respect for parents by their children, which has deteriorated over the years;

Equal justice under the law, not selective political prosecutions;

Faith in a Supreme Being; rather than faith in a society of men;

Responsibility for our own actions, rather than blaming someone else for our failures."

The crowd came to their feet cheering as he pounded the questioner with his answer. They had been told there should be no demonstration for any candidate or what any candidate said. Obviously the crowd thought differently. The reporter threw up his hands in a gesture of surrender and said: "You win Senator, I get the idea." The crowd relaxed and laughed at the reporter's acknowledgement of Michael's thorough and spontaneous answer to a trick question. With his answer he won the crowd and the debate. The rest was academic.

Afterward Mary, the Senator and the debate team adjourned to their suite in the hotel for a postmortem. On television they watched Jocko O'Brian in the spin room where the press goes directly from the debate hall to interview the debaters and their surrogates.

"Who won the debate Jocko? What do think about the not to veiled attack on your candidate's religion? How would you rank the candidates?"

"Gentlemen, I thought they were all very good including Senator Bruck, who made a few tasteless thrusts at Senator Sullivan but otherwise didn't lay a glove on him. As for the Senator he was prepared, as he always is, and I think it showed to his advantage in this debate. I think he held his own."

"Don't you think he won?" they pressed.

"I leave that to you experts to decide," he laughed and moved on to another group of reporters calling for his attention.

In the suite, it was unanimous. "We murdered them," Tom Galvin said and all agreed except the debater who kept his own counsel.

• • •

The leftist press focused on George Bruck's attack on what he called "Senator Sullivan's ties to the Vatican," while a majority of the media covered the debate on the merits.

Of these Michael was declared the winner with Bernard Winslow judged a strong second.

Hanna Hamilton without any creditable opposition in the Democratic primary opened up attacks on all the Republicans running but with special attention to Michael Sullivan who she and her team felt would be her ultimate opponent. They were convinced that the attack on his religion would prove beneficial linked with his stands on abortion and same sex marriage. These two issues, they believed would cast him in an unfavorable light with women who made up over 50% of the electorate. As she roamed the country in a carefully scripted campaign she gave minimal attention to the press who were becoming more disenchanted by the day with her refusal to give interviews and press conferences. Pundits, even though friendly, started to criticize her for not engaging with the people in the early primary states of Iowa and New Hampshire. Her typical day would include only one or two events and those carefully staged with a few people who had been carefully screened. Compared to the Republican candidates who were out every day at as many as five or six events her efforts looked pale in comparison.

At the same time the Republicans continued to drown her in criticism for hiding her e-mails and using a private server as Secretary of State that clearly could be hacked by foreign powers and probably had been; for her cover-up of the Benghazi murders and favors granted while Secretary of State in return for contributions to the Hamilton foundation. Much to the consternation of her supporters, her husband, Frank continued to accept speaking fees and huge donations to the foundation all of which was viewed by the press as cash for favors. In the opinion of many her hubris was uncanny and those who wished to see her the first women President lamented her attitude of being above it all which they felt could spell doom in the general election now only fourteen months off. After the first Republican debate some of the political writers were trying to warn her in their columns that Senator Michael Sullivan would be a worthy opponent and one who might deprive her of being the first female president.

For example, Milton Smith writing in the *Denver Statesman* said, "Like everyone else I watched the two hour debate last night and my immediate thoughts written right after it was over and refined in this column are as follows; Senator Sullivan was the winner but not without worthy competition. In other words they were all pretty effective for their candidacy except Senator Bruck whose sole goal seemed to be to bring down Senator Sullivan at all costs. In my opinion he did himself a lot more harm than good but attacks like his can prove effective with the uninformed voter. If I were ex Secretary of State Hanna Hamilton who has no worthy opponent for the nomination, I would be wary of Senator Sullivan an attractive former trial lawyer, former two term member of the House and just re-elected to a second term in the Senate. He is younger(60) than she(68), quick on his feet where she is more deliberate, looks and acts like a leader and doesn't carry the baggage she is carrying into the general election. I would be mindful of any one of the Republicans, except Bruck."

Thomas McPherson, *Philadelphia Courier*, wrote in the paper's only political column: "Everyone in last night's debate was doing pretty well until Bucky Watson, the notorious liberal commentator, asked Michael Sullivan what he meant by 'values' and Sullivan without hesitation in perfect cadence rattled off twelve or thirteen, such as, protection for the institution of marriage, integrity, respect for women, respect for religion etc. The audience of 3,000 in Cleveland roared its approval and Bucky was forced to throw up his hands in surrender. From that point forward the crowd was listening and looking at Michael Sullivan as their nominee. I could be very wrong about that but that's the feeling I got sitting in press row. Others around me voiced a similar reaction and stated their opinion, some rather loudly, if Hanna Hamilton thought there was going to be a coronation she'd better think twice. And these newspaper reporters were Hamilton apostles who were concerned more about her lack of campaigning than Sullivan's chances to win the Republican nomination.

In early September Tom Galvin arranged for fifty men to come to New York to talk finances and assign quotas for the period ending December 31. Michael flew up for the meeting to speak to the fund raisers. Jocko gave a review of what they had done to date with the money raised and what they intended to do through the end of the year. He also gave out current poll numbers prepared by head of internal polling Truman Foster. The Sullivan team had great confidence in Foster's ability but more importantly his integrity. He never shaved points to please the candidate. Participation in the 2008 and 2012 presidential campaigns provided a solid background of experience needed for the current campaign. He was studious and bespectacled as befitted a man who worked with numbers and the analysis thereof. This is the way he looked but in fact he was a man of great humor, telling jokes, kidding his associates and when it came to numbers---all business. In many ways he was as important to the campaign as the chief fund raiser and even to Jocko. His polling told the campaign where it must spend their resources, where to campaign and when. Where to buy television time. Almost all functions in the campaign depended on the accuracy of his numbers. Michael had developed a real fondness for him and his sense of humor. "It looks like this gentlemen: a two man race Winslow at 28%, Michael at 25%, Batterman at 13%, probably on the strength of his debate performance, Tortelli at 10%, Swanson 7%, Bruck 2% and undecided 15%. With that small number of undecided I believe people are already making up their minds and that could stay that way until February next year when the caucuses and primaries are in full sway."

Tom Galvin reported more than fifty million dollars had been raised to date and another one hundred and fifty had to be in the Sullivan coffers by the end of the year. "That means each of you will have to raise $3,000,000 in the next four months. Does anyone here have any questions? There were none. Everyone in the room knew how important it was to elect Michael Sullivan President. They were not looking for favors from government; they didn't need it. What they did need, and they all believed this to a man, was a leader who could lead the country out of desolation created by President Obama and his dedicated corps of community organizers. From personal contact they believed Senator Michael Sullivan was the one man capable of doing it. They knew there were thousands just like them and if it took half a billion to do the job, they would raise that amount. They were aware Hanna Hamilton would not have to spend very much on a primary but would have a huge war chest for the general election. Whatever it would take they were willing to match her dollar for dollar. When he addressed the group Michael knew he had their loyalty and so he spent a few minutes thanking them and an hour answering questions on issues, where he would be traveling what he thought he needed by way of volunteers both for money and canvassing. They came away charged up by his performance and ready to go back to their respective states and put their shoulder to the wheel in what each considered a crusade to rid the country of a metastasizing cancer.

In late September the second debate was held at the Reagan Library in Simi Valley, California. John Kennedy was the designator hitter to run the operation with Jocko O'Brian and they arrived a day early at the Marriot hotel and took over the top floor, moving in computers, volunteers, copiers and everything that would be required for a full blown press operation. The television spot crew came in the same day to set up equipment that would televise the whole debate later to be cut up into commercials. On the day of the debate Michael and Mary arrived in a chartered aircraft with ten staff and drove directly to the hotel where the debate prep team had a room set up for one last rehearsal. The candidate and his wife ate alone in their room. An hour before the event Mary left him alone. Before any big event in his life, whether it be a trial, a speech, a campaign appearance, Michael set aside some time alone to concentrate on the task at hand. This had always worked well for him because he would become entirely focused to the exclusion of everything else.

The same six appeared before an audience of six hundred with the same format used in the first debate, the only difference being the panel was made up of local broadcast personalities from the Los Angeles area. In the early going Bernard Winslow, the ex governor from North Carolina, seemed ahead on points half way through the session when Michael Sullivan was asked the following question: "Senator as you know the Supreme Court in June of this year declared same sex marriages legal in *Obergefell vs Hodges*. What is your position on the issue?"

Michael had given his position right after the opinion had been issued in interviews and speeches when asked.

This would be the first time before an audience of fifty million people he would have an opportunity to make clear beyond doubt his feelings on the matter. He was aware a deep silence had come over the hall. Many would not like his answer, those present and watching on television. Commentators would dismiss his view as bigotry, discrimination and even stupidity. Nonetheless he knew he was the voice of the silent majority who believed marriage is between a man and a woman and had done so with their votes in state elections only to be overturned by judges. The right to vote on the issue had been taken away by a divided Supreme Court in a 5-4 decision, four Justices dissenting. He had denounced the decision as *"a failed attempt to create a constitutional right without any basis in law."* On subsequent occasions he referred to it as a *"deprivation of the constitutional right of the people to decide the issue rather than five justices of the Supreme Court."* Now he had been given an opportunity to speak out on a subject fundamental to the moral strength of the nation. He intended to give voice to the millions of Americans deprived of the opportunity to voice their opinion.

"Marriage is between a man and a woman and it has always been thus. It is sanctioned by the Creator through natural law not by men. It is the bedrock of all societies. From this union children are born, mankind is perpetuated and the family is formed. Children need a mother and a father. Unions outside marriage cannot produce such a result. Same sex liaisons may be a collaboration, a partnership or whatever the state or the court chooses to call them. But they are not a marriage. The state may confer rights on such combines similar to those granted to the marriage between a man and a woman but the State cannot confer the Sacrament of Marriage on two of the same sex. It is contrary to nature, contrary to reason, contrary to thousands of years of acceptance and contrary to the will of the Creator. Therefore I believe the union between a man and a woman for the purpose of creating a family and perpetuating mankind is sanctioned not by man but by the Almighty. Any attempt to confer the status of 'marriage' on those of the same sex is a nullity." Silence. No one on the panel uttered a word. They too seemed stunned.

The silence was shattered when Bernard Winslow spoke into his microphone with a penetrating voice filling the hall with authority. "Michael Sullivan speaks for me." The first rows began to clap.

"I join in Senator Sullivan's Comments," Patricia Swanson said over the noise beginning to fill the hall.

"I join with my fellow candidates," Sam Tortelli echoed.

Now it was like the "wave at an athletic event; from the front row back they were standing some were yelling, some clapping, some just standing taking it all in.

Hardly heard above the roar Richard Batterman said: "I associate myself with Michael Sullivan's remarks."

Finally, when the crowd understood they were eating into the candidates' time, the hall became quite.

It was then that George Bruck spoke: "I do not share in Senator Sullivan's remarks. I think they are divisive. He would deprive certain citizens the right granted by the Supreme Court. I cannot associate myself with such a position. In fact I condemn his remarks."

It was hard to discern which was louder the boos or the smattering of applause. The moderator stood and addressed the crowd and said: "I appreciate this is a delicate subject ladies and gentlemen but I'm asking you as a courtesy to these candidates to have no further outbursts as we've just witnessed. Thank you." The debate concluded shortly thereafter and the press poured into the spin room for reaction from the candidates and their representatives.

The commentators were beside themselves in chastising Michael Sullivan for his refusal to accept gay marriage. "Disgraceful." "Discriminatory." "He wants to be President, but it doesn't sound like he will uphold the law," said another. If you switched channels you would hear comments like; "Like it or not he called it as he sees it and he's got thousands of years of history to back him up."

"He's put a marker down and it will be interesting to see if he speaks for millions of Americans."

Or another channel where they discussed repercussions: "What are people of religion going to do when they are told they will have to perform gay weddings or that they can't refuse to bake a cake for a gay wedding because it is against their religious beliefs." I think this is going to become another *Roe vs Wade* which has already been going on since 1973 and has divided the country ever since just like slavery did before the civil war."

"More brandy Mikos?"

"Yes, I've had two already and what a joyous occasion this is. Sullivan killed himself in the first debate with that nonsense about values. And now he makes a return engagement with an attack, yes an outright attack, on gay rights." Am I crazy or is he trying to prove how easy it is to lose by bucking city hall?"

Boyden Johnson took a cigar from his guest's humidor, applied his guillotine cutter to the tip, and slowly put the cigar in his mouth, lit it and blew a stream of smoke at his host before answering.

"He's not crazy Mikos, he's stubborn, or I might say righteous. He's not concerned how it looks politically he's interested in telling people straight up exactly how he feels on the issues. He doesn't evolve like most politicians. For him truth is truth and it doesn't change. In some ways I admire him for his candor. He's not your everyday 'which way is the wind blowing' politico. I think he's making a big mistake on the same sex marriage issue and I just disagree with him on almost every issue. I might point out Mr. Bruck is performing just as programed and I think doing a great deal to tear down the halo around Sullivan."

Mikos took a long draught from his glass of brandy and with a smirk said: "I don't mind pouring in the money to Bruck as long he helps the cause. When it's clear the Senator is going to get the nod we'll cut off the funding. He'll have served our purpose."

After the second debate Michael spent a week in the panhandle of Florida shoring up the Republic base that would be vital in the general election. For over a year he and Mary had been taking Spanish lessons from a young Mexican boy working for Michael as an intern while studying law at night at Georgetown University. He and Mary had talked about trying to learn the language and finally decided to give it a try. It came quicker to her but in three months time he was almost as conversant in the language as she. With some trepidation they tried their skills on small groups of Hispanics on the Florida trip and to their amazement and delight the people understood and applauded their efforts.

In the third week the Pope came to Washington, New York and Philadelphia to visit with the President, speak to a joint session of congress and confer sainthood on Fr. Junipero Serra, the Franciscan priest who founded the missions in California. In Washington he stayed at the Vatican embassy on Massachusetts avenue and at the invitation of the Nuncio, the Ambassador to the United States, he and Mary met with the Pontiff the day he arrived for a half hour.

TV trucks parked across the street and two or three thousand people standing down the street witnessed he and Mary arrive in a two car motorcade. With Hanna Hamilton and George Bruck accusing him of being a tool of the Vatican it took fortitude to meet with the Pope for it would only serve to feed the press in its attempt to establish Michael as the "Catholic" candidate and thus drive a wedge between him and the voters.

As they entered the room they knelt for the Pope's blessing and then he gestured them to chairs set up especially for the meeting. Present were the Cardinal Secretary of State and the Nuncio Archbishop, Luigi Sessi. "Michael, I appreciate you and Mary coming. I bring greetings from Peter who I met two months ago when I met with a number of seminarians at the North American College. A fine young man. You must be proud of him."

"Proud yes, but Mary and I are humbled at the thought he has been chosen to serve the Church."

Only twenty minutes was provided for in the schedule and the Pontiff had much he wanted to discuss and the first question he had was how the attacks on Michael were affecting his chances in the upcoming elections.

"They will undoubtedly have some effect but it is too early to know if it will be lasting. My sense is the people are crying out for a leader and they are looking for signs of it in any candidate, and if he or she has it, they won't care what religion they belong to.

"Whoever is elected faces a fractured world everywhere. I feel as you do the world is becoming rootless, refugees pouring across borders, Christians being martyred, I hope the United States will reach that point where it again will become the leader in helping other nations. That God will show you the way. These are difficult Times Michael and we must assume it is the Lord's will, yet no matter bad it gets we must continue to spread His message."

"I agree Holiness and that is why I am basing my whole argument on the need to return to the values we once enjoyed in this country, values which have stood the test of time. If I'm successful we can began to turn back the secular tide."

"I will be watching your progress with interest and be assured that you and the American people will always be in my prayers. Yours is still a Christian nation and has time to avoid the godlessness that has engulfed our European brothers. Mary, my regards to you and your wonderful family and take care of this man he will need support more than ever these next few months."

"Be sure Holiness we will be at his side through it all and if be God's will, he will be the next President."

When a half hour was up they exited into the drive where the two SUV's that brought them were waiting but now a dozen motorcycle police were waiting to escort them back to Capitol Hill. Swarms of press bolted a cross Massachusetts avenue and onto the lawn of the Embassy as they saw the Sullivans emerge from what everyone assumed was a meeting with the Pope. The police kept them at bay; still they shouted their questions; "What did he say? What did you talk about? Is he backing you for the Presidency?" Michael and Mary waved at the press and the crowd across the street which had now grown to six or seven thousand of the curious who had nowhere to stand but on the lawn of the Vice President, whose Mansion was located on the opposite side of the street from the embassy. Like the paparazzi in Europe the press ran after the car until a police car barred their way.

The next day, when the Pope was to meet with the President, the *Washington Star* carried the banner headline:

POPE MEETS REPUBLICAN CANDIDATE SULLIVAN.

The story went on to speculate about what the two men would have conversed about and concluded they were up to no good. Little attention was paid to the Pope's visit to Obama later in the day.

Once a week Jocko O'Brian would meet with John Kennedy and Tom Galvin in New York at an offbeat restaurant on 3rd avenue sometimes joined by Paul Connolly when he wasn't in trial. On alternate weeks, Kennedy and Galvin would fly down to Washington to meet with Michael, Paul and Jocko for a roundup of where they stood with money, and Michael's campaign itinerary. In late November, after Thanksgiving, they held their usual meeting in New York at their club *Patsy Reilly's Pub* where Jocko brought up the subject of George Bruck and what should be done about him since he was starting to damage Michael's persona with *ad hominem* attacks and distortion of his record.

"He's getting his financing from Mikos Tabor abetted by that scoundrel Boyden Johnson. Mikos shells out and Boyden pulls the strings. They're just using this fellow Bruck and he's willing to go along for the ride." Kennedy said this calmly and without any rancor; "like Jack Kennedy used to say don't get mad get even."

"An old Irish trait John which oft times has to be applied. My guess is they're just using him to soften up Michael for the general and have no intention of spending more than they have to." Tom Galvin said with a glint in his eye knowing full well what Kennedy had in mind.

Kennedy glanced at Jocko and asked innocently: "You got any ideas on what should be done?"

Jocko knew how Kennedy worked: by the power of suggestion. By asking the question he was telling the campaign manager to take Bruck out of the race and soon. He just wanted to read about it in the *New York Tribune* and the *Washington Star.* A week after their conference ads began running in fifteen states where the first caucuses and primaries would be held. With pictures and quotes the ads stressed that George Bruck had the most liberal voting record in the Senate amongst the Republicans and ran second to only a handful of Democrats. These ads ran three straight weeks into December. As the date of the third debate approached his numbers dropped into low single digits and it all happened before Mikos and Boyden Johnson could counter it; in the end Mikos was unwilling to spend the five million dollars it would take to rehabilitate Bruck. They had to console themselves with the knowledge Bruck had landed a few punches before he went down.

CHAPTER 6

THE THIRD DEBATE was held Mid November, in Denver, Colorado with all the candidates holding their own except Senator George Bruck, who because of his attacks on Michael Sullivan and the other candidates, coupled with the devastating television campaigned ordered by John Kennedy, found himself far down in the polls. The pundits called it pretty much a draw, with the exception of Michael Sullivan who performed well enough to be declared a winner by a majority of the press. While they were preparing for the debate Mary Sullivan broached the idea with Jocko and the others that she should stay behind in Denver to conduct meetings with Hispanic women while Michael moved on to Wisconsin and Iowa. At first Michael was dead set against it arguing it would be dangerous for her to be on her own. She argued that she, Sally Kennedy and Rita Galvin had been discussing what they could do for the campaign. Their idea was to go to the states with heavy Hispanic population and hold teas just for the women. With her new skills at speaking the language and with added help from the two wives, who also could speak a smattering of Spanish, they could make inroads in that crucial vote. She reminded the team how successful Rose Kennedy and her daughters had been in holding teas all Around Massachusetts when Kennedy defeated Henry Cabot Lodge for the U. S. Senate seat in 1952.

"I remember it well" Jocko O'Brian said. "They started out small inviting a hundred women and fifty would show up. When it caught on they couldn't find houses large enough to hold the ladies so they moved to hotel ball rooms. I remember the Kennedys credited the teas for Jack's victory. I say let her do it."

"What about security and housing?" someone asked.

"I'll make sure they have plenty of security and we will work out a schedule if the idea catches on in Denver" John Kennedy said enthusiastically and turned to Michael: "Can she do it?"

The Senator laughed and said if she and the ladies had the gumption to do it go ahead.

The next day Mary had 200 invitations sent and 75 women came. After tea was served by Mary, Sally and Rita everyone was seated and given brochures with Michael's picture on the front and facts and positions on issues in the inside. In Spanish she told them how important the family was and she described her own family and how they drew strength from each other. With fervor she told them her husband believed the family was the rock upon which the nation was built. She praised them for their love of family. After an hour and a half everyone began to leave but not before they were given a volunteer card to sign. After the food was cleared away they sat in the kitchen of the house and counted the volunteer cards and were delighted that of the thirty five who signed twenty volunteered to host a tea party for Mary and her cohorts. In the next two days they hosted twelve tea parties each one with a crowd larger than the last. Four hundred Hispanic women signed up to go door to door with pamphlets hold tea parties and get out the vote on election day. Mary reported the results to Jocko O'Brian who told her they were all proud of the efforts the ladies were making and to keep it up.

Mary and her companions were tired after the Denver experience so decided to take a few days off and plan an itinerary for the rest of November. It was decided they would skip Thanksgiving and have a turkey dinner with their husbands in early December. All the while Mary was thinking how much fun the tea parties were and to see the reactions of the Hispanic ladies was a special treat. Nobody had ever come around and asked personally for the vote. No one had ever told them what a wonderful job they were doing to raise their families. Mary Sullivan became a heroine to the Hispanic ladies of Denver.

"Michael, Mary gushed, I've been doing well out on the stump and I really believe we're on to something. The reception has been fantastic and with my Spanish I've really been able to talk with the ladies and understand their problems. They are all family. They think same sex marriage is ridiculous and abortion is abhorred. Many had never heard of you and only a few had seen the debates. They are going to get out the vote for you in their neighborhoods. We're going on to Pueblo, Colorado next."

"Sweet heart I only ask that you ladies don't kill yourselves on my behalf. Better we lose than have you in the hospital from exhaustion."

"Don't worry about us; I've asked Kathryn to join us in Pueblo and she's received permission from the firm to be on the road with us for the next two weeks."

"That's great. She'll keep an eye on the three of you. I can't wait to see you. We can have thanksgiving in different motels, a reunion in December then home for Christmas."

Gratified at the result they achieved in Denver they didn't know what to expect in Pueblo. It was better than Denver. 400 women showed up and Mary wowed them with her speech in Spanish. Rita Galvin and Sally Kennedy got into the act circulating amongst the women speaking Spanish. More volunteers were recruited. By this time Jocko was beginning to see the Mary Sullivan operation could be significant and he advised her the campaign was ready to put money behind any ideas she and the ladies could come up with. After a sortie in Las Vegas covered widely by the press their teas broke into the national media with pictures of the event all over television. Back in Washington they sat down and decided to expand the operation to twelve states and enlist volunteers in those states to hold tea parties. Wives of the campaign's fund raisers volunteered to go into the states, several of whom spoke fluent Spanish---all this to be starting January 2, 2016. They were encouraged by polling done by Truman Foster in the areas where they had held teas. The polls showed they were picking up points in the Hispanic population as word spread about Mrs. Sullivan's tea parties.

They all gathered in Spring Valley, except Peter who had to stay in Rome to serve mass at St John Lateran on Christmas day. Jack speculated, with confidence, it would be second to the last Christmas they spent at Spring Valley for at least four years.

"I gather you think your father will win the Presidency next year?" Mary asked in mock shock.

"Indeed I do, Mother. In 2017 I'm bringing the family to the White House for Christmas dinner."

Kathryn Sullivan, who thought her brother Jack was perfect and laughed at all his jokes, said with a look of disbelief, "How are you so sure Jack, we could lose you know, ever consider that?"

"I've considered it and rejected the thought sister. It just seems so natural that I've never given defeat a second thought. Trust me."

It had been almost a year since they had all been together and they relished the opportunity to catch up on family gossip and to forget politics for a few days, with one exception Mary Sullivan, the matriarch, who spent at least two of the days on the phone putting together a team that would take the "tea party" idea beyond the Hispanic community and into the homes of women in at least 20 states. Jocko had given the go ahead on the financing and considered it a small expense for the work they were accomplishing. As had been their habit the entire family including Jack's two small children attended midnight mass at Annunciation down the street on Massachusetts Avenue. Since Michael did not qualify for Secret Service protection before the primaries got underway, Kennedy's group were in all corners of the church with ear phones and for all intents and purposes it looked like a full presidential detail. Michael Sullivan disliked the idea of having protection in the church feeling it was a distraction to the worshipers. Kennedy insisted and the crowd, knowing who he was paid no attention, and in fact it made a lot of them thrilled to have a fellow parishioner who might be President celebrating mass with them.

Christmas morning they were up early to watch the children open their gifts and while everyone was in the living room exchanging gifts and wrapping paper covered the floor, Michael was in the kitchen by himself whipping up scrambled eggs, bacon, sausage, hash brown potatoes coffee, sweet rolls. With the balance of a ballerina he twisted and turned going back and forth watching all his efforts come to fruition. When the feast was prepared he called out to them "breakfast is being served." They all gathered at their seats and the Senator offered a blessing for the food he just prepared. When he was finished the noise level rose and everyone started talking at once. Mary told of her adventures with the tea parties and what was planned, Michael spoke of what he had seen on the trail and the pessimism people expressed about the way the country was going.

"So many are unemployed, they feel like statistics. It's heart breaking to see men in their fifties who once held responsible jobs, out of work for a year sometime two. I've spoken to the families and it has taken a tremendous toll on them and on their marriages. The administration and its press corps keeps telling them how well off they are with the unemployment rate at 5.2%. They know better because they are part of the real unemployment figure of 18%. Obama tells us the economy is growing when in fact we've been in a recession since 2009. The question is will these people turn out and vote or be too discouraged and stay at home?"

"My age group is going to vote and I don't think it's going to be for hard hearted Hanna the vamp of Savannah."

"You're too hard on Hanna Jack," Kathryn laughed, "no pun intended."

"I don't think you can be too hard on her. She's mean and untrustworthy. Four years of her after Obama would put the country under water. Not even dad could bring it back. He's going to have a hell of a time doing as it is."

Michael took it all in as his children and grandchildren joked and argued with each other. What a clan he thought. Here we are about to embark on a journey not knowing where it will lead us and our gang can't wait for it to happen. He was amazed at how Mary had thrown herself into the campaign completely absorbed with getting out with the people and seeing concrete results. If they won she would be a real asset in the **White House**.

"How do you think the others are doing dad," Sharon asked anxiously, hoping to hear he was winning and they were losing.

"I think Bernie Winslow will win in Iowa, and I'm hoping we come in a close second. In New Hampshire, Sam Tortelli has spent a lot of time and is placing all his chips there. If he loses I don't think he has the money to stay in the race."

"How will we do there?"

We have to come in no lower than third. A loss won't kill us because Tom and the fellows have raised plenty of money but it will make the job tougher. My guess is Tortelli will win it and we will be a close second. Next comes South Carolina and Nevada. I think we can win both of those.

In January 2016 President Obama gave his final state of the Union address. Bailey Long, the majority leader, who had to be present due to his position, said it was "pabulum." Others were not as charitable saying it was only loyalty to the institution that caused them to be present. Forty members of the House Republican caucus were absent refusing to bow to precedent. Of this the press made no note, but it wasn't missed by the bloggers who lit up the internet with the news many Republicans had absented themselves from the joint session including Senator Michael Sullivan who was campaigning in Florida. While Mary and her troops had been quite successful in their Spanish speaking forays, Michael had been a little hesitant because he had not mastered the language as she had. Nevertheless, he gave three speeches in Dade County to overwhelming Hispanic crowds. He said, if President, he would not recognize the communist dictatorship in Cuba. He championed the family and condemned abortion. He told them a man and his wife were only ones who should be recognized as married and he reiterated what he told voters all over the country: their marriage was ordained by natural law and no court or legislature could change that fact. Because they too believed marriage was between a man and a woman they listened and cheered hm. The more he stressed these values, and saw how they were received by his audiences the more confidence he had that he was right in speaking out on issues most politicians were staying silent on.

By Mid January five debates had been held and Michael made four of the five concluding it was taking too much time to prepare when his time could be spent more profitably on the road, where he was talking with 25 radio and television stations each day and making four public appearances a day. As the first caucus drew near in Iowa a debate was scheduled on the eve of the vote. All six candidates were on the stage and after five debates they were all getting proficient in dealing with the issues and what counted more and more was how they looked and acted when handling a question. Trial practice made the Senator superior to the others in presentation. He was completely natural and gave the impression when answering a question that there were only two people in the room, the interrogator and himself. He seemingly was totally unaware of the millions watching and the live audience. The viewers got the impression they were looking in on a private conversation. The others made themselves the focus, whereas Michael made the viewer the focus. Finally after the fifth debate the media began to pick up on this trait and commented on it in their columns next day.

Two days before the Iowa caucuses the Sullivan campaign sent two groups of shock troops into Iowa and New Hampshire for the February 9th primary. Their job was to get out the vote by running transportation pools for those unable to get to their precincts, calling down voters if they had not yet voted and urging them to get to the polls, offering to drive them if necessary. In the overall scheme of the campaign it was decided to go light in Iowa and New Hampshire because of the historical unpredictability of those two states voters and put heavy emphasis into South Carolina and the states that followed, the most important of which was "Super Tuesday" with twelve states going to the polls. Michael spent the day before the vote in Iowa flying by helicopters to six towns and the day of the vote moved onto New Hampshire. The press was prepped and in a frenzy over the first contest in the nation. After fourteen months of politics the time had arrived to hear from the voters. On the eve of the vote Truman Foster's internal polling showed: Winslow 38%; Sullivan 35%; Tortelli 8%; Batterman 7%; Bruck 3%; Swanson 2%; Undecided 7%.

That evening as the vote totals came in it became apparent it was a two man race between ex-Governor Bernard Winslow of North Carolina and Senator Michael Sullivan. The race was called by the major networks at 11pm Est.

Winslow	31,206
Sullivan	29,437
Batterman	17,550
Tortelli	15,227
Bruck	15,206
Swanson	12,233

All the analysts agreed it was a minor upset by Governor Winslow and would result in a lot of pressure on Michael Sullivan to win the New Hampshire primary. When asked about it the next morning in Concord, New Hampshire Michael told a gaggle of reporters with a smile; "I feel very good with the vote received in Iowa. It wasn't a first but it was a second so we are going to try and beat that here in New Hampshire and we're hoping for a win in Nevada on the 20th."

"Do you think this race will be over by April or could it go to the convention?"

"I don't think any of the candidates want this to go to the convention; that would only handicap the eventual nominee. No, I believe we'll have a nominee by mid-April." He waved to everyone and departed for the next stop. From the battle plan they had drawn up Michael felt the second in Iowa and a second in New Hampshire would leave him right where they expected to be. Galvin and Kennedy would start the heavy television buys in the twelve states set to cast votes on March 1. That's where the break out would occur. When he arrived at his next stop in Manchester, a phone call was waiting. It was from John Kennedy who sounded calm but alarmed.

"Michael when Mary got back home from Iowa yesterday she didn't feel too well. She didn't want to bother you so she called Sally saying she didn't feel well enough to go to Atlanta. They were going to Georgia today to run their coffee operation. The short of it is Sally took her to emergency at George Washington hospital and they've diagnosed pretty sever pneumonia. I think she needs you."

"John, I'm on the next plane, I'll be there this afternoon. Will you advise the team to get out a press release saying I will be suspending my campaign until further notice."

"That's a little precipitous Michael. I think we should just say Mary has contracted pneumonia from working too hard in the campaign and that you will be spending time in Washington to be with her during this crisis."

"I agree John that's a little softer. I didn't mean to be grandstanding."

"You're not Senator; my reaction would be the same as yours if it was Sally. I think this thing is serious but she should come out of it. And I'm going ask Sally and Rita to carry on the coffee operation from here on out. Now go get that plane. If you need me I'll be in New York for the next few days. God bless you."

John Kennedy arranged for a charter flight to Washington D.C.'s Reagan Airport and Michael arrived at the hospital at 2 p.m. and was greeted by the hospital head, Dr. Philip Wilson.

"How is she Doctor" he asked as the two of them headed to the ICU unit on an upper floor. The press flooded the lobby of the hospital barred from going further by the police. They shouted at Michael as he waited at the elevator with Doctor Wilson. Once in the elevator the Doctor told him she had a severe case of pneumonia and she had been put into the ICU unit to assist her breathing which was labored.

"How serious is it? He asked and prayed to God at the same time that she would live. He felt tremendous guilt in allowing her to go campaigning for him running the coffees in at least ten states. Working herself to the bone she had become a perfect target for a pneumonia infection. He vowed she would do no more campaigning and he would quit the race if it was a matter of her survival.

"Its serious in the sense that she has been hospitalized and put in the intensive care unit. We will be giving her antibiotics intravenously and monitoring her closely for the next forty eight hours. Unless there is further change she should be all right but will have to stay in the hospital for a week to ten days. We will no more in forty eight hours."

"Can I see her?" He asked humbly.

"You can but she heavily sedated and will probably not recognize you. Go on in I'll wait outside for you if you have further questions."

He entered the room and saw her immediately; her head was on a white pillow, her hair arranged on the pillow and tubes in her nose. To him she was a beautiful sight and he felt tears welling up and then surging down his cheeks. He kissed her. She didn't open her eyes so he just stared at her thinking about how much she had sacrificed for her family. How she had thrown herself into the campaign and put together a network that was spreading throughout the country and undoubtedly adding to the votes he would need to win. He kissed her again and left the room wiping the tears from his eyes. When the doctor saw how emotional he was he softened his tone and told him she would receive the best of care and that there would be a pulmonologist and cardiologist on duty twenty four hours a day until she was out of danger.

"I'd like to stay here tonight doctor to be with her is that possible?"

"I will make arrangements to put you up in the room next door so that you are free to go in and check on her with the head nurse's permission."

"Thank you doctor I appreciate all you're doing please take care of her." He put in a call to the children and advised them of the situation. Jack and Kathryn said they would be on the next plane and Sharon was summoned from Georgetown Hospital to mount an all night vigil for Mary Sullivan.

At 7:00 p.m. that evening the hospital issued the following bulletin: "Mary Sullivan, the wife of Senator Michael Sullivan, was received in emergency this morning and was diagnosed with a case of sever pneumonia. As a precaution she was placed in the ICU unit and will remain there until her condition stabilizes."

Speculation was rampant in the media. "Will this hurt his campaign?" they asked each other on the talk shows. "Will he have to drop out of the race?" "Will he suspend his campaign in New Hampshire and leave the field to the other five candidates?" To these questions the campaign responded that the only concern the Senator had was for his wife. Any decisions concerning the campaign would be put on hold.

Jocko O'Brian was in total charge and the advertising was running in New Hampshire, South Carolina and Nevada as though nothing had occurred. Paul, John Kennedy and Tom Galvin made a decision the day Mary went into the hospital they would proceed with the campaign until they heard differently from Michael.

The next morning he was awake at six o'clock and peeked into ICU. She was still asleep and pallor was better than the day before. He decided to get a cup of coffee and started to leave the room when he was stopped by someone with a secret service earpiece.

"Senator, I'm here with a number of other personnel watching out for you and your wife. Can I get you anything?"

"What's your name son?" Michael immediately remembered he wasn't a private citizen anymore and that John Kennedy would have arranged protection at the same time they both knew about Mary. "Bud Merchant Senator, can I be of some service?" he repeated

Bud you can do me a big favor if you'll go down to the cafeteria and get me a roll and black coffee"

The big man (6'4") gestured to another man at the end of the hall, gave instructions to get what the Senator asked for and resumed his seat outside Michael's room. He went back in, sat on the bed, pulled some rosary beads from a suit coat pocket and started praying for his wife. A few minutes later the coffee and a Danish arrived and he wolfed it down forgetting he had not eaten for fifteen hours. About 8.a.m. he heard commotion in the ICU next door and swiftly leaving the room he went next door. She was awake, still had the oxygen mask on, and he could tell him tell she was smiling at him from the twinkle in her eyes. A nurse was in the room taking her vitals, so he excused himself, kissed her on the forehead and left the room. She squeezed his hand and somehow he knew she was going to be all right. The head nurse appeared at the door and politely asked him to leave and come back later as the doctors would be coming to check on her. Out of his element he obeyed and walked down the corridor from his room to the ICU waiting room where Jack, Sharon and Kathryn had been sleeping on couches with two of Kennedy's men sitting on chairs guarding them. Jack woke up when he came in.

"Dad, have you seen her?"

"I have Jack. She's all doped up and has tubes in her but she saw me and smiled. She's sick but she's alive. Thank God for that."

"Can we see her?" At that Sharon and Kathryn woke up and wished their father a good morning.

"You don't look so great dad, you haven't shaved and you look exhausted," Kathryn said with feeling knowing how upset he was about her mother. "Have you had anything to eat? Can I go down to the cafeteria and get you anything."

"No sweetheart, I think if you ask one of these gentlemen to go down and get something for you three, they will be happy to do it. I've had a roll and some hot coffee that's all I want." Kennedy's man brought back rolls, jugs of orange juice and a couple pots of coffee. After they had satisfied their hunger Jack asked if the two guards would step outside the waiting room so they could have some privacy. They discussed how they would handle Mary once she was able to come home and who would stay with her. It was decided Kathryn would stay at Spring Valley with Mary and any necessary nursing help would be brought in as needed.

"What about you Dad, New Hampshire is six days off; will you go up for the vote?"

"Michael hesitated before speaking knowing that it might be difficult for them to understand he couldn't campaign knowing Mary was laying in the hospital still critically ill. The doctors had told him that. They had not seen their mother and when they did he hoped they would understand that the last thing he was thinking about was the Presidency. If for any reason she didn't recover or was slow to recover he would withdraw his candidacy and remain with her.

"Jack I'm not going to campaign in New Hampshire or anywhere else until we have something definitive about your mother. The doctors have told me her condition is serious but she should recover. I can't make any decision until we know how she does the next few days."

"You know best dad; we're with you no matter what you and mother decide."

The girls were not as stricken as Jack at Michael's reaction. For them their mother was more important than any office even the highest office in the land. Jack felt the same way yet he knew his mother and father had worked so hard in doing what they believed was the right thing to do and further that his father was the one man most qualified to save the country from the quagmire it was in. He also knew the decision was out of his hands so he decided to concentrate on Mary's getting well. While the outside world was consumed with terrorists, the election, murders, kidnapping, verdicts, Iran, Iraq and Obama the Sullivans were living in a dwarfed world that revolved around Mary's Room, Michael's room and the cafeteria of George Washington hospital. For three nights Mary was in ICU and on the fourth day she was moved to a private room and the doctors had told the Sullivans she was responding to the massive doses of antibiotics she was receiving. On the morning of the third day Michael was able to spend an hour with her and he told her he had been giving the situation a lot of thought and he had decided to forego the campaign until she was back on her feet. As weak as she was when he suggested what he was thinking about doing, she rose up on her elbows and told him he was wrong to even think such a thing. "You're thinking about yourself she gently scolded. It's God's way not yours. He has sent this illness to me, and I accept it, but your role is to get back on the road and make good on our promise to work for the greater glory of God, *Ad Majorem Dei Gloriam*." He knew she was right and for the first time in a week he felt the clouds clear away.

Sunday night, February 9th he called John Kennedy from Mary's hospital room and put Mary on the line. "How are you Mary dearest," the billionaire said in such a soft voice Mary hardly recognized it.

"John I'm fine in the sense I'm going to make it and will you thank Sally for getting me in here and I hope to be going home in about ten days. My problem now is my stubborn husband has tried to tell me he should stop campaigning while I have pneumonia. I've told him he should do no such thing. I want you to tell him the same thing. To get back in there and start fighting for what we all believe in."

"Mary I'm thrilled to hear the vigor in your voice and I know you're going to be all right, but I would not dare to tell Michael Sullivan what to do when it comes to you. He wouldn't listen anyway. You he will listen to. If you tell him to be here tomorrow morning for the last day of campaigning in New Hampshire, he will come."

"I've told him to get up there and he should be there by midnight. You'd better send a plane to pick him up and I've told him to go in there and win one for the gipper." Kennedy couldn't help but laugh at her spunk and he said: "Mary if we win we owe it all to you."

CHAPTER 7

HE EXITED THE plane and there to greet him were thirty or forty members of the press who had been alerted from Washington he was on his way to New Hampshire. He walked slowly towards the terminal at Manchester-Boston regional airport answering questions as he made his way to a private entrance surrounded by reporters and the ever present bodyguards. "How's Mrs. Sullivan? Do you expect to win on Tuesday? Will you stay in the race if she doesn't get well?"

"She's doing much better and thanks for asking. I would like to win on Tuesday but we'll just have to wait and see. I think she's going to get well and so does she so my answer to that last question is we're not going to have a problem and with a little luck she'll be answering your questions herself." As soon as he made the statement he knew he had misspoke because he had no intention of letting her do any more campaigning on his behalf. A motorcade made up of three SUVs took him to a motel in Manchester where he would catch four hours sleep before appearing at his first stop a breakfast meeting with the chamber of commerce.

Monday morning, February 8th The *Boston Sun* came out with a column on the primary written by Toby Larkin setting out what he considered to be the "morning line" for the race the next day:

Boston: Tony Larkin

"The horses are in the starting gate, the voters are poised to make their bets ----Who will they favor? The polls show

Bernard Winslow, who captured the prize in Iowa, set to claim a second victory. Michael Sullivan was bested in Iowa; will New Hampshire follow Iowa's lead? I would say yes except for the fact Sullivan's wife is in the hospital in Washington with pneumonia and he has been at her bedside all week forgoing waging a campaign in New Hampshire. Will that hurt or help him? New Hampshire is fickle when it comes to Republican primaries. Often times the leader in the polls is upset by someone two or three from the top. They are contrarians. If I were a betting man, which I am, I would put money on Winslow to win, Richard Batterman to place and Michael Sullivan to show with the rest out of the running. I think at 8:00 pm tomorrow night when the polls close at least two of the candidates will be dropping from the race, Patricia Swanson, who has done very well to make it past Iowa and George Bruck, who while well funded, has squandered any goodwill he had with the voters by viciously attacking Michael Sullivan. No matter what happens it has been good for New Hampshire as it has been every four years putting the state in the national spotlight."

As Michael entered the hotel the snow began falling softly. An hour went by; he spoke to packed house, and was on his way to the next stop. The snow was now swirling and coming in sheets with a good two inches on the ground. "How will this effect turnout tomorrow," he quizzed his driver.

"Not too much," the young driver answered, "the folks up here are pretty hardy and a little snow doesn't send them into a panic."

"Well, Jason, as long as you're driving I have no fear of getting to the next stop but I don't know about that press bus that's three cars back. Maybe you should slow down a bit so they don't think we're trying to ditch them." The driver laughed and said impishly: "I've been watching in the rear view and they are having a bad time. We wouldn't want anything to happen to that press bus would we Senator?"

"I take it you're a big fan of the media Jason"

"Not too much senator; I have a bumper sticker on my car that says 'beat the press'"

All day he sloshed through the snow with John Kennedy at his side covering seven events and a 15 minute television appearance speaking directly to the voters. He told them he would restore their health care by repealing Obama Care and returning to the day they could have their own doctor and keep their own insurance something they had been cheated out of by the current administration. He would seal the southern border of the United States and defer immigration from the southern hemisphere for a period to be decided upon. He would immediately cancel cuts in the army made by the Obama administration. He would build our defenses so that aggressors such as China, Russia, Iran and North Korea would think twice before challenging the United States. Domestically he would clean out the Department of Justice and restore it to its rightful place in the scheme of government. He would put an end to federally funded abortion. After the broadcast he and John Kennedy went back to the motel and waiting were Tom Galvin and Jocko O'Brian who had been taking soundings all day on the expected vote.

It was eleven at night and rather than meeting in the bar for a last minute round up they decided to have drinks in Michael's room as the bar on the ground floor was swarming with press most of them feeling no pain after a week of following the six candidates up and down the granite state in snow blizzards.

"You fellows look exhausted" Tom said sympathetically as he notice the lines around the candidate's face.

"We'll be fine Tom, John here is a little tired but he made it thru."

"Listen Tom, I had to carry this guy through the last three stops and I'm older than our candidate. Scotch anyone? They all nodded and he poured it straight out of the bottle into plastic cups he had brought along especially for such occasions. "All right Jocko where do we stand?"

"We won't win but we won't be third. It's a two man race at this point. They discussed the campaign for another hour and retired to await the next day's vote.

The media was surprised by the outcome and barely hiding their bias by hoisting Governor Bernard Winslow as the front runner in the Republican primary. They knew that their champion Hanna Hamilton could probably beat the governor but they harbored serious doubts in their editorial conference rooms whether she could beat Michael Sullivan. Moreover they despised his stance on almost every issue. Stories written in the *New York Tribune* and the *Washington Star* could have been written by the same writer and perhaps they were.

New York Tribune, February 10, 2016:

"Governor Bernard Winslow of North Carolina has put down two markers, Iowa and New Hampshire and now heads to South Carolina---home territory for him---to see if he can make it a triple. Some may argue his win last night was a fluke because Senator Sullivan barely made any appearances the week before the primary due to his wife's illness. Nevertheless his campaign outspent Governor Winslow 2 to 1 yet it was not enough to win. With two important wins Winslow has to be considered the front runner and Michael Sullivan must win in South Carolina or be counted out.

These first two primaries have demonstrated, if anything, there are just two viable candidates going forward, Winslow and Sullivan. Bruck and Swanson will surely drop out as the race heads south to South Carolina and west to the Nevada caucuses. At some point next month Tortelli and Batterman will become irrelevant."

New Hampshire Republican Primary Results

Candidate	Vote
Winslow	75,420
Sullivan	70,405
Bruck	28,756
Tortelli	20,620
Batterman	18,462
Swanson	4,784

In Manchester, the night of the election, Michael met with his supporters thanking them for their efforts on his behalf, gave interviews to all the national television and cable networks, had a short meeting with O'Brian, Kennedy and Galvin and headed to the airport to fly back to Washington where Mary was still hospitalized. When they heard he would be coming the hospital arranged for a room next door to Mary's. In the morning they had breakfast together in her room and he was amazed at how well she looked compared to her appearance before he went to New Hampshire.

"Tell me about it Michael." She propped up her pillows and fell back on them prepared to hear it from the candidate's point of view.

"You know the result," he began, sipping the last of his coffee. We actually did better than Jocko predicted; he was thinking a third place finish was definitely possible so we all thought the close second was good. The voters up there are fairly liberal and they are a demanding group. It's retail politics at the grass roots. We have some terrific people up there working for us and we'll need them in the general. New Hampshire could make the difference. All of us were wading through the snow on Monday and the only one I had a chance to talk to was Bernie Winslow and he was very gracious. I think he knew that day he was going to win so appeared fairly confident. If Jocko is on schedule we'll win in South Carolina and Nevada. Now I don't want to talk about politics I want to know how you feel."

"I'm tired but I know I'm going to be fine; you've all been so good to me. I can't wait to get back to the coffees."

He took her hand in his and said gently: "Mary, my sweetheart, you're not going back to the campaign. I need you well; we all need you well. That's why you're here; you were out there driving to hard."

She knew he was right so made no fuss except to ask how he would feel about her going back in the fall. He got up and kissed her and said: "How do you know we will be campaigning in the fall?"

"Because I know it in my heart and you do to my coy one. You're going to need me as your hostess in the White House so you'd better be nice to me."

"Well if you keep yourself well until the fall then we will let you make some appearances on behalf of the candidate and then you can become the chief hostess at the White House."

"All right, my husband, I'm a little tired now so you go about your business and we'll talk later about what you should do next."

Nobody was paying too much attention to Nevada with only 30 delegates but in Jocko O'Brian's thinking the name of the game was delegates, not how many primaries you win. He had planned to win the majority of delegates in Nevada and the Sullivan brain trust had decided to spend what was necessary to do that if for some reason Michael lost in South Carolina the Winslow bandwagon could be halted in Nevada. First on the agenda was to compete in South Carolina so While Galvin and Kennedy went back on the fund raising circuit, he and Michael made their headquarters in Hilton Head the resort area. Every county was filled with volunteers and twenty professionals were brought in to coordinate the campaign. With two wins behind him Bernard Winslow, the southerner, was in home country and felt he would pick up his third win and be in the cat bird seat going into Super Tuesday. A poll out on February 15th seemed to bear him out. Winslow 30%; Sullivan 25%; Batterman 13%; Tortelli 10%; Bruck 6%; Swanson 3%; Undecided 13%.

Michael worked the state hard hitting most of the population centers, including: Charleston, North Charleston, Greenville, Columbia, Rock Hill city and by helicopter Spartanburg and Mt. Pleasant Town on February 19th, the day before the election. Tom Donovan, a lawyer, and managing partner of at Connolly, Wilson & Riley traveled though out the state with the Senator. In January a decision had been made by Paul Connolly to release Tom from his assignment at the Washington firm to serve the campaign wherever needed. He had been a partner in the firm when Michael was elected to the Senate in 2008 and went with him as chief of staff. In 2012 Paul Connolly decided to open up an office in Washington to accommodate the firm's clients. He chose Tom Donovan to build the practice and within three years the firm went from he and two associates to eight partners and twenty associates. It turned out to be a shrewd move and complimented the 120 person home office.

After the campaign he intended to continue heading up the Washington office. Close cropped hair, blue eyes, mildly graying hair, Tom stood six feet and carried his college weight, a hundred and seventy five pounds. For Michael he was a gift because he had been a championship tennis player at U.C.L.A and frequently played doubles with Michael and Senators Bud Hanson of Georgia and Ted Huntington of Louisiana. A graduate of Georgetown University law school, he worked on the hill for a Congressman for two years and then decided he wanted to practice law as a litigator and so returned to Michael's home town and was hired as an associate at Connolly, Wilson & Riley. At 37, his progression had been rapid. Married with two small children he and his wife, Millie lived in Westley Heights not far from Spring Valley where the Senator lived. It turned out that he and Michael worked well as a team in South Carolina and he was asked to work on Super Tuesday, the next phase of the campaign.

South Carolina proved as Jocko had predicted. Bernard Winslow won but not by much. More importantly Michael gained 15 delegates to Winslow's 35. Three days later Nevada fell into Michael's column so that after four caucuses and primaries the delegate count stood at:

Bruck	4
Swanson	0
Winslow	76
Sullivan	52
Batterman	7
Tortelli	3

March 1, Super Tuesday, was now the crucial date. What the campaign hoped would be the turning point with at least two more candidates dropping out and a head to head battle with Bernard Winslow through March. Twelve states with 686 delegates at stake.

In January they planned to spend nine days after South Carolina in six states leading up to March 1st. Time would be spent in Virginia, Arkansas, Tennessee, Texas, Georgia and Alabama where most of the delegates would be garnered. Tom Donovan would travel with Michael together with five or six aides and the campaign spokesman Dominic Donitelli. North Carolina was left off the list with the knowledge Bernard Winslow would win a majority of his state's delegates. Their first stop was Richmond, Virginia where Michael addressed a crowd of 5,000 Republicans. He told the crowd he would not abide by the deal the Obama administration had agreed to with Iran. The deal was made with a sworn enemy of the United States determined to produce a nuclear bomb. He called negotiations and eventual adoption by the President and the Secretary of State as an act of insanity and he agreed with Congress's refusal to sign on to it. Polling established the country was set against the agreement. Most Republicans and Independents clearly saw the agreement as a "cave in" to the Ayatollah Khomeini and his terrorists colleagues and Michael's denouncing the plan brought cheers from the audience. By February of 2016 the country was no longer listening to the President knowing they would not hear the truth. They craved a new leader. The crowds in Virginia were encouraging and Truman Foster's polls showed they should win in Virginia.

In Little Rock, Arkansas the crowds came out to see Michael Sullivan who had not been in their state for over a year and now he came as a leading candidate for the Republican nomination. Jocko placed the state in the toss up column but that was before Michael got to the voters.

They liked him and no other candidate would be coming into the state before election. The Winslow campaign was putting everything it had into Texas, Georgia and Alabama with North Carolina already a win for them according to the tracking polls. Knowing how important Arkansas would be in the Fall election Tom Galvin and John Kennedy decided to spend heavily, half on Michael's behalf and half attacking Hanna Hamilton; four million dollars was poured in up through election day and the result was an endorsement by the *Arkansas Ledger*. They left Arkansas on Thursday February 25, and flew to, Memphis, Tennessee to meet with the editors of the *Memphis Courier* who proved to be a knowledgeable group of newspaper men and women. The first question asked was why he thought he could beat Bernie Winslow their neighbor and fellow southerner.

"Bernie is a good man and a friend of mine. As you know he beat me for the Vice Presidential nomination in 2012. Since then we have crossed each other's path many times and we see eye to eye on a number of issues. I part company with him on immigration, Iraq, right to work, and numerous other issues. I think the people of Tennessee will agree with my stands on the issues. I also think the people of this state want to win the election this year. I've never lost an election and I don't intend to lose this one. My goal is to restore this country to its proper place amongst world powers and that means beating Hanna Hamilton in November. I believe I can do that."

"Are you assuming you will be the nominee Senator?"

"Gentlemen, I'm not assuming anything but I am confident that after Super Tuesday I will be leading in delegates."

"Can we quote you on that Senator?" Thinking he had set a trap and Michael had fallen into it the editorial board member waited for his answer picturing the next day's political headline: "Senator Sullivan says he will be the big winner on Super Tuesday"

"Yes, you can quote me on that gentleman." The meeting broke up and they shook hands all around. The next day the paper carried the headline Michael thought he would win on Super Tuesday and an editorial read:

"In an interview with the editorial board of this newspaper yesterday we engaged in an extraordinary conversation with Senator Michael Sullivan who was campaigning in our state. We found him knowledgeable on domestic and foreign affairs but more importantly he exudes the air of a man who can win the presidency. We asked tough questions and he gave straight answers. He didn't equivocate and he didn't dodge. We didn't agree with everything he said but in our view he can defeat Hanna Hamilton. This is not to say Governor Bernard Winslow is not a worthy opponent, he is, but we believe the nod must go to Michael Sullivan."

They rolled into Atlanta on the 26th, dropped their bags at the Airport Marriott Gateway, and took a helicopter to the suburb of Kennesaw where a crowd was waiting. He was met at the door by a leading supporter and the minute he appeared at the door to the gymnasium a crowd of 4,000 Republicans came to their feet and the applause thundered up to the rafters. Super charged by the spontaneous reception he slowly made his way to the stage shaking hands all the way.

"What a great reception. Thank you. I'm pleased to be with you today because Tuesday is the day of reckoning and I'm here to ask for your vote. I don't need to tell you the shape the country's in. You're living it every day. It's got to change. The present administration has had seven years to bring the country to its knees. It can be turned around. It starts with a restoration of values. Values we have lost through the secularizing of society. This country is tied together by family. The family is under attack in our secular society. Stand up fight back. Stand up for marriage. Stand up for truth. Stand up for our military. Stand up for America."

That did it. Wave after wave of applause washed over the crowd. Tom Donovan said later it sounded like the roof was going to come off the place. When the crowd grew attentive again he started speaking but was interrupted by voices coming out of the bleacher seats screaming: "Why are you against Gays Sullivan? Why are you against Gays Sullivan?" The crowd got ugly shouting at the chanters. Michael stood very still and then said to the crowd: "Let them speak" They yelled all the more accusing him of being against Gay marriage. He controlled the floor so that in a calm voice he said "You live in America and you are allowed to speak but not to the detriment of those who have come to hear a speech important to them. Nevertheless, I have listened to you now you listen to me."

With the crowd surrounding them, many willing to throw them out of the hall, they stopped their shouting. "I am not against gays but I am opposed to the gay agenda of trying to silence and intimidate all who disagree with them. For me marriage is between a man and a woman and no state or governing body or judicial action can change that fact. Gays should be treated like anyone else no better no worse." He hadn't quite finished when the crowd came to its feet. The protesters were shouted down by the audience. Michael continued on with a recitation of where he stood on the issues and from their reaction they stood with him. The speech lasted only twenty five minutes because he had five more stops in the suburbs around Atlanta: Lilburn, Lawrenceville, Buford, Duluth and John's Creek. They left the high school in Kennesaw by helicopter and flew fifteen minutes to the next stop. Jocko O'Brian had designed the Georgia Campaign to include only the suburbs where the vote was solid Republican and if they were to win Georgia it would be there. At each of the five stops Michael gave what was essentially a stump speech. They came to see him; they knew what he stood for. They knew he stood for them.

Saturday, the 27th, they were in Birmingham, Alabama at an outdoor breakfast served to 3,000 people. He stood behind the counter flipping pancakes with the volunteers and sending pictures back to Mary in Washington. When he started speaking the hecklers started up but the crowd would have none of it; the police removed them quickly and he went on with his speech. Afterward they helicoptered to four other cities and relaxed at the hotel that night. At eleven o'clock just as they were about to retire Jocko got everyone on a conference call to report the overnight polls in Georgia and Alabama.

"We're looking strong gentlemen in the south, which is Bernie Winslow's turf. The newspapers and the so called experts are counting us out because of Bernie's three straight wins but beware the ides of March, we stop him on Tuesday."

"How is it looking in the other ten?" Michael asked.

"All but Oklahoma and Tennessee---too close to call on those two. A loss won't be a shutout because we'll get delegates depending on the number of votes we get. I know you're all tired but we'll have a short break after the first. Good luck in Texas tomorrow, I will call tomorrow and we'll play Monday by ear. Get some rest Michael."

They buckled into their seats for the 7:30 am flight to El Paso, Texas where Michael planned to campaign among Hispanics who made up fifty percent of the population. The decision had been made to send him into El Paso, and San Antonio, Democratic strong holds, not so much to add to his primary votes as to acquaint the Hispanics with the candidate looking to the general election. Tom Donovan decided to sit up in the bleachers during Michael's noon appearance sponsored by the El Paso Republican Club, a group of young professionals dedicated to recruiting and running Hispanic candidates for office. The hall held 5,000 and was three quarters filled due to a week long effort by the club to get their people out. He started out in Spanish sometimes repeating in English. Tom watched the crowd above and below him when Michael talked about the importance of family in Spanish they applauded. When he talked about abortion and the effect it was having in their community they nodded in agreement. When he talked about immigration and what he intended to do about it the reaction was mixed; those who had become citizens the hard way clapped those whose legal entry was in doubt booed.

They listened on the economy because these were hard workers who wanted their children to get ahead. He talked about vouchers that would allow their children to go to a school of their choice. He pointed out the powerful teachers unions and the Democratic Party were against vouchers because they would cost the jobs of inefficient teachers. That they understood and it received the largest reaction of the afternoon. After the speech Michael came down off the platform and plunged into the center of the crowd. Nobody left. They crowded around him wanting to have their pictures taken with him. They liked this fellow; he took the trouble to speak their language, he talked family values, something they believed in. The handlers said it's time to go, but he was having too much of a good time and the crowd sensed it. Tom heard many of them say: *Que es un umbre Bueno* (he is a good man) All this he kept in his head until they were back on the plane to San Antonio, The advance people had done a spectacular job turning out thousands of Latinos and non Latinos. The travelling press in their stories said the crowd was at least 6,000. Michael wove the same themes into his speech and the crowd responded at the same points as they had in El Paso. Headed back to the hotel after the event he and Tom talked about what they had discovered as a result of the two appearances in the Latino Cities.

"I like these people Tom; they were a little stand offish when we started but after the speech down on the floor I felt they liked what they heard and while I might be a Republican I'm not such a bad guy."

"I worked the floor listening after you spoke. Two things stood out for me. One, they didn't leave and two I heard over and over again he's a good man. Michael I think we did some good with the Latinos and the issues they are interested in is education, vouchers, family and their religion, the same as yours

His interest piqued he looked quizzically at Tom and said: "I know they will vote for a Catholic, but a Republican Catholic?"

"A Catholic is a Catholic Michael; you'll get your share and you may even beat old Hanna in the percentages." They talked on until midnight and when Michael finally went to bed Tom sat at his computer and wrote down everything they had learned that day about the Latino vote which he intended to forward to the brain trust for comment. At 3:00 p.m. he fell into bed secure in the knowledge they might be able to get a higher percentage of the Hispanic vote nation-wide than any Republican had ever received in a national election.

Michael and Tom went to early mass in Houston and from there to a fund raiser hosted by Texas oil baron Hugh Munster. Gathered for a buffet breakfast were one hundred men and women who would be responsible for raising five million dollars. The day was cold and the skies gray but for those assembled it was a chance to get some inside information and Michael gave it to them feeling they worked hard for him and had a right to know he was working hard for them and their money was being well spent.

"The latest figures I have on our expenditures is a hundred and twenty five million with ten million in the bank. No one batted an eye at that information. "By the same token Hanna Hamilton has spent two hundred million and she has no opponent. As far as where we are I believe we will finish this second phase of the primaries with a lead of approximately 430 to 260 in delegates." Here he was interrupted by a gentleman in the front row who asked: "Senator you've lost three of the first four contests can you explain how you will wind up after Super Tuesday with more delegates than Winslow?" This question was not asked with any hostility but a genuine concern how the campaign could be losing primaries and still be ahead in delegates.

"Here is the breakdown Andy." Even though there were over a hundred in the room he remembered the gentleman's name and everyone present remarked about that after they left. These were important people in the Houston community and they appreciated the fact Michael would know any of them by name having met them for the first time at Hugh Munster's. "Impressive fellow, Hugh" they said. "We will give what it takes to put him in the White House."

He went on to tell them wins were expected in Alabama, Colorado, Georgia, Massachusetts, Minnesota, Texas, Vermont and Virginia with losses in North Carolina and Arkansas and Tennessee and Oklahoma too close to call. That night they were in Dallas for another fund raiser and an indoor meeting with 4,000 present. He gave his second speech of the day and boarded a plane with Tom for Washington where they would all be gathering at Spring Valley to await the Super Tuesday returns.

CHAPTER 8

THE CROWD AT the American Airlines Center was in a good mood and anxious to vote the next day in the primary election. Holding 20,000, at least 18,000 seats were filled by the time Michael arrived on stage. He spoke for 25 minutes and then answered questions for another half hour from members of the audience. The crowd appreciated it and the press duly noted it was highly unusual and dangerous to speak to a crowd of that size and offer to answer questions.

"Where do you stand on gun control?"

"The constitution provides for individuals to own guns. I support ownership of handguns and hunting rifles. I'm against automatic weapons except in the hands of law enforcement."

"What will you do to protect Social Security?"

"If I'm President I will move immediately to reform it to guarantee it will be available for the next fifty years. To do that age limits will have to be raised and payroll taxes increased. At the same time benefits will be reduced depending on the needs of the beneficiary. Some will get more the better off less. The program cannot sustain itself and will be bankrupt in a few years. Congress has not been able to act. I will lead and ask Congress to follow."

"What about Medicare for the oldsters?" (laughter)

"Going broke; too few supporting too many. Beneficiaries will have to pay more; possibly raising the age limits, cracking down on fraud and cutting the cost of services."

He rattled off his positions on about twenty issues, sometimes giving a short explanation and other times elaborating with more detail. The crowd loved it. On some issues they booed on most they applauded. When they booed he noted there were Democrats in the audience and they laughed appreciating the humor. "All in all a great night Senator," Tom enthused when they got in the motorcade to return to their hotel.

March 1. Day of decision. The team stayed in Dallas to set up for a campaign rally that night, but Tom and Michael and a five man team headed to Metairie, Louisiana for two appearances and an interview with Franklin Dubois of the *New Orleans Times Herald* and then the return flight to Dallas for the Rally. Sensing a victory a large crowd assembled in the ballroom of the Sheraton Hotel in downtown Dallas. A large Screen was placed at one end of the room with the names of the candidates, the states voting, and the number of votes for each candidate. Watchers could see the vote totals as they were posted electronically every five minutes. American flags were draped on the balcony surrounding the room. In the hall outside the press were gathered. The scene repeated itself in Madison, Wisconsin for Senator Richard Batterman, Newark, New Jersey for Samuel Tortelli, San Diego, California for Patricia Swanson, Durham, North Carolina for Bernard Winslow and George Bruck in Knoxesile, Tennesee.

In the suite at the Sheraton Michael, Tom Galvin, John Kennedy, Paul Connolly, Jocko O'Brian Tom Donovan, Truman Foster, the pollster, and Dominic Donatelli, the spokesman, gathered to see if the determined effort they had put in would be rewarded at the polls. As usual Jocko had set up a room next door to the suite filled with phones and computers with his operatives seated before their screens checking the county vote in each of the 12 states posting returns throughout the night. The information garnered would be fed into computer and used in the general election to pin point counties that would receive the most attention in the fall. Food had been brought in on platters and everyone helped themselves. Two barmen stood by to service the needs of the guests. In a corner of the room Michael was trying to talk to Mary filling her in on the day's events and the fact a plane would be standing by at 1:00 am to fly him back to Washington. She insisted he stay the night in the hotel and travel in the morning. He first said "no." Then he thought it over and decided she was right.

The men in the suite were apprehensive but confident the voting would break their way and they would move on to the next round with a lead in delegates. At 7:00 pm, Dallas time, the polls closed in the east and the results were immediately posted on the Board in the ballroom:

STATE	CANDIDATE	VOTE TOTAL	DELEGATES
Virginia	Winslow		6
	Sullivan		43
	Tortelli	3,623	0
	Batterman	6,466	0
Tennessee	Winslow	210,000	25
	Sullivan	85,284	20
	Tortelli	125,632	7
	Batterman	132,361	7
Georgia	Winslow	310,456	18
	Sullivan	335,258	47
	Tortelli	125,821	5
	Batterman	175,233	6

North	Winslow	605,815	42
Carolina	Sullivan	160,426	18
	Tortelli	120,168	5
	Batterman	115,248	5
Massachusetts	Winslow	100,025	10
	Sullivan	175,413	21
	Tortelli	70,268	6
	Batterman	40,482	4
Vermont	Winslow	18,249	4
	Sullivan	30,412	9
	Tortelli	10,620	2
	Batterman	9,452	2

"The eight o'clock vote looks good Michael," John Kennedy barked trying to hide his excitement. A monitor set up in the suite enabled those in the room to see the crowd in the ballroom below and the sight they saw was one of jubilation. These were the first votes coming in on Super Tuesday and to the Sullivan supporters it meant a bandwagon could be starting after the Winslow wins in Iowa, New Hampshire and South Carolina. "It's early, still I think we should drink to this early sign of victory. Anyone care to join me" Tom Galvin said striding over to the bar. With that said the two bartenders feverously began to pour scotch all around. It was 8:30 and Jocko came in from the war room next door to report from what they were getting from key precincts in Alabama Arkansas Minnesota, Texas and Oklahoma.

"Oklahoma and Alabama we may lose but everything else looks good including, the big one, Texas with 155 delegates. We'll know in one half hour how long this primary is going to last." Everyone's attention turned back to the television sets to await the next reports. The politicos were already sounding off, amazed at Sullivan's showing in the first states to report. Some wondered aloud with incredulity that his message of values might be resonating with the voters. Others said Winslow should win Texas a southern state and that would even the score of the eight o'clock vote totals.

Nine o'clock central time and all eyes turned to the Board in the ballroom as the numbers flashed on

STATE	CANDIDATE	VOTE TOTAL	DELEGATES
Alabama	Winslow	220,264	15
	Sullivan	185,614	15
	Batterman	25,264	4
Arkansas	Winslow	50,006	7
	Sullivan	64,276	33
	Tortelli	32,159	4
	Batterman	45,267	5
Minnesota	Winslow	12,513	11
	Sullivan	22,614	20
	Tortelli	8,248	3
	Batterman	9,498	4
Texas	Winslow	240,457	19
	Sullivan	1,256,000	112
	Tortelli	65,000	9
	Batterman	150,654	15
Oklahoma	Winslow	107,245	20
	Sullivan	99,894	17
	Tortelli	50,158	3
	Batterman	52,249	3

"By my tally," Paul Connolly said, standing on a chair in the center of the room looking down on the others studiously, "that's Winslow 187 delegates and Senator Michael Sullivan, 355 with Colorado's 38 delegates to come. I think the tide is turning in our favor!"

"Come down off that chair Paul and celebrate with us," Someone shouted. They watched the celebration in the ballroom on the monitor and Michael announced that he wanted to go down and speak to the crowd. Everyone cleared out of the suite and followed the candidate to the rally. Jocko stayed behind to catch the Colorado vote when it was announced. Michael came through the front door of the ballroom and when the crowd caught sight of him they went wild. "Sullivan, Sullivan" they cried. Security quickly closed around him as he wended his way to the stage. He took the microphone in his hand and spoke:

"I know for certain there are at least five hundred in this room who have worked the towns and streets of Texas and the vote tonight is a product of your work. Thank you. There were eleven other states that voted today and we are hooked up with our workers in those states and I thank them for all the work they did putting up lawn signs, making phone calls, getting people to the polls. All volunteers. I salute you and look forward to doing it again in other states where the outcome is still in doubt. If we are successful, I will be asking you again to help us in the fall. This undertaking is just not about one person running for the office of the presidency. It's about saving our country from the bad hand it's been dealt by an administration that seeks to divide us and weaken us all in the name of equality which for them is a euphemism for taking power from the people and putting in the hand of a demagogue. In November we will take back this country from the demagogue and set the ship of state on a clear course that will again gain the respect of the world. God bless you."

With T.V. cameras focused on his every move, he plunged down into the crowd and was quickly enveloped by well wishers just trying to shake his hand believing they were shaking hands with the next President of the United States and they would never get another chance to be so close to him. Just as he reached the entrance where he had come in, the last tally from Colorado flashed up on the board: Winslow 23,012 votes, 15 delegates; Sullivan 27,926 votes, 18 delegates and 14 delegates to Tortelli and Batterman. When those numbers went up they let out another loud cheer and started up the chant "Sullivan"; "Sullivan."

New Orleans Times-Herald, March 6, 2016 by Franklin Dubois:

"The March votes are beginning to pour in and by the end of the month we should have the eventual winner of the Republican primary. Yesterday Louisiana, Kansas and Maine weighed in with 99 delegates bringing the top vote getters, Winslow with 357 and Sullivan with 446 watching the other four candidates drop out of the race for lack of money or insufficient delegates. Five days ago I had a chance to interview Senator Michael Sullivan and my impressions were these: He's a tall good looking fellow, fastidiously dressed for the occasion, friendly and willing to take whatever time I needed to ask my questions. By trade he's a trial lawyer who after twelve years practicing law with a firm in which he was a senior partner left and built his own law firm starting with two men, He and a gentleman by the name of Paul Connolly, and in seven years built it into a one hundred and twenty five person firm. He had never considered politics preferring the law to all other vocations. And then it was only because a group of his friends encouraged him to run for a vacant seat in Congress arguing he had accomplished much in the law and had a duty to invest his talents in the country. The rest, as they say, is history. He wants to be President of the United States because he and the people of this country see a need to quickly change the direction the country is headed from down to up. He senses a deep unrest in the country bordering on fear and the polls bear him out. In his opinion the country was on an even keel until 2009 when the present administration took office and since that time the country has taken a sharp U-Turn downward with no end in sight. In his opinion it will take a strong leader to reverse course and that can only be done not just by a strong President but he must have a solid phalanx of dedicated leaders in his administration who will follow his lead. He will look for the best people and ask them to serve their country. My impression is he is that man. His whole background speaks to what is required. Worked his way through college and law school, married with four children, a lawyer, doctor, Wall Street broker, and a son studying for the priesthood in Rome. He's wealthy from his work as a lawyer and need not work the rest of his life if he so chose. In some ways being President is like giving up your life for your country----the responsibility is crushing and many men have entered the office with their natural hair color and left white haired looking old. This man at 61 looks vigorous, there is no gray in his brown hair and he has an athleticism about him that speaks of his willingness to engage in the contest and win. He speaks of values unflinchingly when others are afraid to mention them. He is religious and serious about his religion and makes no move to hide it as many politicians do. Yes, it might just be the country is ready for a man of Michael Sullivan's caliber."

March 9, 2016 Headlines around the country:

Chicago Times: "SULLIVAN TAKES EARLY DELEGATE LEAD"

St. Louis Observer: "SULLIVAN SWEEPS HAWAII, MICHIGAN, MISSISSIPPI AND PUERTO RICO"

Washington Star: "SULLIVAN LEADS IN DELEGATES 536 TO 407"

Seattle Messenger: "23 PRIMARIES GIVE SULLIVAN A LEAD OF 129"

Boston Sun: "REPUBLICANS---A TWO MAN HORSERACE"

The day after the March 8th primaries the Candidate flew home to Washington to be with Mary for two days before going out to Florida, Ohio and Missouri to campaign before the March 15 election with 286 delegates at stake.

That night they sat before a roaring fire having a cocktail before dinner. He was relaxed and she listened as he described what had been happening and how he felt about it all. He couldn't be happier with the progress she had made and each day she was gaining more strength. He depended on her judgment and her strength. She knew when to encourage and when to cool him down.

"I miss you out on the stump Mary. It's always easier for me when you're near. I've learned to handle it and if we can talk every night on the road things will work out. The thing that makes it so worthwhile is the people. In our races for the House and the Senate I was meeting people from our state. This is different. You can tell people are different wherever you go. It's opened my eyes to see for myself how good most people are. They know they are getting beat down. After I speak they seem to have hope. Mind you, it's not me per se, it's the message. We're going to clean up the mess; we're going to take charge; we're going to fix the machine and make it run better than it's ever run. They're serious Mary; they want change. Our campaign is furnishing hope and I believe they will come out in droves come November. Then the tough part comes."

"It's still close. Do you think Bernie Winslow can make up the difference and turn it into a horse race like some of the media are rooting for?"

"I don't think so still they will do everything they can to convert it into the race of the century which it is not. Three more contests on 15th, 19th and 22nd will bring us very close to the 1,235 delegates needed to clinch it on the first ballot. That means in two more weeks we can turn our attention to the general and our friend the ex Secretary of State. By the way she has a new television ad out charging me with being a war monger who will bring on world war III because I've said it will be my intention to stabilize our military position in Iraq and Afghanistan."

"We've talked enough; you go to the table and I'll bring two lovely frozen dinners I have prepared for your first meal at home in weeks." All this said with a straight face.

"Surely you would not do that to a travel weary warrior like me." He knew she was pulling his leg but he went along with the joke. A minute later she came in with a beautiful pot roast, mashed potatoes and a salad. "Just kidding" and gave him a kiss. He knew she was still not herself but she had the strength to cook this meal for him. The Irish came out in him and he got out of his chair with tears creeping down his cheeks and took her in his arms and hugged her and could say nothing.

"Now, come on Irish, brush those tears away. You're going to eat this meal and then I'm putting you to bed. You get sentimental when you're tired and you very sentimental now."

"I love you," he said and they ate their meal in a contented silence. Afterward they wrapped their arms around each other and went up to bed thankful they had each other.

He left on Friday to go to Florida where he or Bernard Winslow would win the 99 delegates allotted to the state by winning the popular vote. In his pocket he carried a letter from Peter that he had not yet opened. On the plane ride down he opened the letter from his son:

Dear Dad:

"I'm sorry I could not come home while Mother was in the hospital. Jack called me the second day she was in there and said she would be ok but it would take a couple of weeks. I talked with her a number of times since and Jack was right she's much better thank God. As for you, we've all and I mean all of us here at the North American have been watching the race with great anxiety even the faculty. There are a lot of Democrats amongst the seminarians and the faculty and even they are pulling for you. Yes, praying for you. I know that the fifteenth will be a make or break day for you and mom. If you win Ohio and Florida it seems to me it won't take much longer to clinch it. I know it's hard on mother watching you work like a dog out there, however from the pictures I've seen on television you're good at it and the crowds are spectacular. Here in Rome the work is intense as we are studying the scriptures and it is fascinating what went on before the coming of Christ. I knew a lot before I got here yet I find I knew very little about my religion. The men here are the best and many of them will some day be the leaders of the church in America. I suspect there are some in my class who will even become Cardinals. Who knows someday there may even be an American Pope.

I've also been seeing some mean things said about you and the faith. They seem to want to convince people you will be tight with the Pope and therefore a threat to our plural society. Nothing could be further from the truth;

still there are gullible people who will believe it and vote against you. The ploy won't be successful and you will win. And when you win there will be so much to do to bring the country back from the precipice it stands on now. I hope the Congress can curtail the damage this administration is trying to accomplish in their last ten months.

By the way, I've been watching Bernie Winslow and he seems like a nice fellow. It's great the way neither of you have attacked each other. Bernie might make a good Vice President. I don't want to interfere in the veep pick but I throw that in for what it's worth. Good luck on the fifteenth and again mass will be said for you that day here at the North American College."

Love Peter

He slipped the letter into his breast pocket, sat back in his seat on the aircraft and thought about Peter, his lawyer son, soon to be priest. In Michael's eyes Peter had always been special. A quiet reflective youngster who never gave he and Mary a day's worth of trouble. In high school he was a super athlete, quarterbacking the football team. At Georgetown University he played on the football team as an end because of his size. At law school he was a brilliant student and on the strength of his grades he was chosen to clerk for a federal appeals judge. Everything was going well for him. One day, out of the blue, he announced he felt a calling to join the priesthood. Michael knew this son of his would make a great priest. He was wise and he had compassion. Two strengths that would carry him far in his vocation. Michael knew the fact Peter was going to be a Catholic priest was being used against him in the campaign but he had long ago decided he would rather have a son who was a priest than be President of the United States. To the family Peter was special and they were all proud of the fact they had a priest in the family.

Mikos Tabor, frustrated with Michael Sullivan's march toward the Republican nomination, planned to set a new hurdle in his path before the Florida and Ohio primaries. Through the efforts of the former majority leader of the Senate, Boyden Johnson, a magazine spread was arranged in *Tattle Tale*, a gossip magazine, to appear the day before the March 15th vote. In it Michael Sullivan was pictured with several beautiful women sometimes more than one. The implication being he was quite the man with the ladies, something akin to former President Bill Clinton. The magazine had a small circulation; nevertheless, Boyden knew it would be picked up by the wire services and from there by all the left wing media. A million dollars was given to the magazine to print an extra two hundred thousand copies to be on the newsstands in the supermarkets March 14th. Tabor sat in his New York headquarters waiting patiently for the *Tattle Tale* to take the starch out of the front runner's campaign.

Jocko O'Brian reported to the Sullivan team that the national polls showed Michael up in Ohio and Florida, while Truman Foster's polls showed him doing even better. For some reason, John Kennedy's intelligence apparatus failed to pick up the *Tattle Tale* story before it broke, so it came as a real blow the day before the election. It was on the street being covered by the media in the hopes of turning the vote in favor of Bernard Winslow. Mikos congratulated Boyden in a phone call to the hatchet man in Las Vegas, where Johnson was tied up with a newly formed gambling syndicate intending to break into the Chinese market. Boyden Johnson was out to make big money after his years in the Senate but his hatred for John Kennedy and Michael Sullivan, who he blamed for his defeat as Majority leader and loss of his Senate seat, kept him active in one last campaign----2016.

Taken by surprise by the article the Sullivan forces swiftly convened in a conference call and decided to strike back quickly by calling a press conference in Pensacola where Michael was campaigning for the day. He would deny the implications of the story and demand a retraction from the magazine and if not received in twenty four hours a defamation law suit would be filed immediately seeking general and punitive damages in the millions.

Press, perhaps two hundred plus television cameramen and still photographers, gathered in the hotel ballroom where the Sullivan forces had staked out for the day. Michael appeared in a dark blue suit, light blue tie looking as if he didn't have a care in the world although he realized the situation was dire and millions of people would be watching to see how he handled it and whether the story might indeed be true.

"By now Senator, you've read the story in *Tattle Tale;* is it true you are the ladies man they imply you are?"

"I like women, as most men do since they have daughters and wives and mothers whom they cherish. The answer to your question is I love my wife Mary and she is the only women I have ever loved. This story is a deliberate lie put out by magazine that thrives on false accusations. Check their retraction record. This morning our attorneys have hand delivered to the magazine a demand for a retraction and if not received within twenty four hours a suit for libel will be filed in the Federal District court in Washington D.C."

"Will it hurt you in tomorrow's election?"

"Conventional wisdom says it will; my personal opinion is that it will not and we will win in tomorrow's election."

"Will you guarantee that Senator?"

"Let's say I have great faith in the electorate that they will see through an obvious attempt to smear me at the last minute like they tried to do to both Presidents Bush. I don't believe it will work. Thank you all for coming ladies and gentlemen I must be about the business of winning votes in Florida today. Let's meet again after the vote." And he was gone.

It didn't take John Kennedy long to discover who was behind the *Tattle Tale* story. He guessed Boyden Johnson, but it took a little longer to sniff out Mikos Tabor. Tabor was a left wing scourge Kennedy paid little attention too. Kennedy had caused Boyden Johnson to lose in the 2014 election and now he decided Mikos Tabor should be taught a lesson. The vehicle used would be short selling of his hedge fund shares. He resolved to take care of the Tabor matter after Michael had won enough delegates to secure the nomination.

Sunny skies in Florida, heavy rains in Ohio, Illinois and Missouri. It didn't matter the vote turnout was heavy in all four states. Michael decided to stay in Miami election night because a huge victory party was planned at the Fontainebleau hotel. As they had done in Dallas on Super Tuesday the team gathered in three suites on the top of the hotel, Jocko and his teams of political computer wizzes in one big room and the others in a huge living room for guests who would join the candidate to watch the returns. As the polls closed in the east at 8:00 p.m. first returns showed the vote in Florida: Sullivan---45,000; Winslow---26,543.

"Too early, Michael," John Kennedy said and slipped off to find out more details from Jocko in the adjoining suite. Everyone else, by now a very veteran team, said nothing wanting to see what the next release of votes would show. If most of the votes were from western Florida Michael's initial lead would be insignificant, because Winslow's votes would come in the North and the East. At 8:30 new figures came from the networks and Michael's lead jumped to 150,562 to 75,463 for Bernard Winslow.

"To hell with it" Tom Galvin yelled, "I'm declaring Michael the winner of Florida's 99 delegates. Anyone want to bet on that?" No one did so everyone in the room stepped up to the bar to start the celebration. Kennedy and Jocko came into the room and reported Ohio was a different story. Early returns showed Winslow in the lead: 95,056 to 74,381. Michael again decided to go to the ballroom early to speak to his supporters. On his way down he was given the vote in Illinois: 250,654 Sullivan; 123,289 Winslow; Missouri was going for Winslow 60,453 to 48,236. The crowd gathered knew what he knew. They would win Florida and Illinois, Ohio would be close and Winslow would win Missouri. As a new day dawned final tallies gave three states to Senator Sullivan (Ohio, Florida, and Illinois) and one to Governor Winslow (Missouri). In the all important category of delegates Michael Sullivan finished the night with a total of 197 to Winslow's 89.

The next day the *New York Tribune* editorial summed up the consensus developing around the country amongst the media and the no-it-all pundits:

"The picture is beginning to clear. The Republican primary has a long way to go but a winner is emerging in the persona of Senator Michael Sullivan who now leads in delegates 733 to 496. He has momentum and won decisively in Florida with a closer call in Ohio. Those are two states the Republicans must win to take over the White House. Should the Senator continue to pile up votes against Governor Winslow on March 19 and 22 the outcome will no longer be in doubt come April. The Democratic candidate who is assured of being the nominee of her party is staying out of sight doing little campaigning and mostly defending herself from accusations of untrustworthiness. She should emerge soon or it will be too late. The country want's change and both Senator Sullivan and Governor Bernard Winslow are men who could fill that wish. The Democrat leads in the polls now but she is slipping and will continue to do so unless she gets out and starts mixing it up with the Republicans. 2016 will not be the coronation Secretary Hanna Hamilton thought it was going to be six months ago but she's under the impression it's just a matter of time before she's coronated."

CHAPTER 9

WHEN THE RESULTS were finalized from the March 19 primaries Mikos Tabor decided not to throw good money after bad and so future contributions would be to Secretary Hamilton. At the same time he directed Boyden Johnson to keep searching for material that could be used against Michael Sullivan, reproaching Boyden for the clumsy *Tattle Tale* article. Unaware of what was going to befall him in the near future Mikos continued to think of Michael Sullivan as the enemy, knowing that should he be elected he and Kennedy would be out to nullify him and his affiliates as a potent force on the left. The democrats and the leftists depended heavily on his financing their left wing think tanks, blogs and an array of propaganda outlets. Mikos understood Boyden's hatred for John Kennedy and he was channeling that hatred as a weapon against Michael Sullivan. Four, much less eight, years of Sullivan, would wipe out everything he and Obama had sought to achieve---remaking of the country with power centered in Washington, and the states, weak subsidiaries. He would be able to control a Washington based government but unable to control state government with a Sullivan administration granting more power to the states rather than less as Obama had been able to achieve in seven and a half years. At 80 years old it was his wish to see the capitalist country turned into a socialist utopia. With Sullivan at the helm that wish would never be fulfilled. For him then, it was not a matter of revenge like it was for Boyden Johnson; for him his lifelong dream that Obama had enacted would be shattered and that was worth spending his entire fortune to preserve the status quo.

On March 19, Washington, Wyoming, Idaho, Alaska and North Dakota went to the polls with the result Michael garnered 117 delegates to Bernard Winslow's 28 to bring the count to 850 versus 424---a 2 to 1 lead. Three days later on the 22nd Arizona and Utah delivered 98 delegates to Michael in winner take all primaries. This proved to be the death blow. With 948 delegates Senator Sullivan would certainly be within reach of the magic number of 1236 delegates, so proclaimed the *New York Tribune* in a lead article in the March 23rd edition.

"The writing is on the wall. It would take a miracle and at least one hundred million dollars to turn the Republican race around for Governor Bernard Winslow. Should Senator Sullivan sweep the April 5th primaries, all winner take all, he would have 1,162 delegates---74 short of the number needed to secure the nomination on the first ballot. On April 5, New York should put him over the top with its 95 delegates. This is not 1948 when Harry Truman shocked Thomas Dewey and the Republican establishment in a miracle comeback win. Governor Winslow has waged a valiant campaign and is to be commended, but it is all too apparent that Michael Sullivan will be the nominee. Unless, the Democrats completely reverse themselves, which seems almost impossible, his opponent will be Secretary Hanna Hamilton and the battle will be joined. Hamilton is the early favorite yet there are those on this newspaper who cast the race as a tossup. We will all have to wait and see."

Although victory seemed certain, the Sullivan campaign was taking no chances. After the April 5 primary he spent Monday, April 11 in upstate New York, where a treasure trove of Republican votes were to be harvested, then on to

Indiana, Nebraska and West Virginia where primaries would be held on May 3 and May 10 respectively. While campaigning in Nebraska, he received a call from Bernard Winslow:

"Michael, Bernie. You've been doing pretty good. I'm thinking it's time for me to quit and that's what I'm calling you about." Michael, knowing this was a tough call for Winslow to make started to remonstrate with him but he halted him in midsentence. "No, hear me out my friend. I've talked it over with my wife and all the good people who've been working for me and my decision is it's time to get behind the winner and you've proved with the voters you are there choice. So today I'm holding a press conference concluding my candidacy and announcing I'm asking all my delegates to cast their ballot for you. It's time the party unite behind you because there is nothing more important than taking back the country. You're the man to do that. I'm with you Michael all the way."

"I'm honored to have your vote of confidence Bernie. More than that I appreciated the way you conducted your campaign. All issues no mud. I tried to do the same and you led the way. I agree nothing is more important than beating Hanna. Because of you we will get a head start. Tomorrow we start a new campaign against her and it will be relentless until November 6. I will welcome your support the next six months."

"You shall have it and if your team thinks I can serve as a surrogate I will work my tail off for the ticket. My best wishes for Mary's speedy recovery and God bless you." Michael hung up after a few more words of thanks and arranged for a conference call, with Kennedy, Galvin and Paul Connolly. He informed them of the conversation he had just had with Bernard Winslow and advised as soon as Winslow made his announcement that they go into full campaign mode against

Hanna. Also he called for a meeting in Washington on the 17th of May, the day of primaries in Kentucky and Oregon.

As Promised, after his phone call with Michael, Bernard Winslow called a press conference announcing he was withdrawing his candidacy and giving his support to Michael Sullivan telling the press he hoped his supporters would do the same. It was not a total shock to the media following Winslow and they knew it would be happening but not so soon with a number of primaries still to weigh in. Once the announcement was made they rushed for the telephones, computers and every source to get out the news: All the major media headlined "Winslow drops out, Sullivan the nominee. Or as the *Washington Star* head lined: "IT'S OVER BERNIE."

With Hanna Hamilton a virtual shoo in for the Democratic nomination the political chattering class began the usual round of speculation. The big dailies, hoping for a Democratic win, proclaimed Hanna would win in a walk because the country was so pleased by the programs Obama had put in place they would want Hanna to continue them. (This is the Saul Alinsky approach---ignore the facts and state the opposite). This tack was taken by the *New York Tribune, Washington Star, San Francisco Bulletin* and *Los Angeles Chronicle*. Others were not so sanguine, feeling that Michael Sullivan would give her a good run, and some even went so far as to say he would beat her. The Sullivan team was counting on the Democrats to stick with her despite the baggage she was carrying because her loss would bring down Senators, Congressmen, Governors, and reversals of state legislative control making their task easier to replace Obama's destructive policies.

Earlier in the year at an all day conference in Washington Michael had asked his former law partner Paul Connolly to take over the task of setting up transition teams for all cabinet departments and 20 lesser departments anticipating they would win the presidency and be governing after January 20, 2017. In the past these teams were not organized until after the election in November and the President-elect would then appoint his transition team. As a result the new President started off with few key positions filled because all high level nominations must go through the Senate for approval. For the first nine months of the Presidency deputy department heads---all civil service---and mostly Democrats, run the government. Michael said that would not occur if he won the Presidency. The names of all Cabinet and Sub Cabinet nominees would be sent to the Senate on January 20, inauguration day. The names of 93 U.S. attorneys would go at the same time. Lesser officers, would be appointed within a month. Judicial vacancies would be submitted the first week of his presidency. It was his intent the government would be running within two months with all Democrats released from duty and replaced by carefully selected Republican men and women. A new President has over 3,000 appointments that can be made most of which are filled by the party of the winner. Over a thousand more can be appointed at lower levels. All of this would be a massive undertaking which would have to be paid for by the campaign. Kennedy et al thought it would be of great benefit to the new President and if Michael won he would be entitled to some re-imbursement by the government. The concept was to be ready to go from day one. Two hundred volunteers gathered in mid January to start the tedious yet important task of picking the best people available to spend at least four years working for President Sullivan. In June the press got wind of what was going on and ridiculed the Sullivan campaign for being so presumptuous to think they would even be needing a transition team. When questioned by the Press, Paul Connolly said it was a matter of preparedness not presumptuousness. Some thought it a brilliant idea others thought it arrogant. Cooler heads in the media prevailed and while the concept was novel it became a dead issue since the campaign was paying for it out of its own pocket.

From experience Michael knew the bureaucracy was difficult to move between presidential elections but it slowed to a barely discernable walk when a new administration came to power. That was not going to happen on his watch. He would have enough of his people in place to enforce orders coming from the White House to be acted on with dispatch, not the usual foot dragging. Those who resisted would be reassigned and be replaced by those who would produce. The next four years were not going to be business as usual for the simple reason the country had to recover quickly as though it were wartime. Four years would be barely enough time to get it back on an upward track. The biggest problem facing the bureaucracy was the inability to fire incompetent and disruptive employees. So many obstacles had been set in place to protect the unproductive, including the cost, that many agencies just looked the other way with the result one bad apple would spoil the moral of co-workers. Reform of the system would be a top priority of a new administration. There would be no lifetime guarantee of employment for government employees if they failed to produce. By May of 2016 the transition team with 400 volunteers working out of a building in downtown Washington had made good headway. When Michael captured 303 delegates on June 7 Paul Connolly set up special group to consider who Michael's running mate might be.

Mary Sullivan decided the family, including the candidate, had to get away from the campaign for a few days so she took it upon herself to rent a couple of houses on Kiawah Island, South Caroline where they had stayed years ago, one with a tennis court and a swimming pool owned by Bradley Smith who had offered his houses to them five or six years previously. And a second for Sharon, Kathryn and her friends from New York. Jocko and the rest of the team told Michael to get the rest he would need for the next five months. Kennedy was satisfied the money was pouring in, and Paul was ahead of schedule on the Transition team. So on June 10 they all trekked down to the beach for a five day stay.

Jack and Megan brought the two boys ages three and two and they stayed in the house with the grandparents, and Kathryn brought five friends from New York and Sharon had as her guest a young doctor, by the name of Tim Culhane who had a surgical practice at Georgetown Hospital in Washington. She had been seeing him for about six months and no one knew if it was serious or not. Mary figured they would soon find out. On the day they arrived the sun beamed down on them as if to say "welcome Sullivans." Everyone picked their room, the children ran to look at the pool followed by Jack to make sure they didn't dive in with their clothes on. With the Jack Sullivans settled everyone awaited the others arriving about five o'clock, "Just in time for the cocktail hour," Jack quipped. Sure enough at five a lot of noise came from the parking area and the two girls with their friends in tow came into the living room. Everyone was introduced and Jack proceeded to act as bartender. "I don't know if you noticed but there's an army out there protecting us," Jack said casually just to see if anyone had noticed. "I did," Kathryn said." I just thought they were neighbors; are they part of Kennedy's army?"

"That they are and they will be replaced in about two weeks with the secret service"

"I'd count on Kennedy's army," one of the young men who had come with Kathryn from New York said sardonically. "You know they're known for letting people jump over the fence at the White House" (laughter). Everyone was talking at once, catching up while Michael took the whole scene in. This was going to be fun he thought with the babies around and all these young people. For Mary it will be the best tonic she could have. For me, just sitting around the pool getting some sun is all I need for the last leg of the journey. No one was really paying too much attention to him so he glanced over at Tim Culhane who was in a deep conversation with Mary. He noticed when he first came in the young doctor looked about six foot one with jet black hair and piercing blue eyes. Good looking Michael thought, women would probably call him handsome. Sharon had mentioned casually the last time they saw her that he had graduated from Georgetown and then went to Harvard medical school. Interned at New York Presbyterian and a three year residency at Johns Hopkins. Obviously well qualified. Michael liked his looks and the fact he was a surgeon. In his mind he put surgeons in the same league as trial lawyers. Both species in the arena where the action was. Sharon was listening to him talk and had a look on her face which said I'm very interested in this fellow. So if she was interested, Michael decided, he would be doubly interested.

Mary had arranged to have a cook who would do the cooking for everyone at their house. After dinner everyone went their respective way and Mary and Michael decided to take a walk on the beach to talk over the day's events.

"What do you think of young doctor Culhane?" he asked after they had walked a few hundred yards.

"I like him Michael. He's got an easy way with him. He listens and then speaks. He's definitely interested in Sharon. From what I can tell, quite interested."

"You mean like marriage?" He asked her teasingly.

"I wouldn't go so far as to say that, let's just observe the next few days and see what happens "

They talked about the crew down from New York and decided they were down for a great time and all three of the young men seemed interested in Kathryn and she seemed oblivious to them all, just out for a good time with some friends. For the next two days they developed a routine wherein Michael and Mary would be up at seven for an early breakfast of juice, coffee and a sweet roll beside the pool and by eight Jack and the grandchildren were up and eating at poolside while Michael and Mary read the newspapers. The crowd at the other house would show up around eleven for a swim and then a round of golf in the afternoon, leaving Michael, Mary and Meghan with the children. At six everyone gathered at the main house for cocktails and chatter. Talk of politics was off limits, but no one seemed to pay any attention to the embargo Mary enunciated the first day. Most of the talk revolved around Hanna Hamilton's trouble with the deleted e-mails and the fact her server had been discovered with a second class computer service which had been storing her server in an upstairs closet. The scandal had become so bad the FBI and the Justice department had been called into investigate the situation at the behest of two Inspector Generals.

Congressional committees were hounding her to appear before them to explain why she, as Secretary of State, had used a private server dealing with sensitive documents and not told anyone about it. As the scandal mushroomed she kept up a façade of blaming the Republicans for all the commotion and was getting a free pass from the press until it looked like the Justice department was serious about the investigation in view of the fact others such as General Petraeus had been indicted for far less offenses. The press began to dig up other cases like Sandy Berger's who worked for President Clinton and stole documents out of the National Archives. He was prosecuted and fined fifty thousand dollars and surrendered his law license in the bargain. The words "Nixon stonewall" were being used more and more by the media. Jack Sullivan speculated even an Obama pardon would do little to clear the slate pointing to the bad feeling that developed in 1974 after President Ford pardoned President Nixon. The election was still four months off and still the Democrats made no move to remove her as a candidate. The last chance to do so would be at the Democratic convention starting July 25.

Billy Brogan, one of Kathryn's friends from New York and a fellow trader with her company suggested Vice President Joseph Smith's name would be placed in nomination at the convention but the Hanna forces would be too strong for him. That started a whole new round of conversation with various scenarios being put forth such as: She could be indicted and would have to be removed from the ticket, Smith would be successful and try to run the race Hubert Humphrey ran against Richard Nixon in 1968. Humphry would have won if the election had been two days later. Others suggested the Democrats would nominate her and go down in flames with her taking down hundreds of Democrats with her.

Michael didn't involve himself in these discussions, leaving it to the younger people to worry about it. Instead he had picked up a book when they came down to Kiawah Island by David Halberstam about the Korean War and the role Douglas McArthur played in it. Particularly interesting to him was the conflict between the general and President

Harry Truman. According to the author and assented to by historians McArthur was unaccountable to the military and the President. In Korea, after the North Koreans had been pushed north over the 38th parallel McArthur, against the wishes of the Joint Chiefs of Staff and the President, pushed onto the border with the Chinese who he had completely misread. The Chinese swarmed out of the north overrunning United Nations positions and driving the Americans south at great cost of men and material. McArthur wanted to capture all of Korea. In misjudging the Chinese he failed and was relieved of his command by President Truman. The lesson Michael took from reading this history, is that a President listens to his military commanders but he does not allow himself to be bullied by them. He reflected on that aspect the remainder of their time at the beach.

The sea and the sun had been a perfect tonic for the candidate who had been campaigning for a year and trying to attend to his duty in the Senate. Laying in the sun the last two days he reflected on how far they had come since the conclave held in Spring Valley and what seemed so long ago. All the states he had been in and what the people had told him. He knew they were aching for someone to stand up and say "enough." They knew the Democrats under their leader of hope and change were driving the country into a downward spiral. Paul Connolly was doing a superb job lining up candidates for the judiciary and that Tom and John Kennedy had lists containing names to fill the top jobs. And all of that was good but he knew it would be up to him to restore the faith of the people. He decided as he lay in the sun by the pool to start work on a speech to be given at the convention at which he would accept the nomination of his party. Without any touch of arrogance he started to frame in his mind what he would say at the inauguration. He laughed to himself about even thinking about an inaugural speech when he hadn't even garnered his party's nomination. Still he told himself it was not as silly as one might think. He thought about Kennedy's inaugural address in 1961 which history has recorded as one of the best. The speech laid out a plan, a philosophy that the people could understand. Peace through strength Kennedy told the people. Freedom was a beacon that all could follow if they chose to. Socialism, Communism, Totalitarianism all had failed and Obama's version of Socialism was failing in the United States. He would lay out a road to follow to retrieve American greatness. It would be tough and it would be hard and the people would have to know that from the start. Dividends would come later. If he was able to get the right people in key places in the government, it could be done. He had every confidence of that. At the end of their five day vacation the camp at Kiawah broke up and Jack headed back to his law practice, Sharon to her breast cancer surgeries in Washington, Kathryn to New York and Monday opening on the New York Stock Exchange, and Mary to Washington to work at home planning for teas throughout the Midwest in September and October.

Throughout the spring of 2016 Hanna Hamilton's troubles began to proliferate. Not only did she have scandals from her years in the Senate where she had used her office to grant favors to contributors in return for contributions to the Hamilton Fund, her role as Secretary of State was being called into question on the issue of competency. Who would be so arrogant as to have a private communication system, free of knowledge or control of the State Department and transmit classified, often top secret, material over that system and when confronted deny the fact. Even the press was beginning to see the danger for the Democratic Party. Whisperings could be heard that perhaps the Vice President,

72 year old Joseph Smith, should come to the aid of the party by offering his name at the Democratic convention to be held in late July in Philadelphia. The Vice President was well known having served six terms in the U.S. Senate before being asked by President Obama to be his Vice President in 2008. He was not an overly intelligent man given to making verbal mistakes and a mean streak which he proudly displayed as Chairman of the Senate Judiciary Committee during the 1987 hearings on the nomination of Robert Bork to the Supreme Court. Still it was thought he didn't have Hanna's baggage and if he lost the damage to the party would be far less than a Hamilton implosion.

As July 18 approached, the beginning of the Republican convention began to take shape. The Sullivan team wanted to have a Vice Presidential nominee picked before the party convened in Cleveland. As many as ten were under consideration such as Patricia Swanson who had run a spirited race against Michael in the primary and who had a solid background as a business leader and who would be asked to serve in his administration if not picked for Vice President, Toby Williams, a nine term congressman, the current chairman of the House Foreign Affairs Committee, David Johnson, a veteran of both wars in Iraq and a decorated war hero and recipient of the medal of honor, Peter Walters, Secretary of Defense in the Bush Administration, Senator David Batterman who ran unsuccessfully in the primary against Michael, David Tobias, Governor of Pennsylvania and Bernard Winslow who defeated Michael for the Vice Presidential nomination in the convention of 2012 and more recently his chief opposition for the nomination. Each had their strengths. One would be picked and the others would be asked to serve with Michael beginning January 2017.

The President

Within a week of the convention, it had come down to four: Bernard Winslow, David Tobias, Peter Walters, and Toby Williams. They all had governing experience and most importantly able to serve should any disaster befall the President. In Michael's mind the last was uppermost in his thinking. Someone who could immediately step into the President's shoes. In the end Michael asked Bernard Winslow to run with him. First he liked "Bernie" Winslow, who was around his age and had a business background. Second he had legislative experience, having served in the house and senate in the North Carolina legislature for 8 years and then as Governor for 8 more years. Third he had defeated Michael in 2012 at the Republican convention when John Madden decided to allow the delegates to pick the Vice Presidential nominee. Fourth he had proved a worthy opponent in the campaign and a very gracious loser. Fifth he had offered to campaign for Michael as a surrogate and had done so. "Bernie" was tall, like Michael, and a total southern gentlemen. Mary knew his wife, Beth and they had hit it off from the first time they met each other. They complimented each other in looks, Winslow tall at six feet two inches with distinguished white hair and a handsome face but not soft. High cheek bones and an aquiline nose and cropped hair made him stand out amongst his peers. Geographically he would represent the South, a base for the Republican Party. In picking him they decided he would campaign exclusively in the South as Lyndon Johnson had done for John Kennedy in the campaign of 1960. Because of Democratic strength in the Electoral College, Michael would need all the Southern states including North Carolina, Virginia and Florida that had been lost to the Democrats in 2012. Bernard Winslow would lock those in for the Republican President.

The media saw the danger of Bernie Winslow on the ticket. He would be a plus in the South and a very attractive candidate to run with Michael Sullivan. Both could win notwithstanding the Democrats had a decisive edge in the Electoral College. That edge came from their successes on the West Coast with California, Oregon and Washington and the big states in the East, New York, New Jersey, Pennsylvania and the New England states followed by Minnesota, Michigan and Wisconsin in the Midwest.

To the Republicans pouring into Cleveland for the convention they fully expected to be nominating the next President of the United States and cared little for media predictions of a Hamilton win. Polls showed her leading by one point which equated to a tied election. The press previewed the convention: *New York Tribune* opened with the headline:

"REPUBLICANS GATHER TO CELEBRATE SULLIVAN"

Cleveland Gazette: REPUBLICANS COME TO PLOT HAMILTON DOWNFALL."

All members of the Sullivan team talking to the media said they were quietly confident, but Hanna Hamilton, being the first woman running for the Presidency, would draw a tremendous amount of press and turn out a lot of voters who might not otherwise vote. "Will you win?" they would always ask at the end of the interview. "It will be tough," they would answer "but, yes. Michael Sullivan will win. The American people want a change."

The delegates, alternates, wives, girlfriends, children, whole families, press, guests, politicians, celebrities, the curious, if they could get a ticket and thousands of grass root Republicans eager to boot their candidates home after eight long years in the desert all arrived at the same time ready to hold a grand old party. The first two days of the convention were spent showcasing some of the rising stars in the party and adopting a platform that the ticket would be expected to embrace and run on. The third night was committed to nominating the Vice Presidential nominee and hearing his acceptance speech.

Bernard Winslow of North Carolina strode from the back of the platform to the microphone and for a full minute acknowledged the cheers of the twenty thousand or so gathered to hear what he had to say. His name was familiar to many because he had run as John Madden's running mate in the 2012 election. Four years had passed and people forget. Tonight they would listen to someone who could become one of the new leaders of the country. The ratings bureau predicted at least forty million would tune in to hear the speech set for 9:00 p.m. Central time. The house lights dimmed and Bernard Winslow white haired and distinguish looking was in the spotlight.

"Thank you delegates for doing me the honor of running with Michael Sullivan as the Vice Presidential nominee of the party. I accept the nomination and pledge to you we will fight to retrieve the country from the jaws of defeat." As one, the crowd rocked the rafters and the sound bounced all over the hall thundering from one side to the other. He held up his hand for silence and the noise dropped to a whisper and then total silence. "We gather here in Cleveland at a fateful time in the country's history. This is not the time to celebrate it's the time to dedicate ourselves to overturning an administration that has sought to emasculate the country. It's time to take inventory of how far we've fallen at the hands of an administration that has turned from being Democratic to Socialistic. Yes, in this country "Socialistic," is a scorned word. It started slowly with promises of hope and change. There's been no sign of hope and the change promised has been for the worse. For seven years they have lied to us that things were getting better economically and they are worse. We've been in a recession for over six and a half years. Their policies have cut the middle class to shreds. This was our strongest demographic before they came to power. Ninety five million people in the country who are able to work can't find a job. The government tells us unemployment is at 5.6% and brags of what an achievement that is yet the real figure is closer to 17%. Our college graduates can't find jobs. And those that can are burdened with, in many cases, unsustainable debt. People are working 2 part time jobs because they can't find full time employment. Why are there no jobs? Because this administration has stifled growth, strapped small business with regulations that are killing their businesses. This administration pushes tax increases to cover their mistakes. Tax increases strangle growth. Our economy is shrinking not growing. What have they done to remedy the situation? They've printed 4.5 trillion dollars which has vanished into thin air. They have devalued your assets in order to put off a total collapse. When President Bush took office the national debt was 5.62 trillion dollars. When he turned the Presidency over to the current administration the debt was 9.98 trillion dollars. This administration has plundered the nation increasing the debt to over 19 trillion dollars and they still have a year and a half to go!!! Like Clint Eastwood said in 2012: "if they can't handle the job fire them." The crowd was now standing, all 20,000. In a few short sentences he told those in the hall and the forty million watching how bad the economic situation was despite the lies put out on a daily basis by administration spokesmen. The roar went on for thirty seconds and it was not a cheer but evidence of contempt they held for the Democratic administration.

He lied to us when he said we could keep our insurance and our doctors. (boos) He lied to us when he said the cost of health care would go down under his plan. (boos) He's lied to us about the economy. (boos) He's lied to us about Benghazi as did Hanna Hamilton his secretary of State.(boos) He sold the country out to Iran to burnish his legacy.(boos) He has set race relations back fifty years.(boos) In short he has attempted to divide the American people. He will not succeed. (thunderous applause) Our party will block his every venture until he is gone and we will rebuild the country to what it was before he came. It has been a bad dream but with your help it will soon be over. To carry the torch into a third term the Democratic Party is attempting to foist off on the voters an untrustworthy ex-Secretary of State, and set of leaders with an average age of 75. Our party is fortunate in having a younger generation to lead and we will. In this election we will continue to build on a structure that is being built to last a long time. Politics is fought in the trenches and that is what we have been doing the last five years. It started in 2010 when we captured 63 House seats and six Senate seats. When Obama took office he had huge majorities in the House (257 members) and Senate (60 members). Today they are the minority in the Senate (46) and the House (188). Our base strength is in the states where we control 31 legislatures they have 11. We have it within our power to take the country to the place it should be. With your help, desire for change and a willingness to get out the vote. We must be successful. We will be successful. Thank you and God bless you all."

Again they were on their feet. They came to pick new leaders and Bernard Winslow didn't disappoint. He gave them a factual summary of what had happened to the country and it was presented as an argument that a thinking person could not misunderstand. The speech was meant to appeal to thinking voters not ideologues who stick to talking points and change the subject when confronted with facts and logic.

CHAPTER 10

ON THE FINAL night of the convention everyone showed up; the delegates, the party members, the press, spectators and agitators. About a thousand abortion enthusiasts, Black Panthers, Code Pink, Black Lives Matter, gay and lesbians, transgenders, Planned Parenthood backers, all the usual suspects that appear at conventions were there in force. All in all about 5,000 protesters with their flags and bull horns. When the busses came in with the delegates they made a rush to impede them, but police lines quickly closed and kept them at bay. The television cameras rushed to the scene to try and depict chaos at the republican convention as they met to nominate their candidate to represent the party. American had watched the same scene for years and were no longer fazed by it. Inside the hall 20,000 were poised to hear Michael Sullivan's acceptance speech. In bars, clubs, living rooms, hotels, airport lounges and wherever television sets were turned on 65,000,000 were watching to see who Sullivan was, those who had never seen or heard him before, those who would vote against him, those who would vote for him and those sitting on the fence waiting to be convinced.

Mary and the family were in the VIP box with the Kennedys, Galvins and Connollys. The speech was set for 9 p.m. Eastern standard time, 6:00 on the west coast. After several speeches, Bailey long approached the microphone on the raised dais and the house lights dimmed with one spotlight on him. A silence came over the crowd as he paused and then said in a booming voice: "ladies and gentlemen the next president of the United States." With that the spot light swept over the heads of the delegates on the floor and focused on the back of the hall from which emerged Michael Sullivan the spot light following him in the darkened hall as he worked his way toward the platform. When the crowd saw what was happening they erupted in a chant, frequently heard at his rallies: "Sullivan Sullivan." He went from side to side touching outstretched hands. The roar got louder and louder as he got close to the platform and reverberated around the hall in wave after wave. He mounted the steps to the platform followed by the spotlight in the still darkened room. When he reached the microphone the lights went on and there he stood, tall, in a finely tailored blue suit looking fifty years old, ten years younger than he actually was. For tonight he was their champion and they were going to let the world know it. The greeting went on for a minute and then they came to a respectful silence. He began: "tonight I gratefully accept your nomination. I do so with humility and with confidence that we will leave this hall tonight on a crusade to save our country from the devastation it has undergone these past seven years and will continue to undergo for the next four months when we will defeat the purveyors of this devastation. Last night, Bernard Sullivan laid out the problems the country faces. I will not dwell on those tonight rather I want to talk to you about what we will do to turn the present attitude of defeat by this administration to one of victory. One of the first acts will be to repeal the socialized medicine program known as Obamacare which destroyed the health insurance program we had for fifty years and has driven the cost of insurance out of sight for those who could have afforded it before. It has deprived them of the doctors they had been use to going to. In its place we will propose a plan that will lower premiums, allow for pre-existing illness, end frivolous law suits, prevent insurance companies from cancelling policies, or putting a cap on benefits, allow small businesses to pool and get lower premiums as we allow unions and corporations to do, allow purchasers to buy insurance across state lines, prohibit federal funds to be used for abortion, allow a standard deduction for buying health insurance and providing health savings accounts to pay premiums. In short we will get the federal government out of the business of health insurance and regulations telling patients, who they can see, when they can see them and how much service they can get from their health provider." In a paragraph he synthesized what he would do, they understood and rose to their feet in recognition. After the first few sentences, the anchors in the press boxes high up in the arena noted to the television audience that the speaker was not using notes nor a teleprompter. "Highly unusual for a major speech of this type. Too much room to make a mistake and have it misinterpreted" they said. By the time Michael had reached the part of his speech on health care the audience became aware that he was speaking without notes. This had the effect of their leaning forward to catch every word. Speaking extemporaneously he had the audience in the arena in the palm of his hand. As an experienced speaker he knew that once they saw he was so prepared and speaking without notes they became mesmerized. He continued:

"President Kennedy in his inaugural address asked of his countrymen, 'ask not what your country can do for you but what you can do for your country.' in that spirit I will propose to the congress that we enact legislation that will enlist the youth of our country when they reach age 18 to serve one year in service of the government building infrastructure, working in hospitals, working with charities, to develop a sense of community, teamwork and responsibility. For those who would prefer military service they will be inducted for one year. Both groups will receive credits toward a college education. It is time to train our youth to work together and make a contribution to the country's welfare. They will feel better about themselves and their country.

Our military has been downgraded, forced to fight under rules that prevent them from protecting themselves and generally run rough shod over by this administration. When they took over we were winning the war in Iraq. It's almost lost. It can be saved and become a useful ally against Iran on its western border. We have almost lost Afghanistan on Iran's eastern border. Both these countries surround Iran which is our sworn enemy. Both could be used as bases to deter their further aim of promoting Islamic terrorism throughout the Middle East. We will repeal and not enforce the so-called agreement that this President and his followers in the Senate agreed to with the terrorists in Iran." (thunderous applause) He waited until they became quite and continued; "Our military will start building back January 2017 and they will keep building until they assure us they can defend the country under any contingency." (on their feet cheering) Again a pause. "We do not seek war but we will not shirk from terrorist attacks.

Our government is bloated. I can vouch for that fact as a United States Senator. We have too many doing too little and getting paid too much. I will propose that the Education Department, started by President Carter in 1979, be dismantled. Our children have suffered ever since to the point where our freshmen entering college are having to take remedial reading. (on their feet cheering) The responsibility of educating our children will be returned to the states with block grants to cover the costs. We will scale down, if not remove, the HUD department as a government agency. It has been a source of fraud, corruption, and mismanagement since its inception under President Johnson. We will audit the Department of Agriculture for its effectiveness and for the subsidies it pays out at tax payer expense.

The Department of Veterans Affairs is a disgrace to the men and women in this country who served in the military. There will be wholesale firing of those responsible for the debacle at that agency. (standing ovation) We will protect religious liberty against attacks from those who seek to destroy religion. We will reduce taxes, and reform the Internal Revenue Service which has become a threat to liberty thru its unbridled tactics and a scourge of the people rather than a servant. (Applause and cheers)

Some of these measures may seem harsh or not necessary but I would argue these are difficult times and the time is short to turn the country from going the wrong direction to going in the right direction. The saying is: 'when the going gets tough, the tough get going.' That is the message I bring to you tonight. We will make it if we all buckle down and pull together. There is no alternative. We've seen what the other party has done and the country can't take anymore. Join me in this crusade to bring America back. God bless you all."

Up in the sky boxes the anchors were describing the scene to the viewers. "The balloons, thousands of them are descending on the rostrum and the delegates, confetti fills the air, red, white, and blue, the music is blaring and the families of Michael Sullivan and Bernard Winslow have joined them on the platform and they are waving to the crowd. I would say it is bedlam. Bill (Bill Blatter the anchor for a major network) what do think about what we've just heard from Senator Sullivan?"

"He doesn't fudge, he comes right out and says it. A lot of people are going to be shaking in their boots until election day. You heard him----Agriculture, HUD, Education all are at risk for downsizing or elimination. Veterans Affairs, if he's sincere, will be taken apart and put back together again. The teachers unions become instant enemies. What I found fascinating was his proposal that all 18 year olds serve a year working for the government much as they did during the CCC era in the 30's. It's no secret that the Affordable Care Act needs modification yet he intends to scrap it and go back to where we were with some modifications. Also he didn't refer to it in his speech but part of his platform is welfare recipients will work for their benefits or not receive them. All this is justified, he argued, because the country is in such straits that a belt tightening is required."

"Let's go down to Jerry Simon on the floor for some reaction from the delegates on the floor."

"Yes Bill I hear you and I'm in the center of the Illinois delegation and the noise is horrendous; I am talking to Toby Johnson the head of the delegation. Mr. Johnson would you comment on Senator Sullivan's speech?"

"In my view he hit all the right buttons. This country has been falling apart under the non-leadership of the President. The Senator want's to curb IRS, lower taxes, repeal Obamacare, put responsibility for education of children back with the states where it belongs. And I think the idea of requiring the youth to serve is his most innovative idea. Today's high school graduates are coming out of school undisciplined, uneducated and self centered. Having to work for a year in communities they will learn to work as a team, gain valuable experience and have the satisfaction of serving their country."

Simon turned to the delegates clustered around Toby Johnson and asked: "Do any of you share Mr. Johnson's sentiments on the speech?" In unison they raised their hands, and one shouted out "Toby couldn't have said it better. I think he spoke for everyone in this hall tonight."

"Bill I've talked with some in other delegations just before we came on and I can tell you they said about what Mr. Johnson, head of the Illinois delegation, just told us. For them it's a crusade to win back the presidency and they feel very confident that Michael Sullivan is the man to do it."

"There you have it gentleman and ladies. That's the view of the partisans. What say you?"

"Bill, (comments by Andrew Swartz of the same network) I think he's bitten off more than he can chew. And the first bite I would point out is a draft of the young for a year's service. They will vote against that and the youth vote will count in a close election."

"I disagree Andy.(comments by Hillary Gordon reporter for the *Washington Star*) You are thinking of all those polls in the past where they asked young people if they would favor reinstitution of draft and the answer was uniformly 'no'. We're at a different place now. The youth of today are looking for structure, leadership, a sense of belonging and, yes, discipline which they have not seen much of. Added to that fact there are no jobs for them. It might be very alluring to be part of such a program for a year of their young lives."

"On that point I tend to agree with Hillary. (comments by Barry Jones of the *New York Tribune*) I believe today's youth have had so much freedom and tried every diversion that they are bored. That's a pretty early age to be bored when you have your whole life ahead of you. I think a lot of them would welcome the chance to get some discipline, have the law laid down to them and be with their peers in a community where you learn to act as a team"

"That's an interesting take, Barry, coming from a *Tribune* man I would have thought you would be dead set against a draft as a violation of civil liberties."

"Well some on the paper may disagree with me but I can say at that age I would have probably joined up." (laughter)

The newspapers were not pleased with the programs Michael set out in his acceptance speech.

Atlanta Dispatch: "SULLIVAN PROPOSES UNIVERSAL DRAFT FOR NATION'S YOUTH"

Seattle Messenger: "SULLIVAN WILL ELIMINATE DEPARTMENT OF EDUCATION, HUD"

Denver Statesman: "UNDER SULLIVAN OBAMACARE TO BE REPLACED"

The liberal talking heads were having a field day with the speech lamenting the fact Michael Sullivan would undo their whole agenda they had worked so hard to achieve. On the other side conservative talk shows were raving about the speech and that Sullivan's ideas were sorely needed if the country was to turn itself around and recapture its place at the head of the line. Both sides pointed out the voter would have a clear choice. Hanna Hamilton and Michael Sullivan were far apart on what the nation needed to succeed. There would be no middle ground.

At midnight Michael, Mary and the team adjourned to their hotel suite for a late night breakfast and roundup of the day's momentous events. Kennedy raised his glass in a toast to the couple: "Here's to the President-Elect and first lady."

He led the cheers: "here here." "Do you wish to speak to your subjects Michael?"

"John, I've said enough for one night. Let's say grace over this magnificent spread and dig in. You must all be famished. I know I am." He said the grace and they bowed their heads knowing while they had this food to eat so many in the world did not. His prayer was that each in their own way must work to cure the world's hunger. They ate, talked and drank until two in the morning although the Sullivans retired at 12:30. They were pleased at what Michael and Bernard had said at the convention, Bernie had pointed out how bad the problem was and Michael had followed up with a speech telling the nation what he would do to solve it. It was a tough speech, not condescending, telling the nation there would be some hard days ahead but the result would be worth it. Galvin, Kennedy and Connolly knew they were heading into high seas but for the moment they congratulated each other on how far they had come from that day when Kennedy had asked Michael Sullivan to run for a vacant seat in Congress. That was thirteen years ago in 2003. Now he stood on the brink of becoming the 45th President of the United States. They too had come a long way in the process and they believed more than ever before that Michael was destined to lead. His attitude was perfect. He didn't lust for the office and he had not been hollowed out like so many politicians in pursuit of it. He was himself, and should he lose he would be perfectly content to Join Paul again in the practice of law. They knew in their hearts that was not to be. He would become President, of that they were sure. How it would happen they were not sure.

With the Democratic convention only a few days away Michael and Mary decided to spend a few days in Washington before going back out on the hustings. Two days before the

Democratic convention was to convene rumors started circulating that the Justice Department would be referring the Hanna Hamilton case to a special prosecutor. The day before the convention one of the major networks claimed an announcement would be made that afternoon to the effect a special prosecutor would be named. That claim proved true when the Attorney General named Barton Marshall to be Special Prosecutor to pursue the allegations Hanna had abused her position as Secretary of State under the Espionage Act. They were watching television at their home in Spring Valley when the news broke.

"What do you think is going to happen Michael?" she asked her husband interested in his take on this latest twist in the election.

"I don't see how Justice could have done anything else. As it is they postponed it as long as possible hoping it would go away and, of course, it didn't. It's just too flagrant to ignore. They've actually punted by handing it over to a Special Prosecutor. That may be a huge mistake because he will be coming up with a decision just prior to the election which means she has it hanging over her head if she is nominated next week."

"What do you know about Barton Marshall?"

"He's a Democrat, a good lawyer, and will do a good job to protect his own reputation. Her problem is she's either stupid in not knowing she could not set up a separate communication system from the State Department or she set out deliberately to keep the Department in the dark. In either event she proves her unfitness to be President." He said this as a lawyer and she knew he was right. What neither of them knew at that moment is what would happen next. Michael understood instantly Hamilton's situation would give him a lead in the polls and might even prove determinative of the election two and a half months before it would be held.

"What will she do Michael?"

"She'll try to bluff it through and figure the special prosecutor will absolve her of guilt or the President will give her a pardon before the election."

"A pardon would kill her, Mary said with disdain in her voice. Giving Nixon a pardon caused Ford to lose the election. I think the same would be the result now."

"I agree Mary, you know Hanna has brass for a brain so the only thing she knows is too destroy her opponent and keep driving. It's worked before so she assumes it will work again. This time I don't think so. In fact within a couple hours from now I think we will see a full fledged effort by the delegates to get the Vice President to accept a draft at the convention."

"I'd never thought of that," she said incredulously. At that moment the phone rang and it was John Kennedy: "I've got everyone on a conference call and they all have something to say, are you in the mood to hear it?"

"Good news travels fast John so let's hear what the gang has to say."

"Paul what say you?"

"I say the inevitable has happened and it's going to make our job easier if we go after her."

"I couldn't agree more with that Paul. We have to knock her out of the box as being clearly unfit for the office. She on the other hand will fight like a tigress painting Michael as a war monger, papist and tool of the rich, even though she is richer than he'll ever be."

"Hey, hold on there Tom," Michael cut in, "You're managing my money and I assume I will eventually do better than Hanna with you doing the investing."

"Sorry Michael that was just a figure of speech. You stick with me and you'll beat Hanna twice, first in the election and second in investments."

"John Kennedy here. We are all of the same mind. This may be a break for us but the media is not going to take this lightly nor is the left wing of the Democratic Party. As bad as she is, she's their *Joan de Arc*. They are going to bring on the heavy artillery and aim it at our guy Sullivan. For them this is going to be an election where Socialism is advanced, or it's going to be snuffed out not to be heard from again. They don't care how unfit she is; it's a matter of she may be a liar but she's our liar."

"I agree and so I think Dominic should get out a statement saying this appointment is long overdue and the Special Prosecutor should pursue every allegation. In the meantime we will continue our campaign as vigorously as we have in the past with the intent to win in November relieving the American people of a burden they've had to bear for the last eight years----the Obama administration--- which Hanna Hamilton was part and parcel of."

"I don't have to write it Michael you just dictated it. It will go out immediately over the wire services and a blast fax to all radio and television stations and sundry pundits, mostly ours. Thank you."

They came to their convention with a heavy cloud hanging over the party. Their star was under a new investigation for her misdeeds with her e-mail and private server and the fear they had been hacked by foreign entities like the Chinese, the Russians and Mossad, the Israel intelligence service. This was to be a coronation but felt more like a public execution. It had started out triumphantly with no opponent standing in the way of the first woman President of the United States. Then a 75 year old socialist U.S. Senator had challenged the inevitable and before long he was drawing crowds of 20,000 and 30,000 at one point. How could this be? He had no chance of being the nominee yet he was killing her on the stump without any financial backing. The media, her shield, was no help; they were just as mystified as she was. The answer was fairly simple. The left of her party had become disenchanted with her and was showing their contempt by voting for a candidate going nowhere. Coming to Philadelphia they had to make some fatal decisions. Should the crown go to the socialist, or three non entities who were also running in the Democratic primary getting no traction with the voters. Even as they were arriving by train, plane, and private jets for the big donors, cars for the lesser delegates, there was talk of drafting Joseph Smith, the Vice President. Would he accept a draft? Would it be insulting to Hanna who claimed she had enough delegates to win on the first ballot? Against all odds should they elect the 75 year old Socialist? Gathering on the morning of July 25th all these questions loomed before them.

The leaders in the New York delegation took the lead in circulating a memorandum advocating the draft of the Vice President. They invited some of the party leaders and the heads of the larger delegations to meet in a conference room at the Hyatt hotel. Betty Kozinsky, a leader in the New York delegation opened the session with a straight forward plea for a vice presidential draft.

"I have been a Hanna backer from way back when she was elected to the Senate. I want her to win. She is capable and the only woman who could win the presidency. But she can't win. And it is her own fault. She caused what now has become a real danger for herself and more importantly the party itself. Poll after poll labels her as dishonest in the eyes of the voters. If she goes down many Democrats will go down with her. The polls also show Joseph Smith has high favorables in the party and is not being investigated by a special prosecutor. I say we nominate the Vice President."

Hanna had two of her own operatives in the room and they argued strenuously against Kozinsky.

"She will be exonerated by this Special Prosecutor and she will conduct a far more effective campaign than the Vice President could at this late stage. She has all the money all the organization and he has none. She's ready to go he's not. To draft him at this convention would look like we intend to lose by foregoing the front runner. We've got the delegates. I say we have to go with the Secretary. She can and will win" For an hour it went back and forth and at the end the drafters prevailed and said they would continue to push for a draft although the Vice President had not indicated either way whether he would accept a draft.

• • •

Word got around quickly that the conference at the Hyatt hotel had come to naught and the Smith people were going to put Joseph Smith's name into the ring and that the Vice President was going to go along with the draft. Fevered activity took place all day on the 25th and by the end of the day the Smith forces had enough to block Hanna on the first ballot. They had rounded up a potential 2253 delegates with 2242 needed to win the nomination. The Smith surge was fragmented, handicapped by faulty communications, still they had bought time by circulating the news they had enough to drive the voting to a possible second ballot. The news media liked the idea of competition, because it would drive up the television ratings, yet most of the journalists leaned toward Hanna as most of them were of the same persuasion. The balloting was to take place on the second day and both sides worked feverously all day; Smith trying to wean delegates away from Hanna Hamilton and the Hamilton forces shoring up there conceded strength.

When the voting started Hanna troops were totally organized down to the last delegate. They were pretty sure they could make it on the first ballot mainly because most of the delegates, by design, came from the leftist wing of the party. The Smith forces had argued strenuously that their man had the best favorables with the American people while Hanna was thought to be untrustworthy. Nonetheless she had her troops who were going with her no matter what happened and the consequences be damned. In the end she and her cohorts were too much for the Vice President's loyal and overmatched forces. She won the nomination on the first ballot obtaining the needed delegates three quarters through a call of the states. The Vice President in an effort to heal what was now a large split in the party came to the floor and asked that the vote for Hanna Hamilton be unanimous and that her choice for a running mate, Peter Simpson, the governor of California, join her on the ticket. They made their acceptance speeches promising victory, the balloons came down, followed by the confetti and they all went home praying that their advantage in the electoral college would be enough to carry the day.

Finally the teams were in place for the dash to November 8. Hamilton-Simpson vs Sullivan-Winslow. Michael called for a meeting right after labor day at which all the principles were in attendance and the final plan agreed to subject to the exigencies of a political campaign which could and usually did happen and couldn't be controlled by the contestants. Tactics dictated resources be poured into Florida, Ohio, Virginia, Colorado Wisconsin and Iowa. To win they had to thread the needle and that meant getting Wisconsin or

Iowa and the big ones, Florida and Ohio. Money would be poured into every state to help the ticket from top to bottom. The candidate would spend most of his time in six or seven states with sorties into contiguous states when the schedule permitted. Mary would go with her tea party organization while Michael did a solo until the last ten days when they would campaign together until the end. Everyone was given tentative assignments and they agreed to conference daily by phone. Jocko said the advertising campaign would cover 20 states heavily with the remainder as needed. The theme would be The Secretary of State had forfeited her right to lead the country through her own actions and was being investigated for violating the laws of the United States. In short she was a part of an administration that had botched the job of running the country and to elect her would be to elect someone not worthy to hold the office. For her part Hanna was counting on her leftist constituency to stay with her no matter what the result of the investigation coupled with a vicious attack on Michael for his Catholic religion and his threat to take the country back into war in Iraq and Afghanistan and his insistence on a draft of the youth of the country into what she referred to as his "domestic army"

Truman Foster's internal polls showed them doing well where they had to win, namely Ohio and Florida. The national polls showed Michael with an overall two point lead. She had received a small bounce of 3 points as a result of the convention. The west coast was hard core left with California, Oregon and Washington slipping into her column early. The big states like California, New York and Pennsylvania were already counted in her column.

One week after the Democratic convention the special prosecutor convened a grand jury for the purpose of determining whether the Secretary of State of the United States broke the law in setting up a server separate from the official servers of the State Department and in so doing broke the law by transmitting classified material over her e-mail that was collected on the server and unknown to the State Department. In all quarters political, bedlam broke out. Finally the press began to understand Hanna's denials were just that denials. Now the special prosecutor ominously had enough evidence of wrong doing to submit to a grand jury. Among the press and the media the hard core Hanna supporters began slowly to slip over the side of the ship. The *New York Tribune* considered the Democrats dilemma:

New York: September 2, 2016

DEMOCRATS FACE A CRISIS

By Arthur Hayes, Political Correspondent:

"The Democrats have just concluded their convention nominating Hanna Hamilton, the former Secretary of State and Peter Simpson of California to be their standard bearers. All that is in jeopardy now with the Special Prosecutor appointed by the Democratic Attorney General, summoning a grand jury to review evidence adverse to Hanna Hamilton the head of the ticket. This matter has been hanging over the head of Hamilton since April of last year when it was first discovered that during her four years as Secretary of State she had a secret e-mail account over which classified and secret material was sent. Inspectors General of two agencies referred the matter to the Justice Department for Investigation which lasted almost a year when Justice referred the matter to Special Prosecutor, Barton Marshall. This is a situation we've not seen before in a presidential race; with the election barely two months away what can the Democrats do? They could stick by her hoping for the best and if this was Boston in the era of James Michael Curley who served time in prison, might get away with it. But this is not Boston and the office involved is not that of Mayor. The only possible thing she can do is drop out of the race.

Unless....unless the President of the United States can pardon her for crimes she may have committed. This is not impossible even if her standing with the President is, to say the least, strained. After all she did betray his confidence by setting up a secret communications network contrary to his order to all government agencies. However the fate of his party is at stake and only he can keep her in the race at this time. Bear in mind that in Watergate, Gerald Ford pardoned Nixon from all crimes after he had resigned from the Presidency, and it probably cost him a loss to Jimmy Carter in his bid for election in his own right. Even with a pardon it is not beyond the realm of possibility she could pull victory from the jaws of defeat. Another possibility would be to promote Peter Simpson, her running mate to the top spot. This could presumably be accomplished by the Democratic National Committee voting to do it. With Simpson at the top of the ticket California would definitely go to the Democrats. It would make for an interesting race. A third alternative would be to draft Vice President Joseph Smith as head of the ticket. He would have as much appeal as the Governor of California. There may be other alternatives not obvious at this time. As to which one is more efficacious I cannot say. What I can and do say is none of the alternatives I have mentioned look very attractive. There has been no comment from the Hamilton camp except to say she is completely innocent of any wrong doing and if charged will be acquitted. That would normally keep the wolves at bay but this is the Presidency of the United States and the people are likely to not tolerate a candidate asking for their vote with a possible criminal indictment hanging over her head. Whatever happens you can be sure the Sullivan campaign will not stand still waiting the Democrats to decide what to do. They will treat this as the break it is and run with it. Whatever the outcome we shall certainly know in a few days."

At the White house two views quickly developed: pardon her and save the party; let her twist in the wind and leave it to the party to replace her. The issue for the Democrats they agreed, was could she win if she got a pardon assuming the President would grant one?" Could Simpson or the Vice President make a better showing and even win? She betrayed us some argued. She tarnished the President's administration. Others said she's a household name, she would be the first woman president and with a pardon she can make the argument it was all politics and a Republican conspiracy to bring her down. It might work. We have the Electoral College and we have a built in Democratic Vote they said.

In the Hamilton camp they were conducting business as if nothing had happened. A tactic that had always worked for her in the past. Her camp had made feelers to the White House deciding a pardon was the only logical way she could stay in the race. She was also counting on her financial supporters, and party big wigs to petition the President to grant the pardon as the only sensible way to let the campaign proceed with any chance of winning.

The convening of a grand jury came as no surprise to the Sullivan camp. They rolled out ads that criticized her for Benghazi causing the lives of four Americans, using a private server and e-mail while Secretary of State, using her office for gain by entities making contributions to her foundation in return for favors. The idea was to emphasize she was morally unfit for the office. This attack did not stop when the grand jury was announced. They understood the possibility of a pardon in which case she would continue the fight and they would continue to impugn her reputation for untruthfulness and deceit.

After Labor Day, without warning, the White House issued a press release that a pardon had been granted to Hanna Hamilton with the written explanation that in the President's judgment the Secretary, although making mistakes, did not deserve to be prosecuted. A second reason given was that under the circumstances the country was on the brink of a national election for the next President of the United States; both parties had selected their candidates and were fully engaged in the election process and it should be left to the voters to decide who would serve the nation best. The reaction was as predicted; some in the media thought the President did the heroic thing; let the voters decide. Others said it was another example of Hanna Hamilton being held to a different standard, above the law. The overall opinion said the "pardon" would not help and would in fact hurt her chances with the same result as befell President Ford in 1976. Both camps went into high gear with Hanna reinvigorated with the pardon behind her and Michael out every day preaching values, taking American back from a bankrupt administration of which Hanna was a top official.

As they entered October an accumulation of polls showed Michael with a 4 point lead just outside the margin of error. In October they took Michael off the trail for a meeting in Washington. At the meeting Jocko emphasized the point that they would have to be ready for a last minute appeal for all Democrats to come home to the party. A Republican win would mean death, possibly for eight years. "That's the appeal they will make. They did the same thing in 1968 when Hubert Humphrey went into fall badly wounded by Lyndon Johnson's non interest and the Viet Nam war. Nixon barely held on." Michael had spoken to the point saying there would be no defensive posture hoping to run out the clock. In his opinion Hanna Hamilton would be the worst thing that could happen to the country. "There will be no holding the ball hoping the other side will foul, and we could win on free throws. No we will go all out and portray her for the person she is and when they vote against her they will feel good about it." He went back on the road to set the example for what he had said in the meeting. Watching his tenacity everyone in the campaign doubled their efforts. John Kennedy was spending eight hours a day calling for contributions and they were pouring in fueling huge television coverage in the close states.

Mid October national polls were showing Michael at 44%, Hanna at 40% and undecided at 16%. The internal polls showed Michael at 46%, Hanna at 42% and 12% undecided. For that time in October the polls, in Truman Foster's opinion, were suspect showing such a high undecided. To him that meant the race could be very close on election day since the undecided vote usually broke to the one behind in the polls. He advised they up the advertising in Ohio and Florida emphasizing Hanna's attitude toward the truth and whether that attitude would suffice for the Oval office.

Three debates had been set for the contenders, one in September and two in October. In the first Hanna had come across as stilted treating her opponent as somewhat of a lesser personage. Michael realized after the first four or five minutes the impression she would be sending out to the viewers on television. His mind flashed back to the first Kennedy-Nixon debate. Nixon came over as nervous, over dominant and above all perspiring. For those listening on the radio they had an opposite view. They thought Nixon was the winner. The lesson learned from that debate was it's how you look not what you say. Hanna answered questions in a pompous fashion. On the other hand Michael played it straight giving concise answers while hers were overblown and had to be cut off by the moderator.

Reluctantly the press gave the first debate to Senator Sullivan on points. No knock down or knock out. Privately the Sullivan team thought he knocked her out of the box yet made no big fuss, suggesting to the press: Res Ipsa Loquiter. (the thing speaks for itself) The young journalists had to go to their computers to learn what it meant and when they discovered what it meant they charged the Sullivan team with putting them on. In the second debate, October 1, her handlers had obviously shown her tapes of her earlier per-formance and she modified her approach by trying to be folksy which had the same effect as her first appearance---phony. Michael became specific showing how far apart they were on the issues such as abortion where she favored it and even favored partial birth abortion. He called it mur-der. She hailed the President's agreement with Iran a master stroke. He called it an unmitigated disaster and a betrayal of America's interest and security. She called for a free college education for everyone. He pointed out it would be another entitlement, one the country couldn't possibly afford under the best of circumstances.

By the end of the second debate it was clear the candidates were diametrically opposed to each other on almost every issue except Medicare and Social Security. The media gave the nod to Michael again because of her trying the "folksy" approach when she was anything but "folksy." As the third debate set for October 15 approached the polls showed her trailing by as much as 5 points. Her advisors must have warned her that her last chance to win would be to make a forceful showing, if not win the third debate. On that night she came out fighting like a tigress accusing the Senator as one who would take us to war, a religious fanatic, (presumably because he was a Catholic) would take away welfare, and cut social security to the bone and create a draft against the wishes of the youth of the nation. To each of these thrusts he calmly paried by setting forth his positions and made it sound so logical that her allegations looked like political rantings. In the "spin" room after the debate her people were out in force trying to convince the media she had won the debate hands down. Sullivan's spokesmen merely repeated what they had said after the first debate: Res Ipsa Loquitur.

Washington Star: October 16, 2016........Jorge Pasqual

"The debates are over and last night we saw the real Hanna Hamilton, the one we know as a fighter. Senator Sullivan who's been enjoying a lead in the polls recently seemed somewhat taken aback by the ferocity of her attack. She never let up, pounding him on every one of his stands, branding him as a right wing fanatic. It was really the first time her backers had a chance to cheer---her performance being less than perfect in her first two appearances. Granted, Sullivan counter punched but in my opinion it wasn't as effective as her accusations. There is only a short time left until the election. Concededly she's behind now yet her performance last night should be enough to ignite a fire under her supporters, and as they always do, Democrats will start coming home ala Harry Truman in 1948. This is not to count the Senator out, he leads; but in the next two weeks you will see the polls close as they always do when people start to make up their minds........"

On the 16th Michael and Tom Donovan went to New Hampshire for a last appearance knowing New Hampshire was critical to winning in November. The reception was tremendous with 15,000 turning out in Manchester, unheard of in that state. Hanna was there the week before and only drew 3,000. Afterwards Michael held a press conference and the first question asked was: did he favor women in the military? He understood it was a planted question and he was ready for it. In the back of the hall Tom Donovan gulped hard. He realized as quickly as Michael it was a plant and that it was designed to illicit an answer that would give Hanna a chance to argue he was against women.

"My answer to the question is yes. Let me anticipate the next question. I favor women in the military but not in combat positions. They do not have the physical assets to be in combat. Yes, they have the mental capacity but in combat they are a distraction. They do not have the stamina of a man. It is not necessary. The services have been politicized by this administration in the interest of diversity not to mention votes. In my opinion it has weakened our military and thus our ability to defend ourselves. Prior to this administration women could not serve in combat. If you talk to military commanders they uniformly agree women do not have the same strength as men in combat. Our current military leadership has bent to the will of this President against their better judgement. I will follow the advice of my military commanders." There were more questions but the big one had been answered. Back at the hotel Tom and Michael discussed the expected repercussions from his answer to the question.

"What do you think the media will do with it Michael?"

"The headline will be: Sullivan says women inadequate to serve in combat." He answered laughing.

"Why are you laughing? They're going to kill you."

"I agree they'll be out there tomorrow claiming I'm a misogynist. I'm willing to bet you five dollars the voter is with me on this issue. Jocko has run focus groups on this issue around the country and the result is 8 out of 10 agree with our position. The fact is people are fed up with politicizing the military. Common sense dictates men should fight wars. Women have always been a part of the military but not at the front, firing rifles. Do you accept the bet?"

"I'm not going to bet against you Senator, I know you don't bet if you don't think you will win."

The next day Hanna and her minions in the media took up the war cry: "SULLIVAN VETOES WOMEN IN COMBAT; WOULD REVERSE OBAMA POLICY." Michael would have won the bet when it turned out the issue had a shelf life of two days after the polls showed 69% of Americans agreed with his position, 30% against and a miniscule 1% undecided. Jocko was right on the money.

The last two weeks were to be spent in what the campaign called "must win" states: Colorado, Florida, Iowa, Virginia and Wisconsin. On the 17th Tom Donovan and the Senator were in Colorado for three stops. They first met at the airport in Denver with state director Audrey Dietrich who informed them she had 1,000 volunteers throughout the state ready to act as poll watchers, drivers, sign holders on the major thoroughfares in the largest city and attorneys ready to trouble shoot up to and including seeking injunctive relief in the event of fraud. (The campaign had in place over 500 attorneys in the states to insure against fraud plus 100 attorneys in Washington standing by to give legal advice to the attorneys in the states and or to go to court in the capital.)

Paul Connolly had called key law firms all over the country to secure needed personnel. After the meeting they went to a street rally in downtown Denver. As Michael started to speak hecklers burst on the scene waving Hanna placards and trying to shout him down. He did not engage them but stood silently while the crowd shouted "Sullivan"; "Sullivan." Having run into the same situation on an almost daily basis as the campaign wound down, Kennedy arranged to have his own security force available to remove the "Hamilton Hostiles" as he referred to them while the secret service took care of the candidate. 30 men trained in crowd control swiftly surrounded the hecklers and began to remove them slowly and gently until they were entirely separated from crowd that came to hear the candidate. He went on with his speech as though nothing had happened. The pattern repeated itself in Cincinnati and Columbus, Ohio, with the same result. The papers in both cities were highly incensed at what they referred to as the "high handiness" of the Hamilton forces trying to disrupt the speaker at a political event to which its citizens had come to listen. All in all the campaign thought it owed a debt of gratitude to the Hanna forces for gaining the Sullivan campaign a lot of good will with Ohio voters. Everyone attended a meeting in Miami on Saturday the 30th for the purpose of pulling everything together for the last eight days. Thirty of the key players assembled in a private room at the Fontainebleau, Paul Connolly presiding. Michael and Tom sat off to one side as Jocko O'Brian and Truman Foster explained where they were.

"Polls show us holding sleight leads in our "must win' states. She picked up a little bit in the national polls but we are maintaining a 44-40 lead with 16 still undecided. She's counting heavily on the unions putting all their people in the field on election day to turn out the vote. My guess is she's going to lose some minorities and the youth who don't have the incentive to vote as they did in the last two elections for Obama. The country is angry and they want a change;

I don't think they can pull it off. Michael is killing himself and I hope all of you will follow suit until we can put this thing to bed." The meeting broke up after two hours with everyone feeling all was being done that could be done and rest would be in the hands of the voters.

Meanwhile the Hamilton camp was still confident that with their advantage in the Electoral College they could win narrowly while the Sullivan forces had to run the table, winning Ohio, Florida, Virginia, Colorado, Iowa and Wisconsin, all in the Democratic column in 2012. Her campaign spokesman said over and over to the press: "the Republicans tried to bring her down with a lot of phony accusations and the President beat them at their game by pardoning her before they could do any more damage to her reputation. She was a great Congresswoman, a great Senator, a great Secretary of State and she will be a great President." It was the same rhetoric they had used over and over convincing themselves the people would overlook things she had been accused of. Despite the fact her loss would bring down many Democrats across the country they intended, in their hubris, to defy the odds. Hanna Hamilton was in it for Hanna Hamilton and let the rest of the ticket fare for itself. That confidence would prevail until the day of the vote. Added to her attack on the Republican candidate was a new approach in her relationship to the President. For weeks her theme had been she was independent of the administration. Six days before the election she sharpened her tone saying the administration had made many errors, errors she would correct as President. Some in the media took umbrage at the attack, the most outspoken being Thomas Coburn of the *Los Angeles Chronicle*:

"For some weeks now Hanna Hamilton has been hinting, that as Secretary of State, she often disagreed with the Obama administration's policies. If so, she never voiced them very loudly because they never found their way into the media. These last few days she has become more strident claiming, not only did she disagree with Obama's policies but, they were harmful to the country. These statements, made in broad general terms, do not specify which policies were detrimental. In taking this tack she is desperately trying to put as much distance between her candidacy and her connection to the administration. I believe it is a little too late for that. She voiced no criticism during her four years as Secretary of State and *de minimis* in the four years after. It is counterfeit to all of a sudden proclaim the administration has been guilty of grave mistakes all along. Her opponent, Michael Sullivan has been quick to denounce her hypocrisy in attacking an administration she was a part of when no condemnation of its acts were made during her tenure. She probably understands at this point the President will not be sadden if she loses to Michael Sullivan. In his mind his legacy would be enhanced if his eight years were followed by a Republican administration putting space between him and another Democratic President......."

By Tuesday November 1 Jocko reported that Florida, according to Truman Foster, was safe and that Michael should spend the last six days campaigning with Mary in Ohio, Iowa and Wisconsin. They headed for Madison into the heart of Democratic Country for a series of speeches and then into the suburbs where the Republican vote would be needed to offset the Democratic edge. That night at eleven o'clock they finally met back at the Hyatt Place Madison. A staff of 20 were with them and stayed on separate floors. Secret Service and Kennedy's army guarded the hotel floors occupied by the Sullivan staffers. Since they were famished after a full day of campaigning Mary ordered room service. Hamburgers and hot coffee. When they finished the meal they were so keyed up from campaigning all day they just wanted to talk about what was happening to them.

They laid on the king sized bed facing each other too tired to take off their clothes. "Tell me what your day was like sweetheart?" he said.

"Well actually I had a great time. I spent the whole day at the University talking to small groups and individuals. Mostly, young people. Of course they were all Democrats yet they seemed to like the idea of one year of service to the country. They spoke about discipline. They seemed to have a yearning for it. I found it extremely interesting. I also found out a lot of them are going to vote for you. You know why?"

"No, why?" he said totally baffled knowing that college students, as a group, favor Democrats because of their liberal leaning.

"They like your views on values. They think the country has become too licentious. Can you imagine that?"

"Yes I can. I've sensed it with their parents. The country is fed up with the total breakdown of sexual mores, and the promotion of promiscuity. I think we may be seeing the pendulum swinging back towards sanity and respect amongst the generations, something that's been missing since the '60's"

"Well, whatever it is it renews my faith in these kids. I think they understand the last eight years have been calamitous for us. Let's see if they prove it at the polls. Tell me about your day."

"I was in the city for two rallies, one on the street and one at a high school. The crowds were outstanding. I talked about values and the need to reinstill them in society. The reception was the same as I have had everywhere the last six months. They yelled out: 'give it to them Mikee.' And every time I would mention a value the crowd picked up the chant.

I did the same thing at the high school and they yelled just as loud. It's as though no political figure had ever brought up the need to bring values back into the country's thinking. So what I conclude is we are going to win Wisconsin." On that note they got into their pajamas and fell into the bed happy with the day, events.

CHAPTER 11

WITH FIVE DAYS to go they headed to Iowa because Foster's polling showed they had an excellent chance of picking up six electoral votes. In Des Moines they targeted the suburbs where they hoped to ween votes to offset the Democratic advantage in the city. In a high school gymnasium he told the 2,000 able to get in and the 3,000 outside watching on monitors that his plan to require the youth of the nation to contribute a year of service to the country would prove a benefit to the country and the teenagers in that they would be helping to build the infrastructure so badly in need of repair and serving in the military which would give them pride and a sense of accomplishment that would stand them in good stead the rest of their lives. Values the country had abandoned must be recaptured to enable the nation to build back its strength as example to the rest of the world. Seeking truth and not distorting it to achieve a preconceived end as the administration and the President had done. Lowering taxes for all citizens but requiring all citizens to pay some tax. Protecting religious liberty under attack by the administration and its allies on the left. Allowing people to speak freely and not be intimidated by those who call for political correctness. After each issue he gave his position on the crowd inside and outside the gym exploded with cheers. At the end Mary came on stage and they waved and saluted the crowd who shouted back: "Sullivan, Sullivan." Over the next three days he gave 15 speeches hammering home themes on values, a strong military, repealing the socialistic Obamacare, employment that would reduce levels of joblessness from over 12% to a real 5% rather than the artificial 5.1% contrived by the Administration to leave out of the equation all those who were no longer looking for a job or had been out of a job for at least a year. In Cedar Rapids and Davenport, Iowa the crowds were 20,000 and 25,000 respectively. Feeling his message was getting through to people who really had had enough, he urged the only way their voice could be heard would be to vote on November 8th. "I need your help and that means your vote. Without it I can't win Iowa which we have to win. You can make a difference of four more years of drudgery and failure or a new future for the country." When he waded into the crowd he could tell they were desperate for a change; they grabbed his hand and held on saying they would be praying and voting for him.

Now with three days left they headed for Ohio and the suburbs of Toledo, Columbus and Cincinnati hoping to off-set the city vote with the suburban vote. At the last minute Foster decided they should finish the campaign in Cleveland on November 7. That night the last appearance took place at a large park in the Cleveland suburbs before the largest gathering of the campaign, 35,000. Bone tired when he came on stage, he looked out at the crowd and felt a surge of energy and a desire to speak to each one individually.

"I am overwhelmed at this turnout. I only wish I could talk to each one of you; to personally ask for your vote. This will be the last time I get to speak to any audience before the voting begins tomorrow. There is much to be done. Each day that passes the situation grows worse; I don't have to read off the litany of mistakes and troubles the current leadership has brought on the country. You lived it. I will tell you this can be remedied but it will take leaders who lead not follow. A leader who can persuade the people of the justice of

the cause; a leader who doesn't lie or take polls to determine
what he should do. In short a leader who leads and has the
trust of the people. I am asking you to give me that chance.
I have solutions not excuses. I will make mistakes. I will own
up to them. In the next four years together we can turn the
ship of state around. We will teach our young values. We will
live those values as adults. We will take care of the elderly
we will preserve life at every stage. We will repair our country's defenses. We will take care of those who have served
us in the wars. We will negotiate with world powers from
strength. We will provide opportunity for all not squelch it
with government regulations which has been the aim of the
present administration. If elected I will honor the office not
disgrace it or hold it up to ridicule. No leader can do it alone.
It will take sacrifice. Everyone's sacrifice. If elected I will tell
you what our problems are and I will propose a remedy. I
will never send a soldier of the United States into battle with
his hands tied behind his back so as not to hurt the feelings of some foreign leader." Each promise brought a roar
of approval. He said it all in twenty five minutes and at the
end he brought Mary on stage and they saluted the crowd.
Someone up front yelled: "go gettum Mikee." The crowd
took up the chant: "go gettum Mikee" From one side of the
stage a young boy came over to where Mary and Michael
were waving to the crowd and he handed them a large
American flag. Michael took it and started waving it and the
crowd responded with the familiar "USA, USA, USA." He
gave the flag back to the young man and the magic moment
was over. Due to the late hour they decided to stay at the
hotel and leave election day for Washington. At 6:30 a.m.
a car was waiting to take them to Cleveland Hopkins airport where they boarded a Lear Jet for the two hour ride to
Reagan National. When they arrived the press swarmed all

around and he briefly talked to the reporters saying he felt the campaign had been successful and he looked forward to a favorable result. Then he and Mary and their secret service detail headed to the terminal.

Hanna's advisors were determined to go negative to the end running ads that portrayed Michael as the enemy of women due to his abortion stand; a homophobe because of his stand against same sex marriage; a traitor for being against the Iranian agreement; a danger to the Republic because of his religion and a war monger arguing for maintaining forces in Iraq and Afghanistan. As days wound down she became more shrill in her attacks most of which were being financed by the billionaire, Mikos Tabor thru an independent PAC but carefully coordinated with the Hamilton campaign. On the other hand the Sullivan team had decided to stress the themes he had been talking about the last week and soften the candidate's persona in all their television ads. The contrast with Hanna's ads was stark.

"Peter, the rector wants to see you right away. "Thanks, Sam I'll tend to it." Peter Sullivan was reading Thomas Merton when he heard the knock at the door. He reluctantly put the book down on the desk in his small room and put on his cassock in preparation for the meeting, wondering all the while, what could prompt the rector's request. He had only met the rector one on one on one other occasion. Now he hurried to the fourth floor office of Monsignor Peter Roncalli and knocked on the door.

"Come in," came the soft voice of the rector. Peter Roncalli had been rector for four years and was much admired by all the seminarians and the staff for his good humor and wisdom. At six feet two inches, he looked like a bear of a man, but in fact was soft spoken and a born leader. Under his tutelage the North American College had prospered beyond hope with many generous patrons in Europe and the United States who had taken the college and it's rector to heart and contributed substantial sums to build an endowment. Michael Sullivan's blind trust had been a substantial contributor although this fact was unknown to Peter.

Peter entered the office which was a model of simplicity. A mid sized desk and chair, a small conference table in a corner of the room, a couch directly opposite the desk and pictures of the college and some of the former rectors on the wall. He came from behind the desk as the seminarian entered, welcomed Peter with a hearty hand shake and motioned him to the couch. When they were both seated he asked if he wanted a cup of tea to which Peter answered: "I'd like that Monsignor if you will join me." The big man went to the door, gave an order, and returned to the couch.

"You probably wonder why I sent for you and the answer is his Eminence, Cardinal Boyle of Washington, phoned me about an hour ago and said he wanted you in Washington on the day of the election. He thought it portentous that the family be together on such an important day and I agree. So young man the plan is for you to leave here in two hours and get on a plane at Leonardo da Vinci and be home on November 8."

"This is wonderful Monsignor; I hope you don't think I put my family up to this."

"Not at all Peter, I think I know enough about you that that thought would never have entered my mind. I think the Cardinal came up with the idea on his own and a good one it is. If your father is going to be elected the President of the United States I think it only right that you be present to congratulate him. Be assured our prayers for you and the family go with you to Washington. Skip the tea since it's taking too long and God's speed. One more thing, your family has no knowledge you're coming home, the Cardinal thought it might be a nice surprise for them."

Peter got up and shook the Monsignor's hand vigorously, raced back to his room, alerted his next door neighbor of the situation and was waiting at the Porter's office when a black Mercedes limousine pulled up; he got in with his duffle bag, sat back and enjoyed the forty five minute drive to the airport marveling at the fact he had been quietly absorbed in a spiritual reading by Thomas Merton and an hour and a half later he was on his way home. God works in strange ways he thought. He could hardly contain his excitement as the plane touched down at Dulles International Airport and taxied to the designated parking space where a huge bus took the passengers to the terminal where they were quickly passed through customs and out into the airport proper. As he exited customs a man holding a sign that read "Peter Sullivan" caught his eye and he realized a car and driver had been sent to pick him up. They drove the 35 miles into the city and he was taken directly to Reagan National airport where his parents were scheduled to arrive at 9: 00 am. They were on time and when they saw him they ran and both embraced him at the same time. "What are you doing here Peter? What a joy," cried Mary tears streaming down her face. His father embraced him as they all walked to a waiting car. He explained how it all came about and they laughed at the Cardinal's kindness.

On the way to Spring Valley they decided to vote at their precinct where fifty reporters and still photographers were waiting to capture the moment for posterity and then attend 10:00 o'clock mass at Annunciation, five blocks from home. Only 20 people were in the pews with the secret service stationed in the back. Michael asked that press remain in the vestibule except for those wanting to attend mass. At 10:00

o'clock on the dot Monsignor Vascarelli came onto the altar and the mass started. At the first reading he asked Michael to come forward and read to the congregation. He read the passage with humility and then returned to his seat. The mass went on just as it did everyday yet this was different. It was entirely possible the next president of the United States was sitting in the pews with twenty other people and a smattering of press who accepted the invitation to attend mass with them, all of whom were aware this was a historical moment for the church and for all present including secret service, the press outside on the lawn and across the street on Massachusetts avenue where a crowd of about five hundred people, who heard he was in the church, waited to see the Sullivans as they emerged. As the mass progressed Michael prayed but, as often happens, his mind began to wander and it crossed his mind this might be the last mass he would attend at Annunciation for a while. It sadden him for the moment yet he understood and accepted the fact, as President, he would still be going to mass but it would have to be private so that the presence of the President would not hinder others from attending service without the hubbub that attended every movement of the President. He thought about how life would change for his children who, each in their own way, were pursuing worthwhile careers but would be operating in the glare of publicity should he be elected in the next ten hours. When the mass was over they shook hands with the Monsignor and the parishioners who could not wait to get home and tell friends and neighbors what they had just witnessed. The cars drew up front and as they got into the cars the crowd, now swollen to over a thousand people, applauded and shouted encouragement. Instead of going home they decided to proceed downtown to the Hilton to prepare for whatever was to come.

Mary had arranged to have a buffet supper for thirty men and their wives starting at four in the afternoon in a large banquet room at the Hilton Hotel where the campaign had reserved two full floors. They were the fund raisers, campaign heads and state coordinators who had contributed to what everyone believed had been a well run campaign. In Mary's mind this was a small way of thanking them for all their efforts. Everyone arrived on time and Michael and Mary greeted each guest at the door as they arrived. Later he made a short speech thanking them for all the hard work and then headed up to the war room on the top floor where all the apparatus was set up to chart the election as votes came in from the various states. Jocko had communications set up with 50 individuals in each state who would give minute by minute details on their state vote and the vote in selected precincts. Those would be compared with turn out and vote count in the 2012 election. The first polls closed at 6:00 pm in Indiana and Kentucky and it was expected those 19 electoral votes would fall into Michael's column.

Downstairs the ballroom was decked out in red, white and blue bunting the like of which is seen on opening day at the baseball park, with balloons and confetti festooned to the low ceiling ready to drop when the candidate reached the 270 electoral votes needed to win the presidency. At one end one end of the room a huge board was set up showing the vote totals as they came in, the electoral votes allocated to each candidate and the popular vote accumulation. Large screens were placed around the room so the crowd could watch three networks simultaneously. At the other end of the room planners had arranged for a dance band to entertain until six o'clock when the first returns would start coming in.

• • •

A major network delivered the first returns: "Indiana and Kentucky have closed and the Associated Press is awarding both states to Michael Sullivan for a total of 19 electoral votes." A colleague cautioned that the early returns would be from southern states which would give an early lead to the Republicans and be offset by the eastern seaboard states as the Democrats began to run in big totals. "For Sullivan, his ship has to come in by 8:00 pm showing a favorable trend or the Democrats are going to win this one." Jack Sullivan had been in the war room with Jocko O'Brian phoning into precincts in Ohio and Florida. In Florida he was looking at Brevard County where Michael was getting 60% of the vote compared to John Madden's vote of 56% in 2012. In Broward, the big Democratic stronghold, Sullivan's vote was 47% to Madden's 32%. In Miami-Dade Hamilton was being held to 55% compared to Obama's 2012 margin of 62% to 38% for Madden. He breathed a sigh of relief and checked his figures with O'Brian's state computer contacts. They jibed and the word was passed to Michael and the family in their private suite that Florida was in with its 29 electoral votes. It was only six fifteen but the first "must win" was achieved. Still, Michael felt it was way too soon to let down. The same feeling dominated the room where the family watched with the Galvins, Kennedys and Connollys.

On MBC a panel of political commentators gave their views on what was happening: "Sullivan is expected to get the early vote in Indiana and Kentucky so that doesn't tell us tell us too much. What we want to watch for is what happens in Florida. If Sullivan loses there I believe Hamilton will wind up the winner." "Thanks Bert" said the moderator. At that point, Miriam Watorg, of the *Bradbury Independent* interrupted with what she claimed was breaking news. "AP is reporting that in some of the larger counties in Florida

Hamilton is not doing as well as expected. If that's accurate Sullivan will have met the first hurdle he has to pass." I say by eight o'clock Massachusetts, New Jersey, Michigan and Maryland, Democrat strongholds, will start reporting in and then we'll see where it all stands." At 7:15 CBC called Florida for the Republicans giving Michael Sullivan 48 electoral votes. In Jocko O'Brian's war room his workers were reporting heavy voting in Republican precincts in Georgia, South Carolina and most importantly, Virginia.

With subdued excitement, Truman Foster slipped a note to Jocko which read: "In Fairfax County, Virginia Sullivan is running at 46%, 11 points ahead of John Madden in 2012." Both men knew if that was indicative of the state Michael would win Virginia, a second major hurdle, where Obama had carried the county 59% to 35%. They decided to hold the information for 15 minutes when they would have definitive proof Virginia's 13 votes would go to the Republicans.

In the ballroom new figures went up for Georgia, South Carolina and Alabama, putting Michael in the lead with another 34 electoral votes. The packed room sent up a resounding cheer feeling a release of anxiety ---not victory--just the feeling that things were going well. Up in family suite Kennedy had a score sheet on his lap and announced polls were closed in Massachusetts, Michigan, New Jersey, Maine, Delaware and Maryland, and those states would go into Hanna's column for sure even with Michael doing much better than expected in Michigan and Delaware "That will give Hanna 58 votes to our 82. Our next big one is Virginia. And here's the good news, Jocko sent me a text saying we're in. We will win Virginia and he's predicting we will get over 2,000,000 votes to Hanna's 1,700,000. If I were in Hanna's camp I'd be getting worried." Michael sat quietly on the couch holding Mary's hand, both of them taking it all in watching the excitement in the suite as the states were starting to fill in 100% of their precincts.

In the meantime everyone in the war room was now focused on the linchpin, Ohio, where the polls had closed at 7:30. Jocko and his men were looking at five counties: Butler where Madden had beat the President 62% to 36% and Michael was up over Hanna, 70% to 30%; Cuyahoga where Hamilton's lead in the Cleveland area was down from 68% in 2012 to 55%; Franklin; the lead cut from 60% to 52%; Montgomery, where the President had won in 2012 Michael was winning 53% to 47%; and Summit where he was beating Hamilton 55% to 44%, reversing the vote for the President in 2012. It was now 9:30 and the networks weren't yet focused on Ohio but Jocko phoned to the suite and talked directly with Michael.

"Senator, I think you've bagged the big one. The President won here in 2012 by 100,000 votes with over 5,000,000 votes cast. I'm predicting you will win by 750,000 or more."

"I'll take your word for it Jocko, nice work." He put his cell phone back in his pocket and whispered in Mary's ear. "Jocko says we will win Ohio Mary. That means we are about three hours away from winning the Presidency. I'm going to pass it on to the fellows." John and Tom Galvin were in deep conversation at the bar set up in the suite. Michael motioned them to come over to the couch where he and Mary were sitting. They bent down to hear his whisper, "Jocko says we will win Ohio by 700,000!" They stood up and clasped his hand and both kissed Mary. Without making any fuss they sauntered over to the bar and summoned Paul Connolly and the three ordered their first scotch of the night. "This is really getting to be a lot of fun. Now we only have to sweat out Wisconsin, Iowa and North Carolina.

"This is Aston Smith reporting for the TBC network. It is now 9:40 and we are beginning to get a clearer picture of what is happening. At this juncture the Republican's Michael Sullivan is leading in electoral votes 85 to 43 but the big states of New York and Pennsylvania are still to weigh in and the next crucial state reporting will be Ohio. Bill can you give us the report from the mid- west?"

"Ashton, Ohio polls closed at 7:00 pm and we are getting scattered reports but we do know Sullivan is maintaining a lead of 53.7% to 46.3% with vote totals of 1,718,400 to 1,051,232. If that holds up the odds jump in his favor to become the next President of the United States. Nothing from Iowa, Wisconsin or Minnesota and Michigan is going for Hamilton. Back to you Ashton."

"Well you heard it here first, the state the Republicans must have, Ohio, is leaning to Michael Sullivan. We won't know for sure. Should it turn out Sullivan wins Ohio, it makes it difficult, but not impossible for the Democrat to win.

In the ballroom the crowd was getting louder and louder as cheers erupted every time new numbers were posted. "Sullivan, Sullivan" rang through the ball room packed to capacity with an additional one thousand people in the hall outside, even the lobby of the hotel was beginning to take on a festive atmosphere as more people came streaming through the doors hoping to be with the winner and a part of history. When the Associated Press called Ohio, West Virginia and North Carolina for Michael the ballroom exploded with sound that reverberated throughout the hotel. Hope turned into plausibility and plausibility into likelihood. The crowd smelled blood in the water.

Anticipating a big victory for the first woman President of the United States the Hamilton campaign had booked the

Waldorf Astoria in New York for the night's victory celebration. After Ohio, panic set in but cooler heads prevailed.
Toby Wilson, the leader sat at a table with a map spread out
in front of him. Aides clustered around.

"Ok we lost Ohio but we have not lost. We can still get to
270 by running the table. By that I mean we have to win 16
more states to reach 272."

"What are they?" someone asked doubtfully.

"All states we won in 2008 and 2012. 16 to be exact. For us
the "must wins" are Iowa, Wisconsin, Colorado and Nevada.
We win those four and we win with 272. We lose any of the
four we lose by a nose." In the presidential suite Hannah and
her closest advisers were clustered eyes glued to the television for any hint of good news. With Ohio a somberness
came over the group but when she received a call from Toby
Wilson after the Ohio call she felt better and passed on the
news, "Toby says we can win by winning in Iowa, Wisconsin
Colorado and Nevada. We've always won those states and
there's no reason we shouldn't win them tonight. He said the
other twelve are in the bag."

Boyden Johnson and Mikos Tabor were also in New York.
He had sunk ten million into Hanna Hamilton and earlier
in the evening he was thinking about having a few martinis and a Cuban cigar when she reached 270 electoral votes.
Now he had a fourth martini and was mourning the loss of
his ten million. Boyden was just as despondent on his third
scotch, but he like Toby Wilson saw it was still possible and
feasible for Hanna to win. He had figured out the states they
needed to win just as Wilson had done. He informed Tabor
of his calculations and the billionaire decided to switch to
scotch as a ray of hope formed in his brain. "I think I will
have that cigar now based on your calculations. I feel much
better and there's no use waiting to smoke this cigar. If that

guy Sullivan wins you can count on me to do everything in my power to thwart his every move and I have the money to do it."

Boyden didn't bother to mention to Mikos four crucial states had to be won and he had serious doubts it could be done. Nevertheless, his heart quickened when Mikos said he would spend money to block moves a "President Sullivan" might take to reverse the gains the President had made both before and after he (Johnson) was Majority Leader in the Senate. Presumably he would stay on Tabor's payroll to carry out his wishes which would serve two purposes; make him wealthy and allow him to get back at John Kennedy and Michael Sullivan.

At 9:45 Virginia went up on the board for Michael in what the Democrats believed was an upset; it came as no surprise to the Republicans who were also in the process of taking a gubernatorial seat away from the Democrats and all the state wide offices. The electoral total stood at Sullivan 98; Hamilton 59. Still early in the evening and the polls were still open on the west coast which would bring 74 electoral votes into Hanna Hamilton's column. In rapid succession New Hampshire gave 4 electoral votes to Hamilton and Texas awarded 38 to Sullivan. The television in the suite flashed the vote total on the big board in the ballroom and at 10:15 it stood at:

ELECTORAL VOTE COUNT
SULLIVAN---171 HAMILTON---62

Michael consulted with Mary and they both decided it was time to go to the ballroom to thank their supporters. He gave a signal and a wave of people plus secret service and Kennedy's people headed for the ballroom. An advance team of twenty had gone ahead and cleared a path for the candidate to make his way through the crowd to the stage. Word spread quickly the Sullivans were on their way down. Simultaneously, the network anchors alerted their listeners Michael would be coming into the hall momentarily. On a raised platform to one side of stage a bank of television cameras focused on the microphones from which the candidate would speak. As they came through the door at the back of the ballroom and headed toward the stage the crowd let out a tremendous welcome. The sound was deafening and he and Mary shook hands as they headed to the platform. After four minutes the applause subsided and Michael addressed the thousands of people in the room and the hallway.

"It looks promising! Unbridled noise. I want to thank you all for coming and working for this day. My thanks goes not only to those present here tonight but to all those thousands of people who helped fund our campaign, worked knocking on doors, placing lawn signs and worked in headquarters all over this country on our behalf. I would be remiss if I didn't thank my wife Mary and my family, Peter, Jack, Sharon and Kathryn who are beside me tonight. The key people in the campaign I will not name and you all know who you are. Thanks. It's now 10:35 and we are hopeful of victory but it is too soon to know the outcome. If we win, I will need your continued help and support. (unrestrained applause) We will face tremendous challenges and no one leader or group of leaders can bring the country to its full potential without the backing of the people. Anticipating victory I ask for your help."

At that moment Bernard Winslow, his wife and family came on to the stage and raised Michael's hand in victory. The balloons and confetti plummeted from the ceiling and the room exploded in noise. In the network sky boxes, the anchors seemed stunned by the display they were watching.

"The electoral count is only 171 in their favor and they are partying like they've won. I can't believe it. Have they ever heard of the big Democratic States of New York, Pennsylvania and California."

"Another volunteered: "maybe they know more than we do or maybe they're just happy to be ahead. I always thought the balloon drop came when the candidate reached 270. I guess you can learn something new every day as the saying goes."

• • •

As they left the stage Bernard Winslow invited Michael and Mary up to their suite with adjoining rooms where he and his wife, Beth, were hosting southern Governors, Senators and Congressmen and their wives from the thirteen southern states. The Winslows made tremendous efforts in the south travelling to each of the states at least twice and the last three days in the crucial state of North Carolina where he served eight years as governor. The party was in full sway when they arrived fueled by bourbon and the thought they could be headed for a big win rolling in 175 votes from the solid south. They knew their contribution would merit many important positions in the new administration. At 11:30 the Sullivans bid them good night and headed back to their suite to follow the returns. When they arrived John Kennedy greeted them with the news Tennessee, South Dakota, Oklahoma and Missouri had come home for the Republicans bringing his total to 205. In the war room Tom Donovan and Jocko O'Brian were pouring over numbers coming in from upstate New York and Pennsylvania.

"Tom I've been looking at some of these counties in New York and we are doing much better than John Madden in 2012. More importantly I don't think we'll get Pennsylvania but it's going to be close. I make that proposition based on returns from Bucks and Montgomery counties in Pennsylvania where the Democrats won in 2012 and we're winning now."

"What's the significance Jocko?"

"Just this: the votes we pick up in New York and Pennsylvania will add to the popular vote and if this trend follows in Hamilton's states we could win the popular vote as well as the electoral vote. The significance is if you win both it silences the doubters. Remember in 2000 Gore got the popular vote but lost the in the Electoral College. The Democrats yelled their heads off and made it look like they were robbed. Obama beat Madden 65 to 60 million. I think we're going to invert those numbers to the surprise of the pundits."

"Jocko, if you're right it means the voters have really turned against Obama. A vote for Hanna is really a vote for a continuance of the policies of his administration. It means even voters in the blue states have had it. What else have you detected?"

"The blacks are staying home. They have no interest in Hanna. We'll know more about the Hispanics when the western states report. The Asians voted for Obama. Not this time. We're getting a good portion of their vote and the white vote is up to 64%. To me, the vote in California is really going to be interesting to see how much of the Latino vote comes our way. Michael stressed family and values over and over in his contacts with the Hispanics. If that vote is high in California it will prove Michael was right in his choice of issues to campaign on."

"No point in bringing this up now Jocko but it's going to be interesting going over the vote when this is all over. What's your guess on the outcome?"

"It all depends on Iowa and Wisconsin. Both are going to be close from what we're getting in early returns. I'm sure the crowd downstairs thinks were in but I say watch for Iowa and Wisconsin which we've known from the start were crucial to our winning."

Tom Donovan working with Jocko, knew Kansas and Nebraska were going to vote Republican adding 11 votes to Michael's total. The clock in the war room read 12:30 a.m. and a new day was just breaking with the outcome uncertain. Donovan called the Senator and advised him Kansas and Nebraska were "in our column. The networks won't break that bit of news until one o'clock although they've been conceding both states for the last half hour in their commentaries."

Mary, having been up almost continually for the last twenty four hours kissed Michael and said she was going to bed. "Wake me if we win, let me sleep if we lose." Instead of thinning out the crowd in the suite was growing by the minute. Television Cameras and still photographers were packed in the hallway on the chance the next President was across the hall in the Michael's suite. Secret Service walled off every entrance to the suite and Kennedy's men were inside watching everyone. In the center of the room Michael sat surrounded now by Galvin, Kennedy, Connolly and Tom Donovan. All had cell phones connected to individual workers in Jocko's war room monitoring individual precincts in Wisconsin, Iowa and Colorado.

"It's now 1:00 a.m. November ninth and most people in the east are asleep except a few political holdouts who will not go to bed until a President is elected. Count us among those individuals. It is really getting quite exciting as we near the magic number of 270 delegates needed to win. What is the latest news Ashton?"

The TBC anchor answered: "Arkansas, Louisiana, Pennsylvania, New York and Illinois have all now been called by all networks and the count is 222 for Michael Sullivan and 167 for Hanna Hamilton."

"Can she win?"

"She can, but it will take wins in Iowa, Wisconsin, Colorado, New Mexico, and Washington, Oregon, California and Nevada on the west coast. Early returns from the coast show her winning all three on the western seaboard, although Oregon and Washington will be close. That's 74 votes. Add Colorado, Nevada, Iowa and Wisconsin for another 31 and 'presto chango' you have 272-----she wins."

"Ok. Charles Anderson I ask you what does Michael Sullivan need to win at this point?"

"By my semi-rough calculations he needs to get all the Rockies and Arizona and the plain states and then he only has to win Iowa, Colorado or Wisconsin. Right now I would say his best shot is Colorado where he is ahead. If he wins that, he wins. If he loses Colorado he can still win by gaining Wisconsin or Iowa, traditionally Democratic. On the other hand she has to win all three. This thing could go on until early this morning."

Both camps had already come to the same conclusion by midnight. By one o'clock the ballroom was half empty and people were standing drinking and trying to sleep on hard Chairs. Up in Michael's suite the feeling was tense but confident. The candidate was still sitting at the table with the others and was soon joined by Jocko O'Brian. "The networks are saying it's a tossup; our precinct reporters are telling us the opposite. Iowa will be razor thin; Wisconsin will be a 50,000 plurality. Even if we lose both those states our default is Colorado. In an hour we will know if we win Iowa or Wisconsin. If it's Wisconsin we will have 276 electoral votes; if Iowa 272 votes. From that moment on we refer to our friend Sullivan as Mister President." No one laughed, they were too tired; Michael shattered the somberness asking Jocko if he could now go to bed.

"Can you wait just one more hour Mister President?" With that the whole climate changed and they believed the end was in sight and they would win.

In New York Toby Wilson understood that if either Wisconsin or Iowa went Republican they could close up shop. Their one chance was to win both states and fight the last battle in Colorado. It would mean hitting the trifecta yet all three states had gone democratic in 2012 why not this time? Like their candidate Toby believed they could still win. Returns were streaming in now from all three states, Iowa, Wisconsin and Colorado. At 2:00 a.m. TBC, with Aston Smith in the anchor's chair, broke into a discussion by two political experts to announce: "AP is calling Sullivan the winner in Iowa with 75% of the vote he's leading 775,426 to 690,284, 52.9% to 47.1%. Also Thomas Andrews at CBC is calling Sullivan the winner in Wisconsin with 97% of the precincts reporting: 1,750,531 to 1,097,021.

Toby pulled out his cell phone, told Hanna it was over and suggested she call Michael Sullivan to concede. She wasn't happy but she knew a concession was expected and the sooner she made the call the better she would look in the eyes of the media and the voters. There was always tomorrow.

Jack whispered in his father's ear Hanna Hamilton was on the phone and then turned to the crowd in the suite and signaled for silence. Everyone stopped in mid-sentence sensing the call might be important. "Yes, Yes, and the same to you Hanna." He listened attentively for another 30 seconds and then said "Thanks for the call and the best to you and your family. Yes. Good bye."

Before they could ask he volunteered: "That was Hanna. Called to congratulate me and wish me good luck." The press was notified of the concession, asked few questions and rushed out to start their stories for the morning dailies and the television shows. Michael turned to Sharon and Kathryn who were sitting next to him on the couch and said: "Ladies, better get your mother up I think she should know she's just become the first lady of the land." He stood and shook hands with Jack and hugged Peter and ordered breakfast for everyone in the suite. "Tell the press folks to come on in for breakfast and we'll be doing a press conference at 9:00 this morning. Tom will you ask Bernie if he will join me at nine for the conference."

Mary came out in a beautiful pale blue robe looking like she had just stepped out of a beauty salon and he knew once again why he had married her. She's going to be a great first lady. She was the only woman besides her daughters in the room and he had to admit they made a fetching trio. Apparently most of the men in the room thought the same thing. Someone broke into a song "for he's a jolly good fellow, for he's a joy good fellow. A jolly good fellow is he." And they all lifted their glasses to the newly elected President. Simultaneously four secret service men moved in to separate the family from the others and Michael and Mary knew then life would not be the same.

CHAPTER 12

MARY SILVA, ANCHOR for CBC evening news, explained the election this way:

"At approximately 2:00 a.m. this morning Michael Sullivan captured Iowa and Wisconsin and with it the presidency of the United States. His margin in the Electoral College was 291 to 247 and he also won the popular vote by three million plus. It's safe to say the Obama era is over. Michael Sullivan is sure to lead the country in a different direction if we are to believe what he said over and over again in his campaign. Hanna Hamilton told the country times were good and they'd get better. Sullivan told the country things were stagnant and the country was being led in the wrong direction. The voters accepted Sullivan's view and rejected Hamilton's view. Moreover Hanna Hamilton had been indicted and pardoned. The Democrats thought she had been framed; the Republicans thought she should be put in jail. Somewhere in between lay the truth but the indictment and Obama's pardon had to hurt. So now we will see what the new leaders will do. There were other contests for the House, Senate and the state legislatures and again as in 2010, 2012 and 2014 the Republicans made gains in the House and Senate. The count stands at 55 to 45 in the Senate, a gain of one and 255 to 180 a gain of eight seats in the House. As they have in the past two elections they increased the number of legislatures they control and added two governorships. It has to be said they swept the boards again. The Democrats best bets were Hamilton at 69 and Peter Simpson her running mate 72. In with the new out with the old. Both Sullivan and Winslow are 61 so it could be said the voters went for youth, so to speak. From here it seems the Democrats have to start building back a stable of candidates as the Republicans did years ago. In the Senate they have 23 up for election in 2018 and they surely will lose some of those to give the Republicans a possible filibuster proof majority. No, things look bleak for the Democrats, but they will rise again and for now we in the media should watch and wait to see what President Sullivan will do for the country"

Michael's transition team moved quickly in November and December so that by January 1, 2017 they had Federal Judges, U.S. Attorneys, Ambassadors, Cabinet Secretaries and Assistant Secretaries ready to be submitted to the Senate for confirmation. With control of the Judiciary Committee and the floor of the Senate they could pass all nominations subject to a Democratic filibuster on each one. He felt he would be able to have priority bills submitted to congress by the end of January.

His first appointment came on November 15th when it was announced Tom Donovan, from his old law firm would be chief of staff. By December 1st the names of 26 men and women were announced to serve as assistant to the President. All lawyers recruited from top law firms. The media was stunned by the swiftness of the appointments and wrote dozens of pieces of how the Republicans must have known all along they were going to win, because no party could put in place a government so short a time after the election without starting a year before. Republicans were efficient the press reluctantly conceded. Not as laid back as the Democrats. As the months wore on the media would see just how efficient The Sullivan Administration could be as bill after bill moved through the House and Senate reversing Obama's policies.

He had been a Congressman, one of 435, a Senator, one of 100 and now President of the United States. Now he looked out from a lectern on the West Front of the Capitol facing forty thousand people who had come from all over the country to see and hear the forty fifth president of the United States. The red, white and blue flags of the Republic hung square in the center of the Capitol. Bleachers set up for the occasion held the Senators, Congressmen, Ambassadors, important people in the government and guests, two thousand in all. On television millions watched here and all over the world. A new beginning was about to get under way. What message would this leader have for a world waiting for some sign of hope?

"My fellow Americans. We live in a unique country. A great country! One split in two in 1861 but we recovered and preserved the Union. Called to save Europe in 1917, we responded at a cost of 116,516 deaths of our best men. We survived. A devastating depression brought us to our knees. We managed. When Europe and Asia were being overrun by the Axis powers, Nazi Germany and Imperial Japan, we destroyed them in Europe and Asia, but it cost us dearly. 405,399 lost in the defense of freedom. They fought to preserve our way of life here. One of our allies, the Soviet Union turned into a nation bent on conquering and enslaving the countries of Eastern Europe. We fought a war against Communist expansion in 1950 in Korea at a cost of 36,576 American lives. All in the name of freedom for the people the Communists sought to subjugate. In Viet Nam we fought to stop Communism again. In doing so we lost 58,209 men who made the supreme sacrifice for their fellow men. We lost our pride and it took time but we recovered. In 1990 we saved the Gulf States and Saudi Arabia from the dictator Saddam Hussein. Communism in Russia was defeated in 1990 and in 1991 the Soviet Union was broken up and 13 of its states declared themselves independent republics. In 2017 we are still at war in Afghanistan and Iraq. Through all these wars and economic setbacks we remained the world's leader. How did we reach and maintain world supremacy despite all these obstacles? We had no choice. After World War II Europe and Japan were destroyed. There was a vacuum in leadership. We didn't seek it. We took on the responsibility of rebuilding our former enemies and keeping world peace. We are the most generous nation in the world. We are still a great people but we have forfeited our leadership role the last eight years. For the first time since 1945 we have abandoned our responsibilities. The world's leaders no longer have respect for us. We don't keep our word. We abandon Allies. What has happened?

Others have stepped into the breech. Russia is no longer communist but a dictatorship reminiscent of Joseph Stalin and those of his breed. An Iran seeks to control the Middle East and install a fourteenth century Caliphate. Our government has sought to withdraw from the world and it has proved disastrous for us and our allies.

Our businesses have been strangled with onerous regulations. We have a health Care program based on politics not sound thinking. It is bankrupting the country.

I recite these problems, foreign and domestic, because it is essential you know what we are facing. That you know truth. I will not lie or obfuscate the facts. I will tell you where the country is at any given time. We are not where we want to be now. Yet, as a people, Americans have always risen to face and solve the problems no matter how great. Tell them the problem and they will put their shoulder to the wheel to remedy it.

We must build back and restore our house. The foundation must be a re-affirmation of the values that have made us great. Protection of the family, faith in God, fairness, ethics, goodwill to our neighbors, trustworthiness, respect for religion and respect for life from beginning to end. We have had these values but we've allowed ourselves to be weakened by pornography, devaluation of human beings, relativism, disparagement of marriage, intimidation of speech, sexual promiscuity and materialism. These are the values of those who seek to divide and confuse us. The values of those who hate America and seek power through government to promulgate their agenda which is to subjugate the individual to the whims of government. I believe the people want a country based on time worn values. Values they can pass on to their children and grandchildren. You have chosen me as your President. I will work every day as hard as I can to justify your trust. I will expect no less from those I choose to help me.

I have mentioned the troubles we face. To put us back on the path I will be doing the following: Terminating the hundreds of executive orders that have been used to circumvent Congress. Repeal regulations designed to strangle our free enterprise system.

The health program put in place three years ago has proved to be a disaster, a source of fraud and abuse. It will be abolished and replaced with a new program run by the private sector. Responsibility for education will be returned to the states where it properly belongs. Military preparedness has been jeopardized by cutting our army and navy to the bone. Our safety has been jeopardized. Our armed forces will be built back to levels that will make an enemy think twice before challenging us.

Our young people will be asked to give a year of their time to the community. This will be beneficial to them in learning teamwork and beneficial to the country as we see the results of their work. Many other changes will be made to numerous to elaborate on in this address.

My message to you today is we must start back on the road to restoring our country to its rightful place in the world. People must once again look to us for leadership. Must once again respect the word of the United States. We've done it before. We will do it again------starting now. We don't have a choice. If we want a better world for our children and grandchildren we must start building today. Throughout history values such as self sacrifice, generosity, patriotism and military strength have been the hallmarks of great nations. We must foster and strengthen those principles to be a great nation---a nation that leads the world as we have in the past. Through incentives, opportunity, risk taking, innovation and prayer we will once again be the torch that burns bright for freedom. We will once again be respected by all nations as a power for good and for peace. We will serve you the next four years by saying what we will do and doing what we say. With your help, faith and prayer we will again be a beacon for the world to follow. God bless each of you and God bless America."

The former President of the United States sat dumbfounded as he listened to Michael Sullivan tell the American people his administration had been an abject failure. As a result America had fallen from grace among nations. That values had been lost and must be restored. That definitive steps would be taken to make the nation great again. The tragedy was that everything the new President said was true. When it was over the former President sat in his seat frozen surrounded by a small group of his cronies telling him he was the greatest President the country had ever had---a legend in his own mind.

The stands emptied, the President went into lunch in the Capitol and afterward drove down Pennsylvania Avenue to the White House to review the parade in his honor. They stood four and five feet deep and he walked most of the way marching with the Secret Service. The watching throngs on the avenue and the millions watching on television cheered. There was cause for hope. America was on the way back. Isolationism had been rejected. A great nation does not shirk leadership.

• • •

It was 12 midnight the day of the inauguration; they had danced at three of the ten balls and made appearances at four more and finally they were alone in the White House for the first time. "What do you think of your new house, my darling?" The two of them, the President and the First Lady, sat in the living room of the White House on their first night. She was anxious to know if he felt like she did. Overwhelmed. They had been going since 6:30 in the morning, had met with the ex President and his wife, gone to the inauguration where she had witnessed his swearing in, watched him give his first speech as President, attended a luncheon In the capitol, met thousands of people, watched the parade in his honor and hosted a party for a couple of hundred close friends downstairs. She had fixed him a scotch and soda and one for herself.

"I've tried to take it all in, enjoy the moment, look at everything going on around me, and I must say I have found it overwhelming."

She laughed and said: "we've been married two long: I thought of the same word to describe how I feel."

"I think what's going to be hard to adjust to is people deferring to you, treating you differently. Oh, I realize they are simply honoring the office yet it's going to take some getting used to."

"Well I will be treating you the same Michael and I'm sure the children will also, so you can count on us to keep your feet on the ground."

"To answer your question the new house is bigger than I'm used to but its home for the next four years and we are certainly going to have all the help you would need to keep a house up."

She had asked John the butler to order some ham sandwiches and he arrived with a serving cart and placed food in front of them and bowed out. They were hungry and hadn't eaten since lunch at the Capitol and the minute he disappeared they devoured the sandwiches. The food hit them and they made their way to their new bedroom and fell asleep in each others arms.

At seven thirty the next morning he went down to his office, the oval office. Already at her desk, Maggie Johnson, his secretary since his law firm days at Sullivan & Connolly, advised that General Charles Wilson of the National Intelligence agency was waiting to give the morning briefing. This surprised him somewhat, thinking the Director himself would want to give the first briefing. No matter he thought, the Director will be replaced as soon as possible. He considered that intelligence under his predecessor had been totally inadequate and led to such debacles as the Benghazi affair where four lives were lost.

"Good morning general, can I offer you some coffee or tea?"

"Mr. President I could use a cup of coffee."

"Maggie, ask the steward for a couple of cups of coffee."

Michael motioned the officer to sit beside him on the couch and asked for his intelligence assessment. He began: "In Iraq ISIS is about 40 miles north of Bagdad and getting closer every day. We have 2,000 military personnel there and another 2,000 contractors and Embassy personnel."

"Are they safe for now?"

"For now, yes, but the non-military personnel will have to be evacuated, in my opinion, within a month if ISIS keeps coming." Michael nodded and said nothing. He knew better than this intelligence advisor how precarious the situation was in Iraq.

"In Afghanistan, we have lost control of the south and find ourselves encircled by the Taliban in Kabul. We have outposts with up to five hundred men scattered around the country but they are sitting ducks. In Syria the Russians are in charge with Bashar al Assad as their puppet. The Syrians hate the Russians but don't have the military ware with all to do anything about it.

In Libya the country in on the verge of falling to a mixture of rebels and ISIS who will then probably fight it out for top dog. The Russians are putting pressure on the Baltic States and making constant noises about the Russian speaking minorities in those countries needing protection.

China, with its economic problems, is covering up how bad it is by claiming America is the big threat and calling on nationalistic fervor warning of the growing American presence in the China Sea. Those are the major concerns today Mr. President. Can I answer any questions?"

"How did it get so bad general?"

"Neglect sir. Everything has been politics around here. Not how does it affect the country but how does it look politically."

"Are you speaking for yourself or for the community?"

"For myself and I suspect most of the community. They've watched this thing go down the drain and frankly sir they are hoping some changes will be made. I hope I'm not speaking out of turn."

"That's what my campaign was all about. There will be changes made in direction, policies, personnel and very soon. You can convey that to the community. Thank you for the briefing and you can advise the director I will be expecting you every morning I'm sure he has more important things to do."

General Charles Wilson left the office with the unmistakable impression the Director would not be in his position for long and that he or someone else would be serving as "Acting Director." Pretty smart guy, this President, he understands what a dolt the Director is. Maybe something is going to happen. Maybe the nightmare is over.

The President was sitting in the oval office having a cup of coffee while leafing through a sheaf of memos for his attention only when a buzz came from the outer office. He picked up the phone and heard Maggie say: "Mr. President, I have Justice Elizabeth Goldstein on the phone do you want to speak to her?"

"Absolutely Maggie, put her through." He picked up the ringing phone and said: "good afternoon Justice Goldstein, I'm at your service."

"You're very kind Mr. President, I know you must be very busy so I'll come right to the point. I would rather not discuss what I have in mind on the phone. Would it be possible to meet with you privately at a time and place convenient to you?" The Justice was over eighty years old and had served on the bench twenty years. In most cases she was a liberal vote when it came to the 5 to 4 decisions, but she was an outstanding jurist well grounded in the law. That was the sense Michael had and he respected her for it. He reached into his desk and pulled out a card containing the names of the Justices and their spouses. "I sense some urgency Justice so let me ask could you and Ben join Mary and I at the White House for a quite dinner this evening?" She was taken aback by his no nonsense response and his realization she had something important to tell him. "Why, yes Mr. President I think that is a very gracious invitation and I'll accept for Ben."

"Fine. I will have a car pick you and Ben up at the residence and we'll make sure you get into the house unobserved. We will await you with pleasure and by the way please call me Michael."

With a touch of humor in her voice she said; "Mr. President I will call you Michael and you may call me Elizabeth. We look forward to dining at the White House."

At seven sharp Justice and Mr. Ben Goldstein were ushered into the living quarters and were greeted warmly by Michael and Mary. Over cocktails (dry martinis for the Goldsteins, scotch for the Sullivans they discussed family, Washington rumors, and the recent election. At 7:30 dinner was served in the family dining room. Michael said grace as he did every night over the meal. The Goldsteins were not particularly religious but they admired the President for showing his faith. They felt no embarrassment at the prayer. They had taken a few mouthfuls of food when Michael decided to broach the purpose of the afternoon phone call. He looked her directly and asked: "What's on your mind Elizabeth?"

This was business so she put down her fork and looked at him wistfully and said she was going to retire from the Court. She and Ben had just so many years left and he needed her and it was time to let a younger person take up the heavy duties of a Justice of the Supreme Court. Once she got it out her face took on a glow that was not present when they arrived.

"I never thought you would do it until right now Elizabeth," Ben exclaimed. They embraced each other. The rest of the evening was spent telling stories about the Supreme Court, the Justices and their life together. It was decided she would announce her resignation followed by a letter to the President. As the evening came to a close the men shook hands, the women embraced and the happy couple left to begin a new life together and the knowledge they had two new friends in the White House.

Tom Donovan was in his office when the President walked in unannounced and sat down. It was 7:30 in the morning and he was just enjoying his first cup of coffee. "Got some news last night Tom, Justice Goldstein is going to retire." The chief of staff whistled and then said: "she waited to give you a shot. Doesn't speak to well for your predecessor; I think she's putting country before politics."

"Mary and I had dinner with she and her husband, Ben who seemed like a very nice fellow. She told us she would be making an announcement in a couple of days, noting she had informed me earlier. I'm giving you the task of working with Paul Connolly. He has five names already vetted. When you're ready let's get together and get that nomination up to the Senate as fast as possible."

"You know the Democrats are going scream no matter who we send up so a barrage of artillery fire will be needed before he or she goes to the Senate. The press will sniff the story out by this afternoon so I think it would be wise to have our nominee ready to announce by the end of the week. How does that sound?"

"It sounds fine to me; bring the names and I'll make the choice. Say we meet on the subject in three days." The chief of staff nodded and before he could answer the President was gone.

Tom Donovan, at Michael's request, had traveled with him throughout the last five months of the campaign and had proved invaluable at solving logistics, producing research on a moments notice, and making sure the candidate was always on time for an appearance. He had been an associate at Sullivan and Connolly when Michael was the senior partner. When he was elected to the Senate Tom and four others associates went with him and became an integral part of his senate office. After a few years had passed as a senate aide Paul Connolly offered him a partnership and the opportunity to open a Washington office for the firm. Just before Michael asked him to come on the campaign he had built the firm into a twenty five lawyer boutique specializing in litigation. It was his intention to return to the firm after the election and resume his role as the head of the office and leading litigator. Like Michael, he had a great love of the law and was a fierce competitor in the courtroom. Yet, when he was asked to be chief of staff to the President, he did not hesitate to sign on believing Michael Sullivan was the one man who could turn the country around. As much as he wanted to return to the firm, he felt if he could help as his chief of staff, he would willingly do so.

Five names were proposed to fill the Goldstein vacancy. The President spent two days interviewing the candidates and at the end decided to send the name of John J. Wilson to the Senate for confirmation. His criteria for a Justice of the Supreme Court: a person well acquainted with the law, an impeccable reputation as a lawyer and someone outside judicial ranks, who had extensive experience in the court room. "John Wilson meets all those criteria," he told Paul Connolly and Tom Donovan in explaining his choice "It's been a long while since a man with a litigation background has been on the bench. I think he will bring to the court an expertise they don't have presently among them. The firm he built has a national reputation. The Court is separated from the day to day practice of the law and they will do well to have a man of his talent and background a part of their proceedings."

"It's going to be a rough hoe; the Democrats will scream no judicial experience and a conservative to boot." Paul Connolly was very familiar with all the possibilities, and Wilson would not have been his choice, even though he himself was a litigator. He told Michael as much. On the other hand Tom Donovan thought the approach novel and Michael's argument it would bring new and different perspective to the court made sense. When the appointment was announced Paul's prediction became reality. The *New York Tribune* led the attack:

"The new President has an opportunity to make a real difference in the makeup of the Supreme Court but he chooses not to do so. Most appointees to the Court have come from a judicial background, which in our opinion, furnishes the best background to serve on the Court and more importantly gives the Senate a record of decisions from which they can test the judicial fitness of the candidate. In the case of Mr. Wilson, a good man, it's impossible to judge where he would come down on important cases. His whole life in the law has been spent as an advocate. He takes the side of the client who hires him. He could be an outstanding Jurist or he could be a complete failure out of his league with some of the intellects serving on the bench. There is no way of knowing. The Senate should not take a chance. We urge the President to withdraw the nomination." The rest of the liberal press followed suit while the conservative press praised the pick saying it would bring a dose of reality to the ivory tower.

Michael called the majority leader, Bailey Long and Minority leader Seymour Gottleib advising them of who he was nominating. The result was an affirmation from Bailey and a "wait and see" from Gottleib. Within weeks the minority decided to test their strength with the new President. They announced the possibility of a filibuster against the nominee. With 55 Republican votes and 5 or more Democrats needed to block a filibuster, Bailey Long decided that a positive vote would come from the Judiciary Committee, and at that point the Democrats would decide whether to filibuster or let the nomination come to a vote. If they chose the former He would move to change the rules of the Senate to require a majority vote to confirm the nomination. In such event the new Justice would be confirmed with a vote of 55 Republicans. The Republican leader filed a motion for cloture (cutting off debate) which if passed would allow a vote on the nomination. The motion failed when only 57 voted to shut off debate. As he had warned, Bailey long filed a motion to change the Senate rules to allow for a majority vote. It passed. The vote was taken and the new Justice was confirmed 55 to 45. Michael Sullivan had won the first contest of his presidency. Despite the fact the Democrats had used the identical tactic many times in the past the media condemned the move as unfair. They said it was unfair because a President Sullivan would not use his veto to defeat the vote like his predecessor would have done. To which the Republicans replied: "What's good for the goose is good for the gander."

• • •

Shortly after coming to the oval office, Michael asked Tom Donovan to set up a conference with the Secretary of Defense designee, Robert Butterfield, for the purpose of discussing Iraq and Afghanistan. On the appointed day he arrived well equipped to answer any questions the Commander-Chief might have. Knowing Michael's reputation for being prepared for any meeting, whether it be a trial, speech or campaign appearance he had a briefing book prepared for himself by his staff who would join him at the Department once approved by the Senate which he anticipated would be sometime in February. The first thing he was asked was not whether he had any opinions on the war in the two countries, but whether he would go to Bagdad and Kabul to confer with the military leaders, Generals Mark Barrett in Afghanistan and Bing Smith in Iraq and get their assessment of the situation on the ground and their opinion of who amongst the general staff was best suited to conduct the war against the Taliban in Afghanistan and ISIS in Syria and Iraq. He asked that he report back his findings in ten days.

One of his first acts as President was to request the Defense Department to detail Captain P.J. Johnson as his military aide and raise him to the rank of Major. Johnson had, over the years since he and Michael had been at firebase Apache outside Kandahar, consulted with him as Senator on the status at the Pentagon and the wars in Iraq and Afghanistan. The two, with others, barely survived an Al Qaeda attack that overran the base where the Senator was visiting.

"Sir, I am honored that you requested I serve as your military aide," Major Johnson said as he greeted the President with a formal salute.

"As always, good to see you P.J. I need some information if you have it. My question is this: we've had a series of generals in charge of operations in Afghanistan and Iraq. I believe they have had their hands tied behind their backs in fighting the enemy. The blame can be placed squarely on my predecessor and those who went along with his unwillingness to secure the two countries to prevent a terrorist takeover. First, what is your opinion of Generals Barrett and Smith?"

"They are first class Mr. President but they've been hamstrung by the politics. They can fight if given the opportunity. May I say sir there are a number of highly placed generals currently at top levels who have sympathized with the former president. At the Pentagon they are referred to as 'arm chair generals.' There are at least 10 generals and some full colonels who would be great if you were to decide to kill ISIS and leave sufficient troops in both countries to ensure no terrorist nationalization of either country."

"Major, you've answered the two questions I had in mind. I want your list of who, in your opinion and the opinion of others at the Pentagon, would be the best to take back Iraq and Afghanistan. For your information I've sent the unconfirmed Secretary of Defense to both countries to assess the situation and for his recommendation from the military men who should lead the fight if we decide to 'take back Iraq and Afghanistan' as you so aptly put it."

Major Johnson took a sheet of paper from his pocket and laid it on the desk; with a ball point pen he wrote the names of eight men, five generals and three full colonels and handed it to the President. Without a word, Michael took the paper and put it in his coat pocket. "Thank you Major I will have these people checked out." The aide knew the meeting was over so he stood up, saluted the President and exited the oval office.

Within ten days Secretary Butterfield delivered his findings to the President in a face to face meeting lasting no longer than thirty minutes. He reported that both generals described the situation as dire and if steps were to be taken to salvage victory from defeat it should be done in no less than the next six weeks. Sooner if possible. As to the generals, he found them to be capable of doing the job given sufficient resources.

Michael called in the head of the National Security Council, Myron Poston, the Secretary of State, Byron Titus, and Robert Butterfield. They met at 5:00 p.m. the evening of March 1 in the oval office. The three men sat on two couches opposite the President's desk while he sat on a chair facing them. The only refreshment offered was ice water, coffee or tea. His guests opted for ice water. The meeting started with the President asking: "What do you think of the idea of re-establishing our presence in Iraq and Afghanistan in such a way as to ensure no terrorist regime would ever be able to take over either country and in so doing effectively surrounding Iran on two sides to prevent their takeover of Saudi Arabia, the Gulf States and Jordan?"

For a split second there was no response. Myron Poston spoke first: "It's worth talking about but politically it would be unpopular. That's not to say it shouldn't be undertaken. Our predecessors relied on diplomacy." Byron Titus interrupted with some vehemence: "That's what got us in the fix in the first place, now it may too late to snatch victory from the jaws of defeat." Robert Butterfield repeated what he learned in Iraq and Afghanistan from the two generals. The conversation lasted an hour with the three advisors telling the President what they thought of the idea he had posed. Michael listened and did not speak except to ask a question for clarification. At the end he appointed the three present and added the head of the C.I.A. to form an ad hoc committee to put together position papers on the feasibility of acting on the idea he had brought up for discussion. He asked for a response in one week except for Defense which would be tasked with coming up with the military component that would be needed to accomplish the job.

After a delay of five days the President and his advisors met in the White House situation room on March 15, the ides of March. Poston, Titus, Butterfield, Robert Fenwick, head of the C.I.A., Bernard Winslow, the Vice President and General Peter Bartholomew chairman of the Joint Chiefs of Staff gathered around the conference table in the Roosevelt room with Michael sitting at the head. The President opened the meeting stating: "On the first of March I appointed an ad hoc committee to study the feasibility or re-engaging in Iraq and Afghanistan with a goal of preventing those two countries from falling into the hands of Al Qaeda and ISIS by establishing a permanent force in each country and the further goal of containing Iran which sits between the two. At the same time I asked Bob Butterfield and the Chiefs to come up with a workable plan should we go forward with this approach. Time is of the essence. General Bartholomew will you give us the situation as it exists today?"

The general took a map of Iraq and placed it on an easel. "The red is where ISIS is in control and is gaining ground every day. You will note Fallujah is only 57 kilometers from Bagdad. They could come at the city at any time. In the north the Kurds are holding their own. The south is not presently a target. ISIS controls the oil fields in the north and in northeastern Syria. The map tells you everything you need to know. ISIS wants to control Iraq and so do the Sunnis. Iran want's to control Iraq. If we knock out ISIS we will control Iraq. He put down the map and put up another in its place; a colored map of the Mideast. As you can see Iran is bookended by Afghanistan on the east and Iraq on the west. You control Afghanistan and Iraq and you've got the Iranians surrounded. It is doubtful they could expand into Pakistan or east to Turkey without meeting terrific resistance. I'm not talking about occupying these countries but maintaining a big enough force in each to provide security. How would you go about accomplishing what I've just put forth?" He asked rhetorically

"First, we now have a force in Afghanistan that would have to be beefed up. Maybe 20,000 troops for the sake of argument. While keeping the lid on there, we move into Iraq and start pushing slowly into Sunni country in the west and pushing north to join up with the Kurds. We would put some troops in the north to assist the Kurds and simultaneously secure the oil fields and refineries located there. That would be a complex operation that I need not go into at this time. In summary: oil fields taken and ISIS removed from places they now occupy denying them any territory in which to establish their caliphate. When that is accomplished you turn attention to Afghanistan and put enough troops in there to furnish security against any takeover by Al Qaeda or ISIS. Finally you go after the remnants all over the world and that would be the job of any and all countries that have terrorist cells within their boundaries. That's it Mr. President" He left the map on the easel where it could be clearly seen by all in the room.

For the next hour and a half they digested and discussed what they had just heard. They felt the weight of what they were about to do or not do. It would be costly, and it would cost American lives and they understood the American people were tired of wars, especially wars not won. The Democrats, having failed to solve the problem in eight years, managing only to let it deteriorate, would nevertheless charge the President was taking us back into war again. The question that confronted the men in the situation room was whether they would buckle in the face of an enemy sworn to destroy the west and the United States, as they so often proclaimed, or would they lead and crush the Islamic terrorists before they could spread their caliphate to the entire Mideast and beyond. They had started the meeting at 5:00 p.m. At 10:00 stewards served sandwiches, coffee and tea. By 1:00 a.m., March 16 they had reached consensus. The Secretary of State argued the thrust should be limited to Iraq. Butterfield, the Secretary of Defense, said it should be done as outlined by General Bartholomew. The intelligence people sided with Bartholomew. Vice President Winslow wondered whether either nation, both sovereign and independent, would go along or resist such a plan. Michael said very little during the eight hour session which was by design. He knew these men and trusted their advice. He had chosen all but the National Intelligence Director, a carryover from the previous admin-istration, who in the opinion of the capital's political pun-dits, would soon be replaced. They were unanimous on one point; something had to be done to stop the terrorists from conquering two sovereign nations and turning them into a fifteenth century caliphate.

Michael asked the Secretary of State to stay behind. When the room cleared he looked at Byron Titus in a seri-ous way and spoke in a soft yet commanding tone: "You may have the most difficult job in our effort to defeat ISIS and the Taliban. We need an understanding in writing by the Presidents of Iraq and Afghanistan that the United States will furnish security in both countries, meaning we will not allow Islamic extremists to take over either country to use as a base for their caliphate. That it will be our intent to destroy the terrorists wherever they are. That we maintain our pres-ence as long as necessary to insure that each country can establish and maintain a stable government. In return for providing security we will require that thirty percent of oil revenues be deducted to pay for these services."

Titus was chosen for the post because he was a tough, fair minded a lawyer by training with a demonstrated track record of achievement in foreign affairs under the previous Republican President. When he heard the President say the heads of the two Islamic states would have to be convinced to allow U.S. troops to remain on their soil for what could be an indeterminate term, and for it to be paid for out of oil revenues, it reminded him of going into a cage with two wild tigers without a gun. Unlike his predecessor, a weak, naïve confused Secretary of State, who stubbornly maintained "diplomacy" could be used to dispel the threat of ISIS, he understood the President was giving him a mission that had to be successful. There could be no compromise.

"If they balk, do I have permission to make them an offer they can't refuse and by that I mean telling them they have no option for example: 'We are here and we are staying. It will be in your best interest to have time to stabilize your government, read: you stay in office under the protection of the United States."

"You have my permission to do as you think best to accomplish the mission."

"Thanks Mr. President, I believe you said time is of the essence and the overall plan cannot begin until the mission is completed. I'll be taking three of the best lawyers at State with me to make sure all documents are signed and legal."

"God's speed Byron." They shook hands and the Secretary of State left the oval office with the knowledge the President's plan hinged on his success in laying the ground work for what would amount to a "status of forces" agreement that had been rejected by both countries earlier.

At the behest of the President the Speaker introduced a bill in congress to establish the United States Corps---requiring all 18 year olds to serve the country for one year in the civilian sector or the military. A vote was promised by April 1 in the House. Prior to the bill being submitted, Michael had invited congressional leaders to the White House to take soundings on what opposition the bill would face.

The Democrats told him they would let their people vote their conscience without requiring lockstep opposition. As for the leadership they would oppose because in their opinion no emergency existed that would warrant a selective service draft.

"Gentlemen you've been briefed, furnished copies of the bill and probably discussed it amongst yourselves. What's your thinking?" Michael asked.

Jason Winters, the Minority Leader in the house, spoke first. As he spoke Michael listened intently with the knowledge Winters replaced a fierce partisan in the person of Sheila Berkheimer who consistently opposed any and every Republican measure during her tenure as Speaker and Minority Leader. Winters was not as partisan though a leader in the left wing of his party.

"Mr. President," he offered. "I personally do not favor the coercion in this bill. I could support a voluntary participation but not a draft and that's what it is."

"Are you opposed to the idea," Michael countered, "of our youth giving some time to the country, and in so doing, learning to work together as a team, living in a community and graduating with new skills, a sense of accomplishment and a tax credit to be used for further education?"

"No sir I'm not and I'm sure most Democrats would not. It's the involuntary aspect we object to."

"Will your party oppose as a block?" the President asked.

"In the house I'm going to let people vote as they please."

"How about you Seymore, what will the Senate do?"

"I really don't know, Mr. President, it depends on the bill, of course, and we don't know our position until we caucus on it. I know one consideration will be the cost. How will it be financed?"

Without waiting for the President to answer the Minority Leader answered: "I know how part of it will be financed, agencies will be reduced in size. Savings from that alone will not pay for it. If you're talking about agencies like Education, HUD, Health and Human Services and the like you will get opposition from our party. We will not allow it." Suddenly the Minority Leader was warning the President, on a subject not totally relevant to the conversation, that any attempt to downsize government would be opposed by the Democrats. Sensing the conversation was getting a little too heated, Michael held up his hand indicating he understood their position and it need not result in a skirmish between the leaders. The House Minority Leader told a joke which immediately calmed the atmosphere. Unlike his predecessor who was mean and partisan, Winters was a partisan with a sense of humor who didn't think the world would come to an end if some Democrats voted in favor of a Republican proposal. In inviting the leaders to the oval office Michael meant to sound them out not reach consensus. He knew there would be resistance; he just didn't know how much and this conversation with the leaders gave him his answer. A week later the Speaker told the President the bill would be brought up for a vote on or about May 1 after hearings in the House.

When Byron Titus returned from his mission in Iraq and Afghanistan ten days after meeting with the President and his advisors he reported to the President alone and then with the men who had met in the situation room previously. The meeting took place in his office at State. At this meeting 15 of the top generals and admirals from the Pentagon, other defense officials and members of the NSC were present to ensure everyone was fully aware of the new rules of engagement and what they could expect under the new protocols for the U.S. in Iraq and Afghanistan. For the first time in 8 years the Pentagon experts would be listened to and their advice heeded. They felt free to speak and congratulated the Secretary on his making it possible for them to know where they stood with the Administration and what was expected of them in the two countries. He told them the resources available would be limited but they would not have their hands tied behind their backs and they could use the resources at hand to the fullest extent without worrying about some action they might take would be politically incorrect. In other words they had a President who would back their actions. Much discussion went on about how, when and where military action would start in eliminating ISIS in Iraq. The Secretary assured them that by early April the President will have met with the Chiefs, the intelligence community and Pentagon planners and a definitive plan would be in place. He told them he could not predict when the plan would be executed. Someone asked the Secretary how he managed to convince the Presidents of the two countries to sign an agreement to allow U.S. troops to come back into their countries with a large military presence after adamant refusals to President Obama. Titus got an extremely serious look on his face like he had just been asked to divulge a top national security secret. A sudden calm came over the room and all present expected to hear something so secret that they would be sworn by the Secretary not to even think about leaking it.

"I sat down with each of the Presidents individually and told them the story of Don Vito Corleone." A few smiled knowingly. "I asked them if they understood what kind of a man Don Corleone was. They both assured me they clearly understood. Then I told them Michael Sullivan was the Don Corleone of our country." He couldn't finish, uncontrollable laughter shook the room. Finally they stopped laughing, some clearing tears from their eyes.

"I know this guy. I'm sure Titus did tell them about the Don and worse, Michael Corleone---and knowing his ability to convince people, they believed him. Cooperate or lose your office, your pension and maybe more." The room erupted again. It was a good time to adjourn the meeting and he did so thanking them for taking the time and assuring them they would meet soon when the President's initiative was ready to proceed.

The President met with the Secretaries of Labor, Commerce, Education and Housing and Urban Development and instructed them to set in place a hiring freeze and offer buy outs to many of the senior staff and if that proved ineffective, assignments to places where they could do no harm and might think again about taking a buy-out. In the campaign he had promised to downsize each of these agencies and in the case of the Department of Education, reduce it by seventy five percent within two years. The tenor of the Department would be changed. History of the United States was to be taught in public elementary and high schools, all courses to be taught in English. The use of vouchers would be encouraged.

In New York Mikos Tabor watched with dismay and anger as President Sullivan was dismantling what he and his leftist colleagues had worked so hard to implant in the public school system of the United States. The system preached socialism and collectivism as good and individual initiative and capitalism as bad. That Americans were conquerors, war mongers, that heroes like George Washington and Jefferson were slave owners and thus not worthy of being honored. His immediate reaction was to fund American Teachers Organizations to start challenging the Administration and local school districts, which would be the recipients of block grants from the federal government, to keep curriculums that Mikos and his fellow travelers in the left wing of the Democratic Party had worked so hard to put in place. He saw it as a fight to the death to keep the youth of America marching toward socialism and big government and the defeat of individualism. He decided to fund two "think tanks"; one to propagandize the elementary school system and a second to do the same at the college level, encouraging professors to continue to teach socialist gospel and to lobby and furnish research to Democrat Congressmen and Senators to support his and their left wing ideology.

John Kennedy had hoped for a brief respite from politics and a return to his multitude of business interests but when he and the Sullivan team discovered that Mikos was willing to spend millions of dollars to defend the ideology of the left wing of his party as the prevailing creed in the schools, they decided to put together an organization that would checkmate, if not destroy, Mikos and as a counterweight promote Americanism at every level of the educational system. It had taken years for Mikos and his compatriots to poison the system with anti-Americanism. The President intended to reverse direction, driving out those who taught and inculcated hatred of America in their students.

Five thousand troops joined the five thousand already in Iraq at the end of May. Another five thousand were sent to Afghanistan. Their assignment---to form a protective perimeter around the capitals of both countries. Once in place more troops would be added with the objective of slowly taking back territory captured by ISIS. The offensive in both countries would involve local armed forces in the lead backed by US combat troops. In Iraq, special forces were in the process of securing oil fields in the north, constructing an airfield large enough for cargo planes to land troops and equipment from the 82nd Airborne with which to attack ISIS in the north. The plan, approved by the President, the National Security Council and the Pentagon, was designed to crush ISIS from the north, south and east with the Kurds joining local and U.S. forces. With the sky controlled by the Americans it was anticipated ISIS in Iraq would be annihilated in two to four months after which a consolidation of gains would be made and a contingent of 35,000 troops left in place. In Afghanistan 15,000 troops would be moved to secure the perimeter around Kabul, the capital, and remain in position until ISIS no longer held any territory in Iraq. Then the offensive would commence to destroy ISIS and the Taliban in Afghanistan. The Pentagon estimated both countries would be secure by the end of 2017 with 55,000 troops deployed between the two nations.

In 2010, after Obamacare was enacted by one vote in the Senate, the House of Representatives voted to repeal it by a vote of 245 to 189 but it was too late. The House realized the plan would kill jobs, delay services, sell Americans policies they didn't need as well as services and require higher premiums than under the private sector with deductibles that would leave the insured individual picking up most of his medical costs before his insurance would pay. They said the exchanges (set up to sell and administer Obamacare to the states) would fail despite a loan of $2.3 billion dollars to get them started. The Senate, controlled by the Democrats, failed to act. The critics said Obamacare would increase the states costs of providing Medicade to its citizens shoving 16,000,000 people into state run programs.

Legal scholars opined the plan subverted the power of Congress. The plan set up a governmental agency with appointed members acting in place of Congress, with the Judiciary and Congress without power to control it. In 2013 the Government Accounting Office stated Obamacare would increase the national debt by 6.2 trillion dollars. Obama promised in 2009 "I will not sign a bill that adds one dime to the national debt---either now or in the future." Many prophesied just as many would be uninsured after the plan went into effect as before it went into effect. All the calamities predicted came to fruition. Millions of Americans lost their health plans; those with plans saw their premiums sky rocket. Fewer young people signed up for the program, leaving insurance companies to cover older and sicker people; people were unable to keep their own doctor; those covered by their employers found longer waiting times to get into hospitals or see a doctor; employers had to cut back their employees to part time to avoid penalties set out in the plan. Many employers reduced their staffs to 50 people or under to avoid being thrown into the heavy regulated plan. By 2016 most of the Obamacare plans were failing with many going bankrupt, and insurance companies withdrawing to avoid deep financial loss.

When the plan was originally being pushed by the Obama administration critics pointed out 85% of the American people had heath care plans, leaving 15% uninsured. Obama and the Democrats postulated 45 million people were uninsured but experts disagreed stating the figure was a distortion by pointing out:

1. 14,000,000 of the 45,000,000 chose not to buy health insurance.
2. 10,000,000 were eligible for Medicade or SCHIP (State Children Health Insurance Program) but didn't take advantage of either program.
3. 11,000,000 could get employer insurance but chose not to.
4. Leaving 10,000,000 of the 45,000,000 actually uninsured.

The need for Obamacare was based on a lie: 45 million people in the U.S, were uninsured without recourse.

Immediately after Michael was sworn in as President the Speaker introduced two bills into the House. H.B.1, a repeal of Obamacare and H.B. 2, a substitute health insurance plan based on the free market. The bills easily passed the House with all Republicans and a handful of vulnerable Democrats voting for it. Senate Democrats tried to hold their caucus to vote against cloture but with 23 Democrats up for election in 2018 it wasn't overly difficult to find 5 defectors to allow a vote on the two House bills. In fact, the vote to cut off debate was 63-37. When he signed the two bills into law June 1, 2017 Michael told a press conference: "Obamacare was fraudulently presented to the Congress and the American people eight years ago by the Obama administration as to the number of people it would benefit, the cost and the services it would provide. Like all frauds, it was discovered to be a swindle of all American taxpayers. Because the country was hoodwinked by Obama and his Democratic co-conspirators, Obamacare predictably fell apart costing the taxpayers untold billions. It had to be replaced by a program fair to the patients, health providers, the insurers and the American tax payer. With the passage of these two bills into law, the nightmare known as "Obamacare" is over and hopefully we will never again have such a fraud perpetrated on the people of this country."

Michael's program to draft those between ages of 18 and 21 to serve in UScorps was introduced in the House in early May. By July it had passed both houses of Congress and been put on his desk for signature. The Democrats fought the bill with great vehemence claiming coercion just as their leaders said they would. Nevertheless on the crucial procedural vote in the Senate 8 Democrats voted with 55 Republicans to stop debate and vote on the main question. The bill passed 58 to 42. An administrative process was immediately put in place to register all 18 year olds. Tom Hardy, the first administrator, testified before Congress that under the law and the regulations in effect and to be written, each draftee would serve one year in the Corps at a minimal salary, and would be housed in military barracks around the country. They would live together and be transported to their work sites daily, whether it be a construction site, hospital, charitable institution, county or city projects. They could be drafted for the program between the ages of 18 to 21 but not thereafter. For those who chose the one year of military option they would be assigned to bases stateside to make it possible for regular military to serve overseas both in combat and support rolls. While serving the military option they would gain skills just as their counterparts on the civilian side would be doing. By the end of 2017 Hardy estimated over a hundred thousand youths would be in the Corps with another seventy five thousand in the military.

The President

The media, that had focused on winning the election for Hanna Hamilton and the causes she espoused, now turned their attention on what was happening unabated with the President's agenda. The main complaint seemed to be the Sullivan administration was moving too fast in disassembling what had taken the previous administration eight years to construct. The argument consisted of accusing Sullivan of trying to make America the world leader, a position they disagreed with. Bailey Wilson, writing for the flagship of the left wing press, the *New York Tribune* wrote:

"Obama promised to get us out of war and he succeeded. This new man Sullivan is hell bent on getting us back into it. He's talking about sending thousands of U.S. troops to Iraq and Afghanistan where we will be bogged down for years much as we were in Viet Nam. Is that what the American people voted for in 2016? Under a Democratic administration the nation's schools were prospering under an enlightened Education Department. Now he seeks to tear down that department and send most of its responsibilities back to the states. It took twenty years to build the department into what it is today yet by the end of the year and certainly by 2018 it will be unrecognizable if not completely obliterated."

Other media outlets held a different view similar to those elaborated upon in a story written by Richard Hargrove of the *Boston Sun*: "A recent article appearing in the *New York Tribune* by Bailey Wilson bemoans the fact the Sullivan administration is moving forward on promises it made the electorate in 2016, the chief of which was to make America great again. It appears Bailey and the *Tribune* feel the country was great under Obama. They have not read or refuse to read the election returns that confirmed the voters in the country thought things were going in the wrong direction.

Michael Sullivan and his party have embarked on what the voters wanted and what the country needs; a new direction, new ideas and leadership something sorely missing from Washington these last eight years. With its head in the sand the *Tribune* and Bailey, its spokesperson, have to come to grips with the fact they speak for a minority of left wing ideologues who have had their disastrous ideas rejected. Under President Sullivan the country is moving again and this time in the right direction---up."

Wednesday morning June 1, 2017 the President, Vice President, Secretary of State, Secretary of Defense, CIA director, National Security director, the Joint Chiefs of Staff and a number of aides were sequestered in the situation room in the **White House**, their attention focused on the large screen at the end of the room. They were listening with rapt attention to General Bing Smith in Bagdad detailing what was happening on the ground. The time: 6: a.m. Iraq time; 2:00 p.m. Washington time. "Fifteen minutes ago 25 predator drones equipped with hell fire missiles sought preordained targets in Falluja. There are 3,000 Iraqi and U.S. troops surrounding the city. Our aircraft are attacking the city taking out utilities and ISIS headquarters. Special operations units have entered the city on the south and have advanced an eighth of a mile and are now incurring resistance. Iraqi troops with U.S. advisors are now pouring in from the south. The same thing is taking place in Ramadi. By the end of the day we will know how hard these Islamists thugs are willing to fight. They can be pretty tough when their opponents are unarmed civilians; I'll be interested to see if they're willing to lose a lot of people holding on to the ruins of Ramadi. In the north paratroopers from the 82nd airborne have landed outside Kirkuk with the goal of securing oil fields in Jambur, Bai Hassan, Kor Mor, Palkhanah and Al Qayyarah. They are fighting alongside the Kurdish Peshmerga. As you know the Peshmerga have been starved for equipment and arms and have been fighting ISIS with rifles and hand grenades when they need mortars, trucks and artillery. That equipment is now pouring in. We hope to squeeze ISIS from the north and the south."

The Vice President: "General Smith, assuming you take both towns how will they be held after you move north?"

"Each of the towns will be secured by 2,000 Iraq troops and police with our men in command. That situation will be maintained until ISIS has been driven from the country. When that is accomplished we will set up garrisons in all parts of the country in cooperation with the government. That, of course, is something to be settled by higher authority. Our job is to wipe the Jihadists off the map and that we will do."

Michael spoke: "Bing it's good to see and hear you. It sounds so far so good. I want to hear the bad news as well as the good. We will watch for your reports once or twice a day as you deem necessary. I will be speaking to the American people this evening telling them exactly what is happening on the ground. If anything develops between now and then let me know."

The screen went dark. Michael swiveled around in his chair and faced those in the room. "Gentlemen to bring you up to speed I had breakfast with the Congressional leaders here in the White House at six this morning and advised them an offensive was underway and it was generally agreed I had the power under existing law to proceed. They seemed willing to watch and see how things go. I told them the troops would be on their way to Iraq and everyone understood the goal was to fight the war against ISIS in Iraq not here. There was total agreement it could not be done by air power alone. I said I would keep the four leaders informed on a daily basis no matter how the war was going."

General Peter Bartholomew, head of the Joint Chiefs of Staff spoke up, saying: "15,000 troops will be on their way to Iraq within a week." The meeting broke up on an optimistic note in that they believed the U.S. was beginning to throw some punches rather than taking them as had been the case under the previous administration.

That night Michael Sullivan addressed the nation from the Oval office, his first since becoming President. "My fellow Americans," he began. "This morning at six a.m. Iraq time we sent troops into Ramadi and <u>Fallujah two</u> ISIS strongholds. Simultaneously the 82nd Airborne is moving to secure the oil fields in the north preventing ISIS from selling oil to finance their Jihad. Those troops will move south when the fields are secure. The offensive will not end until ISIS is destroyed. We will continue to pound their positions from the air in Syria. As you are well aware we have suffered numerous attacks in our homeland from these killers. We will continue to run them down in this country; more importantly we will eradicate them on their own soil. This will not be done in a day but it will be done. My chief duty is to defend the country and I assure you that will be my priority until these Islamic fanatics no longer exist and their dreams of a world caliphate are snuffed out like a burning wick on a candle." The address lasted only fifteen minutes and that was by design. What Michael had no way of knowing was that sixty million people were watching and listening to his every word. In bars, pool halls, department stores and in their homes they listened. What were they listening and watching for? The truth. Not some fancy words meant to confuse, to divide and leave the listener as uninformed after the speech as before. What they saw was a sixty two year old man in a dark blue suit and royal blue tie, who looked fifty years old and looked them in the eye with confidence, not arrogance, and who told them exactly what he knew and no more. He gave facts not spin. He looked in charge and he looked like their idea of a commander-in-chief. He would not let them down. He looked and sounded trustworthy. After he spoke they talked to each other in the bars and their homes and said: "finally someone is in charge. Someone is looking out for us. We can sleep tonight because the President understands what has to be done to protect us and our families, children and grandchildren. He gets it." Unfortunately, the viewers got it, but the editors of the *New York Tribune* failed to hear what the man in the street heard. In an editorial the next day they offered their readers a different view of the President's address.

"Hanna Hamilton was right when she warned Michael Sullivan wanted to take us back to war. He says he's going to win an unwinnable war. She called him a war monger. It turns out she was right. She favored diplomacy over guns, talk over missiles. Sullivan's predecessor just got us out of the Middle East with minimal loss of American lives. Now the President has plunged the country back into the mire of Iraq and sooner than later, Afghanistan. We condemn his war policy and hope the Democrats will not cave into the impulse to back him."

After the speech, the President met briefly with his aides and then left the office to join Mary in the living quarters. She had arranged for a late supper of steak, Caesar salad and a glass of wine. He came into the living room and sat down on one of the couches that faced each other. Mary joined him and the butler, John Wiggins, who had worked at the White House for twenty years, brought two scotches on a silver tray, put two napkins down with the

House emblem on them and retired. Michael said: "thank you John," as did Mary. In the six months they had lived in the White House they were scrupulous in treating the staff with respect due professionals. To them the staff had a job to do. And they did too. As far as the Sullivans were concerned they were all in it together serving the country. When a new President comes to the White House the staff is wary as to what to expect. Some Presidents are abrupt and treat the staff as servants. Some of the wives consider the help beneath them and treat them accordingly. Others understood what a difficult job they have and treated them with respect. Michael and Mary were of the latter group. Within the first three weeks they knew almost everyone by their first name and addressed them in that fashion. Deciding it would be a wonderful four years to work for and with the Sullivans, everyone gave a little extra knowing their work was appreciated by the new President and first lady. Below the stairs they were referred to as the "Gentleman" and the "Lady."

They sipped their drinks and after a pause Mary said: "Michael the speech was wonderful, short, factual and to the point. Who wrote it?"

With a mischievous grin he said: "I did."

"Well aren't you the Abraham Lincoln of your time. It was a little longer than the Gettysburg address and not quite as somber but I think it told the people what they had to hear and I think wanted to hear. Somebody is home at the White House."

He loved it when she joked like that. He felt pretty good after his first speech from the Oval office, even a little puffed up and Mary always brought him back down to earth. They chatted about what the media would say and both agreed the conservatives would feel pleased and the left wing disgruntled and life would go on and Michael Sullivan would continue to do what he thought was best for the country.

Then he got serious and asked her: "Mary we've had so little time to talk these last few months tell what's been going on with your campaign to bring all the wives of the congress to lunch at the White House?" In the first months of the presidency Mary decided it would be a good idea to invite the wives of the Senators and the women in Senate to lunch. To make it as intimate as possible she invited ten at a time and the setting was in the living quarters, which many had never seen and would not otherwise have an opportunity to see. Both Democrats and Republicans were invited and the first luncheon drew rave reviews. Politics was mainly ruled out as a topic of conversation and she told her guests she thought it would be a good idea for the ladies to get together, talk about their families and get to know each other better. Strictly social, no hidden agendas. "When I told them you suggested no politics, everyone seemed to relax and we were no longer Democrats and Republicans---just a bunch of women having a great lunch together. While you've been working day and night, I've had seven more luncheons and I'm up to 70 Senators and wives of Senators. I don't know whether it will soften any hearts in the Senate but I do know we all have had a grand time."

"The women run the show Mary, I concede that most of my friends in the Senate would say the same. It certainly won't do any harm and I have the feeling reaching out like that is just what is needed now. I applaud your efforts and hope you're not killing yourself in the process."

"Speaking of killing one's self I'm worried about you my darling. You've been in that office of yours every morning at seven thirty and back up here at seven and eight o'clock. Nobody can keep that pace up and not pay the price. I want you to think about coming home at six every night barring some unforeseen event. Will you do that for me?"

"You're right Mary but there is so much to do and so little time to do it. We're doing well now on our agenda but the opposition will get tougher and tougher and before you know it the election cycle will start up again and partisanship comes to the forefront and legislation grinds to a halt. Right now we've made a start in Iraq and I feel good about that and the new health plan is underway, and successfully. Tom Hardy is working almost twenty four hours a day getting UScorps on its feet and in time I think we're going to get some very positive feedback from the kids who will be in the program. Much more must be accomplished by the end of this first year. You're right though, we've been up to Camp David twice in seven months. What say we go down to Kiawah for a few days. I'll give Matt Doud a call and see if the house is available. Will you check with the Secret Service to see if they can put together a plan?"

"Michael that's a wonderful idea. I can hardly wait. Maybe the kids can join us for a couple of days. It would be a welcome break for both of us and a chance to see the grandchildren.

CHAPTER 13

UNDER THE PREVIOUS administration energy was a major pre-occupation. The President and his administration preferred to put their emphasis on solar, wind and geothermal energy sources at a time when the nation's regular energy sources were oil, natural gas and coal. Even after trying to regulate the coal industry out of business it remained the largest electricity generator in the country. The EPA, the government's energy regulator, used regulations to prevent construction of new coal plants. The agency saw coal fired plants as "dangerous sources" of carbon emissions. As a result hundreds of coal plants had gone out of business and more said they would have to quit the field because they could not meet the new standards demanded by the EPA. In 2009 eighty billion dollars was set aside for Obama's preferred energy sources while coal and oil were being squeezed. Billions of dollars have been lost since then by alternative energy companies going bankrupt leaving the American taxpayer to pick up the tab. For seven years the administration investigated, delayed, postponed and did everything short of denial of a permit for the Keystone oil pipe line that would bring oil to Texas from Canada. Finally in utter frustration the Trans Canadian gave up. Advocates said it would produce 42,000 jobs to build the line and some permanent jobs to maintain. Approximately 800,000 barrels a day would come through the pipe from Alberta, Canada to Texas. Most importantly the line would be privately financed. As part of the transition planning the incoming administration as, Michael

Sullivan had promised, determined to allow the exportation of oil from the United States, Allow the Keystone pipeline to be built and to repeal EPA regulations that were killing the coal industry. When the new EPA Director, Peter Bashor, went before House and Senate committees in mid April he set out clearly the new administration's agenda for energy: pursuit of alternate sources but continued support for oil, gas, coal and research on the possibility of nuclear power. This agenda set off a firestorm in the leftist press and with the environmentalists. Editorials, letters to the editor, petitions and threats came Mr. Bashor's way. He appeared on "Meet the Press" and all the Sunday morning news shows, explaining the rationale behind the agenda. Some of the more aggressive interviewers intimated he and the President were trying to sabotage the environment and tear down all that had been accomplished. He batted these criticisms aside citing facts and figures the American public was probably not aware of thanks to the heavy public relations barrage laid down by the environmentalists during the previous eight years of the Obama administration. Anyone watching these shows would have to admit, the new Director was very intelligent, armed with irrefutable facts and capable of parrying any hostile questions thrown at him. All in all not a good day for the Sunday talk show hosts.

Michael and Mary watched the first show and when Peter Bashor did so well, they watched the other four shows to watch the encores which were even better. He called him later in the afternoon and congratulated him on his appearances "Peter I was impressed. You had the facts; you were better prepared than your adversaries. Must be that Yale law school education."

"Thank you Mister President. I was a little apprehensive going into the lion's den but as it turned out I had facts they didn't have and after the first program it was like shooting fish in a barrel. I don't expect to be asked back anytime soon which is all right with me."

"I think you may be mistaken about that Peter those fellows don't like to be beaten; they're used to doing the beating. They'll brush up on a few facts, do some opposition research and then invite you back thinking they will take care of the wise guy. In my judgement they will be making a mistake but let them find that out for themselves. Again, good job."

Having laid out the plan Peter Bashor went about implementing it. One of his the first acts was to get legislation passed that allowed oil companies to export oil overseas, immediately creating jobs. Planning went ahead on the Keystone pipeline, and almost immediately jobs became available to work on the project. Coal plants in the states stopped going bankrupt and some were laying plans to build more coal fired plants. More permits were being issued for drilling on federal lands. Research was undertaken to determine the feasibility of nuclear power plants.

All these energy measures were passed easily in the House and while the Democratic leadership resisted most of the administrations energy initiatives, with 23 Democrats running for re-election in 2018 and at least seven of those vulnerable for defeat, the Senate Majority Leader, Bailey Long was able to get favorable floor votes on energy related legislation

In early September Michael, the Vice President and others in the intelligence community were in the situation room talking to the head of the Joint Chiefs when the red phone at his elbow rang. He answered and a look came over his face, actually a grimace, like he'd been hit in the solar plexus. He listened for thirty seconds and then placed the phone back in its place. Everyone in the room knew instinctively something was very wrong, not with the President, but with he had just heard. He turned to Tom Donovan and asked him to turn on the television. What they saw and heard created many emotions around the room the most dominant one being anger. A correspondent at the scene in a shopping center in upstate Ohio was describing a shooting that had just taken place.

"As far as we know at least four armed gunman came into the Blakely Shopping center shooting as they came. One was killed by an off duty police officer. At least five people were killed. Three are loose in the center and now we're hearing that they have taken as many as fifty hostages in one of stores in the mall."

In the situation room they heard a tremendous blast coming from the television and the screen gyrated and went out of focus. Seconds later the reporter was back on the screen: "a tremendous blast just occurred about a hundred yards from where I'm standing, people are running everywhere, police are on the scene and swat teams are running by me as I speak. Now I'm hearing that hostages are being shot in the store where they were taken."

Michael turned to Tom and told him to get Brady Wilson, head of the FBI, on the phone. When he got through to the Director he asked for what he knew. He was told up to ten gunman, hooded, with automatic weapons stormed a shopping center in the town of Blakeport, Ohio, population sixty thousand at 3:00 p.m. just a short time ago. They killed the first four people they saw and shot ten more on their way to a building that had probably been staked out in advance. They rounded up at least 40 more and herded them into the store. We believe there were another twenty to twenty five more customers and employees already in there. I'm on a direct line to my men at the scene. They've just heard shooting coming from inside the building so our men and the police are going to break in and try to avoid what happened in Paris in 2015. I'm getting off now and will call you in about ten minutes or sooner when I know more."

They all turned to him when he got off the phone with the Director. No one said anything and he gave a brief synopsis of what he had just heard. His information was at least ten minutes ahead of what the networks were broadcasting. They watched the television. Michael glanced at his watch. Five minutes had passed since he had talked with Brady. He decided to wait five minutes more knowing the Director had his hands full dealing with his men in Blakeport. At seven minutes the phone rang and Brady Wilson told the President the swat teams had busted into the building in three places, and encountered heavy machine gun fire. Two of the Swat team had been killed two badly shot up and eight terrorists were dead and ten hostages had been killed and 25 others wounded by the time the police could get to where they were being held. One of the terrorist had been captured, badly wounded but expected to live. Do you have any instructions sir?"

"No Brady. Secure the situation and then I'd like you to get on a plane and get up there and meet with the press and tell them everything you can without jeopardizing your investigation. I'm going to call this an ISIS attack until you tell me otherwise. If, in fact it is, then the people should be told." He turned to Tom and told him he wanted a national security meeting in the situation room in one hour. He left the room and went directly to the oval office and made a calls to Paul Connolly, the Attorney General, and the Congressional leaders. At 5:30 p.m. he was back in the situation room, with Secretaries of State and Defense present, head of the Joint Chiefs, NSA, CIA and the Deputy FBI director. No longer listening to the television reports he asked each to tell what they had found out since the shooting at 3:00 p.m. The first to speak was the Deputy FBI director: "Witnesses say these men wore fatigues and face masks and were in full battle gear. Many witnesses lived because they fell to the ground acting like they were shot or thought they were shot. They say the men ran by them shooting anyone in their way. Another witness said as they came to the building they eventually entered they stopped and ordered everyone in the area to go into the store with their hands up. Minutes later they heard shots coming from the building and that's when the police crashed in. Brady says everything about the scene speaks of an ISIS terrorist attack." Everyone one in the room was serious and anxious to offer the President their best advice. Some theorized that these men could have come in with refugees on fake passports and hidden out for a time until they were ready to make their move. They all agreed the attack was planned and not some impromptu act after a few prayers at the local mosque. The Secretary of State volunteered that thought should be given to stopping all immigration for at least six months until proper screening systems could be achieved and then continued on a limited basis until ISIS was no longer a threat to the homeland. Paul Connolly said he believed these attacks had reached a point where it was no longer feasible to try the terrorists in federal courts and military trials should take place at Guantanamo Bay, Cuba. That suggestion, after some debate, was endorsed and the President said he would follow the Attorney General's suggestion. The director of Homeland Security reported the southern border was being strengthened yet illegals were still pouring in. The difference being that when caught they were being returned across the border to Mexico. The meeting ended and the President with heavy heart ascended to the living quarters.

"Michael, it is so sad, what are we going to do?" He took her in his arms and just held her for a minute and then said:

"We will continue to do what we are doing only with greater speed and efficiency. The other thing we can do is pray for the victims. Tonight I will put out a short statement offering condolences to the survivors and their kin. Tomorrow morning a press conference to assure the nation we will do everything within our power to secure their safety and outline measures that are being taken to that end. I assume the first funerals will be within a couple of days and I want to attend the first one to meet with the families of those killed. Will you come with me?"

"Of course I will; I think it's the only way we can try to heal the wound and I feel the people would want us to be there to represent the nation."

A couple of days later, after it had been confirmed the attackers were Muslims from Yemen, Pakistan, Saudi Arabia and Syria, ISIS claimed responsibility. Michael and Mary flew to Cleveland and took a Marine helicopter to Blakeport, Ohio to attend a funeral mass for John Wilson, one of the first four killed when the terrorists entered the mall. He was survived by his twenty five year old wife and two small children. St. Mary Madeleine held 400 but on that day 500 were in the church and a thousand outside. The sky was black with rain clouds and a slight drizzle had begun just before the President and Mrs. Sullivan arrived at the church. The hearse stopped in front and the coffin was placed on a cart with wheels. Two men from a local funeral parlor, one in front and one in the rear, wheeled it slowly up the center isle of the church, followed by the family, and behind the family, the President and First Lady of the

United State. When the coffin was resting before the altar and the President seated to the left in the front row and the family on the right, the mass began. At the homily the Priest spoke briefly of how they had all come to be there and then dealt with the question: how could this happen in the town of Blakeport? What did the people do to deserve to be killed in the way they had been gunned down? He confessed he did not have the answer. He reminded his listeners innocents had been killed in greater numbers in Paris and there was no answer for that either. "What we do know is evil stalks the world. These killers were the face of evil. We believe God allows these things to happen. He does not will or commit these acts, mankind does. Mankind has a free will that can be used for good or evil. The scriptures tell us to be prepared for we do not know the day or hour when death will come. We have seen that happen here in Blakeport. It will change us, all of us. It reminds us life is short, almost like the speed of light, compared to eternity. We believe those who were sacrificed last week have gone to a better place with their maker. For that we can be assured. They will be an example to all of us to be the best we can to each other and to our families. They have not died in vain. Their deaths will cause the country to be more alert, and the government to work even harder to stamp out the evil ISIS represents wherever it is found."

Afterward in the church parlors, Mary and Michael met with and offered sympathy to those who were now left to live out the grief that was now a part of them and their city. To each he promised the government would do as the pastor had suggested to them. Stamp out the evil Islamic terrorists.

The network anchors covering the funeral commented favorably on the President's attendance and gave him credit for showing leadership at a time of national mourning, nevertheless, they hastened to remind their viewers of the rumor steps would be taken to limit immigration as a result of the shootings in Blakeport. This they claimed would be a perversion of what America stands for as a nation of Immigrants. The talk was an attempt to preempt the President's call for a moratorium on immigration. Their warnings fell mostly on deaf ears, because after Blakeport, the American people favored such a step by two to one. Legislation was introduced in the House two weeks after Blakeport to cease all immigration for six months in an effort to examine where the breakdown was and to readjust to a favorable balance that would satisfy the need for security and still allow people with proven backgrounds to enter the country. The left exploded. The sponsors of the bill pointed to precedent set in the Act of 1924 when Congress reduced Immigration for a period until new quota could be ascertained and established. Again, Democrats facing re-election read the tea leaves and the polls and voted with the Republicans to put in place a moratorium on immigration.

Mikos Tabor and his leftist cohorts in and out of the Democratic Party launched a twenty million dollar publicity campaign to condemn Congress and its willingness to follow the lead of the reactionary President Michael Sullivan. Aided and abetted by his fellow travelers in the media he was able to throw down a barrage at the Republican led Senate with another twenty million of free advertising.

Not to be outdone John Kennedy countered with a campaign featuring pictures of Islamists who had penetrated our borders and were responsible for killing Americans. An expenditure of 50 million dollars nullified any impact Mikos's efforts might have gained.

Writing for the *Cleveland Gazette*, Bardi Tallifano stated the case for the Administration: "Wisely the Administration and the Congressional majority have called a halt to immigration which is completely out of hand thanks to the Obama administration. Perhaps it was a quest for new votes or altruistic thinking but whatever the motive it has resulted in a disaster. More reasoned heads are now in the leadership of the country and the steps they've taken to quell unlimited immigration across our borders is to be applauded. Note should be taken of, in my opinion, a failed and misguided attempt by the Socialist Mikos Tabor to throw back any attempt to restrict immigration. Republican PACs matched his effort dollar for dollar and in the end his putsch was nullified. The next step is to strengthen the southern border which this President has proceeded to do since his inauguration nine months ago. His first act was to send National Guard troops to the border. Then he redoubled efforts to build a wall that would be highly sophisticated and detect anyone trying to come across. Fifteen thousand new border patrol jobs have opened up with first priority going to veterans of the wars in Iraq and Afghanistan. These men are well trained and will be able to become effective immediately. When the hole in the dike has been plugged and the moratorium on immigration itself is in place the Congress will decide what to do with those illegally in the country. All these steps make us safer and President Sullivan should be applauded for his leadership. Those on the left who accuse him of distorting the country's immigration policy, should be dismissed as false prophets who can only harm the country not help it."

In October the President asked Bing Smith to testify before both houses of Congress on the situation in Iraq. Appearing at separate hearings he told the legislators: "we are winning against ISIS in Iraq." In his House testimony, he spoke of progress and expected outcome.

"We have removed Ramadi and Falluja from ISIS control. A majority of the door to door fighting was done by Iraq Army battalions bolstered by our special force troops. Once the battle was joined Sunni insurgents who fought with us in the surge of 2007 joined the fight. They were invaluable in picking out targets and identifying enemy hiding places. Drones and air power played an important part but the job cannot be accomplished without ground troops. The enemy fought well but at a high cost. We believe they lost over 3,500 men and left only the dead behind. Our losses were 75 Americans, and 450 Iraqis. They were no match for the weapons we were able to bring to bear against them. We surrounded Falluja and like Ramadi the fighting was--- house to house. Again, the Iraq army was the main fighting force. Our special forces were joined by regular infantry and armoured forces. The key is taking out their leaders which we have been able to do with precision drone strikes with hellfire missiles. More Sunnis have come over to our side and by November we will have control of Al Qaim, and Abu Graib. In the north, the 82nd airborne has taken over Samarra assisted by English, German and French troops along with the Kurd Peshmerga fighters. In these battles the enemy has lost another 8,000 and they are not the fighters we faced in Ramadi and Falluja. Not as well trained. Iraq troops have taken control of all the cities that have been recaptured and are being assisted by our troops. Overall, the Iraq Army has sustained losses of over 5,000, while we have lost 650 of our own and another 900 wounded. The next objective will be Tikrit, which has been recaptured by ISIS forces. The enemy has been hurt badly, both in manpower and loss of equipment. Mosul will be the toughest to retake, a city of over 600,000. When that is taken we will have driven ISIS from Iraq.

As for the oil fields in the North, we have secured most of those and oil is being pumped daily; all the revenue is being used by the Iraq government to pay for security and rebuilding areas that have been retaken. We now have special forces operating in Syria directing air strikes against ISIS targets including training camps, supply depots, and vehicles on the ground."

To the question of whether Iranian troops are in Iraq, General Smith answered: "there were some but since our surge to re-establish control of the country they have slowly faded to the south and understand we will be in Iraq for the foreseeable future and that leaves no room for them. I believe when we abandoned Iraq in 2009 the Iranians decided to move in and help the government fight ISIS. Now that we are there and in some force they will stay clear. Assuming we are successful in breaking up ISIS's main force in Iraq and Syria the job will not end there. They will break into smaller guerrilla forces but will be without territory to govern and different tactics will be used to hunt down and kill these isolated forces. As they are defeated and hunted down over time they will attract fewer and fewer recruits. It will take time and patience; it must be done.

CHAPTER 14

THE FAMILY WAS eagerly awaiting Christmas at the White house. Jack, Megan, and their four boys were scheduled to arrive in town on December 23. Peter, studying at the North American College in Rome, and Kathryn living and working in New York were scheduled to land that evening, Peter at Dulles, and Kathryn at Reagan National. Sharon was living in the city which only required a cab ride. It all came together at 10:00 p.m. when Michael took roll and all answered "here" except the baby, John, sixteen months old. At 10:30 the little ones were put to sleep in the living quarters and Michael brought out two bottles of Domaine des Escaravailles Cotes du Rhone Les Antimagnes pronouncing the vintage in broken French. "Are you trying to impress us just because you are the President of the United States," Jack laughed trying to get a rise out of his father. They all laughed, Mary the hardest, knowing Michael had prepared plates of cheeses and crackers of all types and was intending on serving the family a little late night dessert.

"Listen Jack, my boy, the wine may sound fancy but I bought it myself for twenty dollars a bottle and I believe you will find it to your taste. Ask your mother, with the help of the chef I put together the rest of the feast you see before you." He opened a bottle and poured all around, putting the empty bottle on the table beside him and said: "that's one dead soldier. Turning to Peter he asked: "what say you Peter of Rome and the Vatican?

"Things are well but before I forget the Director gave me this to give to you dad. He said it was a letter from the Pope to you." A silence fell over the room. They were all surprised when he opened it up and read it aloud.

"My Dear Mr. President:

Greetings from the Vatican to you and your family on this 2017 Anniversary of the birth of our Savior. I have taken the liberty of having it delivered to you by your son Peter. We are delighted with your advancement to the Presidency of the United States. We will be keeping you and your family in our prayers at the Midnight Mass, Christmas Eve. I ask you do the same for us. We need your prayers.
Francis P.P. I"

"What a beautiful gift to us," Kathryn exclaimed. Mary was next to express her thought: "What a wonderful man to take the time to write us. I loved him when your father and I met him in Rome a couple of years ago. I love him more now. Each expressed a thought of their own then Michael said: "He asked us to pray for him; let's do it now." They bowed their heads and Michael led them in a Hail Mary, Our Father and the Glory be. A warmth fell over the room and they knew it was a special time. Not wanting it to get too serious he opened the second bottle of wine and Peter proceeded to tell them of his Roman adventures and what he was learning at the college.

"I've been fortunate to be working, as an intern, in the Secretary of State's office, in a very low status. For me it's a chance to learn what's going on all over the world. I have a little cubbyhole where they bring memos, documents and complaints from all the embassies throughout the world. My job is to analyze them and then synthesize them for the higher ups. What I find amazing is the Vatican gets more information and intelligence on what's going on than the CIA. I could tell you things dad, I'm sure you don't get in your morning briefing. Like what's going on in Syria and what the Russians are trying to do which is to take over the country and run it through a puppet."

Michael interrupted him to clarify a point: "We know pretty much what Russians have in mind; what we don't know is who they have in mind to be there puppet. Maybe we can discuss that privately."

"The Pope is fascinating. He's a world traveler, a pastor and amazingly a great administrator. We've got a lot of eighty year old cardinals who he is putting out to pasture who have been in the Curia way to long. Younger men in the early sixties are taking over the desks in the State Department and I know a number of men who say they see the same thing happening in their areas. The Church is changing as to its' adherents. Africa is the new missionary country both in priests and congregations. One hundred and thirty five million Catholics and Asia is growing just as fast. We just don't have near enough priests to service them."

"What's the answer Peter?" Sharon asked.

"More deacons to start with. Men who can serve the church doing weddings, baptisms, funerals and they can even give homilies. They can be married only if they were married before they apply to become a Deacon. The field is growing particularly in the United States. Right now I think there are about 39,000 worldwide. Eventually I hope we will be having women serving as Deacons."

The conversation turned to Jack and his family. "Megan and I have four boys and they are a handful. These guys are all competitive even though Brian is the oldest at seven"

"Fortunately, Brian is starting first grade next year and that will leave three at home all day, do you see any gray hair yet?" Megan asked. They all laughed and Kathryn joked: "no gray hair but I see some lines in the forehead." (more laughter)

"Seriously, we're doing great and the law practice is building. We have fourteen attorneys now where we had only 4 when I started nine years ago. Also I'm becoming a politician like dad and I think I like it more than he did when he ran for Congress. Like the people.

When are you going to run for Congress Jack?"

"It's interesting you ask that Peter. To tell you the truth I'm serving the second year of a four year term in the state senate. This year I'm going to try for President of the Senate. If I'm successful there it will be two years before I have to run for re-election to the Senate. If Buddy Forsyth our sitting congressman decides not to run I may consider it, if he decides to run I may run against him in the primary. Too soon to make any plans."

Sharon Sullivan had been listening to them all knowing she had some news that would make news. After Jack summarized his political ambitions, she raised her glass and asked for their attention: I have an announcement to make: Tim and I are going to be married. Unfortunately he was called in for an emergency surgery tonight and couldn't be here but will be tomorrow." The first to hug her was her sister, Kathryn. Michael and Mary hugged her simultaneously and Peter came last and gave his blessing.

"This calls for another bottle of Cotes du Rhone Michael signaled and went about pouring for his excited family. Will it be a wedding in the White House," he asked.

"No dad, reception maybe but wedding mass at St Matthews Cathedral. Is that o.k.?"

"Couldn't be better sweetheart, we would be thrilled no matter where or when. Do I speak for both of us Mary?"

"You do. When will it be Sharon?"

"Probably in May we just aren't sure yet."

The conversation turned to the wedding and while the women were totally absorbed Michael and Jack had a talk about how it was to be President of the United States. Jack joked to his father he had never been very close to the presidents who had served during his life time but he felt very close to the one serving in the office presently. Michael told him that at first he felt fearful that he would not be up to the job because of the heavy responsibilities and then it came to him he was not alone. As a religious man he believed God was with him at all times, and by using reason and common sense he would do the right thing. He reminded himself being President didn't change who he was. He was not ambitious for power, although it was at his right hand, he was ambitious to see the country recover what had been lost and he would do what he believed necessary to do that. That was his guiding philosophy. He told Jack he was not worried about being re-elected. That would take care of itself. What he felt was important now was getting the country back on sound footing which he felt they had made a strong beginning as his first year in office came to a close. He tried out some of the ideas he was thinking about for his State of the Union due in January. Jack told him: "Tell'em what you've done dad, USCorps, the turnaround in Iraq, a new mission in Afghanistan, Protection of the border. Cutting the size of government departments. All these and more show we've turned the corner and the curve is heading upward. There is so much to tell them and I don't mean Congress, I mean the American people. They're the ones that need to hear it."

"Hey what about you Kathryn, Sharon has been getting all the attention, besides making millions what's happening in your world?"

Jack looked at his younger sister with real interest. To him she had always been fascinating. It was unusual for the youngest and the oldest to be close yet they had a certain understanding; she thought him brilliant like her father and he thought of her as tenacious, a risk taker and unafraid something he found admirable. So when he asked the question he really was interested in her life in New York.

"Well, I'm not making millions," she laughed and then whispered in a voice they all strained to hear, "but darn close. Actually the firm has had a very prosperous year and there is even talk of going public. Should that happen, then we will be talking millions."

"Anything else we should know?" he teased, knowing from his mother she had been seriously dating a young lawyer.

"Funny you ask Jack, dear; as a matter of fact John Reilly, who you've met, has been making some overtures lately that sound like proposals of marriage."

Jack indeed new Mr. Reilly. The only time he met him he took an instant liking to him. The thought crossed his mind that Mr. Reilly would be a perfect match for his pal Kathryn. When he got back to his office he looked up Mr. Reilly's credentials in Martindale-Hubble, "the lawyer's bible." born 1985, Boston, Massachusetts, age 34, Partner, Bevins, Williams & Tobin, Boston. Education: Notre Dame, BS; Harvard Law School JD." He never said a word to Kathryn or anyone else in the family not even his wife, Megan. Somehow he felt Reilly, a six footer with black Irish hair and blue eyes, could be the fellow. So his heart jumped a beat when Kathryn told the family.

"Yes, I remember him, Kathryn, seemed like a nice fellow to me, I believe you said he is a trial Lawyer like your brother and your father."

All ears tuned in as they listened to the repartee between Jack and Kathryn. All of a sudden it dawned on the family they might going to two weddings in 2018. Soon after they all retired with new things to think about.

On Christmas Eve the family attended a special mass at St. Patrick's in the city. The church had to be closed off to the public for reasons of security. Located at 10th and F streets in the heart of the city it was first constructed in 1794 and served as the parish for those Irish who were working on the White House and the Capitol. Capitol Hill was not yet the seat of government. The first priest ordained in the United States, Father William Matthews served as pastor for fifty years and was well acquainted with the luminaries of his time, Henry Clay, Presidents, Zachery Taylor, and John Quincy Adams. In 1814 British soldiers attended mass while tending to the burning of the White House and government buildings. The church that stands today was dedicated by President Theodore Roosevelt in 1904.

As they knelt in the pews, the church empty, except for two altar boys and secret service personnel stationed discreetly in the back and side sections, each of the Sullivans prayed for the well being of each family member and expressed gratitude to the Lord for all they had been given. Peter gave the first reading followed by Sharon reading the second. Father Harrington, the pastor gave a very short homily in which he offered a prayer for the family and guidance for the President. In forty five minutes the mass was over and they exited through the front door of the church and to their surprise a crowd of 2,000 had gathered across the street and they shouted "Merry Christmas" when the President and First Lady appeared. Taken by surprise they waved back and shouted back at the crowd: "Merry Christmas to you." Michael had the urge to go across the street and the secret service man closest to him said as firmly as possible: "in the car Mr. President we have no control over the crowd in this situation." Michael gave a last wave and the crowd seemed to understand he wanted to come over a say "hello" but his protectors wouldn't allow it.

"Mister Speakaaa, the President of the United States" so droned the Sergeant of Arms of the House of Representatives, as Michael Sullivan came down the center isle to the cheers of the assembled representatives of the United States, Ambassadors, Justices of the Supreme Court, Cabinet Officers and various and sundry officials who were there as guests. Followed by an entourage of the leaders of the House and Senate, he slowly made his was down the aisle to the dais where the Vice President and the Speaker of the House waited to greet him. Michael looked fit dressed in a dark blue suit, white shirt and striped blue on gold tie, his shoulders squared and a look of ease about his figure as he moved slowly down the aisle in the time worn ritual of the State of the Union address. At the foot of the dais he shook the hands of the Justices and then mounted the two steps to the platform from where he would speak. Once in place he looked to the balcony where Mary and his family were seated. He waved and they waved back and the clapping continued until he signaled he was about to address the House. The year before when he looked out at the scene he was nervous but not outwardly. Once into the speech he had quickly gained his form as a speaker and soon he controlled the room. Now he looked out at his fellow representatives, for that's what they were in his mind, and felt confidence and inner peace.

He wanted to converse with them not speak out or down to them or preach to them.

The next morning the *New York Tribune* summarized the President's remarks:

"Sullivan told the congress, when his party took over governing the country the biggest problem faced was the debt. Noting that when his predecessor took office in 2009 the national debt stood at ten trillion dollars. On the day of his inauguration, eight years later it had more than doubled to twenty trillion dollars thru profligate spending and no attempt at reduction. The annual deficit had ballooned to over a trillion dollars per year. True as far as it goes. He neglected to point out the recession that began in 2009 continued until 2017 when things slowly began to improve. He told Congress there were no good choices. Only tough ones. And he named them. Unfunded liabilities not included in the National debt include: Social Security, Medicare, military pensions, veterans benefits, federal employee pensions, federal guarantees, and many more. The President's remedy: cut taxes and spending. In bold strokes he painted a picture of dire cuts, to the departments, social security, Medicare and pensions. Deficits of a trillion plus could no longer be sustained. His budget for 2019 would be kept under 400 billion. Social Security would be bolstered by raising the amount of payroll tax and extending the age to qualify. The same would apply to Medicare. He conceded these measures would not be popular and might be political suicide yet he looked out at his audience and told them he and they had no alternatives if they cared for the future of the country and those who would come after. "The American people are counting on us to act not put off these decisions any longer to win elections.""

Many first year achievements were noted including strengthening the southern border, curtailing illegal immigration to a trickle, cutting some of the departments such as Education, taking the offensive against ISIS by retaking Ramadi and preparing to do the same in Fallujah and Tikrit, preventing the takeover of Afghanistan by the Taliban and cutting foreign aid by thirty five billion dollars.

All these steps taken were resisted mightily by the Democratic opposition who have always favored higher taxes and unrestrained social welfare spending. They say actions taken by the President will set the country back twenty years. They may be right yet they cannot say with a straight face that their spending ten trillion dollars over eight years of their stewardship produced anything but recession and a 100% increase in the nation's debt. I think most Americans will take a wait and see attitude with the knowledge the president is doing exactly as he promised and he won the election."

"Bailey Long for the President."

"Yes Senator I'll put you right through to President Sullivan.

"It's seven thirty in the morning Bailey, I didn't know you got up this early."

"You've got a short memory Mr. President, have you forgotten so soon those early morning soirees we used to have in my office, some starting as early as seven o'clock before the Democrats got to their offices.

"Now that you've reminded me Bailey I do recall those meetings with fondness. Look where it got us."

"I don't know if you've had a chance to read the *New York Tribune* this morning but when you do I think you'll get a kick out of their take on your State of the Union last night. A tiger never changes its stripes; they say they're going to give you a chance to prove your way is the best way. Pure generosity on their part."

When he got off the phone with the Senate Majority leader he asked Maggie to get him a Tribune and he read the article carefully. Thinking about what was said he took them at their word with the caveat they could turn on a dime and lash out against him as they had done so often in the past.

• • •

After a CIA briefing in late February, Michael asked chief of staff Tom Donovan and the Vice President to come into the oval office to discuss an idea that had been brewing in his head for about three weeks as the offensive in Iraq began to take shape with the next big push being the re-taking of Mosul north of Bagdad. Mosul, the second largest city in Iraq, at one time contained a population of two and a half million that deteriorated to six hundred thousand after its capture by the Islamic terrorists. With twenty five thousand troops in Iraq and the southern portion of the country back in the hands of the coalition the President and his military advisors decided to take back the city. The force to consist of Iraq Sunni forces, regular Iraq Army units and American special ops backed by American Army forces. With the capture of Mosul Iraq would be free of ISIS except for pockets of guerilla fighters who would be hunted down and captured or killed. Tentatively the operation would commence April 1.

Tom and the Vice President arrived at the same time and were treated to a breakfast of Danish, fruit and coffee that Michael had ordered just in case they had not had breakfast. The two visitors ate while the President discussed what was on his mind. "We're scheduled to go into Mosul around the first of April. Easter Sunday is April 1. I have been weighing the advantages and disadvantages of going to Bagdad for Easter then on to Kabul and home. Do you have any initial reactions gentlemen?"

The Vice President whistled and Tom said with a look of conviction. "Dangerous Mr. President, very dangerous. You're no daredevil so what's the thinking?"

"Morale for the troops going into battle. Lift the spirits on the home front. That's my thinking and the reason for going. I'm mostly interested in letting the troops know we care about them enough to come where they are."

"I think its courageous Michael," the Vice President spoke up, "but you have to remember there are three hundred and Twenty five million people here who depend on you to lead. If anything should happen to you, the country would be thrown into chaos. That's something to think long and hard about. That's not to say you shouldn't go because I agree it would be a tremendous boost to the troops and the country as a whole." Following on the Vice President's point Tom offered: "I'm not as wise as Bernie here so I would agree with what he has said. Do the benefits outweigh the costs?"

"I gather," Michael said, "you are apprehensive about the idea. Remember President Bush flew to Bagdad in November 2003 for the same reason I realize the circumstances are different now and the country is a much more hostile environment which is also the case for our troops there. I haven't even brought it up with Mary. If a decision is made to go it has to be shrouded in secrecy with a complete news blackout until we're back home. I wanted to get your reactions and yours are the same as mine would be if Bernie came in and told me he wanted to go to Bagdad."

"That's a good idea, Mr. President, why don't I go. If anything happens to me I doubt whether chaos would ensue."

"Very generous Bernie but you and I know it would not have the same impact not to degrade your popularity." They all laughed and he said he would get back to them in a few days with a decision. The meeting ended and he went to his next meeting.

That night he broached the subject with Mary giving reasons for his thinking on the subject. She listened attentively, as she always did, when he was proposing something of great importance. She asked no questions until he completed his thoughts. "What did Tom and Bernie think?" she asked, knowing full well they would have been hesitant to give him wholehearted encouragement for such a dangerous undertaking.

"Let's say they were hesitant, and I don't blame them a bit. They did agree it made sense as a morale builder for the troops and the nation. I won't go if you say no."

"You know me well enough to know I won't say no. I agree with the thinking; at the same time I share Tom and Bernie's reservations. A mishap would be disastrous for the country. That's the argument against and I assume you've already considered that argument and rejected it, knowing you." She said this in a very matter of fact way knowing of his previous brushes with death in South America, Afghanistan and the Baltics. She was concerned for him and the country and so she said nothing to discourage him. With her blessing he met two days later with the Vice President and Tom Donovan and advised them of his decision to go to the two countries.

It would be his first trip out of the United States since becoming President. He thought it fitting that the first trip would be to the troops at Easter. Tom was instructed that secrecy was paramount and that only people who needed to know be in on the project. He wanted everything in place by March fifteenth. Logistically, it would require a plane, helicopters, fighter escorts where possible, contacts on the ground in Bagdad and Kabul, security arrangements in both capitals and a limited number of people making the trip. A pool reporter or two would be on the flight, with all press embargoed until the President and his party were in the air and approaching U.S. airspace on the way home. A tall order to be accomplished in a short time. He knew Tom was capable of handling the matter discreetly and that was the reason he had been chosen as chief of staff. His instructions were that no one was to know, not John Kennedy, the Attorney General, Paul Connolly, Tom Galvin, not even his own children.

Two individuals alerted to the President's trip General Mark Barrett, in Afghanistan and Bing Smith in Iraq, were directed to coordinate all preparations in their respective war zones. Flying with the President were a contingent of twelve marines who, in addition to secret service, would be his personal body guards, along with Tom Donovan and five White House aides, and two pool reporters. The reporters were carefully screened and their employers sworn to secrecy before boarding the plane at the last moment. The White House grounds were cleared and the press advised that the President and Mrs. Sullivan would be spending Easter at Camp David. In keeping with the story the President and the First Lady left the Diplomatic room of the White House at 10:30 a.m. Saturday morning March 31 and boarded Marine One for the short trip to Andrews Air Force Base just outside Washington. The President and Tom Donovan, dressed in army khakis and indistinguishable from other military were taken into a holding room in the hanger 50 yards from where the helicopter landed. Immediately, once the President was safely in the hanger surrounded by secret service agents, the helicopter took off again with Mary on board for the trip to Camp David. Coffee and rolls were served to the President and the agents and a half hour later they boarded a C-130 J state of the art cargo carrier especially outfitted for the trip to Iraq. The idea behind the use of the cargo aircraft was to make it look like one of the many cargo planes landing every day in Bagdad only in this case it would have F-16's fighter aircraft surrounding it as it entered Iraq air space. At twelve thirty the C-130 was airborne and no one was the wiser as most Americans were preparing to go to the church of their choice the next day---Easter Sunday.

During the flight Tom and the President talked for the first hour and then decided to get some sleep. Separated from their cubicle the rest of the group sat forward facing each other in bucket seats. Some talked some dozed and others, especially the reporters, kept consulting their phones and I-pads to see if any of the news outlets were carrying the story of the President's trip to the war zones. By midnight everyone on the flight was asleep except the pilots, crew and secret service who maintained strict vigilance. The President woke up at 5:00 a.m. still drowsy, and looked out the window in his cubicle and saw the sun coming up, and more reassuring U.S. F-16 Falcons flying cover. Tom woke up after hearing Michael rustling around.

"You OK Mr. President?" Still half bleary eyed he saw Michael looking out the window and wide awake as though he had been up for hours. The younger man roused himself up and offered to get some coffee for the both of them.

"Couldn't be better Tom I can't wait to get on the ground and visit the troops. A cup of coffee would be like manna from Heaven."

The aide left the cubicle and made his way forward. To his surprise most of those in the bucket seats were drinking coffee and chatting. He wondered how long they had been awake and began feeling a little guilty that he had slept so long and soundly. A steward offered to bring back rolls, orange juice and a pot of hot coffee. By the time Tom returned to the cubicle everyone forward was getting the same breakfast and he and the President started to go over the agenda for the day.

At 6:30 they could see Bagdad from 20,000 feet and excitement coursed through the plane as they realized the President's visit would be a complete surprise and they would be a part of it. The pool reporters had been checking their phones all night to see if the trip had been uncovered and to everyone's relief it had not been picked up by any of the news services and in fact the only news of the President was that he and Mrs. Sullivan were enjoying Easter at Camp David. Without any fanfare the C- 130 made a perfect landing and taxied out to the edge of the airfield and came to a stop and the engines were turned off. A bus drew abreast followed by four black bullet proof SUVs. The marines embarked first and quickly formed a cordon around the President. Bing Smith was there to greet the party. The marines got on the bus and the rest of the party climbed into the SUVs and sped across the runways to the Air Base that had to be reconstructed when the U.S. started moving troops back into Iraq in large numbers.

When they arrived at the other side General Smith directed the President, Tom, the White House aides and the two pool reporters into a temporary building much like a the Quonset huts used in World War II. Somewhat primitive, the building had a bathroom at one end and the rest of the room contained a large table with maps on it and chairs all around the table. Two couches sat on one side of the room. He suggested they shave and take a shower if need be and more food would be brought in. When they emerged Michael felt refreshed and had changed into fresh khaki pants, shirt and the combat boots he had worn on the plane. A number of officers were now in the room and the General made introductions all around followed by a light breakfast of rolls, coffee, doughnuts and orange juice. The General announced Easter Mass was being held in a building nearby and invited the President to join the troops at mass. When they got to the building it was packed to the rafters with G.I.s. The minute the President walked in they recognized him and someone began to clap hesitantly, because the building was being used temporarily as a church, and then they started cheering and whistling as if the place was a stadium. After a minute Bing Smith held up his hand for silence and announced: "Ladies and Gentlemen the President of the United States will hear mass with us. Please begin Padre." From that point on they were just 500 soldiers attending Easter services in a hostile country away from home and family with their Commander-in-Chief.

Word spread quickly throughout the base Michael Sullivan, the President, was on the base to be with them. Excitement was contagious. Would they see him? Be able to talk with him? A pretty gutsy move some said. As for his safety, Bing Smith had the entire airport shut down; no flights in or out; three hundred soldiers ringing the base with a hundred military police within the airport ring. The marines that had flown in with the President sat on all sides of him during the mass. At the homily the chaplain thanked the President for coming at great risk to himself to be with the troops on Easter Sunday. "It means a great deal to these soldiers to have their Commander-in Chief with them on the day the assault on Mosul begins."

After the mass the chaplain asked Michael if he would care to say a few words. He got to his feet and took the microphone from the chaplain and said:

"The chaplain mentioned risk in coming here. Any risk taken could not possibly match the risk you are taking to defend us here rather than on our own soil. I know what you are doing and so do your families. The American people know it and they know you will sever the head of the snake known as ISIS. You have the full backing of the people. You will be given the tools you need to win. And there will be no undercutting your commanders by the people in Washington. I can't tell you how pleased I am to celebrate this day with you. God bless each and every one of you."

Some said they thought the roof lifted a couple inches off its base. Others said it sounded like the Boeing wind tunnel. Most settled for the term thunderous applause. They showed their appreciation the only way they knew how; by showering him with the sound of their voices.

The next stop was the mess hall where 800 were being served baked ham, sweet potatoes, pees and salad topped off with pumpkin pie. They knew he was coming and a roar went up when he and Bing Smith stepped into the hall. The President at six feet, one inch, was an inch taller than Smith and as they came through the door into the hall they made an impressive pair, the commander and the Commander-in-chief. The top NCO ushered them to a table where eight service men were seated. Michael sat down and started chatting with them. They knew he was one of them and they were perfectly at ease. He met everyone at the table and then signaled the head of the secret service detail and told him he wanted to move around the room speaking to as many soldiers as possible. At first he was hesitant, but the President assured him it would be all right. To make the agent feel better he asked Bing to come along with him and meet some of his command in person. He got up and started moving around the room with Bing Smith right behind him. He laughed, he joked, they laughed and joked with him, all the while the general seemed to be having the time of his life shaking hands with the men he would be sending into battle. Every person in the room understood what the President was doing; he was not trolling for votes. He was encouraging his men; he wanted to know their names, where they came from? Did they have a family? "Anyone here from Texas?" he would shout out and men and women all around the room would stand and wave their hands. He did the same for a number of states and they all shouted out. They were excited and at the end he made a short speech thanking them for the privilege of sharing a meal with them and that he and the American people would be praying for their safety and the successful end to their mission. As they left the hall they could hear the refrain: "USA, USA, USA."

Before they attended the mass earlier in the day, Bing Smith had spent a private fifteen minutes with Tom and the President updating them on what was happening at that very moment. Mosul was surrounded he said and the road between Samarra in the south and Baiji in the north was in the hands of the Iraqis and American forces. The attack on Mosul would begin at eight points around the city with blocks being taken one at a time. By nightfall the advance teams would have some idea of how tenacious the resistance would be.

At 1:30 p.m. the President's party boarded the C-130 for the two hour trip to Muscat, Oman to avoid flying over Iranian air space. Constantly checking their phones and I pads the reporters passed the word that as of 2:30 Easter Sunday no one was aware of the President's presence in

Iraq. In their opinion it was only a matter of time before the press became aware of the situation as soldiers in Iraq would be calling home to say they had Easter dinner with the President of the United States. Sure enough by the time they landed in Muscat, wire services worldwide were alive with the breaking news the U.S. President was in Iraq and had already left for a destination unknown but presumably back to Washington. After a 15 minute layover in Muscat they were once again airborne for Kabul, Afghanistan and the newly named Hamid Karzai International airport. From the minute they left Bagdad they were joined by a six plane fighter escort that would take them into Kabul. As the plane left Muscat Tom and the President and the two reporters discussed what they had witnessed in the last few hours, most of it off the record. One of the reporters was a Catholic and he expressed how impressed he was at the reverence of soldiers at mass. He told them afterward he talked with several men who said they were not of any particular religion but they understood the concept there are no atheists in fox holes. They said they witnessed the reverence of their Catholic brothers and sisters and were frankly impressed.

"I share your thought, Peter (Peter Isadore of the International Press Service) they were all young and very serious. Many of them will be fighting in Mosul in the next few days and I can only pray for their safety. Everyone I met, officers or enlisted were very professional. I'm confident we are going to crush this Islamic insurgency and that's what it is. They are following the dictates of their religion which is conversion or death to the non-believer. They leave no choice but to be stamped out. They seemingly are unwilling to tolerate the free practice of one's religion."

"Can I quote you on that?"

"Yes, and I'm not speaking of the majority of Muslims, who have shown tolerance for other religions; only those who have taken as their faith the killing of those who disagree with them. ISIS is a cancer we and the rest of the world must cut out or it will contaminate the whole body."

He answered a few more questions and then cut the session short to prepare for the landing in Kabul. The plane touched down at 7:30 p.m. Kabul time and General Mark Barrett and his staff were at the foot of the stairs to meet them. "Welcome Mr. President to Kabul; I've heard from Bing Smith and he said his troops were really bucked up by your visit. We're ready to top his hospitality."

"Not necessary Mark; it was our pleasure to be on the same ground with those fellows. I hope we can meet as many of your troops as possible."

The general introduced his staff and then told the President he was just in time for dinner with the troops. "All press reports I've seen are speculating you're on your way home, so this visit should be a surprise to most of our people. Staff cars were brought up to the plane along with a couple of buses, and before long the motorcade was on the way to the mess hall, where a thousand service personnel waited for their delayed Easter dinner. When they came into the hall a roar went up just as it had in Bagdad. General Barrett introduced the President who apologized to the troops for causing them to wait all day for their Easter dinner. Someone shouted out: "The pleasure is all ours." Michael answered back: "No the pleasure is all mine, now let's hit the chow." Again the room erupted and before long everyone was enjoying the much anticipated meal. Shortly after he was seated with the general and some of the troops, he got up and started around the room stopping at table after table. As they had in Bagdad everyone watched him as he moved about the huge hall. People jumped to their feet with cameras and wanted their picture taken with him. He obliged. He kept it up for an hour having hardly eaten anything. It appeared to Tom and his secret service protectors that he was passionate about meeting with these troops letting them know the folks back home appreciated their sacrifice. They reciprocated with what Tom later told his staff was love "as strange as that may sound." He understood him and they understood him. He cared. That's all they needed to know. He was in no hurry for as far as he was concerned the purpose of the trip was being accomplished.

Before they took off from Kabul General Barrett gave he and Tom a frank assessment of the situation, which in his opinion was dire. Daily attacks in the city. Attacks on bases in the outlands. ISIS dominating Helmand Province and for all purposes controlling Kandahar, the second largest city in the country. He told the President just to hold Kabul, the capital, he would need at least five thousand more troops.

"I realize the Pentagon wants us to hold on until Iraq is cleaned up but I don't think we can hold on that long. I've been sending that message for the last three weeks. Believe me I'm not complaining yet as I said the situation is dire." As he uttered these words he was interrupted by one of his staff officers, who in a calm voice, apologized to the President for the interruption and said:

"There has been a huge explosion downtown, casualties in the hundreds; two suicide bombers drove into the night market and blew themselves up. They are asking if we can bring in some troops to help restore order."

The President looked at the general and said: "You will have 10,000 troops within a couple of weeks. Now you go and take care of business and I will take care of the Pentagon."

The President

"God bless you sir, my staff will see you get on that plane for Washington. I'm on my way down town to help out." They stood. They shook hands and the deal was done. Within a minute the head of the secret service detail was at the President's elbow, telling him they had to get out of Kabul as soon as possible. "Too dangerous sir, we've got to get you on that plane and out of here." He didn't argue telling Tom: "You heard the man Tom it's 6 a.m. in Washington let's head for home. I think we've done some good here and we've learned a lot. We have some good men on the ground out here."

CHAPTER 15

WHEN THEY ARRIVED back at Andrews, Mary, the entire Cabinet and the Joint Chiefs of Staff were on hand to greet them. The Secretary of State thought it would be a good idea to show solidarity with the President and so he called each Cabinet member and requested they be at Andrews when the President arrived.

When Michael saw Mary and his whole Cabinet he felt a surge of pride knowing how unusual it was for a member to show up on such an occasion, much less the entire Cabinet and their wives. He kissed her and shook hands all around and then decided on the spot to have the entire Cabinet back to the White House for dinner. He thanked the press pool and everyone who had been on the trip and then made a short statement to the waiting press which consisted of a compressed version of the journey and the suggestion a better story could be obtained from the pool reporters who had been on the plane. With that he, Mary and Tom were bundled into a marine helicopter for the short ride and landing on the White House lawn where six or seven hundred White House and political employees were waiting to welcome him home.

The *New York Tribune* grudgingly gave their approval to the trip.

"PRESIDENT RETURNS FROM SURPRISE VISIT TO IRAQ AND AFGHANISTAN:

"President Sullivan returned from a whirlwind Easter Sunday trip to the two capitals to spend the day with the troops. The trip was conducted with utter secrecy to the extent the White House put out a story the President and his wife would be spending Easter at Camp David. It turns out she was at Camp David while he was eating Easter ham with the troops in the war zone We commend the President for taking a risky trip to be with the troops. Some on the left have suggested it was a 'publicity stunt.' Whether it was or not is really irrelevant if it brought succor to the troops who were about to engage in the retaking of the ISIS stronghold in Mosul. Those on the left may dispute the motive but in our judgment he showed leadership and that is the point."

While the unplanned dinner that night at the White House was informal it was the first chance the Sullivans had to meet with the Secretaries and their wives though they had done so with individual couples. A warm feeling prevailed and many of the wives had not met each other so Mary took them in hand for a few minutes before cocktails were served. For most of those present it was a chance to catch up on what each was accomplishing in their individual departments. Even Michael was finding more of what was happening across government from talking to the various Secretaries. Dinner was lively with the conversation turning to the war in Iraq. Half way through someone asked Michael to tell what he saw and heard on his trip. He obliged by telling them about the troops, and how much he admired them. "These are just kids in the main. To a man they believe in the mission and more importantly that we are behind them and their commanders. It's made all the difference in the world to not have their hands tied behind their backs as they go into battle. Morale is high and they are ready to take on ISIS. This is what I heard from the troops and their commanders. I am more determined than ever to give them what they need to win."

The Secretary of Defense spoke about the rapport existing between he and the Secretary of State. "You wouldn't believe the tales I've heard at the Pentagon about the infighting that existed between the two during the Obama administration. It was all turf with no quarter given, and to hell with the war. State wanted to give into Iran while Defense saw the obvious need to put troops on the ground to defeat ISIS; Secretary Barry and the President won out by creating a façade that something was being done when in fact they were trying to extract troops from Iraq and shut the operation down."

Jokingly Robert Butterfield said: "Byron Titus and I have had several robust fistfights in his office over certain policies but we always made sure you didn't hear about it and that's what he means when he says we have great rapport." It broke everyone up and in way brought them closer together as a team knowing they could joke with and about each other. Michael loved the team spirit and hoped they could keep it up as so many other administrations had failed to do, resulting in one department holding out on another and cabinet officers competing with each other for power. He believed it had everything to do with the people he had asked to serve. For them it was service to country not something owed to them. After everyone had gone home Michael spent an hour with Mary going over who he met what he saw and what he thought of the chances of driving ISIS out of Iraq.

"We will know in about a week Mary whether we can take Mosul. My guess is those men I saw In Bagdad will take it---how long it will take I don't know. They know they will get what they need. I promised that. They know there is no turning back, no negotiated settlement. Their President is behind them."

After the trip to Iraq and Afghanistan, Michael asked P. J. Johnson to join him for breakfast on April 21. The two met alone in the oval office.

"Major I want to talk to you about Iraq. I learned a great deal from soldiers to generals who I talked to when I was there. We're battling in Mosul right now and so far it is slow going. I'm going to ask you to undertake a mission there which you are free to turn down. First what do you see has been happening before we went into Mosul?" The President was briefed every day on the Iraq situation by the CIA and often by the Joint Chiefs of Staff yet he had great respect for Major Johnson's analytical powers particularly as it pertained to Iraq and Afghanistan so he listened with interest as the Major gave his thinking on the subject.

"Well sir as you know the situation is very complex as to who is fighting who and who wants what results. First of all when we left Iraq, leaving a small force behind, President Maliki cut the Sunnis out and pretty much the Kurds. We had knocked out the bad guy Hussein and Maliki brings in his fellow Shiites into the government and the military starts cooperating with the Iranian government. That generated a great deal of resentment on the part of his fellow Iraqis as you might imagine. It didn't bother the Kurds too much they were pretty much running their own show in the north. Sunni resentment flared up in the form of Al Qaeda in Iraq which turned into ISIS. As to Mosul, the majority are Sunni and they aren't overjoyed at the thought of the Peshmerga and Iraq army taking over the city. When ISIS first started functioning in Iraq they moved against the Kurdish and got as far as Erbil before being pushed back and that has become the status quo with either side just sitting and looking at each other. Remember ISIS took Mosul with about 1,000 men when a 30,000 man Iraq Army dropped their weapons and equipment, or I should say, our equipment and ran south. This gave them a whole new arsenal that they wouldn't have otherwise acquired. The Sunnis in Mosul don't want the Peshmerga in the fight fearing they will make it their territory. Another factor is the PKK which is a Marxist operation run out of Turkey fighting ISIS alongside the Peshmerga but also at odds with the Kurds. The PKK wants a Kurdish state. Added to the milieu is the Turkish Army bringing in troops and equipment around Mosul. I should add the Peshmerga and the PKK are enemies of the Turks. That's the political atmosphere existing when we went into Mosul last week. You may have different intelligence."

"No Major everything I've been informed of squares with what you've just said. Everyone wants a piece of Mosul for their own cause. That will be dealt with once we capture it. Our goal is to make Iraq resistant to Iran, which is spreading terror throughout the region, and strong enough to crush any future caliphate that ISIS or anyone else tries to perpetrate there. With that in mind let me come to the point of why I asked you to come here. I would like you to go to Iraq, specifically Mosul, and become a part of a unit that is fighting to take over the city. Something the size of a squad or platoon made up of Iraq Army troops with one of our own special ops in command. The purpose of such a mission would be to judge the fighting capabilities of the Iraqis under our command. Will they break and run or go forward and fight? The answer to that question is vital to future planning for the defense of the country. Should they broken up into three states, Sunni, Kurd and Shiite under a federated system? Those are policy matters to be decided in the near future. For now it will be enough if we can get your observations after spending a week to ten days with the type of unit I've described. If you choose to go, Bing Smith will be made aware of your presence with precautions taken for your safety. You don't have to give me an answer now---talk it over with your wife and let me know tomorrow."

"I don't have to sir. I will take on the mission." This was said with emphasis and finality.

Michael looked at him and said: "Major I appreciate your willingness. However this is a dangerous mission; there is great risk. I value your opinions and your thinking but I think your wife should have a say in this. You tell her I have asked and refusal will not in any way affect your standing with me. I chose you for the mission because of the trust I have in you. I goes back to Afghanistan where we were both almost killed in that Al Qaeda attack."

The Major had tears in his eyes as he rose, saluted the President, pivoted on a dime and left the office as quietly as he had come in. At eight o'clock the next morning he put a call through to the Oval office; the President took the call and heard him say he was ready to go with his wife's blessing.

P.J. Johnson, a combat veteran, highly decorated for valor in both Gulf wars left for Iraq on a C-130 with a full compliment of infantry soldiers on their way to the front lines in Mosul, Iraq. They flew the same route the President had taken and deplaned in Bagdad and caught another aircraft which took them to an air force base just outside Erbil in northern Iraq inside Kurd territory where the coalition had set up headquarters for the Mosul offensive. From there they were driven to the outskirts of Mosul with a convoy of special operations forces. That night he slept and the next day reported to a platoon headed by special ops first lieutenant George Thompson serving a second tour in Iraq. Thompson had been advised Major Johnson would be serving with the platoon for a few days as an observer and if need be a combatant. The two men bonded quickly, the younger realizing

Johnson had seen a great deal of combat with far greater experience in the field. Early that afternoon the lieutenant informed his men they would be going into the city following on the heels of a company made up of Iraqi Army, Peshmerga and Sunni fighters from Anbar Province who had made an assault on an area south of the city and after a morning of fierce fighting had wrested about twenty five buildings from ISIS control. Their job was to mop up any remaining terrorists. Ahead of the Platoon a Humvee with a fifty caliber machine gun mounted on the top led the way with the men strung out along either side of the street. The lieutenant had told his men not to count on the first wave killing all the terrorists. Often they hid and waited for back up patrols to come into the area and when far enough in they would spring an ambush firing from all sides with snipers pouring fire in from the rooftops. He warned: "take cover until we figure where they are and then we'll a plan to deal with them."

Up ahead of the Humvee a bomb exploded hitting the vehicle but not disabling it. The gunner started firing at buildings on both sides of the street hoping to give the platoon time to take cover. All the men ducked into buildings on the side of the road but not before ISIS snipers had hit two men who were slumped down in different doorways.

"We're pinned down," Thompson yelled at his radio man. "Get air cover in here in fifteen minutes or we will lose half the platoon." After sixty seconds the radio man reported a contact had been made and a apache helicopter promised and on its way with the further instruction to hold positions. Squeezed into the same doorway the lieutenant and P.J. Johnson decided the major, at his insistence, would take an M 4 carbine, race to the other side of the street opposite the doorway and try to pick off the sniper. He ran and shells dug into the street around him. Somehow he made it to the other side and fired a short burst. No sign of the sniper and no incoming fire. Complete silence. Suddenly the sniper rose up to fire his weapon and as he did so P.J. let loose a volley that took the sniper's head off. Another popped up and the same thing happened. Two more in Heaven he thought to himself and motioned the lieutenant to have some men dash over to his side so the platoon would have both sides of the street covered. In the meantime the gunner in the Humvee was laying down a steady stream 50 caliber machine gun fire as the platoon inched its way forward. Half way up the next block three of the men entered what looked to be an empty burned out building and took heavy fire from an upper story killing the first man through the door, a Sunni soldier. Now the apache came on the scene and spotted four men on the roof of the building where the soldier had been killed trying to enter. The rest of the platoon hunched down and watched the roof disappear and the terrorists with it as the Warthog opened up with its 30 mm cannon. They searched the area further as ordered and encountered one more die hard who was silenced after 150 rounds. They checked the body riddled terrorist before heading back to the base. Four hour mission, three friendlies killed, eight terrorists dead they reported. After his report was filed the lieutenant joined P.J. Johnson for a beer outside one of the base buildings using sand bags as chairs.

"I thought your people performed pretty well today, lieutenant are they always that good?"

The lieutenant gave him a quizzical look which he took to mean sometimes yes sometimes no. "The Peshmerga are the most professional; they are real fighters---not afraid of anything. Like our own people. The Sunnis aren't bad and the Iraq army guys are the worst. The one thing that keeps them moving forward in a firefight is the thought they make take a Sunni bullet in the back if they try to run. So far in two weeks they've taken the most casualties because its safer to advance than get shot from behind by a Sunni or a Peshmerga."

"Any danger of getting shot by an Iraqi soldier?"

"No that's not happening up here. They pretty much do what they're told and I will admit after a few of these sorties into the badlands they're getting better at it which is all to the good."

In the next week the major moved to three other outfits, differing in size as the coalition forces moved further into the city and more U.S. troops joined the fray. In the area he was fighting in the resistance had been heavy and the coalition had lost 600 and a 1,000 wounded. Enemy losses were figured at 4,000 killed and twice that wounded. The offensive was two fifths completed with the area taken held by reserve troops. So far the resistance had been stiff without any sign of a break and run on the part of the ISIS fighters. The Major noted that the enemy was mostly very young men, not educated and not good tactical fighters, but willing to die for their cause and that made them dangerous fighters. At the end of ten days he bid farewell to those he had been serving with, checked in with General Bing Smith for a debriefing and caught a military transport aircraft headed for Andrews.

"Come on in Major," the President rose to greet him with a genuine show of affection. I've invited General Bartholomew, head of the Chiefs to hear what you have to say."

Peter Bartholomew, fifty eight years old and a decorated veteran was as gentle as he was tough. He knew how to get the most out of his men. Tall, straight backed with gray hair he was at the peak of his military career at age 58. He spoke his mind and was quick to tell the President when he disagreed. Michael had jumped him over a number of men to make him Chief. Many of those jumped had done the bidding of the previous President contrary to the welfare of the nation. They were re-assigned or asked to retire the first month of the new administration. In their place were a cadre of young men with proven track records. Professional soldiers not political soldiers. P.J. snapped off a salute which was returned by the general who then gave him a sturdy hand shake. Both soldiers knew they were of the brotherhood. They all sat and a steward brought in coffee, tea and cookies. The President opened the discussion suggesting P.J. tell what he saw, did, heard and concluded.

"What I saw was a tremendous amount of destruction of the ground we've taken, and they destroyed as they retreated, you have a great deal of rubble. The streets are passable, mainly because as we take an area the locals are required to assist in cleaning up the streets. We've provided food and shelter for the people in the areas we have captured, mostly away from the city. Our MPs are doing a good job along with the Iraq Army forces in controlling the streets and preventing looting. I found the ISIS fighters to be tenacious but amateurs. They are like the Japanese Kamikaze in World War II. They're fighting to convert those who don't want to be converted. From that standpoint they are in some ways more dangerous than the trained professional soldier."

Both men, the President and the General, were listening intently when General Bartholomew asked: "In your judgment major how long will it take to retake Mosul?"

"At the rate we're proceeding I think another month at least. If they were our troops, two weeks. The trouble is you can't rush these people. Their instincts are not to rush in and get the job done. They have to be pushed although that is not true of the Peshmerga. Those fellows are fighters. I think if they had all the equipment they needed they could do the job by themselves, if they thought they could keep the territory they captured. As far as the Iraqi Army goes they are a reluctant group. They will do a satisfactory job maintaining what we have won back but as for being a fighting war machine---I don't see it."

"How long must they be trained?" the General asked, knowing full well the millions of dollars spent on their training since 2004 had produced mixed results.

"Seeing them in action on more than one occasion I would say at least a year of intense training would be required. One encouraging aspect of the current campaign is the fact battled tested veterans will come out of Mosul and will serve as valuable trainers in the next year or so. Frankly Mr. President and General Bartholomew I think we are going to be successful---persistence being the key."

Watching and listening to P.J. Johnson and realizing the confidence the President had in the man, the General thought to himself Johnson is headed for higher rank. The more Johnsons we have in the General ranks the better off our military will be. Listening to the Major's analysis he could see why Michael had the man as his military aide.

"Let me ask one more question major and it's a political one, out of my realm more suited to the President and his political advisors, nevertheless, I'd be curious to know your views on how the country might be governed other than in its current form?"

P.J. looked at the President as if to ask his permission to voice an opinion. Michael proffered: "I think it is more in your realm than you think Major, after all you've been on the ground longer than the General or I."

Assured he was not speaking out of turn he voiced the opinion Iraq would do better as a federation with three separate states: Kurdish, Sunni and Shia.

"My rationale is the Kurds are essentially autonomous now, the Shia have control of the South and have had since Saddam Hussein was disposed of and the Sunni are going to keep setting off bombs in Bagdad until they get their share of the oil revenues and a great deal of autonomy. Maliki had a chance to make a go of it but he hardened the resolve of the Kurds and the Sunnis by cutting them out of the governing coalition put in place after Hussein was dethroned. I don't know how the thinkers we pay to think would go along with the idea but it makes sense to me."

Michael had been thinking of this solution for some time without discussing it with any member of his administration. He was interested the Major had the same idea. In response to P.J.'s suggestion he merely commented: "You're not alone in your thinking Major; I've read and heard it raised by others." The General again reiterated it was a political and not military decision but off the record said the idea sounded plausible in that it would reduce the number of military needed to provide security for the country. The meeting continued for a few more minutes and then the General offered to give the Major a ride in his staff car back to the Pentagon. He wanted to know more about the man and giving him a lift provided the opportunity to do so.

• • •

Michael continued to follow progress in Iraq on a daily basis with his Secretary of Defense and the head of the CIA. At a meeting May 24 in the situation room with the NSC staff,

CIA, Joint Chiefs, Secretaries of Defense and State and the Vice President Bing Smith brought everyone up to date via secured teleconference. "We've captured roughly five eighths of the city. Resistance continues strong and the Iraqi forces are paying a heavy price while the 82nd airborne and the Peshmerga are inflicting heavy damage in the northern portion of the city. Some of our advance teams have crossed the Tigris River and we control four of the five bridges spanning the river." The General started to continue when the Secretary of State, Byron Titus, interrupted with a question on the number of enemy killed and the number of coalition killed or injured.

"From April 1, when the offensive started, until yesterday approximately 6,000 enemy killed and another couple of thousand wounded. And I should add they don't seem to leave their wounded alive. Very few prisoners have been taken. Our own losses are 600 U.S. Killed and a thousand wounded. The Peshmerga and the Iraq army have lost over 3500."

"Those are heavy casualties General, wouldn't you say?" Titus pressed not unkindly.

"They are Mr. Secretary, but not unexpected. When you're fighting house to house and building to building with booby traps set everywhere in front of you and still trying to preserve some of the city you're going to take heavy casualties. I believe in the next ten days we will have advanced to the western edge of the city where they will try to break out. We have designed a 'rat line' that will allow them to escape to the west and when they get beyond the city that 'rat line' will turn into an inferno worse than Dunkirk. Gunships, F-16's and missiles will rain on their retreat and we plan to decimate the survivors so much so that those who fought in Mosul will never make it back to Syria. At that point we start mopping up Tal Afar and areas northwest to the border with Syria."

"I know you're not known for giving glowing pictures of situations that are disastrous. What you've just told us is extremely encouraging except for the loss of life of our own men and those of our allies. If what you say becomes realty ISIS should be finished in Iraq except for pockets of resistance along the Syrian border. Do I read you correctly?"

"You do Mr. President. The sooner we drive them out the less our casualties. So far everything we've taken back in the country is being secured by the Iraqi army under the leadership of our troops. So I would say by mid-July Iraq should be free of ISIS control and then, if so directed, we will destroy their bases in Syria. I should say sir, I hope, all of this I've said is off the record until we've cleaned out Mosul."

"A good report Bing, and yes, it is off the record and when Mosul is liberated we will want you back here for meetings with Congress and the Chiefs. Good luck."

"Thank you sir. We will continue daily reports to you and the Chiefs." The screen went dark and the President turned to those in the room asking each what they thought about the report they had just listened to.

"I agree Bing is no embellisher, however our sources on the ground tell us, while we are on the offensive and making good headway, it will take longer than the General is predicting. These Islamic fanatics are willing to die and that means you have to kill every one of them to take back territory." Michael had found his CIA Director, Robert Fenwick, to be smart and accurate in his intelligence assessments. And the one just delivered reflected not opinion but fact derived from knowledge from his agents on the ground in Iraq.

"Do you question his prediction of success Bob?" Robert Butterfield, Secretary of Defense queried.

Fenwick turned to face the President before answering: "No. Not the success of the mission only the time it will take. I believe it will take probably until September."

"That would not be good Bob, we all know the temperature is unbearable in the summer and the fighting far more difficult for our troops not used to such heat. I hope Bing is right about finishing in July, Butterfield countered."

Michael was interested to hear what Peter Bartholomew had to say and so waited until all had commented except the head of the Chiefs of Staff. The discussion went on for another hour and when everyone had pretty much had their say the President turned to the General and posited: "You heard what General Smith is predicting would you agree?"

"I do and I also think Bob has a point when he expresses concern about time and the summer heat. It is brutal talking from experience. My suggestion would be to give Bing 5,000 more troops immediately and go all out to finish this thing in a month which would put us into June."

Silence followed his suggestion. Then his boss, the Secretary of Defense spoke up saying: "I agree with Peter and I would suggest we find out from General Smith how and if these fresh troops would affect the time it would take to finish the job." More silence. Then Robert Fenwick broke the silence saying; "I would be interested in what the General thinks. More importantly we haven't heard your thoughts Mr. President."

"Bing will have the 5,000 if he needs them. The decision is made. Peter will you get his answer and get back to me this evening. If we send the troops they should be on their way tomorrow if they are to bring this to a successful close by June."

Within a week, the additional troops were in the battle for Mosul and were making a tremendous difference in the time it would take to drive ISIS out. The Americans brought morale to the battlefield with the result the Kurds and Sunnis doubled their efforts. On June 1, the leaders of ISIS saw they could not hold the city and were left to die in the center of it or find an area they might break out and make a mad dash across the border to Syria. As Bing Smith planned they found what they thought to be a weak spot on the Allied front and began to divert men and materials in an orderly retreat down the "rat line" leaving mainly snipers and suicide bombers behind to cover the withdrawal. The Americans closed in quickly seizing building after building with little opposition. Drones watched the withdrawal and when the main ISIS force of 4,000 men, trucks and armored vehicles stretched out six miles beyond the city limits headed to their home base in Raqqa, Syria they were hit with the biggest air bombardment of the war. Drone directed missiles, helicopter gunships firing at close range, field artillery, warthogs, and carpet bombing B-52's converted the retreat into a shooting gallery and when pursuing allied troops reached the scene of the carnage it resembled a grave yard with thousands of bodies strung out along the six mile corridor and crushed vehicles and equipment, that had fallen into ISIS hands when the Iraqi army abandoned the city in 2015, lay in masses of twisted steel and of no service to any army ISIS or allies. The battle for Mosul ended June 15th 2018.

"CBC network, Mary Silva reporting from Mosul, Iraq: I am coming to you from the war torn streets of Mosul, formerly the second largest city in Iraq. This city has been involved in war for the last two years, the latest occupier being the Islamist terrorist group calling itself ISIS. A campaign by American, Iraq, Sunni, Kurd, French and English troops has been underway to take back the city and after two bloody months for both the coalition and the terrorists the city is in the hands of Iraq and for the most part ISIS has lost its hold on the country. Having driven through the city from end to end I can say the coalition is clearly in control yet it is still unsafe due to snipers and explosives planted in all parts of the city. There was a time when almost two million lived here. No more. The number is closer to four hundred thousand. Will they come back? Authorities here say most will over time. Security is the key. Right now truckloads of Iraqi Army personnel are pouring into the city and we are told within a week every semblance of ISIS will be gone. The terrorists trying to escape the city in what the military now refers to as the 'rat line' were killed by the thousands and all the military equipment they came by when the city was deserted by the fleeing Iraqi army has been turned into clumps of burned out steel littering the road leading out of Mosul to Syria. Haider al-Abadi, the Prime Minister, has declared Iraq freed from ISIS with help of the U.S. and its allies and can now begin to unite the country. Right now Iraq is really three countries, divided between Kurds, Sunnis and Shia. Abadi, Prime Minister since 2014, has done much to bring the three populations together as one; what remains to be seen is whether he can keep Iranian terrorists from infiltrating the government and taking over Iraq itself. For now a great victory has been won and in the process America is safer today than it was a year ago when ISIS reached its apex holding half the country in its death grip. This is Mary Silva signing off from Mosul."

At the end of July Bing Smith reported to the President and then to Senate and House committees the situation on the ground militarily and politically.

"On April 1st we moved against ISIS in Mosul where they had been in control since 2014. Prior to that Ramadi and Falluja had been recovered. Nothing was done about Mosul for almost three years which allowed them time to prepare for our offensive. Unfortunately political considerations by the previous administration caused the delay which in my judgment resulted in costing more lives. Notwithstanding that history, ISIS has now been deprived of all the cities and territory it captured during its occupation of Iraq which began with the capture of Falluja in January of 2014. They continue to occupy territory in northern Syria where they are trying to topple Assad, the Syrian dictator, and at the same time mount a hit and run operation against the Iraqi security forces. As I have previous outlined all the cities we have previously retaken are being protected by Iraqi Army garrisons in conjunction with American forces. This is the type of arrangement we've had in South Korea since 1955. As to whether we will pursue ISIS in Syria; that is already being accomplished on a smaller scale with air attacks and Special Forces operating in limited numbers. Because of the complex political situation in Syria it has not been determined how much force we will have to bring to bear."

Commenting on the General's remarks before the congressional committees, Thomas Coburn of the *Los Angeles Chronicle* wrote in his column the following day:

"Appearing before two congressional committees, General Bing Smith, allied commander in Iraq declared ISIS was essentially defeated in Iraq and that our forces would be there for an indefinite period. I pose the question: is that the right policy for the United States? I don't think so. We've poured billions into a country that has proved it can't govern itself. How many more billions must we pour in and for what purpose? President Sullivan tells us it is essential to keep Iraq and Afghanistan from going ISIS, and thereby blocking Iran from expanding terrorism into a Middle East caliphate. Sounds plausible without considering what it would cost to maintain up to 40,000 troops in both countries indefinitely. Are the radical Islamists that much of a threat? Or have they been pretty much demolished as a result of General Bing's recent victory in Iraq. A valid argument can be made that he did such a good job it will be impossible for them to recruit and build back to where they were. As for Syria the Russians are in the process of killing ISIS there with the intent of propping up Assad or someone of their choosing. They planted the flag first in Syria when President Obama sat by and did nothing to stop them. I say let them have Syria, a country that is destitute and will take years to recover from the war. What I've said others are saying. Where is President Sullivan leading us? To all out war in the Middle East? If he follows through with his plan to duplicate what General Smith did in Iraq in Afghanistan then I think we are headed for big trouble not only with Islam but also with the Russians."

CHAPTER 16

KATHRYN'S INVOLVEMENT WITH John Riley was far more serious than she let on at Christmas. She and Riley had talked seriously about marriage as early as October, 2017. His law practice was booming and she had a net worth of over four million dollars and they both wanted a family so it came down to when to tie the knot. When her sister, Sharon, announced at Christmas she would be married in June the two young women got together and decided a double wedding would be practical. They checked with the husbands to be neither of whom had any objections; so it was resolved that the wedding mass would be at St. Matthews Cathedral in Washington with the reception to be held at the White House.

Mary Sullivan was very excited about the wedding plans and threw herself into helping her daughters prepare for the biggest and most important event in their lives. Michael, busy conducting the affairs of state, was on the periphery of the preparations yet not a part of it. Mary, of course, kept him informed of developments and as the time neared for the event he began to catch some of the excitement pulsating through the entire Sullivan clan.

Part of the protocol required meeting the parents of the two grooms and so they invited the Culhanes and the Reillys, separately, to dinner at the White House.

Tim Culhane came from Green Bay, Wisconsin where his father practiced as a cardiologist and his mother an author of books on travel. Sharon had Tim to the White House on several occasions before his parents came to dinner and the relationship with Michael and Mary was warm the minute they were introduced. He was one of three boys, the other two choosing to become lawyers. Like Michael and Jack the two had graduated from Georgetown University Law School. So when Dr. and Mrs. Culhane came to the White House for dinner it was like home coming weekend at the old school. The evening turned out to be an old fashioned family reunion.

It turned out Dr. Culhane met his wife in New York while completing his third year as a resident at New York-Presbyterian Hospital and she had just graduated from Manhattanville College in New York. She a New Yorker and he from Wisconsin. She was reluctant to leave New York for Green Bay but after living there for 40 years and raising a family, she like the rest, had settled down to being an avid Packer fan and only went to New York to visit family. Michael and Mary were delighted with the Culhanes and the evening was one of merriment, Irish jokes and good conversation about travel and politics and the best time by far was had by the parents of the to-be weds all to the amusement and joy of their children.

The second meeting with the family of John Reilly took place a week before the wedding, again at the White House. The senior Reillys appeared with their son and after introductions were made got down to the serious business of meeting the in-laws. John's father, Timothy Reilly was a small business man, as he referred to himself, in Williamsburg, Virginia. He had attended William and Mary College and upon graduation became employed at the largest hardware store in the area; when the owner died Tim had saved enough, together with some insurance money the owner had provided, to buy the business from the estate. With rapid growth in the historic city he was able to triple the amount of revenue, so much so he was able to put four children through college. The Reillys met in Williamburg and like the Culhanes raised a good sized Catholic family, two boys and two girls just like the Sullivans. Like the visit with the Culhanes, Michael and Mary found the Reillys to be a solid family, a little more serious than the boisterous Culhanes yet fitting in nicely with the triumvirate of Sullivan, Culhane and Reilly.

In view of the wars in Iraq and Afghanistan the Sullivans felt the wedding should be low key and not the huge event the press, especially the Washington press corps, wanted to make it. Instead of being held at the White House as the Tricia Nixon wedding had been in 1971 or Lynda Johnson's in 1967, with great fan fair and publicity, they decided to have the wedding in the church and the reception with 400 guests at the White House.

When the brides arrived at St. Matthew's Cathedral, Saturday, June 2, four thousand people were stacked six deep along Rhode Island Ave. with another two thousand on Connecticut Ave a half block to the West. A fifteen foot platform had been constructed on Rhode Island Ave directly across the street from the church inasmuch as T.V. cameras were not permitted in the church so all the networks had cameras and crews recording the dignitaries entering and exiting the church. Inside the cathedral, originally constructed in 1840 and where the funeral of John F. Kennedy was held after his assassination in 1963, the ushers, grooms and best man all dressed in black morning coats, gray waist coats, striped trousers, gray cravats and black shoes, awaited the brides and the father of the brides, dressed in like attire. At the first strains of Felix Mendelssohn's wedding march the maids of honor and the bridesmaids came slowly down the aisle as 800 heads strained to get a view of the pretty girls smiling and nodding as they approached the altar. Then as the music reached a crescendo down the aisle came the President of the United States, Michael Sullivan, with Sharon Sullivan on one arm and Kathryn on the other. The sight was one so seldom seen that when the guests caught the majesty of it they broke into loud applause and even a few cheers. The newspapers said it was a breakdown in protocol but under the circumstances "very American." The Cardinal said the mass with the assistance of thirty priests and when it was over the two grooms took their brides back down the aisle to be greeted by a crowd later estimated at twenty thousand by the U.S. Park police. Cameras whirred, still photographers captured the scene for posterity and the Metropolitan Police with twenty five motorcycles blaring their sirens cleared a path back down Connecticut to the White House followed by eight limousines surrounded by black SUV's loaded with armed secret service personnel. As the motorcade reached Pennsylvania and 17th, suddenly the lead limousine with the grooms and brides stopped and the brides and their husbands got out of the car and walked to the curb and began to shake hands with thousands of tourists and the just curious who came to see what all the noise was about. Doors flew open on the SUV's and 50 armed agents rushed to separate the couples from the crowd. Concerned why the motorcade had stopped Michael asked the driver if anything was wrong. "I'm getting in my ear Mr. President the lead vehicle with your daughters stopped at 17th street and they are shaking hands with the crowd."

"Tell your lead to get hold of those two and tell them to get back in that car or I will personally leave this car and come down to 17th and spank them both in front of their fans." As ordered he contacted the lead and repeated the President's exact words. Fortunately, the car began to move again and the crisis was over. Mary took his hand and said with a twinkle in her eye: "Michael I've seen you do things like that where do you think they get it from."

"Well," he said a little sheepishly, "when you put it that way I guess it isn't so bad. I'm sure the people loved it, the secret service I'm not so sure."

Four hundred guests watched as the newlyweds danced, the grooms fathers danced with Mary and before long everyone but the White house staff were dancing up a storm. Michael cautioned his daughters not to pull another stunt like the 17th street campaigning and they assured him they would not since they intended to marry only once. With that assurance he joined in the party and had a wonderful time forgetting for a couple of hours the burden he carried as defender of the Republic. In all the Sunday papers across the country a picture was carried on the front pages showing the two brides and their husbands in formal attire shaking hands with the public gathered on 17th street. It seems an AP still photographer was stationed at the corner of 17th and Pennsylvania hoping to get a picture of the President coming back to the White House. When the lead limousine stopped and the bridal party jumped out and started shaking hands with the crowds on the sidewalk the photographer decided to forgo his assignment and capture what he thought might be the picture of the year, maybe even a Pulitzer prize winner. AP had the good sense to put it on the wires and realizing the potential for a picture that showed the humanity of the President's daughters and sons in law editors all over the country splashed it on their front pages. Years afterwards Michael would invariably call attention to the picture as the one thing he remembered most about the wedding.

• • •

Michael Sullivan's election was a stunning setback for the leftist Mikos Tabor, although not a complete surprise. His world view was socialistic. He sought power through redistribution of wealth. It was his intention to back politicians who viewed the world through his eyes and would do his bidding; Michael Sullivan was the antithesis of Mikos and what he stood for. The day after Michael Sullivan became President-elect Mikos Tabor began putting together a plan that would stymie his every move. To accomplish this goal he called on the former Democratic Majority Leader, Boyden Johnson, to spearhead his plan of attack. With the election of the Republican Sullivan the Democratic Party was left leaderless and with no one on the political horizon who could lift them from their travails. With such a vacuum the Republican Party could redo everything that had been accomplished by Barack Obama. To Tabor's mind two things had to be accomplished to stop a Republican steamroller. First the Democrats had to win back the Senate to stall legislation. With the Senate holding down the fort, the Democratic Party would have to build back up from the grass roots and promote candidates with national reputations. Mikos, a billionaire many times over, had the resources to finance dozens of senate races which would take place in 2018 when the Democrats would have 23 seats to defend. With the Senate held by the Republicans 52 to 48 it would be necessary for the Democrats to hold all their incumbents and pick up five Republican seats to take control of the upper house. He realized the House of Representatives would be in Republican control for at least six more years so the firewall had to be in the Senate.

Three weeks after the election in November 2016 Mikos called together in his New York apartment the heads of think tanks, newspapers, magazines talk shows, many of which he financed totally or partially and all of whom relied on his financial support. Along with this cadre he asked Boyden Johnson's lobbying group centered in Washington D. C. to head and coordinate the group. Having been bested by John Kennedy on numerous occasions he advised the group of his plan and an added feature that would consist of a smear campaign against Kennedy and then tying him to the Republicans and particularly Michael Sullivan. Boyden Johnson would be in charge of finding strong Democrats to run against Republican Senate incumbents and orchestrating a smear campaign denigrating John Kennedy and then tying him to President Sullivan. He told the group money would not be an object. With lucrative contracts in their pockets they left New York to put the Tabor plan into effect.

As promised, in 2017 Mikos's plan to paint a sordid picture of John Kennedy went into full sway. First stories started to appear about the "Man behind Sullivan." Kennedy was pictured as a robber baron who had plundered, and cheated his way to his fortune. A man who controlled President Sullivan from the very start of his career. All of a sudden, after a year of pummeling, John Kennedy was as well known as most movie stars. A couple of months after Tabor's minions started their campaign Kennedy discovered who was behind it and called in his aides to plot a counter attack. Sloan and company was called in to get stories in the press and media telling the real story of Kennedy the self made man. A man of integrity wanting nothing for himself but everything for his country. By midyear of 2017 stories were planted in newspapers throughout the country telling the public of the plan of the socialist Mikos Tabor to tear down America and transform it into a socialist country. That his strong arm man was the notorious ex Democratic Majority leader, Boyden Johnson;

naming the various radical media outlets he controlled. So that by the end of 2017, both men who preferred to operate behind the scenes where suddenly thrust into the limelight as public figures. As much as he detested the publicity Kennedy, with superior forces, came off as a hero and Mikos as a predator. Realizing Mikos would not go away Kennedy kept his forces at work exposing the Tabor network and what they hoped to accomplish at every opportunity. Despite Kennedy's campaign Mikos kept to his goal of capturing the Senate. If he could accomplish that he could succeed in stopping Republican legislation and more importantly appointment of Republican Judges and most of all Supreme Court Justices of which Michael Sullivan would have at least three more opportunities. So the battle raged on.

Come August of 2018 President Sullivan went back on the hustings to promote Senate incumbents and those challenging the 23 sitting Democratic senators. Mary Sullivan went to Kiawah, South Carolina to be joined by Megan Sullivan and her four children where they planned to stay until the President and Jack joined them for the Labor Day week-end. Tom Donovan was left to run the White house, while Michael and four assistants to the President headed for Pennsylvania to a fund raiser in Pittsburgh, where one million dollars was raised for the party followed by a huge rally in Philadelphia where Michael urged the 5,000 attendees to elect the challenger, Connell, arguing that the Senate had 55 Republicans and needed 5 more to be able to cut off Democratic filibusters and pass laws with a majority vote. As he travelled to Delaware, Indiana, Michigan and Virginia his message was the same "give me a filibuster proof Senate and we will pass the laws that will promote economic growth." In Montana, North Dakota and Missouri he told them the country was coming back economically as a result of cuts in the income, corporate and capital gains taxes. Offering proof of his claim he told the crowds the Gross Domestic Product would reach 3.8 % in 2018, the highest since 2007.

After a fund raiser held Richmond, Virginia, John Kennedy who had been instrumental in setting up such events all over the United States, stayed overnight with the President at the White House and after a steak and potato dinner they adjourned to the family living room to enjoy an after dinner brandy and in Kennedy's case a Cuban cigar, the President confining himself to a domestic corona.

"Michael how are you doing physically after twenty five cities in fifteen days?"

"I find it invigorating John meeting the people who are helping our cause and, as for the crowds I sense, from their enthusiasm and reception we've been getting, they feel things are getting better economically. When our Trade Representative got tough with the Chinese our exports started moving. Their idea of getting ownership in every business we tried to set up over there was nothing less than extortion and they've been doing it for years. No more. It's the age old story---push and the bully backs down. Sure I'm a little tired still I'm heading out to Missouri, North Dakota, Minnesota and Nevada next week. We've got to increase our Senate majority with the possibility of appointing two and maybe more Supreme Court Justices this term. And to change the subject how do like your new celebrity courtesy of Mikos Tabor?"

A dark look came over Kennedy's face before he answered. Michael was sorry he asked the question when he saw the other man's look. Nevertheless the entrepreneur answered with a big smile: "It's a pain Michael. It's tougher to do business because they know too much about me. I guess once you get involved with politics it happens. My only regret is that the little guy is trying to target you by tarring me. You'll notice, however my men did a job on him that makes the devil look like a saint compared to him. I don't mind beating his brains out but he just keeps coming back pouring money into his left wing outlets. I guess that's the price we pay for being on top. I'm sure he will be around the next four or five years although he's about 84 years old."

"The trouble is you can't get rid of the socialists, or Democrat-Socialists I should say. When Mikos dies some-one else will take up his cause," Michael philosophized.

"I know you probably haven't made up your mind whether or not to run for re-election but on the assumption you are, Tom, Paul and I are already laying the ground for the re-elect campaign."

"To the contrary, John I have made up my mind, sub-ject to Mary's veto or Divine Intervention. From my present vantage point there is so much to be done that it can't be accomplished in a four year term. The last four years, if we are successful, will be the toughest if the Democrats gain the upper hand in either house. If they don't we will be able to set the course for the next fifteen to twenty years should they gain the White House in 2024. I'm thinking I could appoint three more Justices to the Supreme Court and at least two thirds of the Circuit Courts of Appeal. That's why it so important that we add to our Senate position. The Democrats have wasted years on feathering their Washington nests paying no atten-tion to building back their party from the ground up. The best they could put forward in 2016 was Hanna Hamilton and no one coming up from the farm clubs. So I'm optimistic about winning a second term."

"Well our friends will delighted to hear that; with your acquiescence I will pass the word and we will start mov-ing at a faster clip." That was settled as far as Kennedy was concerned so he, Paul and Tom Gavin would be free to, first re-start the financial superstructure that had proved so effective in Michael's 2016 campaign and second to start picking those who, with Jocko O'Brian, would form the nucleus of the Re-Elect Sullivan campaign 2020.

"Can I offer you another brandy, my friend since there just the two of us we might as well relax a bit." He had never known the Irishman to turn down a brandy so without his replying he poured two brandies for them and sat back down on the couch in a relaxed position facing Kennedy sitting in the chair opposite. After a couple of cocktails before dinner, wine with and a brandy Kennedy felt in an expansive mood and gestured at the room around him after he been handed his drink by the President of the United States.

"Can you believe this Michael, here we are sitting in the living quarters of the White House drinking brandy and smoking cigars and you the most powerful man in the world according to the pundits and me a little fellow who made good. Could you ever foresee something even close to this when we met and decided you should run for congress?"

"Tell you the truth John I thought it was a big step into the unknown when I left a booming law practice to run for the House. All because you said I had a duty to serve. As it turns out you were right. I've been able to do more for more people than I ever could have done practicing law. Besides I will only be 69 when a second term is over and I'm sure Paul would take me back into the firm."

"Take you back to the firm, are you crazy? Having a President of the United States as senior partner in a Washington law firm! Who wouldn't kill for that privilege?"

Michael laughed at his friend's enthusiasm and at the same time realized it would be a long struggle before he was ever able to go back to practicing law but the thought of it gave him a comfortable feeling knowing there could be life after the presidency.

"I'd be curious Michael, what do feel now after having been in the office over eighteen months is the greatest geopolitical threat to us?" This was a question of real interest to John Kennedy, from a business standpoint as well as a military one.

"When we were campaigning I thought a great deal about that but seldom if ever got into it deeply. I feel the same now as I did then. It seems to me there are three spheres of influence that will have to be considered in the next few years: Europe and the threat of Russia. They are far less potent now than at the end of World War II, still with Putin as the duly elected dictator for the next few years, they will try to push into the Baltics, Finland, and Ukraine. If not stopped they will invade Poland as impracticable as that may seem now.

The second sphere would be Asia where the Chinese are willing and able to make some loud noises and even invade Taiwan, Formosa. They can even make trouble through their client-state North Korea. You'll recall the Chinese did a great deal of the fighting for North Korea in the 1950 Korean War. I think they are going to be bogged down trying to keep a billion and a half people happy and under communist control, plus they are trying to practice communism and capitalism at the same time and from what we know of their economy they are not too successful at it.

The third sphere is the Middle East, and that's where we are now beginning to get a plan in place. Our sworn enemy there is Iran and their great plan to turn the area into a fifteenth century caliphate. By being present in Iraq and Afghanistan we have Iran surrounded. Of the three I consider Iran to be the most immediate threat if they get a nuclear bomb. In my judgment they are every bit as reckless as the North Koreans. The trick here will be to disable their bomb making facilities before they can threaten Israel and the entire region with surrender or annihilation. Those facilities will have to be taken out by us or the Israelis. The other option would be to have people on the ground in Iran who could get into the facilities themselves and blow them up."

"It's that serious Michael?" Kennedy asked genuinely concerned from the look on his face.

"My predecessor fooled around too long and has put us in great jeopardy. Action will have to be taken."

"My God Michael if we did something on our own or with the Israelis it could result in Armageddon."

"Granted and if done correctly with a surgical strike that completely disabled their ability to retaliate they would be finished as a threat in the Middle East and hopefully leadership would revert to Egypt and Saudi Arabia as it was after World War II. I don't know the answer yet but I do know the only thing these people understand is force."

By this time it was almost midnight so it was decided Kennedy would stay overnight and leave in the morning. When he finally got into his bed he lay awake thinking about his discussion with the President of the United States. One conclusion he drew was he would not like to be in his shoes. The President clearly had a grasp of the geopolitical problems facing the United States. Solving them was another matter. He knew the can had been kicked down the road for years by the Democrats yet from the way Michael described the situation kicking the can would no longer suffice. He wondered if the American people even guessed how dire the Iranian problem was. He finally fell into a troubled sleep.

• • •

As promised Jack and the President made it to Kiawah Island for the Labor Day weekend and were blessed with sunny skies and little or no wind on their three days at the beach. With secret service agents on the beach in bathing suits surrounding them Michael, Jack and the four grandsons attacked the waves with vehemence and the laughter and yelling could be heard up where the houses were, though not on the beach that had been cleared for their use. Because the public was not allowed while the President or his party used the beach, Michael made it a point to fight the surf which he enjoyed immensely for a limited amount of time and then go back to the house so neighbors could share in the enjoyment without secret service in sight with their famed ear pieces. Making a note to himself, he intended to speak to the head of the service next time the family came to Kiawah island to make arrangements for the public to use the beach at the same time as the President and his party.

Nothing of any great note happened while he was at the beach so it turned out to be a short but beneficial vacation playing tennis with Jack every day and romping in the ocean with his grandsons. When the time came to go everyone was just a little sad to leave the island and talked about coming back for Christmas when the girls and their husbands could come and maybe even Peter could make it back from Rome. That was the hope they all carried with them as Jack and Megan Sullivan went back to their home and the law practice and the boys back to school. Mary went back to the White House and Michael flew to his first fall campaign stop in St. Louis, Missouri where the five special assistants had been working over Labor Day to turn out a crowd of 10,000 at the Family Arena in St. Charles across the river from the city.

When the President and his men arrived they could see the advance team had done their job with what the fire marshal later admitted to the press was at least 12,000 people and people still in line. On this day he was touting the incumbent Senator who was in a close race with his Democratic opponent.

When Michael strode on stage after an introduction by the Senator he went right to the speaker's stand, unscrewed the microphone from its perch, went to the front of the stage and said: "We will win this race, we will add Senators to our current number and we will continue to build this country back." They roared back at him: "YES WE WILL, YES WE WILL."

That set the tone for the rest of his speech in which he explained how important it was to have the Senators needed to confirm appointments to the Supreme Court of which there could be at least three more. He explained, with majorities in the House and Senate, he would seek and pass the laws they had elected him to pass. He had cut and would continue to cut the thousands of regulations that his predecessor had written that were smothering small and large businesses alike. And finally when introducing the incumbent he told the cheering throng he needed their Senator. It was all said in twenty minutes and the crowd loved it. The Senator went on for a half hour, but the crowd didn't mind; they'd come to see the President and they were not disappointed. Two days later the polls showed the Senator had increased his lead to nine points. The press gave due credit to Michael's coattails and in their columns said he could be the one weapon the Republicans had to insure the Congress and the Presidency would be of one party for the next four years.

Michael moved on to Minnesota, North Dakota, Florida and Maryland thru the first ten days in October. As he moved from state to state and city to city the crowds got bigger and bigger. In some ways he was leading his incumbents and challengers against the Democrats and by mid-October he had so many requests to speak Tom Donovan was busy turning them down telling the senate campaign chairmen he would only go into those states with the closest races on the last two days before the election.

In the meantime, while on the road, Michael had all the facilities at hand that would be at his disposal in the White House. Every day no matter where he was a CIA briefer would give him overnight developments from every part of the world including the battlefield in Afghanistan. Peter Bartholomew reported by secured phone while he was in Florida that with the addition of 15,000 troops to the 5,000 already there they were beginning to push in Helmand province north of Kandahar, with casualties light compared to the territory they were taking back from the Taliban.

Progress in the two war zones gave Michael a sense that things would work out in the battle against ISIS; that by the spring of 2019 they should have a strong foothold in both countries allowing the country to turn its attention to other ISIS enclaves in an ongoing effort to stifle the advance of radical Islam. As ISIS continued to attack in the large cities of Europe and parts of the Muslim world itself, countries began to see they were as vulnerable to the terrorists as the United States and therefore the enemy of the United States was also their enemy.

For the moment he had to turn his attention away from the wars and concentrate on the campaign that would decide whether his party could continue to hold the Senate or not. As expected, a call came to go to New Jersey two days before the November 6 where the Republicans had a good chance to take the seat away from the incumbent Senator. The polls showed Republicans would hold on to their 55 seats and with luck would pick up two more one of which would be the New Jersey seat. Michael asked Mary to go with him convincing her she could do more for the challenger Sheila Thompson than he could. No one could tell later whether it was the two stirring speeches Mary gave in Newark and Jersey City or the fact the President came to campaign in the state. In both appearances she introduced him and in the process managed to get in a ten minute speech she had written herself praising Sheila Thompson as a women with impeccable credentials: lawyer, successful politician, Secretary of State, married and the mother of five children. In a nuanced speech she subtly pointed out the incumbent Senator had a cloud over him which she did not mention and that Sheila Thompson was unblemished by any scandal and had proved her trustworthiness as a public official. It was a tough act to follow for the President yet he tried to tailor his remarks to dovetail with his wife's. Whatever the case, their appearance and remarks contributed to Thompson's upset win. And it was so acknowledged by the *New Jersey Journal* on November 7:

"The polls were razor thin when President and Mary Sullivan came to New Jersey to speak on behalf of Sheila Thompson the new Senator-elect. A lot of voters told our correspondents after hearing the two of them make their plea they actually switched their vote at the last minute. Some credit the President but the women we've talked to say it was Mary Sullivan who pushed the Secretary of State over the top. Who are we to judge."

Back at the White House election night, the Sullivans invited the Kennedys, Galvins, Connollys and twenty other couples to a buffet supper followed by watching election returns. The East room had been set up to mimic what a campaign election night hotel ballroom room would look like. A bar was conveniently placed at one end and tables with light food sprinkled around the room. A large screen was mounted at the other end so that the guests could mingle and converse while keeping one eye on the screen. Strategically placed couches and chairs completed the décor. At seven o'clock polls in the east started to report in and from the very start of the evening the various senate races wove back and forth as one party would win a seat and the other party would lose. At one a.m. the next morning the last race was called, ironically enough, in New Jersey with the final result the Republicans picked up two seats and held all their own to increase their margin to 57. In the house they added to their majority making it 260 to 174. The next morning the *New York Tribune* carried the headline:

DEMOCRATS LOSE AGAIN

"Admittedly, the Democrats had far more Senate seats to defend than the Republicans, still conventional wisdom and history dictates they should have cut the Republicans hold on the Senate to 53 instead of adding to their majority. They did better in the House capping Republican gains to six seats. It all goes back to 2016 when they ran a weak candidate for President because they had no alternative. The party still has not learned the lesson the Republicans learned back in 2008 when they lost the election. They started building from the grassroots, so that when 2016 rolled around they had a surfeit of candidates at every level ready to run. The result: 30 governorships and thousands of legislative seats all over the country. Now the next election is 2020 and there is still time to build a cadre of candidates to match the Republican effort. If they don't, you can be assured the Republicans will be the governing party for the next six to ten years. For the Democrats there is no time to lose."

Michael left the party at 11:30 election night and with a staff of five including Tom Donovan started making congratulatory calls to all the winners in the Senate and the house---fifty in all with the last call to Bailey Long, the Senate Majority leader, at two in the morning. Bailey had been doing the same thing letting the new comers know he would be on hand to welcome them and extending an invitation to join he and the President at the White House prior to their swearing in. It was hard work yet it had to be done to insure party unity.

With the election over Washington's attention turned to phasing out the 115th congress with the passing of minor legislation and preparation of the beginning of the 116th session and the State of the Union Address. Michael had achieved repeal of Obamacare, drafting high school age students to serve the country for one year, reversal of hundreds of executive orders, appointment of a Supreme Court Justice and downsizing many of the government departments. It had been an exciting time in Washington for the new administration still there was a never ending agenda to accomplish so with the ending of the 115th congress, the President and the two houses of congress began to slow the pace, rest over the holidays and come back strong for the new session commencing January 5, 2019.

CHAPTER 17

"PETER, THE SECRETARY would like to see you in his office." The Secretary happened to be Pietro Cardinal Lombardi the newly appointed Vatican Secretary of State, a man who had served in diplomatic posts all over the world but mainly in South America. To the core a diplomat yet a man of humble demeanor. Rare in a Vatican Secretary of State but perfect for the Pope he was serving. Peter, the fourth year student, and part time worker in the Secretary's vineyard, made his way to the Cardinal's office in quick time and he was barely over the threshold of his office when the Cardinal met him arms outstanding giving him the European "faire la bise" kiss of welcome. Motioned to sit down Peter took a seat next to the Cardinal in an office that was quite simple lacking the grandeur of his predecessor who had a flair for French antiques and large expensive paintings. He had not met the Secretary since the appointment so this was a good opportunity to size the man up. Roughly about 68, perfect posture, chiseled features with a prominent Italian nose which in a strange way made him look like someone's idea of a Roman warrior. He had served all over the world in many positions both Apostolic Delegate and Apostolic Nuncio and you could tell from the lines in his face he was a hard worker. When he addressed Peter it was with a soft spoken voice tinged with steel. By reputation he was much like the Pope himself. Humble, conveyed no airs or superiority despite his esteemed position as the number two man in the Catholic hierarchy. Peter felt at ease the minute he sat down.

"How does it feel to be the son of the President of the United States?" This was said in a kind way with a genuine curiosity. Peter understood the priest was truly interested although it seemed a bit forward on a first meeting between the intern and his boss. Nevertheless he took it in the spirit in which it was asked and told the Secretary: "Eminence I really don't think about it that much. My father has been in politics for some years now and the family is pretty used to it except having secret service protection all the time is a little cumbersome. The rector has been very good about having them at the college so everyone there thinks nothing of it after three years. I'm proud of my father and what he has accomplished and that's about it." "I have a feeling Peter your father is a humble man and at the same time some would say the most powerful man in the world. A good quality that spells well for your country. I've read through your dossier and I detect you have your father's humbleness. Am I right?"

"That's for others to judge Eminence. I think I'm a hard worker and we all got that from our parents. Their motto has always been '*Ad Majorem Dei Gloriam*' and we all try to live up to that."

"That's a wonderful motto Peter I would hope we all can live up to it. I asked you to visit for two reasons; first I wanted to meet you because I think in days to come we may be seeing more of each other, although you're not yet a priest and secondly our Holy Father would like you to be a courier to your father with this letter." With that he handed him a packet and said with a twinkle in his eye "Don't lose it although I'm quite sure if you did there is nothing in the letter that would be embarrassing to the Holy Father or your father. Can I trust you with it?" Again a twinkle in the eye.

"I've been a messenger before Eminence and my record is clean so far." They both laughed. Peter got a hand shake and was out the door before he knew it; when he looked back he saw the Cardinal already back at his desk working through a stack of documents. The young man left the Secretary of State's office with a warm feeling about the man. He was older than his own father by eight years yet he seemed so much like his father. Peter took an instantaneous liking to the new Secretary and looked forward to perhaps being able to work for him after ordination still a year off. He had expressed the idea it could happen and the Cardinal didn't seem to be the type who said things to flatter or gain favor. For no plausible reason he felt the man he had just met could possibly be a future Pope. More like a kind parish priest than an important Cardinal as the many Cardinals in the curia, he had met, thought they were. He went back to his desk thrilled at meeting the Cardinal and looking forward to his trip home the next day to celebrate Christmas with his family.

The Sullivans decided to spend Christmas in the White House and all showed up except Jack, Megan and their grandchildren. Michael and Mary were disappointed, but understood the parents felt the boys should have Christmas in their own home and besides they intended to come to Washington for Easter. Sharon and Tim Culhane announced their first child was on the way, and not to be outdone, Kathryn and John Reilly announced she was pregnant. It was with real joy in their hearts that the Sullivans, Culhanes and Reillys attended Midnight mass Christmas Eve at St Matthew's Cathedral with the general public, each of whom had to pass through a magnetometer to be seated, a price they were willing to pay to hear mass with their President and his family. With the exception of a hundred secret service men and women spread throughout the church and a battery of television cameras located midway down a side aisle the service was like any other being held all over the city. The homily given by the Cardinal of the Archdioceses of Washington went to the core of what Michael Sullivan believed. He told of the birth of a child in a stable who the prophets foretold would save the World. He grew to manhood, gathered 12 men around him and preached peace, forgiveness and redemption. He said He was the Son of God and His mission was to redeem men from their sins offensive to His Father. The Cardinal said God was angry with the men he created because of their sinfulness and worshipping of false gods yet he loved them so much he sent his Son to be offered as a sacrifice to placate His anger. Why did He want to save mankind? He wanted man, who He created and loved, to have the opportunity to be with Him for all eternity by returning His love and obeying His commandments on earth. As the priest turned to continue the mass, Michael thought to himself it's so simple---- do good avoid evil---- that's what the Lord asks of us. But he knew, as all men know, that is the battle each man must fight for himself and it is a struggle that goes on until there is no breath left in a man to do battle.

Peter gave his father the letter from the Pope the moment he got home and Michael took it and read it privately, disclosing to no one except Mary its contents. In the letter the Pope offered congratulations for Michael's first two years in office saying the U.S. had recovered from its doldrums and appeared working its way back to leadership of the free world. Once again America had become a symbol of hope to the world's oppressed and the threat to religious liberty, which gained a beachhead under the previous administration, has been checked under his leadership and for that he expressed thanks. He went on to say that from a geo-political perspective he feared China posed a threat to

America's leadership and that he should be vigilant and firm with the Chinese who, with internal unrest, would resort to distract its citizens from their plight by telling them the United States is a military threat they must prepare for. On the other hand he asserted China has approximately twelve million Catholics the majority of which are "patriotic Catholics" who follow the tenants of the government the rest "underground Catholics" who owe their allegiance to the Pope. The Pope expressed in his letter that it is a hopeful sign the Chinese communist government allowed any of its citizens to practice their religion. The letter ended with wishes for a prosperous new year for the country and for Michael as President.

Based on the letter Michael requested a briefing paper on the conditions for Christians and particularly Catholics in China surmising the Pope had opened a new outlook on that country, one that had not been highlighted or even mentioned in briefings received from the CIA or any of the Catholic prelates he had talked to in his first two years in office. He decided it could be an issue on which the two countries could reach some common ground.

With the holidays drawing to a close and the beginning of the 116th congressional session Michael began to work on his third State of the Union speech. Tom Donovan worked with the speech writers to come up with some general ideas that had been discussed with the President in informal discussions. In the last few days he had re-written sixty percent of the speech to reflect his approach to informing the nation. As always, preparation was everything. Facts and figures had to be checked and rechecked. Practicing the speech was paramount to effective delivery. He did this over and over until he was satisfied he could convey his message with sincerity, conviction and most of all clarity.

The President

On the night in question he strode into the hall shaking the requisite number of hands, greeting both Democrats and Republican alike, and mounted the steps to the speaker's platform and looked out at the men and women of the new congress which would be in session until adjournment in 2020. After the applause tapered off and he had the complete attention of the room he began by acknowledging appropriate guests and then began to give his speech which would last no longer than thirty minutes where most such addresses lasted at least an hour.

"This evening I wish to discuss with you the State of our Union. It's on the mend. It was badly wounded but I can report to you progress has been made on a number of issues and foreign matters we've had to deal with since taking office two years ago.

Domestically radical changes have taken place in health care; the program known as Obamacare has been scrapped and in its place a private approach has been undertaken in which you can choose your own doctor and buy insurance across state lines which means competition is now a factor and almost everyone can buy insurance if they wish to; it is not mandated. For those who can't afford it a form of subsidized insurance is available protecting against a catastrophic event.

Taxes have been lowered for both individuals and corporations. Formerly 45% of Americans paid no taxes whatsoever. That is no longer the case with every citizen now sharing in the burden even if it be a small sum. Moreover, this year we will be proposing that corporations that have been banking profits overseas and thereby paying no taxes here will be able, under legislation that I think has bipartisan support in the congress, to bring that money back to the U.S. and pay a tax which will be reduced from what it has been for years and which gave companies no incentive to return off shore profits. It will provide a very significant one time boost to tax revenues.

Our military establishments were down to the bare bone at the end of 2016; tonight I am thankful to report the congress has authorized, on a bipartisan basis, a buildup of our Army, Navy, Marines and Air Forces together with the equipment we will need to defend this country and to pursue the Islamic terrorist threat we currently face.

We have put in place the program known as UScorps which consists of a draft of our young men and women to give one year in the service to their country in the military or domestically before they go to college or resume their lives without further education. By doing this service they earn credits towards further education if they choose. The results have been gratifying. They are living together, working together, learning new things together, and working in hospitals, non-profit charitable institutions, building roads, bridges and houses. There are two million of them contributing to the welfare of the country.

The military has asked that women not serve in combat positions and Congress has passed this legislation which I have signed into law. I believe this will strengthen our ability to defend the country in time of war. It does not affect the promotion opportunities of women as some have argued.

With respect to education by using block grants we have returned money to the states so they can run their educational programs at the level the citizen will have a say rather than mandates coming from an all knowing Education Department in Washington forcing all states to conform to some education method having no relevance to what the state deems best for its students. Moreover the Department of education has been reduced in money and personnel to one half of what it was formerly and it will be our intent to reduce it further until its status is one of coordination with and between the states not setting education policy as it has done in the past.

Government itself has been downsized in every Department except defense and Health and Human Services. For quite some time government employees have received higher pay than those in the private sector and had the added advantage of job security. It has been almost impossible to fire incompetent government employees. The first problem has been partially solved with such employees no longer getting automatic raises which has been the case for years. Raises are now based on merit. Something entirely new for the federal worker. Legislation will be offered this year to streamline the ability to discharge incompetent employees by cutting down the number of hearings and options an employee has to delay the firing for years at great expense to the government. We want the best people we can get in the government and we can get those people with paying fair wages and a measure of job security.

We will be submitting to Congress legislation to address the shrinking funds available to sustain Medicare and Social Security. Those proposals will include such changes as increasing the age of eligibility as our life expectancy grows. Raising the rate of contribution. These matters may no longer be neglected and congress knows this and I believe will respond to sensible changes that will restore the financial integrity of both programs. This will be the top priority of this administration

When we took office our national debt was twenty trillion dollars. Ten trillion of that was run up between 2009 and 2016. The budget we will submit to the Congress this year will have some deficit but it will not be adding a trillion dollars of debt per year to the national debt as was the case in the last four years of the previous administration.

We have worked on immigration. A wall has been erected on our southern border, with National Guard troops and immigration officers patrolling, backed up by drones and other devices that have proved effective with the result illegals crossing border have dwindled to almost nothing while at the same time thousands of illegals with criminal records have been disported along with thousands more that have come here illegally. So that after two years a total of one million two hundred thousand illegals have been returned to their country of origin. At the same time we have stopped immigration from the south for an indefinite period and adjusted quotas from other countries to restore balance in our immigration policy. Under congressional authority we have stopped issuing V1 visas that deprive Americans of jobs in favor of those from other countries.

Our economy is beginning to recover and economists are predicting the GNP will reach 4.1 for 2019 which would mean the country is back on sound footing. Polls have told us the American people feel things are getting better and that we are moving in the right direction which is a complete turnabout from two years ago when our people felt we were going in the wrong direction----downhill rapidly.

Turning to foreign affairs and defense of the country I can report to you finally the problem of ISIS and its Islamic terrorist network is being addressed militarily overseas and domestically here in the United States with the addition of more F.B.I. agents being hired and our intelligence agencies gaining more expertise as well as new tools to work with in tracking down ISIS cells as well as lone operators. Abroad we have driven the terrorists from Iraq and are on the threshold of making Afghanistan free of terrorist's domination. As you are well aware ISIS has suffered heavy losses in Syria and we continue to bomb their facilities located in eastern Syria. A new Haven has sprung up in Libya and we have commenced bombing sites we have identified as training camps. This is all taking place against an enemy determined to defeat us and has wrought immeasurable harm against us here and abroad and we have no choice but to hunt them down and destroy them as we would any life threating disease."

After every issue he reported on, the Republican majority rose to their feet and applauded loudly while half the Democratic side arose. Still there was a tangible evidence of bi-partisanship as both parties realized things were improving and they could reach common ground on some issues.

Even the editorial writers were willing to surrender some of their partisanship in favor of a more even approach to what was happening under the new administration.

The *Washington Star* commenting on The President's State of the Union wrote:

"The President's address last night to the 535 legislators making up the House and Senate, was probably the shortest on record. He spoke thirty five minutes and made use of every minute detailing in concise language what his administration had accomplished in two years. It was impressive. Many in the opposition would disagree that the changes made were to the advantage of the people. They should have no complaint. Everything he discussed last night he promised he would do as he campaigned for the presidency. The Democrats campaigned on a platform of higher taxation and more spending Republicans campaigned on less government and lower taxes. The Republicans won. So far the country is doing better than it did before President Sullivan came into office. Not even the loyal opposition can deny that. If things keep getting better, even slowly, the President could well be looking at a second term if he chooses to run. Time will tell"

In like manner the liberal flagship of the left, the *New York Tribune*, on their editorial page made like sentiments but more tepid.

"We followed closely the remarks delivered last night to members of the 116th congress at the annual gathering known as the 'State of the Union.' Some would say it was short and sweet, certainly the Republican members would say so, not so much the Democrats. All must admit we are doing better as a country now than we were under President Obama. In President Sullivan we have a man who has come in with the intent of changing the direction and the philosophy under which the country is to be guided. More than that he has proven to be a leader as opposed to leading from behind. Many disagree with his approach and his conservative ideology still it cannot be argued the man has not set the tone and he is a leader. This is not to endorse him for there is much that is undone both here and abroad. But for his first two years it cannot be denied he has taken the reins of government and is riding herd on the bureaucracy and the military with uncommon results. We don't always agree yet we applaud his efforts."

• • •

They were gathered in the Roosevelt room across from the oval office: the Secretary of Defense, Robert Butterfield, Robert Fenwick, Director of the CIA, Myron Poston, Head of the National Security Council, Byron Titus, Secretary of State, Peter Bartholomew, Head of the Joint Chiefs of Staff, Tom Donovan, Chief of Staff to the President and the Michael Sullivan. The subject: Syria. Having called the meeting the President acted as chair and asked Myron Poston to present the Syrian problem to be followed by a discussion of what steps to take vis a vie, Syria.

Poston, a man of fifty, had been in his position as head of the Agency for only two years, still he came to the position with a wealth of experience having served as deputy under the previous Republican President and before that as a top CIA agent serving in posts all over the world. Totally familiar with the world situation and America's friends and her enemies; a graduate of Georgetown's Walsh School of Foreign Service he first served in the State Department overseas and in that position became familiar with various CIA station chiefs resulting in his switching to the CIA and subsequently to the National Security Council (a position held by Henry Kissinger and Condoleezza Rice in prior administrations.) A man of few words he was always well received due to the accuracy of his assessments and the rationale used to back them up.

He began: "We all remember when Syria was the force behind Lebanon in 2006 when they engaged in a one month war with Israel. Bashar al-Assad was the President of Syria, having succeeded his father, Hafez al Assad who ran the country for 30 years. Assad is a doctor with a specialty in Ophthalmology and is not to be underestimated. All was going well for him until 2011 when, in conjunction with the Arab Spring and the overthrow of Zine el-Abidine Ben Ali in Tunisia, Murbarak in Egypt, Muammar Gaddafi in Libya and Ali Abdulla Saleh in Yemen, some of the natives became restless which led to a minor uprising followed by a heavy handed crack down by Assad and from there into a full fledged civil war. At first there were just the Syrian rebels. Then others joined in against the Assad Royalists. The Shia militias backed by Iran's revolutionary guards came in on the side of Assad. Then ISIS got into the fray followed by the Russians who backed the government. This map I've put up shows who is in control of Syria now. In the north central part of the country ISIS is in charge and strings out south to the southern border marked as black on the map; eastward from ISIS are the Kurds all the way to the eastern border of Syria which they control. The Kurds are marked in yellow. Along the far western boundary are the royalists in red and the Syrian opposition in the green. In the lower southeast you again have the royalists in red and opposition forces around the Golan Heights. Under the previous administration confusion reigned and we tried to train and equip some of the rebels hostile to Assad and that turned into a fiasco. As you are well aware the Russians moved in when we failed to act and now they run the country with Assad the nominal head. For how long we don't know. He seems content to take orders and as long as he does they will probably let him stay. This was a country of 22 million; half had to leave their homes, 250,000 have been killed. What we are concerned about now is ISIS is still operating in Syria. Do we continue to bomb, send in ground troops or limit ourselves to special ops just to keep them off stride?"

Myron Poston spoke first. "We have developed a plan where we bomb and use Special Forces. First we want to block them from running guns and personnel into Iraq. That we have pretty much accomplished by securing the Iraq border. The bombing and special ops part would amount to a guerilla war against ISIS chiefly around Raqqa where they maintain what they call their 'capital.' All this has been worked on with Defense and State." Both Secretaries nodded toward the President letting him know Myron was stating their thinking as well as his own. "At this point I will end my contribution to the discussion."

"We've considered an option of sending in troops and have actually game planned how we would do that and how many troops would be needed although we have concluded that is a last ditch option and not practical at this point." From his seat in the center of the table the Secretary of Defense went on to explain in detail what Myron Poston had laid out in summary.

At that point the Secretary of State spoke up saying: "let me play the devil's advocate about continued activity in Syria. The question I raise is whether we run into the Russians on purpose or accidently and all of a sudden we have a potential shooting war between them and ourselves? Anybody care to address that point?" The Secretary of Defense looked around the table to see if anyone was going to jump in to answer the question and seeing no hands and hearing no sound and the President content to await an answer he volunteered: "Byron you raise a valid point. Let me see if I can address it. Going back to President Bush, the son, our policy has always been we will go after terrorists where they are and we will pursue them in any nation that harbors them. I grant the previous administration did nothing to adhere to that policy being content to sit around and make threats with no follow up, still the policy laid down is as valid today as it was in 2001. Therefore I would think it wise to advise the Russians of our intent. That we are not interested in overthrowing Assad, nevertheless, we do intend to destroy our enemy wherever we find him. Accommodate us, we have no quarrel with you."

"And what if the lads in the Kremlin say stay out of Syria---we're trying to rebuild the country; towns and cities held by ISIS are part of Syria; we feel Assad can bring these towns back within his orbit with our help."

Anticipating this reply Robert Butterfield's demeanor took on a different look. His eyes hardened as he looked around the table focusing principally on the President before he spoke. He knew that in answering this question he would be suggesting policy the United States should follow in any confrontation with the Russians in Syria; still he did not hesitate to speak about a subject he and generals at the Pentagon had given a great deal of thought to. After a pause he said: "in that case I would advise the Russians we will bomb and send special forces into Syria as long as it provides a safe haven and jump off point for ISIS fighters to enter Iraq; if problems arise in the pursuit of this policy we will be happy to work it out to avoid any military confrontation between us and them."

"I think that's a pretty good answer Byron, what do you think?" Michael asked.

"I think Robert is a good lawyer, Mr. President, fast on his feet and I think he has raised a valid point one that has to be considered when we come to how we solve the Syrian situation."

They were two hours into the meeting when a knock came at the door. Everyone look startled at what could possibly be so important as to interrupt what everyone in the West Wing knew; that a strategic conference of the highest importance was being conducted in the Roosevelt Room. The President calmly said: "come in," knowing whatever it was that was coming would be of high priority since no one working in the West Wing would dare to interrupt the discussion for some trivial matter. A young man came in and went directly to Tom Donovan and handed him a note. He turned and exited the room as quickly as he had entered. All looked at Tom. "The Associated Press is reporting that Iran has captured, and that is the word they used 'captured' one of our patrol boats that travel between Kuwait and Bahrain,"

All eyes were on him with no words uttered by anyone at the table waiting for him to finish. He continued: "They are getting this from Iranian news services saying all on board had been 'captured' and would be held in Iranian custody until further notice. That's it."

Everyone's mind fastened on the images seen on January 12, 2016 when the Iranians took eleven U.S. sailors off their patrol boats and held them for twenty four hours before releasing them. The present dispatch sounded more ominous in that the Iranians were talking of holding them for an undisclosed period of time. Michael Sullivan immediately took over the meeting. Speaking softly and calmly he asked them to cancel any further plans they had for the evening.

"We will meet in the war room at 8:00 p.m. In the meantime I want all of you to contact your agencies, garner all the information you can and ascertain exactly what the situation is. We need to know when, where, how before any steps are taken. Once we have the preliminaries we will have a statement for the press and the country."

The Secretary of Defense was ordered to return to the Pentagon and return that evening with the military personnel required with a plan for retaliation if need be. The intelligence agencies were ordered to bring the latest intelligence to the meeting. Tom Donovan was ordered to alert the speech writers to prepare a short speech to the American people alerting them to the situation and what the President intended to do about it. All White House staff was ordered to stay in place until further notice. Peter Bartholomew was ordered to put all military on standby until further notice. Finally leaders of the House and Senate were to be alerted for a meeting with the President at eight a.m. the following day. As for the President he made his way from the oval office to the living quarters to prepare for the 8:p.m. meeting. Tom Donovan was asked to take any messages to the President.

"Michael this is very serious isn't it?" Mary asked the minute he came through the door.

"You've been watching it on television?"

"The Iranians have released pictures of the men captured and it shows them on their knees just like they did in 2016. It's disgusting. What can we do? What will you do?"

"It's very serious Mary; my thinking now is the only thing they understand is force. First I want to know whether they will release our men immediately. If not, then I will convey to them there will be severe consequences if they do not. If they still refuse there will be retaliation far beyond what they could possibly imagine. I've called a meeting for eight o'clock this evening to get some advice on how to proceed. By then we should have enough facts to make a decision. I've left word to notify me here if anything breaks. Why don't we order a couple of sandwiches and watch the television to see what they're showing."

She switched it on and flashing across the screen was a military man identified as General Ahmed Latifpour, head of the Quds force, the special forces unit of Iran's Revolutionary Guards at what looked like a press gathering in Tehran with an interpreter speaking over his voice saying the twelve Americans had been captured at sea and they would be held and tried for spying activities. That the American government was being notified of the capture and the consequences.

"Turn it off Mary. I'll know a lot more from our own people when I get downstairs."

"Michael after you eat, please lay down for a few minutes for a short nap. I'll call you before its time to go to the meeting. The next twenty four hours are going to be demanding and you're going to need all your strength. Will you do that for me? I promise I will wake you up."

"Ok sweetheart get me up at 7:30." Mary was as solid as a rock and he always followed her advice. She knew this was akin to the Russian Missile Crisis that Kennedy faced in October 1962 and knowing his thinking she knew he, like Kennedy, would not back down. He had run for the presidency to rebuild America from the disaster it had undergone for eight years when weakness became America's calling card. The Iranians were testing this President thinking he would make idle threats and not follow through. They were about to find out in a crushing way how mistaken they were.

All participants were seated in the situation room when the President entered at 8:00 o'clock sharp. He took his seat at the head of the conference table and began asking reports from his agency heads and military commanders. After everyone contributed to the store of knowledge gleaned from inquiries at their agencies Michael summed up what appeared to be updated facts. "4 IRGC boats surrounded our vessels in the middle of the Gulf not far from Fair Island, where the Quds maintain headquarters. As you know the Quds are Special Forces who report directly to Ayatollah Ali Khamenei and the kidnapping could not have been done without his approval. We don't know where our men have been taken or how they are being treated but the Iranians have put out videos showing them in captivity and indicating they will be tried for spying. We have had no direct contact with the Iranians. Discussion."

The Secretary of State, Titus, gave his view to the effect we should establish contact with the Iranians as soon as possible and start negotiations for the return of the American sailors despite propaganda by the government of Iran. When asked what the U.S. should do if the Iranians refused to negotiate the matter, he expressed a preference for some sort of military action.

Likewise the Secretary of Defense said he favored a military response and he and the generals from the Pentagon were there to suggest options should the President decide to take the military option. Others advised caution reasoning a military action could result in a strike by Iran raining missiles on Israel as well as our bases in Iraq. Whether for or against military intervention all agreed the Iranians should be contacted immediately either directly or through diplomatic intermediaries and made aware no ransom or other consideration would be paid for return of the men and if their return was not secured within a defined amount of time retaliation would ensue. Until midnight the discussion continued until the President having heard all sides and multiple options decided Iran would be given twenty four hours to arrange a release without conditions. If they failed to comply extensive bombing of military installations would take place along with nuclear facilities and cyber attacks on their grid system. Michael concluded the meeting requesting the following orders be carried out. He would call congressional leaders to the White House advising them of his plans to take action against the Iranians if talk failed. The Pentagon would put in place aircraft to carry out the attack. The Cyber Command would prepare to invade Iranian infrastructure. The Secretary of State was directed to contact our agents in Switzerland requesting that they advise the Iranian government of the U.S. demand for the release of our military men within 24 hours or face serious retaliation. A press release would be put out at 3:00 a.m. advising all media of the demand by our government and the threat of retaliation. Tom Donovan was directed to seek air time from all the networks for the President to address the nation at 11:00 a.m. on the developing crisis.

Phones began to ringing all over the place in Washington from 3:30 a.m. and Michael finally got the congressional leaders in his office at 4:30 a.m. instead of 11:00 a.m. and filled them in on the conversations and decisions that had been made three hours before. Jason Winters, minority leader, was skeptical about the decision to take military action. He favored talk even if it took a couple of weeks. The Senate Minority leader, Seymore Gottlieb, expressed fear that retaliation would bring on the destruction of Israel by long range missiles. They did agree something should be done yet shied away from a military response. On the other hand Bailey Long, Michael's long-time friend in the Senate and the Majority Leader, voiced the opinion they could not back down for to do so would wreak havoc with allies and the American people who had stood by and watched the government do nothing when the Iranians took the U.S. embassy workers hostage in the Carter administration and our sailors during the Obama administration. Other members of the leadership committee present voiced concern and anger at the audacity of the Iranians. All, to some degree, understood they could not stand by and do nothing. With all orders being given and a decision to go forward made, Michael, bone tired went upstairs to a waiting Mary, a bit of food and a chance to get some sleep having been on his feet for almost twenty four hours.

The news rooms around the country and the world were alerted at 5:30 a.m. Television producers began calling "experts" to appear on the morning shows to discuss, postulate, and speculate about what was happening. The *New York Tribune* hit the streets with an early edition proclaiming the country was on the brink of war with Iran. Taking their cue from the press release from the White House they speculated the U.S. would strike the Iranians militarily if the men in custody were not released. They saw it as a possible start of World War III. The *Tribune* cautioned against precipitous decision making by the President. The more conservative outlets said the President should brook no defiance from the Iranians and if need be hit them with whatever force necessary to recover our seamen. The battle of the air waves ensued all the rest of the day with everyone's eye on the clock which would reach the twenty four hour mark at three or four in the early morning. Would the Iranians buckle or would they renege on their threat? For the press the world hung in the balance.

After a two hour nap Michael got on the phone with the Prime Minister of Israel, Aron Cohen telling him of U.S. plans for retaliation should the Iranians fail to release the captured sailors. Cohen listened and when he understood the gravity of the situation he agreed the Iranian action could not be allowed to stand. To do nothing would encourage further hostage taking not only of military but civilians as well. Then Cohen told the President that Mossad, Israel's intelligence service, had knowledge from within Iran that they were months away from getting a nuclear bomb. That for some years Mossad had been working with the National Council of Resistance (NCR) an organization of dissident Iranians with a large intelligence set up in Iran placing workers in Iranian nuclear installations and in particular Fordor and Natanz the latter a deep underground bunker. That several of those workers together with a team of Israelis had been working for years at these facilities and given the word would blow them up. While they could not completely destroy them it would take years to build them back up.

"Mr. President we are ready to go forward and the fact you may have to do the same is fortuitous for us but it is something we were planning to do for our own survival. They are months away and we cannot wait any longer or it will be too late for us."

Michael made no attempt to dissuade the Prime Minister from the course he was outlining and told him the sole purpose of his call was to alert him to the potential of the U.S. bombing Iranian targets and the repercussions it might have on Israel.

"I'm fully aware of the consequences to my country Mr. President by taking the action we are about to take yet for us it is a matter of survival."

Michael told Aron Cohen he understood his position and that risks were being taken by both countries and if successful it would bring stabilization to the Middle East and diminish the Iranian threat to the region.

Receiving clearance from the President, Byron Titus flew to Switzerland to meet with Iran's representative and negotiate with him directly rather than through a Swiss emissary which would normally be the protocol since Iran and the U.S. did not maintain a diplomatic relationship. Almost 15 hours had elapsed since he and the others had been notified of the capture of 12 American sailors by Iran. Now as his plane landed in Bern, Switzerland he gathered papers he had been working on in preparation for his meeting with the Minister of Foreign Affairs, Hassein Kahn who arranged for the two to meet at the Federal Palace, site of the Swiss Parliament. Twenty minutes after deplaning he arrived at the Palace only to be greeted by a swarm of television cameras and shouting reporters. "What's America going to do? Who are you meeting with? Are the Iranians going to back down?" He smiled and kept walking ignoring their pleas and headed straight for the meeting.

While on the plane he reviewed a complete dossier on Hassein Kahn prepared by the CIA. From his reading he knew the man was a hard liner and had served for some years in the Office of the Minister of Foreign Affairs as a minor deputy rising to become the Minister in 2016. He received his orders from the Aytollah Khamenei, the head of State. Short of stature, balding with a mean look about his eyes he could be a formidable adversary in discussions as portrayed in his dossier. When he greeted Byron Titus he had a big smile on his face, as though the discussion to take place was to be friendly and the American would be sent on his way with the message the Alytollah meant business and while talking might achieve some breakthrough it would take months and perhaps some concessions from the United States before an arrangement could be worked out for release of the captives. However, Byron Titus was not of the same mind set and when they came together he gave Kahn a firm hand shake and motioned him to a chair on the opposite side of the conference table. The Secretary had two aides with him in the room, one an interpreter, the other, a potential witness to the proceedings. Kahn had at least eight aides all primed for a long conference with the American Secretary of State.

The Swiss had provided a large conference room for the convenience of the parties complete with note pads, pens and bottled water. The Iranians were in a jocular mood anticipating listening to the Americans begging for release of the prisoners and Hassein Kahn telling them it would be a long time, if ever, before any serious discussion could take place leading to their release. Hassein began the discourse by explaining to the Secretary Iran's version of how and why the capture took place and that it would be necessary to conduct trials of the prisoners for spying on Iran. After a half hour of Iran's position the Minister of Affairs asked the Secretary if he had any disagreement with what he had just heard.

Secretary Titus came forward in his chair, put both elbows on the table, hunched forward looking directly at the Minister and began to speak very slowly so the interpreter could hear and translate it for all the Iranians in the room. The Minister interrupted him saying that he spoke and understood English very well and there would be no need for a translator. Byron Titus cut him off: "I will have the interpreter repeat what I say so that all your aides understand it as clearly as you do what I have to say." He began again: "Mr. Minister I have come a long way to deliver to you and your leader, Aytollah Khamenei, a short message." Kahn's facial expression went from smiling to frozen. He sensed immediately that the man sitting across the table from him was not there to bargain or plead only to deliver a message. The other Iranians were not so perceptive and they were sitting back waiting for the American to beg.

Titus continued: "the message is spelled out clearly on one page in front of me which I will give to you when I conclude saying it verbally so your assistants can understand clearly what I have to say. I have signed the message as agent for the President of the United States and I speak for the President of the United States. You have taken without provocation twelve men of the United States Navy. You have 24 hours to release those men to our custody." He let the translator slowly repeat what he said. For the first time he looked at the Iranians on the other side of the table and he saw they no longer had smirks on their faces but understood something very bad was happening. The man sitting opposite from them was not going to be doing any begging. He was making a statement and most of them were smart enough to realize the meeting was not going to be pleasant. They waited for the Secretary's next statement feeling sure Hassein Kahn would deal swiftly with the American if he became too belligerent.

"If our men are not released within the time frame I have set forth there will be retaliation by the United States at a time of our choosing. I can assure you it will be painful."

Hassein shot back at him: "Are you saying you would take military action against my country----which would be an act of war?"

"I've said what I came to say Minister and unless you have something to say as to when our men will be released I have nothing further to offer.

At least 30 seconds went by in silence. Each side just looked at the other understanding that what the Secretary had just said could lead to Armageddon in the Middle East. Then quick to realize this would be no bargaining session the Minister said: "I will take your message back to our leaders and we will let you know our response in good time." He started to get up and motioned for his aides to do the same planning to walk out of the meeting without any further discussion.

The Secretary remained seated and just as they were about to reach the door of the conference room he said in a loud and unmistakable voice:

"I said you have 24 hours to respond. If we don't hear your response in that time frame there will be retaliation. We don't pay ransom." While the Minister thought he could bluff, the aides knew the American meant what he said and what was supposed to be a lark had suddenly turned into a nightmare. None of them envied the Minister of Foreign

Affairs having to give the Secretary's message to the great ruler, Aytollah Khamenei

The Iranians left the Palace and when Byron Tyson and his associates finally took their leave they ran into a gaggle of reporters waiting outside. "The Minister of Foreign Affairs told us you Americans were being stubborn and wouldn't listen to reason," one shouted. "What did you tell the Iranians?" The Secretary stopped and twenty microphones were thrust at him and sound booms dropped around his head. He talked at the microphones saying: "I advised the Minister that Iran had 24 hours to release our naval personnel." With that, he began inching his way toward a waiting black limousine. Just as got seated in the back seat a reporter stuck a microphone in through the window and asked: "What will America do if they don't comply?" As the window rolled up the Secretary smiled and said: "I suggest you ask the Iranian Foreign Minister."

Once on the plane the Secretary contacted the President over a secure phone in the car and described the meeting and what was said emphasizing the Iranians were completely unaware of what U.S. reaction would be. He said they were taken aback and tried to show some bravado when they were given the message and appeared in shock when they got up and left the meeting confused and stunned by what they had been told. Based on the Secretary's call an emergency meeting was scheduled for eight o'clock in the White House situation room. All the usual participants were present including the Secretary of State whose plane landed at Andrews and he was helicoptered onto the White House lawn ten minutes before the start of the meeting. He gave a complete briefing of his meeting with the Iranian Foreign Minister. Wheels were put in motion for Air Force and Naval units to be prepared to launch an attack within 24 hours of the warning given in Switzerland. General Bartholomew said it would consist of an air, cyber and sea attack.

"Our Stealth bombers will fly from bases in Iraq and Afghanistan. Submarines will fire cruise missiles from the Persian Gulf. Targeted will be the Frontier battalion, Army garrison at Bampur, Allah Akbar garrison, Eslami Rnam Raza garrison, Hashemabad Air Base, Parchin Military base and about another dozen sites. Nuclear sites hit will be Nantanz and Fordor with Massive Ordinance bombs that can penetrate deep enough to do extensive damage. We have been advised the Israelis have some of their own people working inside the plant at Fordor and will be sabotaging the works regardless of what we do. The Israelis will also be hitting military bases and air defense sites other than our targets. All this will commence at a signal from the President. Initially there will be two waves. The first an all out attack. The second will be undertaken if the Iranians fail to capitulate and return our personnel."

"What are the chances of this setting off war in the Middle East?" someone asked. The President answered:

"That's the question of the hour. The truth is we don't know. It's a gamble and the payoff for us will be a very badly disabled Iran unable to advance their aim of conquest in the area or an all out war where they launch long range missiles against Israel along with Hezbollah firing at Israel from the north. I don't think the Israelis would have any difficulty knocking out rockets coming from the north but they would probably take a lot of "incoming" from Iran. As far as Russia is concerned they back Iran; still they won't be too upset to see the Iranian program knocked out."

"What about the public relations debacle we will face if Iran doesn't buckle?"

At this point Michael broke in to answer the question directly. "Whether we are successful or not, initially the press will attack with a vengeance claiming bombing Iran as punishment for taking our personnel is over reaction comparing it to Lyndon Johnson's using the sinking of one of our boats in the Gulf of Tonkin to up the ante in the Viet Nam war. I think the situations are demonstrably distinguishable, even so, the comparison will be made by the pundits. I don't think good or bad press enters into play here. Our objective is to prevent the Iranians from getting a nuclear bomb and if we can do that we will have achieved stability in the Middle East. The Jordanians, Egyptians, Saudis and the Gulf States will welcome the defanging of the Iranians I can assure you. As Jack Kennedy used to say: 'victory has a thousand fathers but defeat is an orphan.' If we succeed in blocking the Iranians they will say we should have done it a long time ago instead of creating fictitious red lines and then backing down as Obama did. If it goes awry we will be the goats. I think we have to take the chance."

That evening the President went on television in a short address to a nation that had been following the Iranian narrative closely. As always, he gave them facts in which he summarized the situation as Iran unlawfully taking U.S. personnel from their vessels in the Persian Gulf under threat of force and threatening to detain them and according to their spokesman, try them in an Iranian court. That the Secretary of State had advised the Iranian Foreign Minister in Bern, Switzerland that if the men were not released to U.S. custody in 24 hours there would be serious repercussions. At the time of his address he told the nation four hours had already elapsed toward the deadline. He stressed this was not an idle threat and the country should be prepared if the Iranians should not comply.The President's reaction to the taking of American seamen caused a bolt of lightning to come down from the throne of the *New York Tribune* in the form of a lead article on the right side of the paper's front page by Sophie Goldfarb one of their top columnists challenging the President's decision:

"Some seven or eight hours ago President Michael Sullivan addressed the nation in a short fifteen minute speech which will have repercussions far beyond his simplistic approach to solving the problem of the capture of our military personnel by a brazen Iranian government. Instead of trying to negotiate with the hostage takers he chooses to threaten them with massive retaliation if our men are not returned within a 24 hour time frame. Is that any way to get them back safely? No. He chooses to put their lives in danger and produce a catastrophic war in the Middle East which we will undoubtedly be dragged into if Iran strikes back from our bombs by raining missiles on Israel. Have the allies been consulted? Has anyone been consulted? If so, we haven't heard about it. We think the President's position is reckless and will only lead to war with Iran and a conflagration of the entire Middle East. In short we condemn his unilateral action and we hope wiser heads in his administration will speak up against it."

Other media of the leftist persuasion took up the chant even before the 24 hour ultimatum exhausted itself. The "main street" press and conservative pundits on television and radio massively came to the President's defense best enunciated by an editorial in the *Cleveland Gazzette*:

"Iran with great hubris, and an obvious sense of invincibility, decided to 'capture' twelve seamen of the United States Navy and put them trial as spies. How could they do such a thing? The answer can be found in recent history when they did the same thing and got away with it dealing with a weak American President. They got away with the theft of the century when they conned the weak President and his even weaker Secretary of State into a deal that allowed the Iranians to do anything they wanted to do to develop nuclear capabilities under the guise of just using nuclear fuel for peaceful purposes. Fortunately this President and the Congress rejected this one sided agreement in 2017. Even then the Iranians didn't get it and continued pursuit of the bomb and spreading terror through the Middle East by backing ISIS Islamic radicals. They apparently think they are still dealing with former President Obama. They will find to their chagrin they are not. Michael Sullivan has drawn a line in the sand and unlike his predecessor will not back down from it. The leftists in this country are afraid to face facts they have not made up. The rest of the country is not. We predict the people will back this President and say 'it's about time.'"

While the media battle raged the President and his advisors were awaiting developments in the situation room. In Iraq and Afghanistan aircraft were armed and awaiting the order to attack as were submarines in the Gulf. At the 10 hour mark Byron Titus reported there had been no sign from the Iranians they intended to release their hostages or even discuss the matter. Fifteen hours after the ultimatum was issued Iranian television announced through a series of speeches by government officials that the ultimatum issued by the United States amounted to a bluff which they intended to call. Their message: "We will proceed as planned." Some in the room said they have spoken let's proceed. The President said: "No we will wait the full 24 hours. I suggest we meet back here this evening at 6:00 p.m. and a final decision will be made."

They met as agreed and when nothing was received from the Iranians Michael gave the order to strike. They struck with great force at 4 a.m. Iran time March 15th 2019. All targets were hit with precision and surveillance showed the missiles and aircraft had done as intended. Several hours after the attack a tremendous underground explosion was detected which meant the Israelis were successful in their sabotage efforts at the Fordo complex; that and with the bombs dropped by the Stealth B2s, American and Israel intelligence estimated the nuclear facilities would be out of commission for years. Sitting in the situation room everyone was waiting for an all out counter attack from Iran. Nothing happened in the first hours after except two long range missiles launched into Israel one of which was shot down and a second doing minor damage. Hours passed. Iranian television, picked up all over the world, condemned the action as a cowardly attack and said there would be consequences. No word came concerning the hostages. On the 17th a second attack was ordered more punishing than the first. On the 18th Iranian officials by way of a back channel through the Swiss signaled the hostages would be released in return for a cessation of attacks.

All the key participants were in the room when the Iranian message was received. The President asked those present to say a silent prayer of thanks for the success of the mission. The Iranians had backed down and the President's gamble had paid off. Iran would no longer be a threat to the world with its nuclear ambitions. The victory was not without loss. Ten American pilots went down with their aircraft and the Israelis had at least 50 people give up their lives in the sabotage effort at Fordo.

World reaction was expected and it came with an onslaught of condemnation. The Russians led the attack claiming the strike against Iran was an outrage and compared it to Hitler's attack on the Soviet Union in 1941. China and North Korea chimed in. After a week passed the Allies, one by one, began to breath a sigh of relief and with Iran neutralized praised the United States and its President for the courage to brandish the bully. Some European Capitals went so far as to state that America, after a hiatus of eight years, was back in place as the world's leader. More time passed and by summer people were holding their heads high knowing they had leadership at the helm in Washington.

CHAPTER 18

AT THE SAME time Iraq was being secured the President authorized 20,000 troops to Afghanistan, the objective being to clean out Al Qaida and a growing ISIS threat. For that reason he requested General Mark Barrett, his commander in Afghanistan and his wife to join he and Mary at Camp David for a week end of talk and relaxation. He and Mary went up early on a Friday by helicopter and were joined that evening for cocktails and dinner by the Barretts. Michael had met the General in Kabul on his trip to Iraq in April of 2018. Instinctively they liked each other the General being younger by ten years. The conversation led to talking about their children; the Barretts had four sons, one of whom was serving In Iraq, two in college, one at the University of Southern California the other at U.C.L.A. and the youngest at a Jesuit prep school in California near his brothers. His wife, Donna, lived in Los Angeles while he was overseas. It turned out He was a top flight tennis player who starred in his days at West Point. Donna, a Vassar graduate, dated him her senior year in college and they were married upon his graduation from the Point. Over a few drinks before dinner, and later a meal of steak and baked potatoes, they talked about children, grandchildren, life in the army, travel, and history. For a few hours they forgot the presidency, the war in Afghanistan, and the state of the world and just talked about their separate but similar life experiences. Barrett was a decorated Viet Nam veteran who had participated in numerous battles, all in positions of command and had survived, though wounded three times. He carried scars on his back from his wartime experience. Serving in first Gulf war he rose quickly in the ranks and by the time of the second Iraq war he made Brigadier General. The men arranged to play tennis in the morning while the wives went for a hike followed by about 15 secret servicemen in jogging clothes.

On the court the General proved an able adversary. Watching him warm up Michael knew he was in for a battle. Mark Barrett had been far too busy running the war in Afghanistan to play much tennis, even so, once he started to hit the ball the old rhythm came back and it was obvious he had played a lot of tennis in his time. For his part Michael had tried to play once a week at the White House with the result he was playing very well. They started. Michael served and took the first game. The General served and took the second game and the next five to take the first set 6-1. When they sat down for the break Michael apologized for winning only one game.

"All right Mark," he said as they took their places for the second set, "I think I've figured out your game and I'm going to do a lot better this time." The General laughed and said: "I'm not in that great of shape you may win by default. They started and Michael broke his serve in the first game. Then they reached 3-3 when the General broke back. They battled back and forth, slice back hands, drop shots, overheads, chip returns pounding forehands; both men were completely caught up in the game. It was not a General and the President of the United States playing tennis, it was two men battling each other to win, the older holding his own against the younger man. At 6-6 they both sat on the bench resting before the tie breaker. After a minute Michael got up and said: "Come on Mark this is for the money."

Opening with a big serve Mark took the first point and then the second. 2-0. Michael rushed the net on his own serve and volleyed away a backhand passing shot. 2-1.With a punishing serve the General won the next two points to go up 4-1. Michael won the next point when his opponent rushed the net and he hit a beautiful passing shot down the line. The count reached 6-3 in favor of the General, with Michael serving. He fired an ace. Feeling he could do it again he hit it down the center of the service court and the General reached it but could only net it. 6-5. Still set point with the General serving. Michael set his jaw and decided to block the serve back and come into the net. It worked. 6-6. Now they were even. Mark faulted his first serve and then hit a soft second serve that Michael jumped on with a forehand cross court for a winner.7-6. This was it for both men. Michael served for the set and the General hit a crushing return sending Michael back to the base line where he was able to hit a high lob. What should have been an easy point for the General, instead of waiting for the ball to drop and then hitting an overhead, he decided to hit the overhead while the ball was still in the air. He missed and suddenly it was over. Exhausted they both staggered over to the bench and sat down.

"What a match Mr. President I haven't played that hard or as well in years." "I tell you Mark I haven't had this much fun in years, I thank you. When you come back from Afghanistan we'll have to do this again. For me, I going to rest on my laurels; I couldn't go a third set."

Back in the main house, it was General and President again as though the tennis match between the two men had never happened. The two couples spent Saturday evening talking about everything except the war. It turned out the General was an avid student of the civil war and he regaled

Michael and Mary with little known stories of that era. In turn he and his wife were fascinated when Michael told them of some of the adventures he and Mary had during the 2016 campaign. At 10:00 o'clock both men conceded they were too tired from their morning tennis match and asked to be excused. Permission was given and the wives talked until midnight when they decided even they had reached the point of exhaustion.

• • •

The next morning at 10:00 a.m. the President and the General met at Laurel Lodge a quarter mile from Aspen Lodge, the residence. The day before they had been equals on the tennis court, today they were Commander-in-Chief and General Mark Barrett, commander of allied force Afghanistan. They sat side by side in the large conference room with a map of Afghanistan lying flat on the table in front of them. The general proceeded to explain the situation on the ground and his thinking on what should be done to quell the Taliban and ISIS.

"You'll recall your predecessor called for a drawdown when we were at 13,000 troops in country. By 2014 we were down to 8,000 troops, barely enough to keep the lid on; then you, sir, upped US involvement to 20,000. That's still only enough to hold the line. Politically the country is a disaster---weak central government with President Abdul Ghazan and what they have chosen to call a chief executive officer. Hamid Karzi, the previous president, who has been referred to as the "Caped Crusader," left the country paralyzed with corruption. War lords in the north run their own shop though antagonistic to the government in Kabul. The Afghanistan National Defense and Security Force is poorly led despite the training they have received from us. We refer to this force as the (ANDSF). They are deployed in Helmand Province mostly as a blocking force from Al Qaeda expansion into the north."

Pointing to the map he explained the Taliban, calculated to number about 15,000 in November, had taken over large swaths of property and controlled the cities of Sangin, Gersesk, Khanastin, Nawjad, Marjah, Bagram and Baghlan in the north.

"The Taliban we fought after nine-eleven were Afghan who wanted to overthrow the government and create their own caliphate. Over the years that original group has pretty much split up, with the originals being led by Ayman al-Zawahri, some defected to ISIS and the remainder joined up with the ANDSF. While Al Qaeda and ISIS are opposed to each other they are both aligned against the government and will fight each other over control of the country. Of the two organizations ISIS is much better organized. I should point out that ISIS is also thriving in Pakistan under a weak government and it will be interesting to see how they handle it.

Coming back to Afghanistan, as you know large quantities of opium are being grown in Helmand Province producing three billion dollars a year for the economy. In 2008 we had 40,000 troops in Afghanistan and part of those troops were used to eradicate the opium crop. As much as seven billion dollars was spent and we were successful but failed to stick with it so that today opium is back in full production. If we interdict the drug traffic we will effectively deprive the Taliban and ISIS of their chief source of revenue which is financing their insurgency."

The President mentioned to the general that he, while serving in Congress, had been sent to Columbia to look into the drug growing epidemic existing at the time; eradication was being conducted by defoliation with great effect except farm crops were being destroyed as well as the opium crop. As a result the Columbian government with the US as partner went to ground and started taking out the plantations one at a time. He thought, in time, the same tactics could be used against the Afghan opium trade.

"Actually sir we've done what little we could, with minimal effect, against the warlords, ISIS and the Taliban who thrive on the drug trade. The government has looked the other way since too many officials, government and military, have a stake they don't want to forsake."

Looking at the map Michael stated what he saw as the problem in Afghanistan. "Mark it looks to me like the Taliban and ISIS are based mostly in Helmand Province with Kandahar being the ultimate target. Again in the northeast they control the area encompassing Ghazni and a couple of small areas in the northwest. I think all that is manageable over the long run by continuing to engage them with the Afghan army backed up solidly by our forces. We have a status of forces agreement with the government which in many ways allows us to control how much pressure is put on the Islamists. I've seen no evidence the ANDSF can accomplish, by itself, the goal of keeping Afghanistan in the hands of a secular government. That means we have to have enough troops in there to insure they will have the backbone to do what is needed with the help of our special ops and regular American troops backing them up. That's to be distinguished from our goal in Iraq which is to deprive ISIS completely of any portion of that country while at the same time giving the government of Iraq time to stabilize. I'm not so confident the Afghans can establish a stable government any time soon. I'm satisfied Iraq is under control and the goal now is to make it impossible for the radicals to take over Afghanistan as their new caliphate. My question to you is:

given the objective I've set out how many troops do you think you will need in Afghanistan?"

Knowing how important it was to give an accurate answer, and knowing full well Michael would go over the same ground with the Joint Chiefs and all their advisors, he said he would need 30,000 with 10,000 in reserve. Explaining his choice of numbers he carefully set out his rational for the request.

"We will need 15,000 to 20,000 of the ANDSF plus about 10,000 of our troops assisting to take Helmand Province and draw a perimeter around it. Once successful we will have to garrison in outposts all around the perimeter; 20,000 ANDSF and 5,000 of our own. Between garrisons around the country, special ops, and trainers we will need about 40,000 US troops. Once that is accomplished we move to the smaller occupied areas in the center of the country and duplicate the Helmand operation. The two small areas in the north we will work with the warlords to put down Al Qaeda and ISIS. All the while we will be running special operations against top targets, radical leaders and training camps wherever they are set up. It seems to me this struggle will go on indefinitely until the ideology itself is stamped out."

Now the President spoke: "I hear you Mark, and since I've been given this job working with our military I've learned about what they do, how they go about it, and I've learned to trust their judgment if it makes sense. I will, of course, be discussing this with the Chiefs, State, Defense and the NSC what we've been talking about this morning. Before you head back to Afghanistan I would appreciate it if you would visit with Peter Bartholomew and his people laying out your version of what will be needed in manpower to get the job done. Moreover, I think the opium problem is a hindrance to what we want to accomplish and its spreading poison into Europe and our country. We will do the world a service if we can cut the trade to nothing. That's an entirely different problem and I'm going to get another branch of government to undertake that job."

With that they concluded their meeting with a hand shake and Michael put his arm around the General's shoulder as they headed back to the main house. There he and Mary saw the General and his wife off and then they took a long walk around the grounds. The air was bracing and they walked over a mile before calling for a golf cart to return to the residence. They read the rest of the afternoon and at six o'clock Mary handed him a scotch and soda fixed one for herself and came and sat beside him on the sofa.

"I thought Mark and Betty were very sharp" Mary opened the conversation, hoping he felt the same way. "I agree, Mary. Mark has a real grasp of what's going on in Afghanistan and besides He's an excellent tennis player although I value him more as a military expert. You spent all the time with Betty; I gather you think she's pretty sharp too?"

"We talked about their children and how it's been difficult with him serving in Afghanistan for the last year and a half. Beyond that she's been involved with helping wives whose husbands are serving with the general and she considers that a full time job although without pay. When she described what she was doing I had the greatest respect for her and considered Mark lucky to have her. I think we should have Bing Smith and his wife Sandra up here to get to know them better; the fate of Iraq is in his hands and it would help you to get to know him better."

"Good idea. Why don't you call Bing's wife, Sandra, and arrange to have them up here. By the way, I've been so wrapped up in this ISIS fight that we've never really talked about what you think about the strategy we're using in Iraq and Afghanistan?"

"I dislike the idea so many civilians are being caught in the crossfire. Oh I know it can't be helped nevertheless it makes my heart ache. And I don't like the beating you're taking in the press for going after ISIS so hard but I also understand it's the price you pay for leading. To answer your question I think the tactics being employed are the only sane ones, and if they had been used before you arrived on the scene we might not be so far behind in defeating the radicals."

"Believe me Mary, I got used to critics the first year I was in Congress and have never looked back. You know me. I marshal the facts apply what I hope is common sense and make a decision. Once made there's no turning back. If I'm criticized by the left I know I'm doing the right thing, no pun intended." She laughed.

"I've asked the chef to prepare two New York Strip steaks, French fries and a salad with tomatoes. Are you game?" Knowing he loved steak and French fries she decided to splurge because the chef at the camp had instructions to go easy on the steak and French fries for the President who, if left to his own resources, would have it for dinner every night. He suggested they have another scotch since he felt relaxed and wanted to catch up on family gossip. After he prepared their drinks she brought him current with the comings and goings of the children. "Jack and Megan have decided he will run for Congress next year I think you should give him a call and see what his plans are. I don't think there would be a conflict with you running for re-election yourself next year."

"Hey, hold on there Mary," he said in mock surprise. "I've never said anything about running for re-election. You're making a big assumption there."

"Don't you try to fool me Michael Sullivan; I've been talking with John Kennedy and Tom Galvin and they are already setting up the machinery and don't tell me you don't know about it."

He smiled weakly and said: "well I've heard some rumblings from those fellows but I've never come right out and said I would be running for re-election."

"Well, are you?"

"If you say so."

"I do say so. And just to be sure you don't change your mind I'm going to call John Kennedy when we get back to Washington and tell him what you said."

"That settles it, he said with a laugh and got up and kissed her, returned to his seat and said: "next subject."

He suggested they have another scotch before dinner since he was learning about family doings and he wanted to hear more.

"Sharon called two days ago and said she's pregnant and the baby is due around March next year. No word yet from Kathryn but I expect to get a call any day with an announcement."

He laughed and said: "those girls have always been competitive; my guess is they'll have four like we did and call it a day. And by the way Peter is going to be ordained next year in Rome and I intend to be there in the front row at St. Peter's and the press can make whatever they wish of it."

"Do you honestly think they would be critical of you going to your son's ordination?" she said with a look of surprise on her face.

"Anything to do with religion they will be critical of. You remember how they made a big fuss when we met with the Pope. Called it a 'secret meeting.' Expect the same treatment when we go to Rome in the middle of a presidential campaign. Next year will be a busy one for us Mary, with Jack running for Congress, me for re-election, at least one new grandchild and maybe a second and Peter becoming a priest. Will you be up to it?"

"Anything you can do I can do as well," she laughed and told him dinner was ready and they got up and made their way to the Dining room.

It was early in October and the President and the Vice President were having lunch outdoors in front of the oval office; a get together they indulged in at least three times a month. It provided a good opportunity to bring the Vice President up to date on everything crossing his desk. Michael had felt from the beginning of his presidency that it was important to keep the Vice President appraised of everything in case anything should happen to him. Bernard Winslow appreciated the President's concern and often times found he could be of real help in giving advice. Besides both men liked each other and both felt at ease in each other's presence.

Looking out they saw the beautiful south lawn freshly mowed, the trees beginning to lose their leaves and far off to the south a view of the Jefferson Memorial. That view was always inspiring to both of them and they often commented on it every time they met. Talking about nothing in particular, they were interrupted by the serving steward who asked if the President would take a call. Asking who it was the steward told him it was Tom Donovan.

"I'll take it Samuel. The steward brought the phone to the table. "Tom, what's up?" he asked the chief of staff. The Vice President watched him as he listened to Tom Donovan; his expression unchanging although Bernard Winslow knew Michael well enough to realize he was getting some important information whether good or bad he could not decipher. The conversation lasted no more than a minute and when he put the receiver down he looked at his Vice President and said in what sounded to Winslow as a sad and mournful voice:

"Tom Watson has been killed in an automobile crash on I-95. It was a head on; both he and his wife were killed instantly." Winslow said nothing and sat there stunned. Thomas Watson had served on the Supreme Court for thirty years and was conservative in his approach to the law. A brilliant legal scholar and perhaps the best writer on the court. When he wrote dissents, which he often did, the majority felt the sting. He would point out with surgical precision what they tried to hide in verbose language. After a minute or two passed Bernard Winslow broke the silence and said simply: "He will be missed Michael, how do you replace a man like that?"

"You don't Bernie, he's irreplaceable. There will be a firestorm no matter who I nominate. The leftists want his seat and will do everything they can to block a conservative. What I will look for is a person who knows and respects the law and will interpret not legislate from the bench. I suggest we adjourn this lunch so that we can get back to the problems at hand. Touch base at the end of the day with any thoughts you have on a court nominee. In the meantime I will be meeting with Paul, Tom and some of the leaders to get their ideas. Some important cases are on the docket this year one involving abortion. It could be a case that will require looking at Roe vs. Wade to see if that decision should be overturned. The political implications are huge not to mention the legal consequences should it be overturned in a presidential election year." The President walked back into the Oval office and Tom Donovan was already there and ready to discuss the ramifications of what he had just told Michael.

"What a shock Mr. President. It's made me sick. The Watsons were hit by a drunken driver who crossed over into their lane and hit them head on. They were dead almost instantaneously the State Police reported. There will be a week of mourning with the funeral next Saturday morning at the National Cathedral. I assume you and Mrs. Sullivan will attend."

"I will be there and so will the Vice President and all Cabinet members and you can put that out to everyone this afternoon. Also ask Paul Connolly to come over here as soon as possible. Arrange for a call to the Chief Justice; I want to express my condolences and assure him I will be acting as quickly as possible to nominate someone to fill Justice Watson's seat. Tom left and Michael sat in the oval office by himself thinking how unpredictable life was. Here was a man at the top of his game living a fruitful life making great contributions to the law of the land and all of a sudden no more. For Michael it was just another example of how tenuous life is. Death has no respect it cuts down the mighty the young and the old. His religion taught him this was the way it was meant to be. Be ready for you never know when that time will come. He was not afraid of death for he believed time spent on earth was simply a prelude to eternal life promised by the Creator. With that passing thought he said a silent prayer for the Watsons and then made his call to the Chief Justice. The Attorney General was ushered into his office at 4:00 p.m. and he motioned Paul over to one of the two oval office couches facing each other.

"Mr. President I've been on the phone since Tom called---all with the press. They want to know when you will nominate and who is being considered. My answer to all and sundry was I have no information on that and I haven't spoken with the President. So now that I'm here have you got someone in mind?"

"I have about ten people in mind that I would like you start vetting. I'll give you a list. Next, maybe as soon as tomorrow we can get together with the Republican leadership in the House and Senate. If John Kennedy and Tom Galvin are available I would like to meet with them. If we can arrange both meetings tomorrow, I think we can make some preliminary decisions. I'm sure you've had a thought or two; anyone you have in mind?" Paul didn't hesitate and gave him the name of Brad Burrows.

"Interesting Paul, we've been together so long we think along the same lines. Brad crossed my mind after I finished lunch with the Vice President today. We were about half way through the meal when Tom called us with the news. The fact you thought of the same name means he will in the top five."

The Attorney General responded, "He's a top lawyer not only in trial but in the appellate field. The court could use a Justice with court room experience plus he has a brilliant mind. Those folks at the Court are mostly in the tower and I don't think any of them have had courtroom experience at the Federal District Court level. I remind you the academics will scorn someone who has not been on the Circuit Court of Appeals; fortunately they don't have a vote in the matter. And remember Brad Burrows will be the second person you've nominated for the court with court room experience and there will be backlash on that."

Michael's prediction about reaction on the left to the vacancy on the Supreme Court proved accurate. Leading the way the *New York Tribune* sallied forth with a warning to the President and the Republicans.

"We had a court on which the conservatives had a 6-3 majority following the resignation of Justice Goldstein and the appointment of Justice Wilson. The Republicans threaten to maintain that edge by nominating another conservative to replace the late Justice Thomas Watson. Should the President and the Republican Senate be successful in this endeavor it will be a devastating blow to the Democratic Party, the entire Liberal movement and most of all too American women. We urge the leaders in the Democratic Party to fight to the death whoever the President nominates, for to be sure, it will be a rock-ribbed conservative who will vote to overturn Roe vs. Wade." More conciliatory and open minded was the liberal *Minneapolis Leader* whose Marilyn Sussman wrote:

"Normally we agree with the *New York Tribune* on policy. Suffice to say we do not agree with it on the comments made in their editorial columns about the danger of the President nominating and the Senate confirming a conservative judge. If the *Tribune* means by 'conservative' a judge who interprets the constitution and does not act as a legislator; then we totally agree with them. The trouble is that is not their definition. They insist on a Justice who is willing to go beyond the words of the Constitution to fit a liberal theology. Unlike our brethren we value a Justice who interprets laws and does not try to make them. We've had plenty of those. We value a Justice who will Interpret the words in a statute not twist words to satisfy some personal idea of what policy should be. That's the kind of Judge we favor no matter the party he or she may belong to."

Back and forth it went as the President and his team researched, interviewed and finally decided on Bradley

Burrows. Burrows, the 55 year old founder and senior partner in the New York law firm of Barrows, O'Hare, Rosen,
Wilson & Gottlieb with over a 100 lawyers specializing in
litigation was vetted, interviewed and finally chosen to fill the
Watson seat. Barrows, a brilliant trial lawyer, also excelled
as an appellate advocate, having argued 13 cases before the
Supreme Court while submitting 30 briefs and amicus briefs
to the Court on behalf of his clients. In addition he had tried
cases in Federal District Courts all over the country as well
as presenting oral arguments before five Federal Circuit
Courts of Appeal. Michael had made his acquaintance
before he entered politics when they were both becoming
nationally recognized trial lawyers. Over the years they had
renewed the acquaintanceship at various annual American
Bar Association meetings. The formal announcement of
the nomination contained information he was married, had
four children, belonged to the Presbyterian Church, graduated from Vanderbilt University, The Wharton School of
Business at The University of Pennsylvania and Harvard Law
School. Before Michael initiated the search to replace Justice
Watson, he asked Paul Connolly, the Attorney General, to
have his staff prepare a memorandum on the subject of abortion beginning with *Roe v. Wade*, the 1973 case permitting
the absolute right to an abortion in the first trimester of a
pregnancy.

Knowing cases would be moving through the Federal
Courts based on a state statute outlawing abortion or in
some cases forbidding doctors to perform abortions he
wanted to know the current status of the law. Within two
weeks of the request he received a memo from the Attorney
General's office outlining the issues dealt with by the
Supreme Court in the case, the decision, dissents, and the
aftermath.

Michael J. Walsh

To: THE PRESIDENT, OF THE UNITED STATES

From: OFFICE OF THE ATTORNEY GENERAL OF
        OF THE UNITED STATES

Subject: ROE v WADE, 410 U.S. 113 (1973)

Argument was held before the court December 13, 1971. A Texas statute was appealed to the Court which prevented a women from getting an abortion. (The law in most states at the time.) Seven Justices sat for the argument while two more awaited confirmation. The vote was 5-2 to strike down the statute. Justice Blackmun, was assigned by the Chief Justice to write the opinion. Since there were two vacancies on the court it was decided to hold the case over until the next term and have it reargued when there would be a full court. Blackmun's initial effort was considered implausible in that it had a bare conclusion favoring abortion unsupported by any part of the Constitution.

On October 11, 1972 the case was reargued before the full court with the result unrestricted abortion was allowed in the first trimester of a pregnancy; some restrictions could be applied in the second and the state could pretty much outlaw it in the third. Blackmun based his right of privacy argument on the case of, *Griswold v. Connecticut*, 381 U.S. 479 (1965) a case in which the state tried to restrict use of contraceptives. Others in the majority argued the fetus is not a person and therefore not entitled to protection under the Constitution. Another reasoned the woman had a 'right to liberty' under the Constitution. The two Dissenters argued: there is no right of privacy in the Constitution (Renquist);

Justice Byron White went further: "The Court, for the most part, sustains this position: prior to the time the fetus becomes viable, the Constitution of the United States values the convenience, whim, or caprice of the putative mother more than the life or potential life of the fetus......" and further:

"I find nothing in the language or history of the Constitution to support the Court's judgment. The Court simply fashions and announces a new Constitutional right for pregnant mothers {410 U.S. 222} and with scarcely any reason or authority for its action, invests that right sufficient substance to override most existing state abortion statutes.......As an exercise of raw judicial power, the Court perhaps has the authority to do what it does today; but, in my view, its judgment is an improvident and extravagant exercise of judicial review that the Constitution extends to this Court."

In *Thornburg v American College of Obstetricians and Gynecologists*, 476 U.S. 747 (1986) The Court addressed a Pennsylvania Law that required informed consent be given before an abortion could proceed. By a 5-4 vote it struck down the law as being inimical to its prior holding in *Roe v. Wade*. Justice White called for Roe v. Wade to be overruled asserting it was bad law when announced and remained bad law. He argued: the Court retained the ability to set aside prior decisions when those decisions overturned laws representing the will of the people, by finding principles not in the Constitution as the basis for their decision. In this regard he wrote:

"...Decisions that find in the Constitution principles or values that cannot fairly be read into that document usurp the people's authority, for such decisions represent choices that the people have never made, and that they cannot disavow through corrective legislation. For this reason it is essential that this Court maintain the power to restore authority to its proper possessors by correcting constitutional decisions that, on consideration are found to be mistakes."

He called for overruling of *Roe v. Wade*: "In my view the time has come to recognize that *Roe* v. *Wade* no less than the cases overruled by the Court in the decisions I have just cited departs from a proper understanding of the Constitution, and to overrule it."

Abortion next received review before the Court in *Webster v Reproductive Health* Services, 492 U.S. 490 (1989) where the State of Missouri sought to limit abortions by not allowing public employees or public facilities to be used to assist in abortions not required to save the life of the mother, prohibiting counseling to have an abortion and requiring physicians to perform viability tests on women twenty or more weeks into their pregnancy. The issue thus framed was: did these restrictions violate a woman's right to privacy or the Equal Protection Clause of the Fourteenth Amendment? In a confusing decision the court upheld most of the restrictions but refused to address the question of whether *Roe v. Wade* should be overruled. Some of the Justices were inclined to reverse it, however Justice O'Connor, the swing vote, wanted to avoid confrontation and so rendered a meek opinion allowing restrictions to abortion but not tampering with the original decision leaving abortion on demand viable.

In 1992 the case of *Planned Parenthood v. Casey*, 505 U.S. 833 (1992) was argued before the Court. The question presented was whether a woman wanting an abortion must have informed consent, and wait 24 hours or if a minor obtain parental consent. The Court in a 5-4 decision upheld *Roe v. Wade* but allowed the Pennsylvania restrictions on abortion to stand. Justice Scalia criticized the majority opinion for failing to address the central issue whether *Roe v. Wade* was bad law and should be reversed.

Eight years later the state of Nebraska passed a statute prohibiting partial birth abortion. Under the standard of "undue burden" formulated in *Casey* the Court held that not allowing the practice would be an "undue burden" on a woman's right to abortion and therefore struck down the statute. In a cogent dissent Justice Scalia lamented the fact the majority again refused to face the fact *Roe v. Wade* lacked legal authority. He suggested:

"Today's decision, that the Constitution of the United States prevents the prohibition of a horrible mode of abortion will be greeted by a firestorm of criticism as well it should. I cannot understand why those who acknowledge that, in the opening words of Justice O'Connor's concurrence,"{t}he issue of abortion is one of the most contentious and controversial in contemporary American society, "ante, at 1, persist in the belief that this Court, armed with neither constitutional text nor accepted tradition, can resolve that contention and that controversy rather than be consumed by it. If only for the sake of its own preservation, the Court should return this matter to the people where the Constitution, by its silence on the subject, left it and let them decide, State by State whether this practice should be allowed. Casey must be overruled. *Stenberg v Carhart*, 530 U.S. 914 (2000)

In response to *Carhart* Congress passed the Partial-Birth Abortion Act in 2003 which was immediately challenged as an unconstitutional burden on a woman's right to an abortion. In a 5-4 decision, the Court in *Gonzales v. Carhart*, 550 U.S. 124 (2007), ruled the ban was not unconstitutional and did not place a burden on a woman's right to an abortion.

Much of the legal community and constitutional scholars have said *Roe v. Wade* is on a death watch, lacking any legal support from the Constitution. Some have compared it favorably with the worst decision in the Court's history---*Dred Scott*, 60 U.S. 393 (1857) wherein by a 7-2 vote the Court held that negroes were not citizens and therefore had no standing to sue in Federal Courts. (Dred Scott had sued for his freedom from slavery)

In the aftermath of *Roe* 59,000,000 million infants have been aborted. Broken down by race the percentages are: 37% White; 37% Black; 19% Hispanic; 7% others. Abortion has had the largest impact on the black population compared to their numbers in the general population.

At the time Michael interviewed the five candidates for the Supreme Court he had in hand the Attorney General's memorandum. He believed the abortion decision an aberration, however, in conversations with each he avoided reference to issues such as abortion that had come before the Court or would be coming before the Court including an abortion cases. He found it distasteful and unprofessional when members of the Judiciary Committee would ask the nominees appearing before them how they would vote on certain issues knowing full well the nominee could not give an opinion on a case or matter before him or her. What he did do was talk generally about the law, ask them their view on how the law should be applied, and from these discussions he was able to get a sense of where they would fall in the political spectrum. Of the five all were capable yet Michael felt Brad Barrows could bring the most to the bench and could eventually turn out to be another Thomas Watson. In any event he felt very comfortable with his pick and looked forward to doing everything possible to insure his confirmation before the Senate.

After he introduced his choice at the White House, the media broke from the room and that night the leftist attack began, followed by the print media the next day and the columnists the day after. "Brilliant"; "Accomplished lawyer"; "highly regarded by his peers" they spoke and wrote, the only problem they lamented -----he was too conservative too suit their taste. Someone closer to the center or left of center would be the consensus pick by the Democrats and their media allies. On the conservative side pundits, talk show hosts and Republicans mocked the media-Democrat position for praising the nominee as a "great lawyer"; "well qualified" while objecting to the appointment on the grounds he might turn out to be a Judge like his predecessor Tom Watson, brilliant but conservative

Michael discussed procedure with Bailey Long, the Senate Majority Leader. They decided to hold a hearing before the Senate Judiciary Committee as soon as possible in as much as Seymore Gottlieb, Senate Minority Leader, had advised his party would not support the nominee and he had the votes to block a vote on the merits.

Hearings went on for two totally partisan weeks with witnesses, called by the Democrats, protesting the appointment as putting in jeopardy *Roe v. Wade* and a host of other cases and the Republicans testifying to the nominee's prowess as a leader In the law who would be a credit to the Court. By a vote of 11 to 9 the Judiciary Committee sent the nomination forward with a "do pass" recommendation. Well aware the Democrats would vote against cloture (cut off debate) Bailey Long decided to convince three Democrats to vote for cloture which would allow the Senate to proceed to a vote with 51 votes needed to secure the nomination. The three Democrats chosen were up for re-election in 2020 in Republican dominated states and would be most susceptible to outside pressure. Television ads blanketed the vulnerable Democrats in their home states; donors threatened to withhold contributions to their campaigns. It all proved too much when Seymore Gottlieb was unable to stop four defections from his party which allowed the cloture motion to pass setting up a perfunctory vote on the merits. Bradly Barrows, by a vote of 57-43, became the second Justice appointed by President Sullivan in his first term in office and the 116th Justice appointed to the Supreme Court. The media was not happy so they decided with a collective sigh to take a wait and see approach and if the confirmed Judge turned out to be a true conservative in his decisions they would then apply a scorched earth attack as they had on many of Thomas Watson's decisions.

CHAPTER 19

In the two and a half years of his presidency Michael Sullivan held 40 press conferences which he found instructive, and as President, an opportunity to pretty much talk about what he thought was important and treated the press as a professor would teaching a law class. Once a date was picked he would begin preparations which included reviewing press books and going through what amounted to a moot court exercise.

Members of his staff would pepper him with questions for forty five minutes which would be taped and reviewed prior to the conference. On the day designated he would go to the White House Press Room and take his place at the podium. The room was built over a swimming pool installed during the administration of Franklin Roosevelt and remained as such until 1969 when President Nixon had it covered over and the current press room built to be used as the official room in which press conferences would be held. Seven rows of seven seats brought the room's capacity to 49. Prime space was taken up by correspondents from the major networks and the associated press sitting in the front row.

From the start, the President was able to memorize most of the names and faces and after the first few conferences he knew the personalities and backgrounds of most of them so that when a question was asked he knew pretty much what to expect from the questioner. At least half the correspondents were in their late twenties or early thirties, all of whom considered themselves as hard boiled reporters when in fact they often had little experience and less knowledge than their predecessors in the 80's and 90's. The other half were somewhat older with a little more experience and some re-treads waiting to retire. What Michael liked the most was taking questions from the young ones. At the first conferences, they were all anxious to box him in on a question in the hope of making some news and enhancing their own reputations. Because he was so well prepared he would kindly answer their questions leaving them flummoxed and unable to dispute him with a follow-up question. Most of them came out of left wing backgrounds, both in their education and then early in their careers, working for leftist media. At the outset they resolved to bring this new conservative President down, soon however, they discovered, at least the older ones, this could not be accomplished; the man was to fast on his feet and had a sense of humor that disarmed them. The younger ones took a little longer to figure out they were not dealing with an equal in the give and take of a press conference. When a reporter asked a stabbing question sure to set the President on his heels, the answer would be short and concise, absent verbosity, and to the point leaving reporter unable to challenge. The President would relieve the reporter's frustration by adding a little joke or kidding the reporter so that he or she didn't look foolish in front of his or her peers. After a while some of the younger reporters began to take a liking to Michael Sullivan telling themselves he was a pretty smart fellow who maybe they could learn something from. Before long the President sensed this change and began to take on the role of teacher to the point where the younger reporters began to treat him like a professor who they could learn from. Many of their stories reflected this new discovery they had made in the Republican President. As he neared the end of his third year in the office, the press corps began to understand the President might have a different political philosophy than theirs but he took them seriously, treated them with respect and always gave them straight answers whether the news hurt him or helped him. Most of them were used to being lied to but this President didn't lie. When he told them something they could print it as fact and not have to spin it to their readers.

The press was always skeptical, after having been lied to by previous Presidents and their front men, the press secretaries. Not with President Sullivan. It took some time to get used to his style---telling the truth even when it hurt so after the first year they realized he wasn't spinning facts, keeping things hidden and when someone in his administration fouled up he owned up to it----not claiming executive privilege.

Thus it was in early October 2019, while Michael was holding a press conference, that a question was asked by the TBC correspondent about whether the U.S. was going to put troops into Syria as well as maintaining the status quo in Iraq and fighting a war in Helmand Province, Afghanistan.

He thanked the reporter for the question and welcomed the chance to answer it. For weeks the Pentagon had been working on a plan to triple the number of special operations forces on the ground in Syria and increase targeted air strikes with planes and drones. The President gave the following answer reported all most verbatim in all the leading newspapers and major cable and television networks.

To Ashton Smith of TBC he responded: "Ashton, thank you for asking that question; it is important and needs to be answered. Your premise about holding to the status quo in Iraq is correct. We have taken back the major cities in Iraq, including Mosul. The Iraq border with Syria has been secured so that ISIS fighters are on longer crossing the border into Iraq. Oil fields have been revitalized and oil is being exported at an increasing rate and revenue from the oil is being distributed by the central government to the three states of the Federation, Sunni, Kurds and Shia. The Federation is in its infant stages yet its working better than the mostly Shia government that proceeded it. We have twenty thousand troops stationed all over Iraq under our status of forces agreement. In Afghanistan we have undertaken the mission to clean out ISIS in Helmand Province which covers the southern portion of the country then move against strongholds in the east and finally neutralize ISIS in the north by cooperating with anti-ISIS tribes who have been fighting them for years. I can say that ISIS no longer exists as a fighting force in Iraq. We hope to achieve the same result in Afghanistan. The last remnants of ISIS strength lies in Syria. There we are attacking them in the one place where they still have control--- Raqqa. Iran, the sponsor of ISIS, has been set back in its program to form a world caliphate as a result of our recent bombing to curtail their nuclear program. Russia maintains its power in Syria, still they are no friend to ISIS and our enemy is ISIS not Russia. ISIS is being slowly strangled as a military force that could take over a country, yet they still pose a threat to Europe and the West, in that, while diffused as a fighting force they still have great potential to disrupt, using terror tactics as a weapon they hope will eventually win them a victory."

While Michael Sullivan was totally absorbed running the country, his son, Peter was in training to be a Catholic Priest at the North American College in Rome. In his third year of theology, he was trying to do two jobs and succeeding at both although he found it was taking a toll on his health. During a good part of the day he was at his studies at the College and beginning at three o'clock in the afternoon he trooped over to the Vatican to serve as a junior intern in the Office of The Secretary of State. On an afternoon in mid-October, while sitting in the chapel at the college praying, he felt a sudden pain in his lower right abdomen. It hurt though not excruciatingly. When he knelt down he felt a jarring stab of pain so strong he fell back on the pew and tried to lay down to relieve the pain. One of his fellow seminarians praying in the back of church heard him cry out in pain and ran to where he was laying, saw the situation and ran to get help. Three big seminarians came running, picked him up and got him to the infirmary before the Rector was aware of what happened. Once he arrived on the scene he knew instantaneously Peter needed medical attention. Arrangements were made to take him by ambulance to Agostino Gemelli University Polyclinic, where the Popes are taken when ill or in need of surgery. Before leaving with Peter in the ambulance, the Monsignor left instructions that Mary Sullivan be notified of her son's hospitalization and that he would call her in Washington once he had more information on Peter's condition. When they arrived three surgeons were standing by to operate as necessary. After a quick examination they all agreed he was suffering from a ruptured appendix and the decision was made to operate immediately since an infection was spreading quickly throughout his abdomen. The Monsignor was told that he had peritonitis which could be life threatening.

By the time he reached Mary through the White House switch board she had already been contacted by representatives of the college just as the rector had instructed and had also been contacted by Pietro Cardinal Lombardi, Vatican Secretary of State, reassuring her the best doctors were available to care for Peter, and that he himself was on the way to the hospital and once there would get the full story from the rector of the college.

The Monsignor gave Mary the story as he knew it, about the ambulance ride to the hospital, the working diagnosis once he was examined and the decision to operate immediately to prevent the spread of the infection. He also assured her he would remain at the hospital through the operation and would call her after it was over.

She hung up, called Michael and was immediately put through even though he was in conference with a head of State. "Michael, Peter has been taken to a hospital in Rome and will be operated on momentarily for a ruptured appendix. Can you arrange a flight to Rome as soon as possible?"

Knowing Mary, his mind immediately focused on the news he was hearing and he first answered her question before requesting more information.

"Mary I hear you. I want you to hold on. I'm going to make arrangements right now to get you on a plane for Rome in the next two hours. He picked up a second phone and asked Tom Donovan to come into his office. "Tom I want Mary on a plane for Rome in two hours. Peter has been taken to the hospital there in an emergency situation. Can you arrange it?"

"Sir, tell your wife a plane will be standing by at Reagan National Airport in two hours and a car with escort will be standing by at the south entrance to take her there in forty five minutes and anyone she wishes to accompany her." He asked no questions and immediately set out to make good his promise.

Michael resumed the conversation with his wife: "Did you hear all that Mary, the plane will be ready in two hours and you will be picked up at the back door."

"Yes I heard it; tell Tom he's wonderful. I don't know if Peter is in grave danger or not, I do know he has an infection in the stomach and they are going to have to go in and take his appendix out and try to stop the infection. I've talked with the Rector who took him from the North American to the hospital. He told me Peter collapsed in the chapel and was discovered by three fellow seminarians slumped on a bench writhing in pain. They first got him down to the infirmary and then figured out they better get him to a hospital. I've also had a call from Cardinal Lombardi who said he was on his way to the hospital and would let me know what was going on from there."

All the while Michael stayed silent listening to her knowing she did not exaggerate and always set out the facts of a situation quickly and with accuracy. When she finished he said: I'll pray, you go throw some things in a suitcase and get on that plane. I'm going to ask Jack to be there with you if he can make it. Once you get there if you think Peter is in any real danger call me and no matter what I'm doing I'll be at your side. I'm starting the prayers now for you and Peter and know I love you. Take care of our son."

"I love you too Michael and I know he'll be all right but I have to be with him now. The minute I talk with the doctors I will call you."

"Mary, I just had an idea. I'm going to see if I can get Greg Marshall, the top surgeon, at Georgetown to go with you?"

"Michael, you can't do that, he's as busy as you are and I'm sure he has all kinds of surgery lined up. Besides they will have operated on Peter by the time I get there."

"All well and good Mary, still I would like to have my own man there should anything go wrong. If he can go he'll be on the plane with you to Rome. Trust me and keep going or you will miss your plane."

"You are impossible Michael. I will discuss this with you when I get back home. Pray for me."

As strange as it may seem Greg Marshall had four days before his next surgery and did not hesitate when Michael asked if he could be at Reagan in two hours to fly to Rome with Mary.

"Greg, I can't thank you enough, I know it's an imposition and Mary said I had no right to ask, nevertheless, I want someone on the ground who knows what's happening and no one can fill that role better than you. Mary and I will be forever grateful. While you're there we will have people to assist you in every way and I guarantee we'll have you back here in time for your next scheduled operation."

"Thanks Mr. President, I'm pleased to do all I can and will call you when I have any news. And don't worry. It does no good. I'm sure the Lord is going to take care of Peter." The call ended, and as promised Mary, the doctor and a friend were on board a plane bound for Rome while Peter was being operated on.

He next called his son Jack, filled him in on Peter's situation and asked if he could join his mother in Rome as a stand-in for himself. Without hesitation he told his father he would take a plane out that night and be with his mother in the morning. Finally he placed calls to Sharon and Kathryn, both with new babies and brought them up to date on what had happened to Peter and that Mary and Jack were on their way to Rome to be with him.

By the time Mary arrived the next morning the operation had been completed and the Italian doctor who performed the operation said the cavity was drained, the appendix removed and anti-biotics were being administered by infusion. He deem the operation a success. Greg Marshall went over the records of the operation, talked with several Italian doctors and examined Peter himself. All this he passed on to Mary, telling her proper procedures had been followed and that Peter should be better in about a week. Jack arrived later in the day and arrangements were made for Mary and Jack to stay in rooms adjacent to Peter's private room. Later in the afternoon he had recovered enough to speak with his mother and brother and told them he felt sore and a little sick yet confident he would be all right. After the second day Jack flew back home to continue his campaign for congress, feeling Peter was out of danger and it good hands at Augustino Gemelli hospital. On day three Peter was lucid and talking but told his mother he had no strength. The next day, the doctors told Mary Peter was not responding as quickly as they had hoped; and that the anti-biotics were not having the desired effect. That night she was dozing in the room when a nurse came in to take his temperature. When she had completed her task she exited quickly from the room, not without Mary asking if Peter was all right. The nurse mumbled something she could not understand and within the next minute two doctors came into the room and began examining the patient. She knew something was wrong the minute they entered the room. She stepped out into the hall while they completed their examination; and when they emerged she confronted them and asked if everything was all right. They were evasive in their answers and before she could press them for an answer the senior of two secret service agents posted outside Peter's room stepped in front of the doctors and repeated in a menacing voice: "The President's wife would like to know if her son is in any danger." This was said in such a manner that the doctors understood a straight answer would be required or there would be serious repercussions both for themselves and the hospital. Deciding truth was the better part of valor they told Mary Peter had acquired a fever of 105 and that the infection was raging in his body. That they were calling for medical back up from an infectious disease physician to see if he could get to the problem before it was too late. Pulling no punches they said Peter was in danger of death. Mary fainted and the secret service had the doctors revive her enough to ask the agents to notify her husband and tell him what she had just been told.

The call was made to the White House and then patched into the President on Air Force One flying over Colorado on his way to California. The agent repeated verbatim what the doctor told Mary about Peter's condition: "danger of death,"

Michael was put through to the Vice President and gave the following instruction: "Bernie, my son is in danger of dying in Rome. We're over Colorado right now and I've ordered the pilot to put us on course for Rome. Tom is in Washington and will assist you as he would me; you are in charge of the country for now. I'll be back in Washington as soon as I can."

"Michael, this is heart breaking. Go with our prayers for Peter. Take care of Mary and God bless you and your family. We will take care everything at this end. Do what you have to and we'll keep in touch. I will alert Tom as soon as I get off this call, and the country should be alerted to the situation and I assume you would want this out as soon as possible."

"It's a personal matter Bernie, nevertheless, I think the country has to be aware of why the President is out of the country and that you are handling matters in Washington while in daily contact with me in Rome. Take care."

He slumped down is his seat and started to cry thinking about Peter and what a great son he was. "Please God, if it be your will, let him live he has so much to give."

The Vice President released the news to the press and the reaction was immediate. With few exceptions the working press as well as the columnists were sympathetic to the news the Sullivans could be about to lose a son. Some went so far as to suggest the country pray the young man's life be spared. Others said the President was the bearer of many burdens as leader of the country and this could be a burden too much to bear. A few covered it as a political story, speculating that if the young seminarian should die, the President might be inclined to forfeit a run for re-election. The nation as a whole offered prayers for the young man's recovery.

Air Force One touched down at Fiumicino, Rome and the President went immediately to a waiting U.S. Army helicopter for a six minute ride to Roma Ciampino Airport and from there into the city to Agostino Hospital. From the airport into the heart of Rome traffic had been cleared so that the motorcade arrived at the hospital seven minutes after leaving the Ciampino. The advance team had signaled the President was five minutes away so Mary was at the hospital to greet him and they went up to Peter's room immediately. On the way up in the elevator she told him quickly while they were alone that the Physicians had said they could do no more and that he had a short time to live. Awaiting them outside Peter's room was the Rector, Monsignor Brian Moore, Cardinal Lombardi and several doctors.

They wanted to take Michael to a nearby conference room to brief him on Peter's condition; he first wanted to see his son and asked everyone to excuse he and Mary while they went into Peter's room. Michael was shocked at his appearance; he was white as a sheet, had obviously lost considerable weight and his hair was matted on his forehead wet with sweat and fever. He bent and kissed his son and whispered his name but no response came nor sign of recognition. Mary held his hand as the tears streamed down his face. "God can save him Mary I know God has work for Peter to do. Let's pray for a miracle." They left the room and went a few steps down the hall where the doctors and the priests were waiting for them. The conference was short. They said they had done what they could do medically and if he was to be spared it would be the work of the powerful anti-biotics they were pouring into him. The head physician said: "I have suggested Mr. President that your son be given the last rights of the church. I myself am not a Catholic yet I know when a Catholic is near death this is proscribed by the faith." Michael and Mary felt fear for they knew the last rites meant death is near. They acquiesced, and the Cardinal assured them the rite would be administered within the hour as a "precaution" as he phrased it not wanting Mary and Michael to think he too thought death was imminent.

They said they would wait in Peter's room. Once in the room they knelt at the foot of the young man's bed and prayed. Now it was dark in Rome and the lights of the city had come on. The hustle and bustle of the night was in full sway; in the dark hospital room the President and his wife sat in the semi-dark, with just a shimmer of light coming through the half opened door. Outside two armed secret service agents sat just outside the door. Four more were at either end of the hall. Fifty more were in and around the hospital all to protect the President.

At nine o'clock Michael, who had been dozing from sheer exhaustion and sadness, heard voices coming down the hallway from Peter's room. He looked over and saw that Mary had fallen asleep in a chair. Suddenly there was a knock at the door, Michael opened it and an agent with a look of urgency said: "Sir, I believe the Pope is coming to this room; agent Jones at the end of the hall said he's sure it's the Pope and there are just a couple of People with him." The couple of people turned out to be the Rector, Monsignor Moore and Cardinal Lombardi.

Just before they arrived at the room, Peter shook Mary gently and whispered in her ear they had visitors. Michael went to the door and just as he was about to open it the Pope stood in the doorway. At the sight of Michael he put out his arms and wrapped them around him as a father would a son. Then he stepped back when he saw Mary coming toward him and took her in his arms and the tears streamed down her face in gratitude. The Pope told them he had been asked by Cardinal Lombardi to administer the last rites to their son Peter and now he was here to give the sacrament of Extreme Unction to this son of the faith. Like any parish priest he brought along a little black bag with what he would need to perform the solemnity. Much like a physician carries a black bag with his tools to cure the body, the Pope carried his tools to cure the soul. As the Pope drew alongside the bed all in the room knelt down. The priest began the ritual with a few short prayers and then administered the holy oils on his forehead. Had he been conscious he would have heard his confession and given him the Holy Eucharist. After reading the final words of the sacrament of Extreme Unction he put his hand on Peter's head and gave him the Papal Blessing, and motioned Michael and Mary to step outside the room with him. Once in the hall he took both their hands in his and said: "Michael and Mary, do not be afraid, I believe the Almighty has much work for Peter to do in the Church. I have prayed that if it is His will, that your son be spared. They knelt for his blessing and he was gone.

Mary spoke first: "Michael I know he's going to be all right. When His Holiness took my hands in his I felt something come over me and I can only describe it as a sense of peace."

"He's God's representative on earth Mary; he said 'do not be afraid' and I'm no longer afraid. He said Peter has work to do for the Church. I believe him. To show how much faith we have let's leave it in God's hands and get some rest. Tomorrow is the first day of the rest of our lives."

A doctor and two nurses manned the watch all night, constantly checking on their patient. At two in the morning he seemed to be sleeping peacefully something he had not done since the operation. At four he asked for a glass of water and after drinking the full glass he fell back on the pillow as one would do and went back to sleep. When the nurse came in at seven to check on him he was wide awake sitting up in bed. "How are you this morning?" he greeted her. She looked at him as though she had seen a ghost. She barely got out "good Morning Father," before she ran out of the room and down to the nurse's stand where she called the doctor and asked him to come immediately that the patient was sitting up in bed talking. They came running, doctors and nurses, to see if the woman knew what she was talking about. When the doctor reached the room Peter wished him a good morning also and asked if he could have something to eat.

"Do you know how sick you are young man what are you thinking of asking for breakfast?" "Well doctor, I actually feel pretty good, I'm awfully sore all over probably from being in this bed for a while."

By that time two other doctors had joined the cast and one of the nurses had awakened Michael and Mary and told them of what was going on in their son's room. With only their pajamas on they rushed down to Peter's room. When

they arrived he was sitting up in the bed the doctors probing him all over; he was able to give them a wave as they
came through the door. The minute they saw his face they
knew he was going to be all right. Without saying anything
to each other in their hearts they knew a miracle had been
wrought. The doctors told them they had no explanation for
his apparent recovery from death's door. They didn't use the
word "miracle" yet they had no other explanation.

By word of mouth the news spread throughout the hospital and on to the street and into the news rooms all around
the country. The people whispered "miracle"

The major newspapers in Italy splashed headlines across
headlines:

La Osservatore Romano: "MIRACLE, PRESIDENT'S
SON LIVES"

La Repubblica: "DOCTORS HAVE NO ANSWER FOR
RECOVERY"

IL Tempo: "POPE ADMINISTERS LAST RITES TO
PRESIDENT'S SON

IL Messaggero: "PRESIDENT'S SON SURVIVES—
SOME CLAIM MIRACLE"

The parents were overjoyed and decided Mary should stay
in Rome until Peter returned to the college. Sharon and
Kathryn, who had flown from New York, decided to stay
a week before returning home; Michael and Jack planned
to fly on Air Force One the next day to Washington, satisfied Peter would be back at the seminary in a few weeks and
ordained as scheduled.

The following day as they started to leave the hospital Michael and Jack shook hands with the Italian doctors who operated on Peter and the nurses who watched over him through his ordeal. All streets around the hospital were blocked off and the road to Roma Ciampino Airport cleared by order of the President of Italy. In front of the hospital a motorcade awaited led by twenty motorcycled Carabinieri and fourteen SUVs, `which would surround the President's limousine front, back and both sides each vehicle loaded with heavily armed secret service agents. Snipers were posted along the route he would travel.

As they came to the front entrance they could see the hospital staff, all dressed in white, waiting to catch a glimpse of the President of the United States before he entered his waiting vehicle. At the door Mary kissed him goodbye and he turned and started to take the four steps to the car.

It all happened so quickly no one had time to move. Witnesses later said a man in a white doctor's coat, his hand held high over his shoulder clasping a knife plunged it into a man, who, seeing the knife, stepped in behind the President, and took the slash in the shoulder. Others said the man was immediately pounced on by three men in dark suits (secret service agents) before he could reach the President, who turned when he heard the scuffling behind him. As he pivoted to look behind, Michael saw the agent starting to fall to the ground and a man in a white coat holding a blood soaked knife coming at him. Before the man could reach him secret service agents had wrestled him to the ground. Michael knelt down to see how badly the agent was hurt and simultaneously he was surrounded by secret service with automatic pistols drawn ready to fire. Frightened, the watching crowd dispersed in all directions not realizing what was happening.

"Mrs Sullivan get in the car with the President we're heading to the airport," an agent shouted and the motorcade pulled away from the hospital curb and sped through the streets of Rome on the preordained route.

In the afternoon edition of the *New York Tribune* a banner headline read: "ATTEMPED ASSASSINATION OF PRESIDENT SULLIVAN FAILS," followed by the lead story describing what happened:

"Four hours ago U.S. President Michael Sullivan was threatened by a knife wielding man dressed in a white coat masquerading as a doctor at the entrance of Agostino Gemilli Polyclinic, Rome, Italy. He was just leaving the hospital where his son is confined and was about to enter a waiting limousine when a man, broke from the crowd of hospital employees gathered in front of the hospital to see him off and attempted to strike him with a knife but was thwarted when one of his guards stepped in and was stabbed, saving the President. We have since learned the authorities have the man in custody and sources close to the police say he identified himself as Farid Aboud. These same sources say he has told the Italian police he is a member of ISIS and has implicated others in a plot to assassinate the President. Police squads have been moving through the city of Rome hunting down co-conspirators. The agent who saved the President has not been identified, however, the agency has said he will recover from the wound he received in the stabbing. Mr.Sullivan was quickly evacuated to Fiumicino Airport to board Air Force one for the trip back to Washington, while Mary Sullivan will remain in Rome until her son is completely recovered. In the meantime Italian police are systematically rounding up all suspects who have been under surveillance for suspected terrorist activity. We are now able to say the war on terror has come to Rome as it has to Paris,

Belgium, Denmark, Germany, England and other European cities. Romans beware of the enemy."

Of course the American media and commentators covered the story from all angles including the fact ISIS would have the capacity to get near enough to the President to assassinate him. They called for greater security and a renewed effort to ferret terrorists out overseas and in the country. More police, more deportation of illegals, greater surveillance along the border. Some, on the left, suggested beefing up security too much would result in infringement on the privacy of Americans and prove to the terrorists they were succeeding in sewing fear among the populace.

CHAPTER 20

WHEN MICHAEL RETURNED to Washington he was satisfied Peter was out of danger plus Mary decided to stay in Rome until he returned to the college, yet he felt a melancholy never experienced before. His son's brush with death had a profound effect on him; nothing seemed as important as it once had. What seemed so urgent before didn't seem so urgent in the light of what he and Mary had just gone through in Rome with Peter's illness. It dawned on him they almost lost their son. He knew that if the Lord had taken him they would have accepted that and their faith would make life bearable. Still, death makes everything else seem small and unimportant. Intellectually, he knew he had to throw off the feeling of sadness because, as President, he didn't have the luxury of grieving over his son's plight. For Mary it took longer to recover from the experience of seeing her son almost die.

The day after Michael returned to the oval office he wrote a letter in his own hand to the Pope which he had hand delivered in Rome. It read:

> The White House
> Washington D.C.

Holiness:

I write in gratitude for your coming to the hospital to administer the last rights to my son Peter. My wife and I, rightly or wrongly, credit his recovery to your act of kindness and the will of the Almighty. It is our strong belief he was spared to make strong contributions to God and to the Church. Mary and I keep you in our prayers everyday knowing the burdens you carry for the faithful. With best regards,

Michael Sullivan

In return through the Papal Nuncio he received a reply:

VATICAN.VA

Dear Mr. President:

Thank you for your gracious note regarding your son. Before he was sick we had met here in the Vatican. A fine young man and I agree with you, he is meant to serve the Church in a most meaningful way. We will be watching over him in his recovery and will have you and Mary in our prayers. Likewise I appreciate your keeping me in your prayers.

Francis

Shortly after she returned to Washington they were enjoying a late supper when Mary broached the subject of how Peter's near death experience had effected them.

"Michael, everything seemed so clear a month ago and now I'm not so sure about a lot of things. Do you know what I mean?"

He looked at her lovingly and reached across the table and put his hand on hers. Then he tried to answer:

"I do know what you mean. I was so sure before Peter's illness and the attempted assassination it was right to run for re-election. Now I'm not so sure it is that important. I've thought about going back to practicing law and having time to spend with you, see the grandchildren lead a normal life. It would be so much easier. Something like what happened to Peter and I makes you stop and think what's important in life."

Tears came to her eyes as she said: "Michael you must not think that way. There is no easy way for us. We have to do what God wants us to do. You won the Presidency for a reason, and so far you've been given the strength and the wisdom to bring the country back from the brink. Good things have been happening, despite what the press says; we're winning in Iraq and now Afghanistan, USCorps has been a huge success, and the college presidents are raving about how much more mature the students are having served in the Corps, just to mention a few things. I feel a little down now; the thought they tried to kill you and Peter almost died. We'll get over it and be better for the experience and so will the whole family. Peter's come back was a miracle and I honestly believe when the Pope gave him the last rights it was a turning point. You escaping death from an insane terrorist. Surely a miracle. No, practicing law would be the easy way. We've never taken the easy way and now's not the time to start. Do you hear me Michael Sullivan?"

"Wipe the tears away, I said I thought about going back to join Paul and the law firm, yet it was a fantasy, knowing full well I could not leave the presidency just when things are really began to turn around. Too much at stake. Every President faces the possibility of assassination; I don't fear death. If we run and lose, that's one thing. Practicing law would be legitimate. Short of that I will run and win if it's to be."

"Good, my darling, you've wiped my tears away. I think we're just going to have to work very hard to get back into the stream of everyday life and thank God he's spared our son and he saved your life."

One of the President's top priorities when he took office was to revamp the State Department which in his view and the view of many others contained deadwood in the middle and incompetence at the top. To accomplish this task he appointed Byron Titus, Secretary of State and a lawyer with a background at the State Department. In the early months of the administration Titus assigned a task force of three lawyers to go back over the history of the State Department from 1940 to the present. Their instructions were to compare the type of Personnel being hired over the years, the manner in which the successful Secretaries had managed the affairs of the Department and current status as to personnel, mission accomplishment and overall effectiveness. Reviewing the report that was put together over a three month period he felt things were worse than expected.

Foremost the State Department had grown tremendously over a span of 70 years from its early days in the War Department located in the Old Executive Office building on the grounds of the White House. In 1940 it numbered 1,968; 13,294 in 1960; 15,751 in 2,000 and over 19,000 in 2016. Written as a memorandum, the report covered the terms of the various Secretaries of State commencing in 1937 coming forward to the present. It read as follows:

To: The Secretary
From: William Bennett III

CORDELL HULL (1933-1944) lawyer, U.S.Representative, Senator and the longest serving Secretary appointed by Franklin Roosevelt in 1933. Japan's invasion of China in 1931 was the only thing of consequence going on at the time internationally. Adolf Hitler would not come to power in Germany until 1933. Neither of these two developments caused any stir at the department which at this time was small and not interested in entanglements in foreign matters. At the time of Pearl Harbor, in 1941, Hull was negotiating with the Japanese. As war raged in Europe he did see the need for re-armament and used his influence as Secretary to bring it about. His real achievement was to set the stage for the founding of the United Nations. Under Secretary Hull top flight personnel were hired and that remained so through the end of World War II.

STETTINIUS JR. (1944-1945); JAMES BYRNES (1945-1947); GEORGE MARSHALL (1947-1949)

DEAN ACHESON (1949-1953) became the primary advocate and architect of the cold war against Russia and one of the authors of the Marshall Plan designed to stop Soviet influence in Europe after World War II. At the time of the Korean War in 1950 he signed off on General McArthur's crossing the 38th parallel into North Korean territory which was a tragic mistake because it brought the Chinese communists into the war causing great loss of life by American forces. He was accused of sheltering communists in the department, culminating with Alger Hiss being found a communist and a traitor. After the war Congress passed the National Security Act which required more agencies than State to participate in decisions. Acheson was able to bypass the (NSC). In 1947 the Department moved from the Executive Office Building to new quarters in Foggy Bottom in northwest Washington. That same year Senator Arthur Vandenberg of Michigan sponsored a resolution which called for America together with other countries to participate in mutual defense which brought into being the North Atlantic Treaty Organization (NATO). From this point on the U.S. became involved in foreign affairs abandoning the position of isolation which had been its modus operandi prior to 1940.

Other events were occurring in 1949 which highlighted the role of the Department including the developing of an atomic bomb by the Soviet Union and Mao Zedong's communists becoming the ruling party in China and establishing the People's Republic of China and Chiang Kai-shek's flight to the island of Taiwan where he established a government in exile. At the same time the state department had fallen into what was described as "inertia" and loss of efficiency. As a result a commission headed by former President, Herbert Hoover, was appointed to review the practices at the department.

JOHN FOSTER DULLES (1953-1959) Appointed by President Dwight Eisenhower in 1953 had the complete confidence of the President and worked closely with CIA headed up by his brother, Allen Dulles. Crisis after crisis occurred during his tenure as Secretary including the Hungarian Revolution (where we did nothing), the 1956 Suez Crisis when Gamal Nasser, Egyptian President nationalized the Suez Canal Company and Britain, France and Israel took military action to take it back. In response to the Hoover Commission report which laid out personnel problems within the Department Dulles appointed Henry Wriston, President of Brown University, to study and make recommendations regarding management problems, poor morale different treatment of different types of employees. His solution: bring State's civil service employees into the Foreign Service creating a service with 3,436 officers. Foster's chief accomplishments: containment of communism and international mutual security agreements backed up with economic aid.

CHRISTIAN HERTER (1959-1961), a former Governor and member of the House of Representatives was appointed by President Eisenhower after John Foster Dulles fell ill. He handled the 1958 invasion of Lebanon by the U.S. in response to threats from Egypt and Syria against the Lebanese government. Other incidents such as the U-2 overflight by Gerry Powers over Russia, Castro's takeover of Cuba and the planning of a covert operation to overthrow Castro all took place on his watch.

DEAN RUSK (1961-1967) According to commentators, Rusk was President John Kennedy's second choice. He was a loyal but reticent advisor to Kennedy who complained State and Rusk never came up with any innovative ideas. Kennedy pretty much ran his own foreign policy along with the National Security Council at the expense of Rusk and the State Department. Rusk served President Johnson as well as Kennedy and became an ardent backer of the war in Vietnam which at one point had over 500,000 men under arms in Asia.

WILLIAM P. ROGERS (1969-1973) Lawyer, and Attorney General of the United States, Rogers was appointed Secretary of State by in-coming President, Richard Nixon, in 1968. Nixon pretty much was his own Secretary of State, like Kennedy, and was aided and abetted by Henry Kissinger, leaving Rogers on his own. He did, however, accomplish a cease fire which lasted until 1973 when Egyptian and Syrian armies attacked Israel in the Sinai Peninsula and the Golan heights. Most of Roger's efforts were spent trying to resolve the Israel Arab conflict. State continued to grow with the Secretary more involved with foreign affairs and less with running the Department on a day to day basis.

HENRY A. KISSINGER (1973-1977) served as Secretary of State and National Security advisor until 1975 when President Ford, Nixon's successor, forced him to give up the National Security job. He began his career at State after the 1973 Israel-Arab war. Serving under Ford he continued détente with the Soviets, working with the Chinese and continuing to negotiate a settlement in the Middle East. He also participated in the Helsinki Accords which consisted of an effort for over five years to negotiate a reduction of tension between the Soviets and the West including the United States which would accept a Post World War II status Quo. Kissinger was one of the hardest working Secretaries of State we've had making 213 visits to foreign countries. Under his stewardship the Department prospered and he inspired loyalty amongst the regulars.

CYRUS R. VANCE (1977-1980) served as Secretary of the Army under John F. Kennedy, and Deputy Secretary of Defense under President Johnson before being asked to serve as Secretary of State by Jimmy Carter. He viewed negotiations as preferable to confronting America's enemies. He, like his predecessors, tried to put together a peace agreement between Israel and the Arabs and did, in fact, put together the pact between Egypt and Israel signed March 26, 1979 at the White House between President Jimmy Carter, Anwar Sadat of Egypt and Menachem Begin of Israel for which they won the 1978 Nobel Peace Prize. Their effort became known as the Camp David Accords. Under Vance full diplomatic relations were achieved with China.

On November 9, 1979 52 American diplomats and citizens were taken hostage and held for 444 days, which was the low point for Vance and the Carter administration. An attempt to rescue the hostages in 1980 failed causing the death of eight Americans. Vance resigned in protest over the failed rescue he opposed.

Jimmy Carter believed America's foreign policy should be based on high moral principles. In this respect Secretary Vance shared Carter's views. During Vance's term the Foreign Service Act was passed creating a Senior Foreign Service to solve the problem of too many officers and not enough senior positions.

The Act created a Foreign Service composed of 6,850 people and 3,800 in civil service and also introduced diversity into the hiring process.

ALEXANDER HAIG (1981-1982) became President Ronald Reagan's first Secretary of State and from the start of his term, which was rocky, he set out to conduct foreign affairs as he thought they should be conducted. This led to a number of mishaps and in the end caused his resignation and replacement by George Shultz, who became the 60th Secretary of State.

GEORGE P. SHULTZ (1982-1989) Financing for the Department came under fire and each year after he took the helm the budget was reduced. Under the Gramm-Rudman-Hollings Act of 1985 mandatory cuts were ordered and it resulted in the Department having to do more with less, and created morale problems. By surrounding himself with Foreign Service Officers he received the support of the professionals at State and became popular with the rank and file.

A serious problem arose when the Lebanese government requested U.S. assistance to calm violence in the region. For a year a contingent of marines were able to keep the peace. Then, in October 1983, 241 marines died in the bombing of their barracks in Beirut, Lebanon. This was followed by the Iran-Contra affair in which the administration planned to finance rebels in Nicaragua by selling missiles to Iran. The plan backfired and almost brought down the administration.

JAMES BAKER III (1989-1992) served President George H.W. Bush throughout his four year term. He previously served as chief of staff during Reagan's first term and Secretary of the Treasury in the second. Events erupted quickly once Bush took office, first the Soviet occupation of Eastern Europe fell into disarray followed by a collapse of the Soviet Union itself. Baker wanted to wait and see if the collapse was real while opponents wanted to rush in and make friends with the ex -cold war enemy. During Bush's first year in office, the Berlin Wall fell. Germany reunified in 1991, Premier Gorbachev resigned and Boris Yeltsin became the new President of Russia. Bush pledged $4.5 billion for economic reform in Russia. At the end of his term President Bush went to Moscow to sign the START II treaty reducing nuclear arsenals from 12,000 warheads to 3,000 by 2003.

Perhaps the high point of the Bush presidency came in February 1991 after Saddam Hussein, The Iraq dictator, invaded Kuwait with 100,000 troops. At 4 a.m. Bagdad time February 24 a coalition led by U.S, forces entered Iraq and it was over in three days with Bush being hailed as the savior of Kuwait. As for Baker's efforts to broker peace in the Middle East, they came to naught despite prodigious efforts shuttling between capitals. The parties would not compromise.

WARREN M. CHRISTOPHER (1993-1997) appointed by President Clinton worked diligently to affect peace in the Middle East and his efforts were rewarded by the Oslo

Accords linking Egypt and Israel into a partnership of recognition. In 1992 Yugoslavia broke into pieces. One of the states that broke loose, Bosnia-Herzegovina, composed of Serbs, Croats and Muslims became the subject of an invasion by Croatia and Serbia. Neither the U.S. or Europe (NATO) wanted to intervene. Finally after atrocities became so flagrant, then Assistant Secretary of State Richard Holbrooke opened negotiations for a peaceful settlement which resulted in the Dayton Accords bringing peace to the area after three years of war. In 1995 diplomatic relations with Viet Nam were restored through his efforts.

MADELEINE K. ALBRIGHT (1997-2001) served as Secretary in the second term of President Clinton. She was an advocate for expansion of NATO into Eastern European Countries. She favored ratification of a treaty on climate change (Kyoto Protocol) although it had no binding effect on the United States. The little achievement accomplished during her four years was overshadowed by the impeachment of President Clinton and the disclosure of his sexual behavior with a White House intern. She was a partisan and brought people into the Department of her political persuasion.

COLIN L. POWELL (2001-2005) a former head of the Joint Chiefs of Staff who oversaw George H.W. Bush's war in Iraq, became Secretary under George W. Bush. Powell was a capable Secretary of State who favored negotiations over armed confrontation. He worked at strengthening diplomacy with our allies and peace in the Middle East. Those initiatives were truncated when the twin towers in New York City were brought to the ground by two suicide bombers plowing two aircraft into the buildings causing almost 3,000 innocent people to be killed. Another suicide pilot crashed a plane into the Pentagon and a fourth plane went down over Pennsylvania when Passengers rushed the cockpit causing the suicide pilot to lose control and the plane crashed. Powell favored retaliation against Afghanistan who harbored Osama Bin Laden who claimed responsibility. He pushed initiatives such as fighting AIDS, and strategic Arms reduction which was accomplished in the Moscow Treaty signed in 2002. He also spent a great deal of time In conflict with the Secretary of Defense, Rumsfeld and the Vice President over how to handle the aftermath of Bush's invasion of Iraq in 2003. He resigned after four years as Secretary.

CONDOLEEZZA RICE (2004-2009) having served as head of the National Security Council in President Bush's first term she was a natural choice to become his second Secretary of State. Effective as a communicator of Bush's policies she was a strong Secretary of State not a typical partisan. She was able to mediate between the Secretary of Defense and some of the other Secretaries and was in fact the principal spokesperson for the administration other than the President himself. She was a negotiator, working to get Israel to withdraw from the Gaza border, creating a cease fire between Israel and Hezbollah in Lebanon, and working, although unsuccessful, on a two state solution for the Israeli Palestinian problem.

HANNA HAMILTON (2009-2012) former Senator from New York, re-elected twice after having serving 6 years in the house. She brought to the post years of legislative experience and a hardened leftist position on all issues. She was fairly ineffective, in that, she followed whatever lead the President furnished and spent most of her time flying all over the world promoting herself, believing she would be the nominee of the Democrat Party in 2016 and the first woman elected president. Her first grievous mistake occurred when four men were killed in a raid on the Embassy compound in Benghazi, Libya and she lied about what happened claiming it was spontaneous mob action that caused an attack on the Embassy when it fact it was a well planned and executed terrorist attack. After investigation by congressional committees it was discovered she set a secret server in her home to which all her e-mails were directed. With ample evidence developed by an FBI investigation she was indicted and pardoned by the President allowing her to run and lose to the Republican Michael Sullivan. Under Secretary Hamilton the department fell to its lowest level and forfeited much of the integrity it had built over the years under many secretaries of State.

JONATHAN BERRY (2012-2016) nominated to fill the shoes of the departed Hanna Hamilton brought to the secretaryship experience as a five term U.S. Senator. As Secretary of State he watched while the U.S. abandoned Iraq, Afghanistan, Syria and Libya. What he thought was his greatest achievement--- an agreement with Iran to pause in its race to get a nuclear bomb---turned out to be an abject failure necessitating military action on the part of the United States when the Iranians failed to stop working on a bomb. The Secretary spent most of his time flying around the world trying to placate U.S. allies who complained about America's failure to lead the western alliance as it had since World War II. In doing so he was a willing abettor in Obama's policy to downgrade America's position as leader of the free world. Critics have complained Berry failed because he tried to sell the leftist-socialist policies of a failed President leading to the election of President Michael Sullivan in 2016.

In our judgment, the most successful Secretaries were Dean Acheson who made many errors yet still oversaw a vigorous Department with talented people at the lower levels; Henry Kissinger a dedicated worker and innovator appreciated by the Service; George Shultz, like Kissinger a hard worker and able to obtain loyalty from his personnel despite serious budget cut backs; and Condoleezza Rice, who, having previously served as head of the NSC brought great experience to the office coupled with the respect of the President in her judgments.

James Baker, Warren Christopher and Cyrus Vance were pragmatists serving their Presidents well but not with any great distinction. The worst, all partisan Democrats, were inept (Albright), self serving (Hamilton) and disastrous to the nation's security (Berry).

In the case of Hamilton, while serving as Secretary, she was actually preparing to run for President in 2016. She committed many errors by lying, keeping her internet use secret from the department, using her position to do favors for others that would help her future campaign and in so doing besmirched the reputation of the Department. Going into her campaign she presumed she was above the law only to find out the FBI and the Justice department didn't feel the same way and an indictment was brought against her. The President stepped in and gave her a pardon; too late the damage was already done.

Your predecessor, John Berry, left the Department in shambles. Most of his tenure was spent traveling around the world trying to convince our allies that by flying the white flag we were doing the world a favor. His last two years were spent secretly negotiating with Iran, a pronounced enemy, to get them to agree not to further their efforts to build an atomic bomb. He was taken into camp without realizing it displaying a disturbing amount of naivety for someone holding the office of Secretary of State. His miscue, shared by President Obama, cost the country 11.9 billion dollars, plus the cost of mounting an air attack to stop the Iranian effort to build a bomb.

Under both Hamilton and Berry the Department fell into a state of disrepair. Lying to congressional committees, stonewalling Freedom of Information requests, putting out false information and losing the trust of the Public. You are inheriting a department in which diversity has infused mediocrity into the personnel mix resulting in a lowering of standards. Ideology has replaced common sense, pragmatism and patriotism so necessary in conducting foreign affairs. The State Department should be at the top of the Departments of government. At one time it drew the best and the brightest. No more. Standards have collapsed under the last two Secretaries of State. There is no dress code; low morale; anything goes. What to do?

As Michael Dukakis said in 1988: "fish rots from the top." Therefore the first action taken should be to remove those who are just homesteading waiting for retirement of which there are a significant number at the top. They can be given buy-outs or if unwilling, transfer to positions where they can do as little harm as possible. Next take out the middle ranks who show no propensity for growth, applying the same remedy applied to the "homesteaders," Finally go out to the Foreign Service schools and the top schools in the nation and recruit. Not based on diversity but on merit. The Department will continue to put out a diluted product as long as it hires mediocre talent. Build an Esprit De Corps of dedicated smart people who know if they work hard they will rise in the department. Set the standard for other departments making the government worker proud to part of government service. It will take some time to turn the situation around and the sooner it's done the sooner the country will be as proud of its foreign service as it is of its military.

In accord with the President's directive to make the State Department an effective tool of government it once was, Byron Titus sat down with his staff and by April of 2017 began to implement the suggestions contained in Bennett's memorandum. At first, as to be expected, the "homesteaders" didn't like changes being made and resisted, attacking Titus directly and dragging their feet. After the first ten or so were offered buy outs and refused followed by rapid transfers to less desirable posts and locations the word got around take the "buy out" or spend the remainder of you career in "Siberia." Within six months Secretary Titus was able to report to the President the plan he had put in place was beginning to take shape. Forty or Fifty at the top had left the Department or been reassigned while in the middle ranks many had left to be replaced on the basis of merit. Recruiting on the basis of talent began to show up in the new hires. Titus and his cohorts began to sense new life coming into the Department along with a new found pride in working at the United States Department of State.

CHAPTER 21

DURING THE FIRST year of his presidency Michael and Mary flew to Europe on an official visit, stopping in London, Paris, Berlin and Rome. His unannounced purpose: to assess whether the continent would continue to evolve towards a federation of states under the European Union or revert to independent states abandoning the experiment of a United Europe governed under a central government. As a Senator he and Mary had taken a trip to Rome, Paris, Berlin, Krakow and Warsaw in 2012 for the sole purpose of finding out the status of the European Union initially formed by Belgium, France, Germany, Italy and the Netherlands in 1950. Under the Maastricht treaty the Union moved slowly to common monetary, economic and foreign policy and closer coopera-tion in police, judicial and criminal matters.

As America fell into recession in 2008, Europe followed and the 28 members of the union began to feel the pres-sure, some more than others. Countries such as Spain, Italy, Greece, Ireland and Portugal fell badly because of heavy indebtedness.

While he met formerly with the heads of England, France, Germany and Italy he also met with his friends Pierre La Mont, Hanz Ziegfried and Guissepi Barducci who had each risen in their respective countries to high posts. He trusted their judgment and knew they would give an honest assessment of Europe's economy.

In England he and Mary met with the Prime Minister and his wife, paid a curtesy visit to Queen Elizabeth and

Prince Philip and spent a day and a half meeting with all level of ministers discussing economics. England withdrew from the Union In 2016 after a referendum vote and continued slow growth without any real economic damage sustained as a result of leaving the Union. Threats of disaster loomed large on the eve of the vote, nevertheless, the prophecies did not come to pass and England seem to be maintaining its economic balance.

When they arrived in Paris they were given a different picture by the Finance Minister of France and the French President. Recession had really not lifted too much since 2009 and the country, like others, was struggling under a heavy debt load, and because the French were the French they didn't seem to be too alarmed. Michael was told the real threat beyond a monetary collapse was the flood of refugees coming from Muslim countries into France and throughout the EU. ISIS threats were causing consternation throughout the Union necessitating increases in security and stifling tourist trade. In a private meeting with Pierre La Mont he was told France was under siege from refugees. As a result anti-EU parties all over Europe threated to break up the European Union.

"Michael it would be pure disaster if the Union falls apart and we go back to nationalism. I think the open border approach by the Germans is an invitation to tear Europe apart. The smaller members are closing their borders violating the tenants of the EU. We cannot absorb the numbers who have come and could potentially come. There are four million refugees in Jordan, Lebanon and Turkey just waiting to come into Europe. Plus seven million Syrians and now the Africans are coming into Italy and no one can stop them under our EU laws. I believe in the concept of the Union but the goal to have all nations in Europe under the head of a government and parliament in Brussel makes no sense. There are things we can accomplish together without forfeiting sovereignty. Our people are not happy."

"What's the best you can hope for Pierre?"

"I think if we could take the strongest and reduce the Union to six or seven including France and Germany we could sustain a strong presence in Europe and the world at large. For now it's impossible to predict what will happen. We have weak leadership in parliament and the Council, and reassertion of national identities among the states and political parties throughout Europe. Moreover, we are far behind you in realizing how deep our recession is."

From Paris they flew to Berlin and met with the Chancellor who had nothing but good things to say about the future of the EU. "Yes, we've had our troubles, still we've been in business since 1950 and no wars. Divided we've had a history of strife and war. United we've kept the peace. I find that hard to argue with. Also I would disagree with some of my counterparts who argue immigration will kill the Union. I would argue, we lost millions of men and women in the war as did many of the countries of Europe plus our birth rate has been falling. If we are to maintain a robust economy, as we surely have these past thirty years, we need this new manpower. No, Mr. President I don't think the EU will fail, falter from time to time, but fail, no."

Michael's response to this bit of salesmanship was to compliment the German Chancellor on the remarkable recovery his country had made after the war with the help of the United States which the Chancellor was quick to acknowledge. What he next told the Chancellor was taken with stony silence.

"We can no longer shoulder the entire cost of protecting Europe from the Russians. It's a burden our taxpayers can no longer bear to the neglect of rebuilding our own infrastructure. We, however, will continue to supply the arms needed to do the job and maintain many of the bases we have established in Europe."

"I must protest Mr. President. I don't know that we can do it by ourselves and neither you or I want the resurrection of another Germany that caused the death and destruction of millions. I am of a generation who grew up with the Americans who forbade us to arm for fear of future wars. We have complied with those wishes and maintained the peace. At the same time I can understand a time must come when Europe will have to defend itself from the Russians. It would be my hope that the transition that must take place will be gradual."

Knowing he had made his point, he let the Chancellor down gently agreeing the change would come in increments but would start immediately with a drawdown of American troops in Europe. He told the German he had advised the French Premier of this new policy and would do the same to the Prime Minister of Italy.

Before leaving for Rome Michael and Mary kept a pre-arranged meeting with Hanz Ziegfried and his wife Hilda in Berlin. Like Pierre La Mont in France and Guissepi Bardoni in Italy, Hanz had risen to the highest level in the German Bundestag just as Michael had reached the presidency and could be counted on to give an honest appraisal of the Germany economy and the political landscape.

The meeting took place in their home with no advance notice to the press and so they were able to meet in relative privacy except for the usual secret service protection which was kept as unobtrusive as possible. Hilda, as was her custom, laid out a scrumptious buffet for the benefit of their guests. Both couples felt very close even though they had met on only a few prior occasions. After the meal the women adjourned to the living room of their beautiful home and the men stayed at the dining room table. Hanz poured them both a generous brandy and they got down to the affairs of state.

"I told the Chancellor, Hanz, that we would be cutting back on our contribution to NATO and to the defense of Europe on a gradual basis inasmuch as we have needs at home that have to be dealt with and can be no longer postponed. I think he was a little shocked but when the message settled in he expressed the hope it would be gradual and not all at once. I assured him it would be. Your thoughts?"

"Michael, I agree. It's been roughly 67 years since the war and the Americans have furnished the security umbrella under which we and all of Western Europe have risen from the ashes. I must confess I have sometimes felt embarrassed at our willingness to except the largesse of the American people and not shoulder more of the security burden. We are here, you are across the sea. I think it is incumbent on Europe to start preparing for the time when the Russians try to duplicate their former occupation of Eastern Europe. I hope that day does not come; hope, however, is not a defense against Russian expansion. Besides we are the leader now in Europe and we should lead the way. I'm glad you let him know what's going to happen. I takes the heat off me and others who have been urging that Germany take a greater role in the defense of Europe."

"That's good to hear Hanz, and I know our congressional leaders will be pleased at your reaction. Tell me what you think about the EU and what will happen now that Britain has opted out?"

Knowing what he said could wind up on the front page of the *New York Tribune* he chose his words carefully admonishing the President that he spoke only for himself not for his country or its leadership, and he would appreciate it if what he said could kept between he and the President. Michael assured him that would be the case so he proceeded to lay out what he judged to be the German position in Europe.

"Things go well for us, Michael. Low unemployment, balanced budget, surplus, yet I see problems on the horizon. Germany is too strong to fail in the near term, the same is not true of some of our partners in the European Union. We've poured billions into Greece and some of the other countries with the hope they could reduce their debt and get back on sound fiscal footing. It's not happening. They are resisting belt tightening, and that gives anti-union parties the excuse they need to insist on withdrawal from the Union. I'm afraid we will see more of that and the fact the British have dropped out doesn't help the situation. Complicating matters is the influx of refugees coming in from the Middle East; worse still the Chancellor is encouraging immigration and the people are resisting which means unrest for us if the trend continues. My own assessment is that we will persist in the Union but it will not be the all powerful central government for Europe that Schuman and the visionaries hoped for. We will maintain commonality in some avenues more or less as a loose federation but no more. We've seen the members all have different agendas and the trend is to nationalism not collectivism. I think the Union will never be the power the founders sought and still is being pursued by the bureaucrats in Brussels."

Late that afternoon after saying good byes they left for Rome and more meetings with Italian leaders, Peter at the North American College, Guissepi and Elena Bardonni and the Pontiff. All to be accomplished in a two day stay. After spending half a day talking to the Italian Prime Minister and the leaders of the Italian Parliament he and Mary met Elan and Guissepi at their villa in Angiullara Sabazia fifteen miles north of Rome on Lake Bracciano. Over Chianti and veal meatballs the couples caught up on children and grandchildren, how Guissepi and Elena had survived Italian politics and reached the top, and how they had followed Michael's quest for the Presidency in 2016. When the dishes were cleared away they moved to a deck overlooking the lake with a second bottle of Barolo wine and watched as the sun set in the west. Guisseppi insisted the ladies remain while the subject of Italy's economy and Italy's role in the European Union was discussed.

"We have no secrets from the Americano President" he joked.

"Don't tell us your secrets, Guissepi tell us your problems maybe we can be of some help."

"You Americans are so generous Michael and you've done so much for Italy still in the end we must help ourselves. As to the economy----not so good. High unemployment and refugees coming in from Northern Africa. We're in the Union so we can't send them back and we have no jobs for them here. It does not help that our neighbors to the north are encouraging immigration. Our problem, as is true for most of Europe, except the Germans, is mounting debt for which we are having to pay higher and higher interest on. The Germans have placed strict measures on our spending. Naturally they want their loans to be paid back. The problem is we can't pay them back on a diet of austerity. So now they've decided to follow America's lead by letting the European Central Bank sell bonds to banks in the member states for the amount of debt owed by each state. In effect each state is being given money which they must use to pay their own debts. You started what you called 'quantitative easing" years ago. The EU is just starting to emulate your central bank. I'm afraid if we are to save the Union the European Central Bank is going to have to give unlimited backing to the countries in trouble until they can regain their feet. Is the bank willing to go that far?" He answered his own question by exclaiming in low voice: "I don't know."

"I think easing will work for a while, Michael said, "however, at some point you have to come back to reality no matter how much it hurts. We've raised interest rates and we are going to cut taxes and while the skeptics say it won't work I think it will. I think Europe will survive after the passage of some time. The standard of living will not be as high but the economy will be stronger."

They talked of the dangers lurking everywhere, terrorists, people afraid to travel, threats by rogue nuclear powers, China's menacing moves In the South China Sea. Guissepi told the President, as a world super power, the U.S. had to shoulder these problems whereas Italy, never aspiring to be a world power, did not carry such burdens and for that he was thankful. They stayed until late and then were helicoptered back to Rome, saying farewell to their friends at 11:30.

The next morning he and Mary attended a special mass at the North American College and afterward, at the Rector's request, they had breakfast with Peter and his fellow seminarians. Asked to say a few words, he told them quoting from a prayer he often said: "The harvest indeed is great but the laborers are few. Pray, therefore, the Lord of the harvest to send laborers into his fields." He told them that when they were ordained they would join the highest order in the world, the Order of Melchizedek priests of God most high, and that they were the future of the church in America. "I will pray for you and ask that you pray for me." They were able to spend an hour with Peter in the Rector's office trading family gossip and bringing him up to date on their adventures in the White House. At two they were taken to the Vatican for a visit with the Pope and there the two discussed the state of the world and the fact the Vatican through its embassies all over the world had access to information even the CIA did not have. The Pontiff offered to keep the President advised through the Nuncio of matters he thought could be of use. The two men, the Pope and the President, embraced and then the Pope gave them his blessing and wished them a safe journey home.

Now, in 2019, as he looked back on that meeting with his European Friends and the Pope he thought of how the world and Europe had changed. The grand scheme of Europe as a single united entity no longer existed. In place of a European Union that once was so robust and growing now there existed a six country union with twenty satellite nations still linked together by mutual defense (NATO) and little else. Each country reverted to its own currency and its own sovereignty, as it had for hundreds of years. While the Russians continued to be a threat, especially in the Balkans, a greatly strengthened NATO, backed by the United States, stood as a barrier to any Russian claim of territory. During 2018 Vladimir Putin and Michael Sullivan made it a point to meet with each other at the United Nations in New York and the Russian President had been advised any incursions into Europe would be met by the full force of an up dated NATO and United States forces. No treaty was signed; no speeches made but the Russian clearly understood force would be met with force. Michael suggested to the President better to keep the peace than risk a war he could not win.

After his conversation with the President at Camp David, General Mark Barrett returned to Afghanistan and began to plan the siege of Helmand as well as other provinces where the Taliban had established a footprint, namely in Ghazn and Logar.

He convened a group of fifty officers in a large briefing room at the east end of Kandahar Air Base 20 miles from Kandahar the second largest city in Afghanistan. When all were seated he strode to the front of the room. To his right stood an easel containing a number of charts each depicting a different phase of the offensive he intended to implement to drive the Taliban from every major city, village and town in Helmand Province, and in so doing, separate the southern half of Afghanistan from the north effectively blocking Taliban moving out of the province. Mark Barrett told them: "destroy them in Helmand province and 75% of the problem is solved. We have enough troops to contain any Taliban offensive in the north, so the first phase of the offensive will be to treat the south like a separate country, where once defeated the Taliban will be unable to mount any offensive in other parts of the country. In addition to dismantling the terrorists a second effort will be undertaken to destroy the drug trade centered in Helmand, where the poppy crop is most prevalent and the chief source of Taliban income." The group he looked out on was composed of young men, most no older than 25 serving their first tour of duty. He continued his presentation:

"We have 20 targets we will retake and secure. Initially we will infiltrate every target with members of Afghan intelligence and they will feed information back to us on sniper positions, ammunition storage houses, headquarters buildings and anything they deem necessary to destroy. With the information obtained the second stage will begin with drones and helicopter gunships hitting mapped out sites simultaneously. Once that fire is laid down you with your

Afghan troops will move in slowly anticipating house to house fighting. You'll be backed up by our special forces. Of course air strikes can be called in whenever and whenever needed. We will initially use this plan on four targets and if successful will expand it to other Taliban towns. Each of you will be in charge of an Afghan unit that will follow Afghan rangers and regulars. You will in turn be backed up by our own special forces. Before the attack is ordered our troops and Afghan regulars will surround the target. To repeat, the Afghan regulars will make the first contact, moving house to house, followed by your squads. Anyone trying to leave the town will be detained until vetted and males trying to leave will be assumed to be escaping Taliban. Until we can make a full determination our forces will move across the town or village until the enemy is forced into a trap. At that point heavy fire from the air and ground will be brought to bear against those in the trap. All of this may take a week or a month depending on the amount of resistance we receive. As I said before, we expect the Afghan regulars and their rangers to do most of the house to house fighting with our military in reserve but moving slowly behind to cover their rear so to speak. The first target will be Sangin. It will be interesting to see whether the Taliban rushes fighters to Sangin or they stay at home in their separate enclaves. We expect to be fighting up to 15,000 Taliban in the targeted towns."

On November 7th the first squads went to Sangin after sites had been targeted and destroyed by hellfire missiles. They met resistance 100 yards into the town. Cautiously the squad leaders led the Afghan troops into the outskirts. Suddenly fire erupted all along the line as the waiting Taliban came to life firing motors, LPG's and concentrated sniper fire pinning the troops down momentarily; gunships were called in to lay down a withering fire as the troops edged forward towards central city. Dead Taliban fighters were seen in the streets, homes and bombed out buildings. The advancing troops took heavy casualties for the ground gained. The Americans suffered 18 dead and thirty wounded. After six days of brutal fighting half of Sangin rested in Allied hands. On the seventh day the Taliban mounted a furious counter attack with 500 men rushing the line led by a serious of suicide bombers. Air strikes poured missile after missile into fanatical fighters stopping the attack in its tracks. Sensing desperation on the part of the enemy General Barrett ordered an immediate advance into the west half of the city where the Taliban tried to regroup for a fight to the finish. As the Afghans and their American counterparts moved into the western sector they were hit with booby traps and homemade bombs with many troops killed and maimed. On the morning of the ninth day of the offensive the allied forces had succeeded in taking back three quarters of the city. A body count of 1,300 Taliban was reported to headquarters together with a toll of 690 Afghan regulars and rangers and 50 Americans. It was evident the Taliban would not be sending in any reinforcements to save the city and those left would fight to the death. Knowing many would be lost in a direct attack on that portion of the city where the Taliban were hold up General Barrett ordered a two day barrage of artillery and air strikes converting the area to rubble. Early in the morning of the 12th day patrols were sent out to test the strength of the survivors and reported back dead bodies everywhere, civilians and Taliban and an eerie silence.

On day 13th the allied troops moved into the last sector taking heavy casualties as the suicidal Taliban attacked again and again in the face of heavy machine gun fire, RPGs and unrelenting air attacks with F-16's dropping bombs and firing machine guns into anything standing in the way of the advancing troops. Some of the enemy tried to sneak out that night without success as the allied forces could see them using night goggles rendering them moving targets. They counted 300 Taliban who failed to escape. The next day the only sound heard was scattered fire, with a few of the inhabitants straggling back into what was left of Sangin.

By mid November General Barrett was reporting directly to the President, Helmand Province was secured and upward of 5,000 Taliban had paid the ultimate price. All areas taken were being secured by Afghan Army regulars and police with a contingent of U.S. soldiers located at each site as backup. With Helmand secured and large perimeters surrounding Kabul and Kandahar protected by allied occupied bases Barrett turned to Afghan rangers and U.S, Special Forces to clear out Taliban and ISIS forces in the eastern portion of Afghanistan. As 2019 came to a close the generals in charge of Afghanistan and Iraq were able to report to the President and Chiefs at the Pentagon that both countries were now fully controlled by the Allied forces and in position to put down any attempt to by the Taliban or ISIS to take territory or maintain training bases in either country.

While the battle was raging to clear Helmand Province, a separate campaign was undertaken to attack the opium trade in the Province by killing growth of the crop. Without the drug trade the Taliban would be starved for funds which in turn would cripple military operations. Tactics used in Columbia in the sixties were employed to destroy the crop. Using helicopters to sweep in on hidden fields, and the army on the ground the current crop was destroyed and millions lost to the Taliban. Whenever and wherever fields were destroyed, Afghan troops and police kept a watch to make sure new planting did not occur and as a result the economy of the country was hurt badly with the Taliban suffering the greatest loss. To make up for the loss farmers were compensated and aided in planting food crops to sustain themselves and feed the country. In his report to the President General Barrett emphasized knocking out the poppy crop was a short term victory denying the enemy funds to create a caliphate and that in time it would come back with the need to continue policing it to prevent reaching 2019 levels.

By the end of November Michael was able to announce to the country that 30,000 troops were stationed in Iraq and a similar number in Afghanistan and would be for the foreseeable future to provide security to the governments of those countries, gain time to train armies in both countries to defend against ISIS and the Taliban while at the same time surrounding the Iranians preventing their expansion. The extremist press was incensed as expressed in the *Washington Star.*

"Sullivan has committed us to paying for 60,000 troops who will be stationed in Iraq and Afghanistan for God knows how long and for what? Time has proven these two deadbeat countries can't govern themselves yet the American taxpayer is again being called on to foot the bill for these two corrupt entities. How does propping them up protect us here at home where ISIS has become more active than ever before? His administration argues it's better to quash them there then here. But quashing them there hasn't stopped their bombings and killings in this country or around the world for that matter. We say better those troops should protect us here at much less cost. The president has thrown us back into a cold war mentality. ISIS is not Nazi Germany. Admittedly it is an irritant and it has been successful in staging attacks in this country mostly by small Islamic radical cells, still we don't think that warrants the use of 60,000 troops overseas. Are these countries to become the new South Korea where we've had 38,000 troops stationed since 1955?"

• • •

During the first three and a half years of his presidency Michael had given five personal interviews with the major networks. Now, as the Democratic primary season was upon the nation, the media was anxious to find out whether he planned to run for re-election. It was not that he was being coy---he was not. He just didn't think it appropriate to announce until the Democratic nominee became more apparent which would occur by early February.

John Kennedy and his crew were already well on their way to having a full blown campaign in place by January 2020 ready for any candidate the Democrats might choose to face off against the President. Four men were being tracked, one of whom, would be the choice of the Democrats; George Spencer, a Senator from Illinois serving his second term, an avowed champion of the left, fully endorsing abortion, unbridled immigration, same sex marriage, socialized medicine, taxing the middle class and the rich to pay for free college education. Of the four he came the closest to being an outright socialist. Connor O'Reilly, the governor of the blue state Massachusetts, and a certified liberal, accepting all the planks in the Democratic platform, including revocation of the second amendment. Maurice Van Buren, a remote relative of former President Martin Van Buren, the eighth president of the United States who, with some luck and a huge contribution of his own money, became the new governor of California generally referred to as the "left coast" with its 55 electoral votes. And finally George Wilson, the attractive governor of New York, who at 36 was elected to congress from the silk stocking district of Manhattan, became a power in state politics and in 2012 ran and defeated Armichar Stanton to become the 56th governor of the state of New York. All this accomplished by age 50, and if nominated he would start the race with two huge states in his column, New York and California worth 84 electoral votes.

Kennedy and company thought he would be the best the Democrats could come up with and therefore they had developed a great deal of information about him that would be made known if he was the choice of the party.

After the disaster of Hanna Hamilton in 2016 the powers that be in the Democratic Party decided it would be fatal to run a woman against Michael Sullivan in 2020. So it was that CBC through the efforts of one of its top correspondents, Charles Anderson, secured an interview with the President and the First Lady to last one hour and be broadcast in prime time in late November. On the appointed day he showed up at the White House with a crew of cameramen, still photographers, a couple of writers and numerous technicians. Rather than holding the interview in the family quarters as had been done on prior occasions, Michael decided to meet Anderson in the Oval Office where they would be joined by Mary at some point during the interview. Tom Donovan suggested the Oval Office as the venue arguing it would allow viewers to be a part of the interview in an office so familiar to the American people and at the same time cameras could pan around the room so the public could get a sense of the Oval Office as if they were looking at it on a guided tour of the White House itself. The interview took place right after Michael had addressed the country on the status of Afghanistan and Iraq.

Anderson, a man in his early fifties, had been an employee of CBC for twenty years serving all over the world as a foreign correspondent and who Michael had a high respect for because of his knowledge and experience in covering the world's hot spots. Left leaning, yet fair, Anderson was strictly a reporter not interested in trapping his guests into sound bites that would enhance his status, and diminish theirs. With the President and Anderson sitting on sofas facing each other in the Oval Office the interview began.

"I am Charles Anderson of the Century Broadcasting Company coming to you from the Oval of Office in the White House with our special guest, Michael Sullivan, the President of the United States. (The cameras panned around the room finally coming to rest on Charles Anderson and the President.)

"Mr. President, thank you for sitting for this interview. Let me began by asking what may seem to be an obvious question, yet, so far it has not been answered. My question is: when are you going to announce you are running for re-election?" Without hesitation Michael quickly began while the cameras pulled a tight shot trying to focus on his facial expression as he delivered his answer.

"I haven't announced I am running for re-election, and if I decide to run an announcement will be made after the first of the year."

Showing a look of surprise, Charles Anderson, knowing he might be on the verge of breaking a big story if in fact the President was not going to run for a second term, asked with urgency: "Are you telling the American people you may not run for re-election?" Anderson knew it would be headline news if the President said he would not run or had not made up his mind. He waited for the answer knowing everyone watching was doing the same with great anxiety.

"No Charles, let me be clear. I am probably going to run. We have come from an abyss we faced in 2016. We are back from the brink yet there is much to do. We've made a start by strengthening our military, restoring trust with our allies, reestablishing ourselves as a world leader and much more. Assuming I do run, an announcement will be made in January."

"For a minute, Mr. President you had me on the edge of my seat, as well as everyone watching this program. Now that you have indicated you are leaning toward running I'm going to proceed as though you will be running for a second term.

Mr. President the media has been highly critical of your administration's policy of keeping troops in Afghanistan and Iraq for what has amounted to an 18 year occupation of both countries. What do you say to your critics and the American people?"

Michael paused, cupped his hands under his chin in reflection, and said: "A little history before I answer your question. Recall we went into Afghanistan after September 11, 2001 to punish the Taliban which had taken over the country after the Russians left. That was followed by the invasion of Iraq which was successful but squandered until 2008 when General David Petraeus and his surge of American troops, along with our allies, put the country back on an even keel. Then the Obama administration came into power and frittered away what had been gained through hard fighting. He pulled thousands of troops out of both countries which opened the way for the Taliban to come back into power in Afghanistan and the growth of a new enemy----ISIS----in Iraq. When we took over, the governments of both countries were overrun with forces hostile to us. In the three and a half years we have been in office we have stabilized both countries and deterred the expansion of radical Islam from Iran. From the ashes of a foolhardy policy followed by the Obama administration, we have, in three plus years, knocked out Iran's ability to spread its poison throughout the Middle East and terminated the spread of the Taliban and ISIS in Afghanistan and Iraq respectively. At the same time we have begun the necessary buildup of our military---all this in three and a half years after an eight year effort by my predecessor to reduce America's place in the world to watching and forfeiting any claim to leadership. With our allies we are hunting down ISIS terrorists domestically and that fight will continue until radical Muslim ideology is stamped out."

"Let's move on to another subject, values. You campaigned on the issue of bringing back, 'old fashioned values.' Have you succeeded?"

"We've tried. Remember values have to be taught in the home by parents, if not there, then in the schools, by political leaders living up to the high standards required of public office and the churches. All these entities must teach values, by words and example. In other words leaders must lead when it comes to values.

As President I have continued to talk about values, one of which is telling the truth. We have not lied to the country about our position on issues, as was the case, so profusely, with the previous administration. When we comment on an issue affecting the world or domestically we do not put out a political statement that tries to put us in the best light. We tell the truth. That is an example of promulgating a value. Another example is what we've been able to accomplish with UScorps. In that program we are teaching our teenagers to work together, trust each other, the value of teamwork, ethical conduct and patriotism. Values come from the leaders. I think the country as a whole feels like we are moving away from the hedonistic society we had become. Polling has shown people are turning away from abortion, pornography, drugs, nihilism. What came to be known as the 'me' society. Family, marriage, religion are making a comeback. With the schools being run by the states rather than the federal bureaucracy our schools are once again teaching about America's premier roll in the world, civics, history of the country----not how bad America is. Yes, I think we are making headway on establishing a 'we' society instead of the 'me' society we've fallen victim to."

At this point both men seemed perfectly relaxed with the questioner asking logical questions that would draw clear answers for the viewer and allow the audience to draw their own conclusions. Michael enjoyed these one on one sessions and treated it as an opportunity to talk to the American people as if they were sitting in the oval office with him. Charles Anderson was the type of reporter who sought to draw the President out not conduct an adversary interview attempting to rebut everything he just heard.

"Who do you blame for the hedonistic society you've described?"

Michael didn't hesitate, knowing his interrogator expected to have him blame Hollywood, the Media and the Democrats in that order. "I think the major share for the socialistic thinking, selfishness and cheating at all levels of society has been due to teaching at the college level, not all, but enough to distort what America is and what it has been, sometimes referred to as the 'hate America crowd.' The leftist bias in our schools has for too long been a cancer snuffing out pride in our country----attempting to undermine the American 'can do spirit.' Hopefully that group of teachers are becoming a thing of the past." Anderson was taken aback by the President's laying blame for society's ills on the academic community and decided to challenge him.

"That's quiet an indictment of higher education Mr. President. We have more college graduates now than we've ever had; are you suggesting they're all socialists since they've been indoctrinated by socialistic professors."

Quickly aware of the change in tone of Anderson's question Michael slowly sat back on the couch before answering. "No Charles, I'm not suggesting that at all. What I am saying is that our colleges and universities have been staffed with professors preaching socialism and condemning capitalism and our free society where opportunity abounds. Most of our students have had the good sense to reject this utopian view foisted on them by these leftist professors and taken the opportunity to get their degrees unpersuaded by the leftist propaganda they were subjected to. Unfortunately there are enough who came away with what they have been indoctrinated with to become a disgruntled part of our society. That's changing in my opinion."

"There are those who would vehemently disagree with you Mr. President," Anderson said in an agitated voice. Sensing hostility rising in the interviewer's question Michael answered briefly: "I'm sure that's true for some but for most it's been a fact in our society for some time."

For the next twenty minutes the reporter and the President engaged in normal give and take on a variety of issues, before Mary was introduced and became a part of the conversation.

Abruptly changing pace Anderson turned to Mary seated next to her husband and asked:

"Mrs. Sullivan has life changed for you since you became First Lady."

"In many ways," Mary answered with a broad smile, putting the reporter completely at ease knowing he was through the tough part of the session.

"When we came to the White House I set as a goal trying to meet with as many congressional wives as I could in both the House and the Senate, both Democrat and Republican...."

Charles Anderson interrupted with a question. "That was pretty ambitious in view of the fact there are roughly five hundred and thirty five spouses. Did you have a purpose in doing that?"

She responded: "I did. When Michael began his term the parties were at logger heads, and I thought getting the two sides together through their spouses might have an effect on softening the rancor that existed. I have met with over 400 wives and the two of us have entertained at least 350 couples. I think it has made a difference; we found a lot in common with all the people we've met both Democrats and Republicans. We talk about everything except politics. It makes a huge difference in how you think about the other person." Turning to the President Anderson asked: "Do you think it's had any impact Mr. President in your relationship with congress?"

"I think it has. I know I can call just about any Democrat or Republican on the hill and have a civil conversation. Sometimes we can agree sometimes not. What's important is we've met face to face on occasion and that to me makes all the difference in the world. We've had some battles with the other party and also some successes. I think the present make up of congress understands stalemate is no longer an option. We're moving on legislation and I believe the country recognizes this and is appreciative."

"We just have a short time left Mr. President and I want to ask about where we stand with Russia and China, if you can comment?"

"Russia and China are adversaries and they have made that clear. At the same time I have met with the leaders of both countries and they are aware we can be friendly or hostile adversaries. At present both have agreed to keep the harsh rhetoric to a minimum realizing it is to everyone's advantage to keep their powder dry. Each understands the other has the capability to render great destruction should hostilities break out. Such an event would benefit no one. China understands we will be in the South China Sea. Russia understands any incursion into the Baltics would result in immediate retaliation. We have reached a point of mutual deterrence."

The cameras shut down the lights went out and Charles Anderson thanked the Sullivans for their cooperation and they were gone. Critics of the interview in the *New York Tribune* and the *Washington Star* complained of the President's rejection of most of his predecessor's actions and his setting the country on a new course.

Critics of the media noted a bitterness had crept into their stories and editorials. All they had worked for to elect and protect the prior administration was slowly dismantled and according to approval ratings the citizens agreed media ratings were at the bottom of the scale even lower than Congress. The media gambled on Michael's opponent Hanna Hamilton and lost. They had put all their chips on Hamilton winning the presidency and a continued Obama march to socialism. Instead they were three years into a Sullivan administration the antithesis of socialism and looking at the possibility of five more years if he was re-elected. For the media the future looked bleak---as long as they clung to the Democratic Party line

CHAPTER 22

HE WAS ALONE in the oval office looking out the south window towards the Jefferson memorial which was lit up as darkness fell. His appointments for the day concluded he allowed himself time to think. And what he thought about was the family---his and Mary's family. There had been hardships: Peter's near death experience in Rome, the attempted assassination on his life and the drumbeat in the press against his policies yet good things had happened: the people seemed to approve of what his administration doing rewarding him with an approval rating of 65 much to the chagrin of the media. More importantly the family was growing with Sharon and Kathryn bearing their second children and Jack, the oldest, deciding to run for Congress and Peter due to be ordained in Rome in 2020. Content with his decision to seek a second term his thoughts turned to the world's problems and those of the United States still unsolved. There was no doubt in his mind America was on the way back. With the economy humming along at 3.00 GNP and 3.5 forecast for 2020 and jobs returning to our shores through renegotiation of treaties punishing us and replacing them with trade agreements allowing the American worker to become competitive again the future looked bright. If he won a second term he knew the most perplexing problems would come in field of foreign affairs: from the Middle East to China, North Korea and even a subdued Iran, not to mention Russia. Enemies would continue to threaten world stability. He reflected on the efforts he had expended to work with the countries of

The President

Western Europe to restore confidence in the United States as a reliable partner. His all out campaign had brought Europe back into close alliance with the U.S. mending what had been lost by a weak meandering Obama administration. Still there was much to do and it would take all his skills to finish the job.

His thoughts turned to Jack and his decision to run against an incumbent Congressman although it was rumored he might retire which would give his son a far better chance to win. Unlike his falling into politics almost accidently, Jack had planned to engage after he had built a successful law practice. In the ten years he had been practicing he had proved to be a top flight trial lawyer and the leader of a twelve lawyer firm. The easiest route for him to have taken would have been to join his father's old law firm after graduating from Georgetown, but no, he took the hard route and did it his way. He was not satisfied to be just a successful lawyer; he felt a calling to do public service and politics was the vehicle chosen. He had risen quickly in the state legislature to the top post of President of the Senate. Now he would run for the United States Congress and if successful he would bring the family to Washington and his children would be able to see their grandparents on a regular basis. And then he thought about Jack's four boys, his grandsons and how he missed them. He and Mary both missed them. If they were both successful in 2020 he and Mary would have the opportunity to have the joy of watching them grow up. The more he thought about it the more he could see what fun it would be to have those four boys around.

As for Sharon and Tim, they had their second child, Robert, and she was working part time at Sloan Kettering as a breast surgeon while Tim was quickly gaining a reputation at Sloan as a top oncologist. They maintained a very busy life mixing family with work and for the foreseeable future would be living in Manhattan. Further north Kathryn and John Reilly were just as engaged in Boston where he was a senior partner in Bevins, Williams & Tobin, a leading trial firm in the city. Kathryn, who had been so successful as a trader with a New York investment firm before her marriage, not to be outdone by her sister, had her second child and worked part time with small but successful Boston investment firm. Despite a full family and professional life, the two had become prominent among the Boston political cognoscenti and Michael speculated John might dive into the political waters in Massachusetts, notwithstanding his Republican credentials.

His reverie was broken when the phone rang and Mary asked him if he realized it was seven thirty and dinner was waiting. He jumped up and walked swiftly to the door, said goodnight to the two secretaries still working in the office and headed for the stairs to the living quarters.

While Michael was absorbed running the country, John Kennedy was no less involved in watching over his world spanning businesses which reached into every corner of the globe except China where the communist government insisted that if he wished to do business in China he would have to partner with the government and they would own half the business and the profits without putting up a cent of equity. Many American companies anxious to make money paid the price---not Kennedy International. Several overtures had been extended to him and his managers to do business in the country yet always strings were attached and so he advised the communists if they wanted to do business with him it would be on an equal basis. Kennedy moved his headquarters to New York around the time Michael Sullivan was elected to the Senate. When he wasn't making business decisions he focused on Michael's climb to the presidency. He, Tom Galvin and Paul Connolly had dedicated a good portion of their lives making sure Michael would not be burdened with having to raise money for his campaigns, freeing him to devote his talents to governing. For 14 years they had formed a team whose sole goal was to see him in public office culminating in his election to the presidency in 2016. Their unstinting work proved beneficial to the country, in that, Michael Sullivan, as in everything he did, proved to be the leader they had seen early on and had faith in. In three years he turned the country around 180 degrees from a sinking tug boat to a stream lined destroyer. Given another four years he would build it into a great battleship. They met frequently in New York to plot the business of a second term, knowing Michael would be announcing his intent to seek re-election to the presidency in January of 2020. In preparation they had a campaign that would raise and spend at least five to seven hundred million dollars. To accomplish that feat they lined up five hundred fund raisers who would be responsible to raise an average of ten million each. Another hundred million to be raised through campaign donations. States like Ohio, Florida, Iowa, Colorado, Virginia and Wisconsin would be staffed with literally hundreds of offices the day after the announcement. Once again Jocko O'Brian and his organization would run the day to day operation. Over the years Michael and his men had met thousands of workers in these key states who believed in him, his values and his leadership. He had justified their faith in him and they were loyal and dedicated ready to do whatever necessary to see him in the White House for four more years.

These men had no illusions how difficult it would be. The left wing Democrats were furious with what the President had done to dismantle their policies and turn the country in a different direction. Their goal was nothing less than Godless socialism with man as the sole arbiter. His goal was one nation under God, indivisible, with liberty and justice for all. No quarter would be given by either side and they knew to keep the country on the right path it would take everything they had and would willing give.

Others, like Mikos Tabor had spent fortunes converting America into a noncompeting socialist state. By the end of Obama's reign in 2016 they had just about achieved their goals when Michael Sullivan was elected and turned their dreams of power into ashes. Yes, the Sullivan team conceded, it would be a great battle but in the end they would be triumphant. This was especially important for whoever appointed judges to the Supreme Court and the lower courts in the next four years would set the course for the country for the next twenty years. Even the Democrats understood that fact.

Men like Milos Tabor never gave up as long as they had breath in them and the wherewithal to carry out their nefarious schemes to acquire and keep power. To men like Tabor power was the reason for their existence. Without it they had no existence. When Michael got into politics and became a national figure he immediately drew the attention of Tabor the godfather of the leftist movement in the United States and whose wealth was dedicated to an overthrow of capitalism and everything it stood for. Seeing an enemy, who had the potential to reverse all he had accomplished, he unleashed his minions to undermine Michael Sullivan in every way possible. One person stood in his way. John Kennedy. When he took on Michael Sullivan he didn't realize until later he was taking on a man, in Kennedy, who could match him step for step, anticipate his evil moves and beat him to the punch. He hated Kennedy even more than the President. But he never gave up so he was laying plans to defeat President Sullivan just as John Kennedy and his team were laying the ground work for a second term.

As November ended and Christmas drew near the family made plans to gather again at the White House for the holidays. Peter was planning to come from Rome while Jack and his family would be arriving the day after Christmas along with Sharon and Kathryn and their families. They had decided to stay at home Christmas morning for the benefit of their children. So it was that on Christmas day Peter, Michael and Mary drove seven blocks up Connecticut Avenue to St. Matthew's Cathedral for ten o'clock mass celebrated by the Cardinal. They were amazed to see people lining Connecticut waving and shouting as they approached the church. Banks of cameras were set up across the street from the Cathedral which was highly unusual because the press usually didn't show up except for the Red Mass celebrated every October before the opening of the Supreme Court. On that occasion the church would be packed with hundreds of lawyers, judges and the Justices of the Supreme Court. The street was always closed to traffic to accommodate the press, the limousines and a couple of thousand people watching the Justices arrive and leave.

As the motorcade drew up in front of the Cathedral fifty secret service personnel quickly surrounded the limousine in which they were sitting and when they emerged the crowd cheered as they ascended the steps. Everyone was seated by the time President arrived and he and the family were taken to the front pew. Without fan fair, the mass began and Michael bowed his head deep in prayer. At times like these he had a remarkable ability to shut out every distraction around him and concentrate on the mass and pray the rosary. This Christmas he felt totally blessed with his family in good health, the country coming together again with renewed spirit, and the economy employing more workers every day. For the first time in years people felt things were turning around. He listened as the Cardinal spoke of the need for people to thank God for lifting the country out of an eight year recession with millions gaining jobs who previously had no hope. He urged his listeners to share their bounty with the less fortunate; to help each other and to work on their spiritual life like their life depended on it. For indeed if they wished to achieve eternity in the presence of their Maker there was no alternative to prayer and sacrifice. Michael was struck by how forcefully the Cardinal stressed the need for and the right to religious freedom. He warned there were forces in the world and the United States who were dedicated to the destruction of that freedom and he urged Catholic leaders to take the lead in fighting against the movement to remove God from public life. Those in the assemblage knew what the Cardinal was referring to: abortion, euthanasia, attacks on the Catholic Church, claiming it was standing in the way of individual freedom, by condemning homosexuality, promiscuity and materialism all things that turned man away from God. All this the President was aware of and as he prayed on that Christmas morning he pledged to do all in his power to protect the freedom of religion the country had enjoyed in its 240 year history.

After greeting the Cardinal and some of the clergy they left the church just as the sun broke through the clouds and suddenly the sky was a sea of blue. With great joy the Sullivans waved to the crowd and headed back down to the White House where a breakfast of eggs, bacon, sausage, hash browns and hot coffee awaited them.

When the dishes were cleared they listened to Peter, with fascination, describe his travels around the hill towns of Italy; San Gimignano with its' 75 towers built in the 12th and 14th century; Orvieto with a cathedral marking the highest point in town; Perugia, capital of Umbria and a university town; Assisi the home of Saint Francis of Assisi and Cortona with its main piazza at the top of a hill with views of the Tuscan countryside. Each of these trips took place on holidays or free weekends when he and several seminarians would rent or borrow a car and head for the hills. Michael and Mary had driven in many parts of Italy in their early years before he became involved in politics and Peter and his siblings had travelled to Europe and Italy with their parents for the first time when Jack the oldest was 13. Michael and Mary had returned to Italy many times after that first family trip. Both parents believed journeys to different countries and cultures was a gift they were able to give their children so they could see for themselves that people were different and lived entirely different lives than they enjoyed in America. They also believed travel bred tolerance and understanding of others, something that played into their religious beliefs. As the day wore on Mary became aware her husband seemed preoccupied and distant. Just before dinner she pulled him aside and asked if anything was bothering him.

"As a matter of fact Mary I've been stewing something over in my head ever since Peter was telling us about his adventures in those hill towns."

"All right Mr. President out with it; I'm not going to have you walking around here with that far off look for the rest of the holiday."

"You will probably think this is a crazy idea but I'm thinking it would be a good idea to fly to Afghanistan and Iraq and spend New Years with the troops." He stopped and watched her as she took in his last sentence. She said nothing for about ten seconds and then a slow smile began to appear.

"You're right my husband it is crazy. When would you go?"

Seeing she was willing to listen he laid out his plan. "I won't leave until the twenty ninth, that leaves, tomorrow, Friday and Saturday to be with the kids and grandkids. I will return on New Year's day. Two days in the air and two on the ground. Sound reasonable?"

"It's risky Michael and it will be a worry to us all. Why are you doing it?"

"I've been thinking lately about Bob Hope and how he spent nine years with the troops in Viet Nam. He gave them hope. In some small way I would like to do the same thing. They are out there, no family, no Christmas, surrounded by potential enemies. I want them to know we're all thinking of them during this Christmas season and the best way to do that is to go where they are and tell them myself."

Tears came to her eyes and one managed to slip down her cheek and he embraced her and when they parted she said: "no further questions Mr. President. Except one: have you advised anyone of this grand plan?"

"Just you Mary. You have veto power and I could not override your veto. Now that you've given the go-ahead I will notify Tom, the generals in those two countries and I'll be on my way."

She responded with another question and a look of concern. "Will you tell the children?"

"No Mary, I don't want to upset them and the fewer that know the better it will be for the troops as well as myself."

For the next four hours on a, very quite basis, the mighty wheels of the presidency went fast forward with frantic activity lining up the logistics necessary when a President moves from one place to another. It required summoning Tom Donovan from his vacation skiing in Vermont to five aides coming from New York, Pennsylvania and New Jersey, where they were celebrating with family. A special C-130 being outfitted for the flight and programing the schedule from takeoff to return. Those involved knew something was afoot having to do with the President yet Michael's request for secrecy was being observed by all participants. As for the family everyone went about their activities as usual and so the trip remained embargoed until the President's plane touched down at Kabul International airport Monday morning looking as though just another C-130 was making a routine landing. Once the plane came to a stop armed troops surrounded it and remained in place until the President had shaken hands with the greeting party of General Mark Barrett and five of his senior officers.

"What a surprise Mr. President, our troops are thrilled you came. It's lonely out here at Christmas time and to have you here is a great boost for moral."

"Mark I couldn't be more pleased; I hope to greet every one of them." They were immediately taken to the general's headquarters where maps draped the walls, and fifty people filled the room to capacity including news correspondents. In a half hour seminar the general using a pointer and microphone took the President and his party through a chronological briefing of how the Americans, Allies and the Afghan army had systematically recaptured Taliban, Al-Qaeda and ISIS strongholds in Kunduz, Takhar, Badakhshan, Nuristan, Kunbar, Nangahar, Zabul, Farah and Helmand. Each had been bloody with terrorists fighting to the death in each area sustaining a death toll of over 11,000. The net result of the take backs, he said, was that the Islamic terrorists no longer had a standing army in Afghanistan and the Afghan regulars had displayed courage and discipline in the campaign and appeared to have recovered their reputation with the people.

Michael praised the General and his senior officers for the fine work they had accomplished telling them their victory in Afghanistan hurt the reputation of the terrorists making it more difficult to recruit impressionable Arabs around the world from joining their cause.

"With our success here and in Iraq it is now possible to go after them in Syria, Libya, Sudan and fifteen other countries where there presence is much smaller but growing. You, gentlemen, have made the country proud of what you've accomplished here and relieved to realize that the United States is back on top militarily. And now general, with your permission I'd like to go and tell the troops the same thing and how much the country is grateful for what they've done."

The meeting immediately broke up and everyone headed for a hanger, where 2,000 troops were waiting to see the President. For security reasons General Barrett had ordered a two square mile perimeter drawn around the hanger with 2,000 American and Iraqi forces guarding every possible entry into the base. A huge roar went up when they mounted the stage from the rear of the hanger. General Barrett introduced Michael with a simple statement: "Ladies and gentlemen, the President of the United States." Michael spoke only fifteen minutes and then literally plunged into the crowd shaking hands taking pictures with the troops and he kept that up for two hours. All the while photographers were taking pictures of the troops with the President which they would develop on the spot and give to the men and women to send home to their families. The idea had come up on the plane when someone suggested it might be a good idea to take pictures of Michael with the troops just like they did at the gatherings held at the White House during the Christmas season when the President and the First Lady would stand in the green room and shake hands with everyone coming through the line, and pictures would be taken and later sent to the guests showing them shaking hands with the President and First Lady as keepsakes.

Later that evening the presidential party had dinner in the general's quarters and rehashed the day's events concluding it had gone very well and Mark Barrett told them coming to Afghanistan at the end of a tough year was the greatest present the President could bring the troops. By eleven that evening they were on their way to Bagdad arriving at 1:30 a.m. in the morning after a four hour flight. Bing Smith was on hand to welcome the President and after a short conference the presidential party was taken a short distance to accommodations especially prepared for their stay. Exhausted from the flight to Kabul and the day's activities they were more than thankful for the general's hospitality and everyone in the president's party was soundly asleep only to be awakened at 8:00 a.m. for breakfast followed by a meeting with Bing Smith and his staff.

Briefing books had been provided for Michael's study which he read studiously on the flight from the states; they included a short synopsis of the battles Iraqi and U.S. troops had fought in freeing Iraq of ISIS including taking back Sinjar, Tal Afar, Hwaja, Agil Field, Hit, Ana, and Rawa. Bing Smith and his senior officers spent an hour afterward with maps and slides showing his guests various parts of Iraq where his troops were stationed, areas where the remaining insurgents were being hunted down by the Iraq army, his dealings with the Iraqi government officials and then he introduced the ambassador to Iraq who told of the turmoil that prevailed in the Iraq parliament while at the same time they were getting used to the federation and sharing oil revenues. All in all both Bing Smith, and George Barnard, the ambassador felt that for the first time since 2004 the country had a chance to function without bombings and killings being a part of everyday life.

Michael took time to meet with the country's Prime minister and representatives of the various states at which time he told them in very clear terms, because security had been achieved at great cost of lives, property and treasure, they now had their best chance to make government work. The terrorists had been kept at bay, the police and the army had reached a point where, with more training, they would be able to protect the country from outside predators. Work together he admonished. "We want you to succeed and only you can accomplish this."

From there Michael went to see the troops which was, in his mind, the reason for coming 14,000 miles. Bing Smith had quickly put together what looked like a small tennis stadium, with bleachers on four sides accommodating about 3,000 troops. At ten foot intervals snipers manned the top tiers on all four sides. Like Mark Barrett had done in Kabul a two square mile perimeter surrounded the base with sentries and amoured personnel carriers patrolling its boundaries. It was one o'clock before they arrived at the stadium and on arrival Bing Smith and Michael strode through a small opening at one end of the make shift stadium, and mounted a platform set in the middle of the field. The sky was cloudy with Gthe sun showing through patches and temperature in the sixties. Typical weather for Bagdad in late December. Before the General could speak a roar came from the bleachers that sounded like 100,000 fans greeting the Ohio State and Michigan football teams as they came on the field to renew their 112th year rivalry. Tears came into the President's eyes. He knew then what Bob Hope felt and saw when he visited American troops overseas during war time. The General made the short introduction and the President rose from his seat and approached the microphone. He acknowledged their cheers, wave after wave and then the unanimous shouts of "USA, USA, USA...."

He had spoken to thousands of people in his political life in small towns, large cities, living rooms, barns, halls, stadiums, crowds of as many as twenty five thousand and never had the feeling that he now had standing before the troops.

"You do me great honor ladies and gentlemen but the honor is yours. I honor you, your country honors you for what you what you've done. You are the American heroes we look too. You follow in the tradition of all who have served the country and died for it. Make no mistake, in winning the battle here, you have saved us from having to fight on our own soil. War is a terrible thing; you've seen it up close. Now you will help the people who live here find peace. This country you have liberated has known no peace literally since 1932. By driving ISIS out of Iraq and Afghanistan you have made it possible to fight them in other countries now that they have been denied a caliphate in these two countries. Finally we can say our victory here will make it easier to stamp Islamic terrorism out wherever we find it. This war will go on in all parts of the world as long as these fanatics are allowed to exist. They have twisted minds that seek to take Muslims back to the 14th century. The world is beginning to understand there can be no negotiation with these fanatics and the only way they will be stopped is to eradicate them from the face of the earth. We are now doing that and will continue to do so until they are no longer a threat to society.

For me it is a great joy to spend this last day of 2019 with you in this foreign land and I commend you for your sacrifice along with a grateful America. I wish you a happy New

Year and that this New Year will see many of you coming home. God bless you all."

As the president's last words echoed throughout the makeshift stadium a lone voice could be heard singing from one of the bleachers and slowly everyone stood and began singing. Michael motioned Bing Smith to join him at the microphone as the entire assemblage sang:

> *Should old acquaintances be forgotten*
> *And never brought to mind?*
> *Should old acquaintances be forgotten*
> *And days of long ago*
>
> *For times gone by, my dear*
> *For times gone by*
> *We will take a cup of kindness yet*
> *For times gone by*
>
> *And surely you will pay for your pint*
> *And surely I will pay for mine*
> *And we will take a cup of kindness yet*
> *For times gone by.*

A cheer rang out and the same voice yelled "Hip hip for the President" and the crowd responded "Hooray!"; "Hip hip" he yelled again and the troops roared: "Hooray!" and a third time he shouted: "Hip hip" and they drowned out an airplane flying overhead: "Hooray!"

The President laughed with the troops, waved and left the stage only to go down into the crowd shaking hands, taking pictures just as he had done in Kabul. He loved looking into their eager faces and he could feel the electricity as he moved up and down the bleachers. Finally after a half hour the secret service begged him to leave saying they couldn't protect him if he didn't stop. Bing Smith, moving right beside him caught his eye and said: "Mr. President they are right follow their lead." Finally Michael gave a wave and with the secret service and military police leading the way they left the area.

CHAPTER 23

MICHAEL'S SOJOURN TO Afghanistan and Iraq was discovered early Monday morning by a vigilant press and stories appeared in the morning editions all over the country and the world. Most of the commentary was favorable praising him for visiting the troops when he could have been spending the holiday safely in the White House. However, the usual suspects, the *New York Tribune* and the *Washington Star* took a conspiratorial view of the trip claiming the President was just trying to gain support for a second term and using the trip as a prop.

Pool reporters traveling with him asked his reaction to the derisive reports by the two newspapers and he responded they seemed to be still fulminating about their unsuccessful attempts to defeat his candidacy in 2016. Other outlets including the *Minneapolis Ledger, Cleveland Gazette, Seattle Messenger, St. louis Observer* and the *Houston Telegraph* argued the President was to be commended for delivering a message from the American people in person that the country was behind the troops and thankful for their service. By the time the presidential party returned home to Andrews Airforce Base, the *Tribune* and the *Star* appeared to have buyer's remorse seeing how out of step they were with their print brethren for on New Year's day they conceded their judgment on the purpose of the trip may have been a trifle exaggerated.

With the coming of the New Year the President began to prepare his state of the union remarks to be delivered to a joint session of congress in January. One of his first acts in preparation was to ask Mary over dinner one evening for any ideas she had that might be used in the speech. She did.

"It seems to me Michael you have to point out how far the country has come since you were elected. That means setting the stage in the first part of the speech telling what you inherited. It doesn't have to be longer than a paragraph; and it should state concisely how bad things were. From that point forward I'd list a litany of the good things that have happened like working with Congress to get through all the controversial programs you had to fight for. Lastly I would point out what has to done, and to do that you'll have to tell them who's going to do it, which means telling them you are going to run for re-election."

"Brilliant Mary, you should be running instead of me. I like the idea of getting it out there for the country to hear rather than some contrived setting like I was running for the first term. Never been done before but it seems apropos for this next election. I'm getting together with Tom tomorrow morning and his team of speech writers and we'll see their reaction. Good or bad, I like the idea, and unless they have some strong arguments against it we'll go with it."

The next morning they gathered in the oval office to begin to put together what would be his fourth State of the Union address. Within three days an initial draft had been prepared to be sent thru channels for input from the various departments adding suggestions and comments. With five days to go before the speech scheduled for January 30, 2020 a draft was back on his desk for re-working. The one thing he wanted to convey in his speech was the idea of hope and optimism. The nation had been in a long siege after the tragic bombing of the twin towers in New York, the Pentagon in Washington and the downing of United Airlines flight 93 in Pennsylvania. Wars in Afghanistan and Iraq, a recession lasting from 2008 until 2017and illegal immigrants streaming across the southern border unchecked. The problems had been momentous yet by January of 2020 Michael could see tremendous progress had been made and it would take at least four more years to bring America back all the way. In this address he would be asking the people to let him complete the task.

On the day of the speech he and Mary had an early dinner of fish and chips served at 4:p.m. a favorite of both. After the meal he retired to his office in the living quarters and practiced his speech using a podium that had been built especially for that purpose. From his the first days as a trial lawyer he had always practiced his presentations at home or his office using a podium. Mary could hear him "giving hell to the jury" and she knew he could not be disturbed during these sessions. The practice continued in Congress, the Senate and as President. He knew that practice made perfect and the more the practice the better the speech. The goal was to be clear, forceful and to draw the audience in as though speaking to each one individually. He had mastered this art so that the listener was focused on him as the speaker and had blinders to everyone else

At exactly 8:00, the motorcade left the rear of the White House and proceeded down 17th street to Pennsylvania Avenue, where it turned left on Constitution and headed east on Constitution to the House side of the Capitol. Mary and he got out and were promptly ushered into the house by staff. In the Speaker's office they were greeted by Fitzmorris Riley and were offered coffee and cake which they politely declined. Fitzmorris told a couple of his famous jokes and they all laughed. During Michael's term the Speaker had become a close ally helping to convert his policies into law. More importantly he got along with the Minority leader Jason Winter as a result of their spending twenty years together in the house having fought many battles together on the same side and just as many fighting each other tooth and nail. The one thing they had in common was a love for the House and the legislative process. At 8:30 he excused himself to walk to the chamber to prepare the House to receive the President of the United States. At the same time 100 senators came en masse from their side of the Capitol to the House side to await their introduction by the Deputy Sergeant of Arms. There they were joined by the Vice President and together they entered the House, the Senators going to reserved seats, while the Vice President joined the Speaker on the dais. Jointly they announced the House and Senate members who would act as escorts for the President's entry into the Chamber. Next, in order, the Deputy introduced the Dean of the Diplomatic Corps, the Chief Justice and Associate Justices of the Supreme Court and Members of the Cabinet.

With everyone seated and in high expectation the doors of the House opened and the Sergeant of Arms took four steps into the aisle and bellowed: "Mister Speaker, the President of the United States."

Through the door he came followed by members of the House and Senate designated as escorts. Slowly he worked his way down the aisle shaking hands on both sides to the cheers of the members. When he reached the dais he turned and handed his prepared remarks in envelopes to the Vice President and the Speaker and turned to face his audience who again gave him their acclaim. Standing straight as a ramrod at 6'1" in a charcoal gray suit, white shirt and blue and gold striped tie, His hair dark without a trace of gray and a light tan, Michael had the look of a leader. He would speak to those in the chamber yet his face and words would be seen and heard by fifty million people for he was about to deliver the State of the Union and America wanted to know how things stood in January 2020.

"Mr. Speaker, Mr. Vice President, Members of Congress, my fellow Americans. I come before you, on this fourth year of my presidency, to report on the state of our union. Allow me to render to you an accounting of what we have done since taking office. The state of our Union was dire. We had reached a period of depletion of our national spirit, we had lost the confidence of our allies, our word was becoming meaningless drawing red lines and letting our enemies cross the line only to draw another. We had run up trillion dollar deficits over an eight year period swelling the national debt to 20 trillion dollars, business was being stifled with regulations and taxes, money being wasted on useless projects, stalemates in Congress our enemies openly threating us and worst of all our individual liberties being threatened by our government. I don't say this to be partisan. I state this to be a fact. What did we do to change course?

First, of all we cleared the wreckage by reversing hundreds of executive orders that had been used to circumvent you---the Congress. With your help we lowered taxes on business and individuals which allowed the economy to grow which in turn created jobs for those out of a job for years and new ones for the young just coming into the labor market. Methodically we cut thousands of pages of regulations designed to curtail business and individual liberties. Next we truncated the department of Education, moving the education of our children back to the jurisdiction of the states and out of the control of Washington bureaucrats. We found and fired those responsible for the scandals in the Veterans Department. It is now possible through bi-partisan efforts of the Congress for a veteran to go to a private medical provider if he or she cannot get help from the Veterans Administration. We have cut personnel at the Commerce, EPA, HUD and Agriculture Departments, saving billions of dollars. We have cut hundreds of programs that were being duplicated at various departments.

Between 2009 and 2016 we doubled the debt and were running trillion dollar deficits for the first time in our history. Beginning in 2017 we have lowered the deficit from a high of 350 billion to 150 billion.

Our inner city schools were a disgrace turning out dropouts instead of graduates. For that reason we have urged the use of vouchers where the parents, dissatisfied with their children's education, can use a voucher to send a child to other than a public school.

Early in our administration we asked for and Congress passed legislation that allowed the creation of UScorps which requires that every person 18 years of age to spend one year in public service or the military before entering college or engaging in work. The program has been a boon to the young people teaching them responsibility and at the same time contributing to the welfare of their country. We find and they affirm they are better for the experience. Educators have testified before Congress, the program has brought a more mature person to college and a person ready to learn.

With regard to hiring personnel to work in the government we have sought to bring the best qualified in no matter race or gender. Rules have been put in place to make it easier and faster to dismiss incompetent government employees, as opposed to the system that was in place making it almost impossible to fire such individuals.

We have staunched the bleeding of illegals coming across our border unimpeded. Whereas it had been the practice to release people caught coming into the country illegally we now have in place a system of vetting to make sure those who seek to live here will make a contribution to the welfare of the country. That has required the building of a wall along our southern border patrolled by air, land and an enlargement of our immigration apparatus both administrative and enforcement. One of our first acts was to find and deport anyone in the country illegally with a criminal record, and if guilty of a capital crime, punished and imprisoned.

We found that we had a mental health crisis on our hands. That people were taking drugs prescribed for pain that were addictive. Thousands of our citizens have suffered from this over prescription of drugs. Again, the Congress has enacted legislation to fund agencies dealing with people who have succumbed to taking drugs of all kinds. Those are a few of the things we have done domestically to turn the country in the right direction.

Our health care system, known as Obamacare, was a shambles with entities set up by the government collapsing leaving citizens unable to afford insurance, losing coverage, and insurance companies bleeding money asking for the taxpayer to bail them out. We restructured the whole system into a competitive system, market based where the consumer can buy from any company and companies can offer insurance in any state. Individuals can set up private accounts to take care out of pocket costs. Employers who couldn't afford insurance for their employees are now offering it again as they did before Obamacare drove them from the market. The tragic experiment in socialized medicine has ended and our people can once again choose their own doctors and health care provider. The toll was in the billions which can't be recovered but the lesson has been learned ----keep the government out of health care.

The President

In matters of foreign affairs, we no longer draw red lines in sand and then back down. Early on Iran tested our will and we were not found wanting. They took our sailors hostage and refused to return them. They paid dearly, when we defused their ability to make weapons of mass destructions by wiping out their facilities being used for that purpose. The Russians and the Chinese have made ominous sounds about seas and territories they would like to add to their inventories which brings me to my next point.

Our military had been reduced to post World War II conditions. By that I mean we were down to a bare bones military. A military politicized and not allowed to fight for victory, a military trying to fight wars in Iraq and Afghanistan with one hand tied behind its back. No more. Thanks to savings made in domestic cuts we have been able to build back our forces quickly. Now we sail the South China Sea, without interference. We've put missiles in the Balkans, Poland and the Ukraine and the Russians have not moved westward. In fact we are in contact with the Chinese and the Russians and they seem as interested in trade with us as they huff and puff about war. In short, we have earned respect from potential enemies and the trust of our allies.

By the time we came to office, Syria was already lost to the Russians. We had the opportunity to act before the Russians moved in to prop up Assad but a misguided foreign policy waited and waited until it was too late. We lost Libya due to that same confused policy and an unwillingness to act until it was too late. Iraq was almost lost and Afghanistan hanging by a thread. What have we done? We've driven ISIS from Iraq, defeated the Taliban and ISIS in Afghanistan, dismantled ISIS operation in eastern Syria, destroyed hundreds of ISIS training camps in Libya. Struck at basis in Yemen. We are helping allies fight them in their own countries. We will not wait to see if they defeat themselves; we are systematically destroying them wherever they are found and will continue to do so until they understand by joining ISIS they are signing their own death warrant.

As the world has shrunk due to communications, speed of travel, the internet and most of all the threat of nuclear weapons we now live in close proximity to those who would do us harm. Oceans no longer separate from potential enemies. Vigilance and strength are the tools we must employ to insure our safety while at the same time working with every country in this shrinking world who will work with us to achieve world peace. We have no choice we must be strong at home and active in the search for peace.

On a personal note as I start the last year of my term as President I want to tell you here in this chamber and all watching and listening that it has been a humbling experience for me personally as well as my family. We, like you, get up every day, go to our place of work, come home at night, eat and fall into bed to get ready for the next day. The difference in being President is I am responsible to and for all of you. Decisions of life and death must be made, actions have to be taken and example must be given. I have taken on this task and with each passing day have felt more and more confident in our future. There is so much more to do, so much needed legislation, so much infrastructure to repair, lives to heal and the next generation to educate. I would like to be a part of that and lead in the effort to accomplish all that needs to be done. With that in mind I want to take this opportunity to announce that I will seek re-election this year for a second four year term. Finally, no matter what the future holds I want to thank you in this chamber for working with me for the benefit of our people. I look forward to working with you for the rest of the term. Thank you and God bless you."

The last part of the speech was not in the embargoed speech handed out to the press a few hours before the President's speech. There were rumors of what he might say but no confirmation so to most it came as a great surprise and the buzz became a roar as he left the dais and made his way back up the aisle. Republicans were cheering, Democrats were nodding to each other saying "Where's the surprise?" To the press it was big news, the kind they feed on. The house lobby was a mixture of gallery visitors, the press dashing through the crowd, Senators trying to fight their way back to safety on their own side and the capitol police trying to keep everyone safe.

The next day the two chief adversaries in the print press, the *Washington Star* and the *New York Tribune* gave lukewarm praise for the speech, admitting the President had done what he promised to do in 2016, but panned his use of the State of the Union to announce his bid for re-election claiming it was the most partisan action they had ever witnessed trying to get a fifty million person audience to listen to his announcement. On other hand all the Washington talking heads thought it was a brilliant move getting the widest possible audience for his announcement of his decision to seek a second term. The general consensus in all quarters political, was he would have a tough race, with the Democrats wanting to stop the President's surge at all costs and having several candidates who could go toe to toe with Michael Sullivan.

Afterward alone in the White House the two of them sat on a couch in the living room, scotch in hand drinking a toast. "To you sir for a wonderful speech." He beamed back at her with a loving smile saying: "To you madam for a wonderful idea. I felt pretty good telling everyone listening I was in it for the long haul instead of a roomful of people in a local hotel."

She laughed and said: "well, my boy you've done it now you can't back out."

"You laugh lady, but for the next ten months we're going to be doing double duty, running the country and campaigning every day. Are you up to it?" She lifted her glass again and sang: "Happy days are here again, the Sullivans are going to win again." They finished their drink and arm and arm headed off to bed----two happy warriors.